SILENCE

IS

GOLDEN

SILENCE

IS

GOLDEN

Robert Thier

2017

First Printing: 2017

ISBN: 978-3-962600587

This book is also available in eBook format. More information on this and any other subject connected with Robert Thier's books on: www.robthier.com

Dedication

Knowledge is power is time is money. Why waste precious time and ink on a dedication? This story is dedicated to no one!

Just joking. After all, I'm not Mr Ambrose and can be as loquacious as I want. This story is dedicated to a lot of people. First and foremost among them are the fabulous proofreaders who have helped me polish this story: Iris Chacon, Svasti Sharma and Nela Korenica. Without them, this book would never have made it to publication.

Next, a big 'thank you' goes to you. Yes, you, dear reader, along with all the other awesome fans and ifrits who purchased this book or previous books of the *Storm and Silence* series, thus supporting my professional writing career. It is thanks to you that I can continue towards my dream of being a professional writer.

Lastly, a big load of thanks goes to my fans in general. For three consecutive books, you've all been supporting this series on social media and various online writing platforms, and I wouldn't be where I am today without your spiffing support!

CONTENTS

MY SCANDALOUS, HORRIFIC CRIME

The bailiff stared at me down his long, hooked nose. It wasn't particularly difficult to stare down at me, because he was sitting high up on the bench behind the massive judge's table, whereas I – well, I was sitting in the dock.

'Why is he staring at me like that?' I whispered to my friend Eve.

'Perhaps because you're staring at him, Lilly,' she whispered back.

'I want him to stop.'

'Well, then maybe you should stop first.'

'Ha! In your dreams! I won't be the first one to give up!' And I intensified my glare. Eve sighed, leaned back and fished two knitting needles out of her bag. They were accompanied by what looked like a cross between a spider web and a patchwork quilt, but was probably supposed to be a sock. Her fingers started to move faster than my eyes could follow, and the clicking of needles echoed through the courtroom.

On my other side, my friend Flora sat, her lips trembling, trying not to cry. And next to her, on her other side, sat my best friend Patsy, who was busy throwing Flora thunderous looks, threatening death and damnation if she let as much as one tear slip. Patsy was of the firm opinion that a girl should always behave with strength and dignity – particularly when she had just been dragged into court by a bunch of chauvinistic bastards!

I, on the other hand, was of the opinion that Flora badly needed a hug. The dock didn't really allow enough room for that, so I leaned over and patted her on the shoulder.

'Don't worry. We'll be all right. You'll see.'

Glancing up, she gazed at me with moist, fearful eyes. A tiny smile lifted one corner of her lips. She might have actually believed me except, at that very moment, from somewhere at the back of the stately room, the sound of an opening door reached our ears. The bailiff rapped his knuckles on the table to call for attention.

'The court is now in session. His Lordship, Justice of the Peace Winston Montgomery Murgatroyd presiding. All rise for his Lordship, Justice of the Peace Winston Montgomery Murgatroyd.'

Flora shot to her feet.

I remained sitting. Patsy remained sitting. Eve kept knitting and remained sitting.

'*All rise* for Justice of the Peace Winston Montgomery Murgatroyd,' the bailiff repeated, his voice a little louder.

Patsy waved him off. 'We heard you the first time.'

'If you do not rise, Miss,' the bailiff said, stiffly, 'you shall be held in contempt of court!'

'Goodness! Now you've really frightened me.'

'Patsy!' Flora plead-hissed. 'Please!'

Patsy gave Flora a long, hard look. Then she exchanged one with me. I shrugged and nodded. Rolling her eyes, Patsy pushed her considerable bulk into a standing position. I followed, and so did Eve, after making sure her monster-sock was safely tucked away.

Footsteps sounded through the room. A tall, portly figure in black appeared behind the massive judge's table and settled into the big chair. He picked up the gavel, and it smacked down once, hard, on the wood.

'You may be seated,' announced a voice that was about as dry – and as friendly – as old bones in a graveyard.

We all sat down again. Except Flora, who remained respectfully standing just to be on the safe side and had to be tugged down into her seat by Patsy.

The bailiff cleared his throat. 'The case before the Court is the matter of the Crown versus Miss Eve Sanders, Miss Flora Milton, Miss Patsy Cusack, and Miss Lillian Linton.'

'Did I hear correctly, Winslet?' The figure behind the judge's table sat up straight and stared down at us accusingly. It had an even longer and more hooked nose than the bailiff. 'Ladies? We have *unmarried young ladies* in the dock?'

'I'm afraid so, my Lord.'

'Good God! What is the world coming to?'

'I would not know, my Lord.'

Magistrate Hooknose sent us another stare and in his bone-dry voice asked, 'What, pray, are they accused of?'

The bailiff cleared his throat again.

'The accused are charged with wilfully, deliberately, and with malice afore-thought on 9 February 1840 to have–'

Abruptly, his eyes went wide and he cut off, staring down at the documents in front of him. Quickly, he showed them to the court clerk next to him – who dropped the glasses he was just polishing and nearly fell off his chair.

'Well?' the magistrate demanded impatiently. 'Of what are they accused?'

The bailiff whispered to the court clerk. The court clerk whispered back at the bailiff. Both of them threw a horrified look at Patsy, who cocked her head and gave them a cool smile.

'Well?' the magistrate's voice didn't sound quite so dry anymore. In fact, one could say it sounded almost alive. Almost.

'I...' Nervously, the bailiff glanced around. 'I would not like to...in the open...you must forgive me, my Lord, it is just so shocking, I cannot–'

'What were they doing, man? Out with it!'

The bailiff took a deep breath. Resigning himself to his fate, he made a brave face, and sat up straight to do his duty, horrible as it might be.

'Bicycling, my Lord.'

'*Bicycling?*"

'Yes, my Lord.'

'*Females?*'

'Yes, my Lord.'

'*In public?*'

'I'm afraid so, my Lord.'

The elderly court officer who stood at attention behind the magistrate cleared his throat. 'Forgive my interruption, my Lord...but may I ask, what is this "bicycling"? It sounds extremely dodgy to me.'

'It is, Rogers.' The magistrate gave a small shudder, as if someone had walked over his grave. 'It involves movement through the use of a certain means of transportation commonly known as a "bicycle", that seems to be abominably popular with young people these days. You may have heard of the contraption under its original name, "velocipede".'

The court officer's eyes went wide.

'You don't mean...?'

'Yes.'

'They were moving around on...?'

'Indeed.'

'Using the pedals?'

'I assume so.'

'And with their *unmentionables* spread?'

The magistrate closed his eyes in pain. 'Please, do not make me think about it.'

'Hey!' Patsy called. 'They're called legs! We all have them, you know, not just us girls, if you haven't noticed! You can call them by their real name!'

'Or poles, posts, props or shanks,' I suggested. 'Those are perfectly acceptable, too.'

The two men threw us scandalised looks.

'Only listen to how they speak!'

'Deplorable, isn't it?'

'When I was young, under old King George, things like this wouldn't have been allowed to happen. Girls knew what proper behaviour was back then.'

Patsy opened her mouth, probably to tell the two where they could stick their proper behaviour, but I grabbed her arm. 'Keep your mouth shut, will you?' I whispered. 'For Flora's sake.'

Patsy hesitated a moment, but then closed her mouth again, grumbling.

'Where did this outrage occur?' the magistrate demanded of the bailiff, nearly quivering with moral outrage. 'In a back yard? A garden?'

The bailiff reddened, but bravely cleared his throat and answered, 'No, my Lord. In Green Park.'

'In Green P–! You mean to tell me that these females bicycled *in public*?'

'Indeed they did, my Lord.'

'With children present?'

'It pains me to say so, but – yes, my Lord.'

'And they witnessed these females moving around on their bicycles, moving their unmentionables and sitting on saddles in a way that was totally...*bifurcated*?'

The bailiff nodded gravely. 'Yes, my Lord.'

Slowly, the magistrate covered his face with his hand. 'Good God!'

For a few moments, sombre silence reigned in the court room – except for the incessant clickety-clickety-click of Eve's knitting needles. Finally, the magistrate lowered his hand. His gavel hit the wooden block, and in his driest, most graveyard-like voice, he proclaimed: 'I will need some time to contemplate the sentence. This court is adjourned for five minutes. No, on second thought, ten minutes. These females should have some time to contemplate the gravity of their crime. Officer, stay here and watch the criminals. I would not put it past such perverse, corrupt creatures to try and escape the justice they deserve.'

'Yes, my Lord! Of course, my Lord!'

A few moments later, the door closed behind the magistrate. Eve's clickety-clickety-click carried on as if nothing had happened. I turned to Patsy and said, 'So, you perverse, corrupt creature, you have to admit that I won the race to the duck pond.'

Patsy crossed her arms over her ample bosom. 'I admit no such thing!'

'Eve? You were there, weren't you?'

'Hm?' *Clickety-clickety-click.*

'There, at our bike race! You saw who won, didn't you?'

'Mhm.' *Clickety-clickety click. Clickety-click-clack-click.*

'Well? Who won?'

'Hm-hm.' *Clickety-clackety-click-clack.*

I sighed. Apparently, I wasn't going to get any answers from this quarter. Turning, I focused my gaze on Flora. 'You were there, too! Who won?'

I knew who had won, of course. Patsy would just not admit it, because she'd rather swallow her parasol sideways than admit anyone had beaten her at anything. Flora knew that, too. And to judge by the colour of her face, she wasn't all too fond of the idea of having to tell Patsy she had come in second place.

'Um...well, Patsy, you know.... It's not always about the winning...'

'Yes it is!' Patsy contradicted her.

Flora tried again. 'I mean, you two weren't serious, you were just having fun...'

'No, we weren't!'

'Oh, um, I see. Well, in any case, I'm afraid that – mind you, the light wasn't very good, and I wasn't looking closely – from where I stood, it, um, looked like...like Lilly won.'

Patsy nailed her to the bench with the deadliest of deadly stares for a few moments. Flora quailed, but didn't lower her eyes, which I thought was an enormous achievement.

'Admit it!' My grin was broad enough to split my face. 'You lost!'

There was a long moment of silence, then: 'Fine! Yes! I lost! But only because that policeman pulled me off my bicycle first.'

I conceded with a gracious nod. 'I bet he wished he hadn't when you landed on top of him.'

Patsy barked a laugh. 'Oh yes, he did!'

We lapsed into silence again, but this time it was utterly companionable. The clickety-clickety-click of Eve's knitting needles still sounded in the background, and to my satisfaction I noticed it was slowly driving the bailiff insane.

4

'So,' I mused. 'What do you think I'll get?'

'Hey, we didn't agree on a prize for the winner! It was just for the fun of it.'

'I'm not talking about the race, stupid! I'm talking about my sentence!'

'Oh.'

'Do you think we'll all get the same?'

'Impossible!' Patsy declared. 'I have a much more impressive record than you! No matter what you get, I'll get at least twice as long.'

'Long?' Flora's eyes went wide. 'What do you mean, *long*? Surely, you don't mean....'

'Yes,' Patsy confirmed with grim relish. 'I do.'

'No! Surely they're just going to give us a fine.'

'Are you kidding?' Patsy laughed. 'They have to set an example against independent women like us, or their whole chauvinistic system will collapse! It's chokey[1] for us, ladies. At least a week. Maybe even two.'

Flora nearly fell off the bench. Even Eve stopped knitting and looked up.

'*Two weeks?* They're going to throw us into jail for *two weeks*?'

'Oh God!' Covering her mouth with both her hands, Flora did her best to try and vanish into thin air. When that didn't work, she curled herself up into as small a ball as possible and hid her face behind her hands. 'I don't want to go to jail! It'll be dirty in there, and cold! And they have rogues and thieves and cutthroats everywhere!'

'Are we really?' Leaning forward, Eve grabbed Patsy and me, drawing us closer. 'You two were listening to what the stuffy old tomcat with the gavel was saying! Are we really going to go to jail?'

'Don't worry.' Seeing the fear in Eve's eyes, I patted her hand. 'I'm sure they don't put girls in the same cells as dangerous criminals.'

'I'm not worried about *that*.' Eve waved away dismissively the idea of being stuck in a cell with a rapist or murderer. 'Don't you understand? If we get thrown into jail, we won't be able to attend the Royal Wedding on Monday!'

I rolled my eyes.

'Oh, of course. The Royal Wedding. How could I forget?'

It was a legitimate question, considering that Eve – and, in fact, most of the city of London – had been talking about nothing else for the last three months.

'Wedding – bah!' Patsy snorted. 'It's disgraceful! We have a woman at the head of the nation for the first time in how many hundred years, and what's the first thing she does after ascending to the throne? She gets herself a man! Pathetic!'

She looked at me for confirmation.

'Um, yes. Very pathetic,' I assured her hurriedly. But to judge by the suspicious glare she shot me, I suppose she could tell my heart wasn't really in it. To tell the truth, no matter how much I tried to ignore the Royal Wedding of Queen Victoria and Prince Albert, in some secret corner of my fiery feminist heart, I was looking forward to it. Maybe because Prince Albert was rumoured to be a specimen of that extremely rare species known as 'nice men'. Or maybe it was

---

[1] A British slang term for 'prison'.

because it hadn't been he who had asked Victoria to marry him – no, it had been the other way around. She had gotten to decide, an idea which I found extremely appealing. I suppose there were certain advantages to being queen.

'It's not pathetic!' For one moment, Eve looked affronted, but it only took seconds before her eyes started to glaze over and assumed a glamorous gleam. 'It's romantic! The most magnificently madly romantic thing there has ever been in the history of England and the Empire! Prince Albert is so dreamy! I saw a photograph of him in the *Spectator,* and he's just the handsomest man who ever lived! Mr Darcy can't hold a candle to him! And besides, Mr Darcy is only a fictional character and Prince Albert is real. He's a handsome prince, and he's real, and he'll be married in three days!'

'And not to you,' Patsy pointed out in a dry tone.

Eve threw her a dagger-like look. 'Thank you so much for reminding me.'

'You're welcome.'

'Anyway, you see why we can't go to prison for two weeks, don't you, Patsy?'

'Oh, of course.'

'I mean, it's a Royal Wedding, for Christ's sake! How often in our lifetime will we be able to attend a royal wedding? We simply can't go to prison! We can't!'

'Absolutely not. I'm sure if we explain to the judge, he'll let us off with a reprimand so we can go shout "God save the Queen" together with the rest of London.'

Eve gave Patsy a suspicious look. 'Are you making fun of me?'

'Whatever gave you that idea?'

They started to bicker, and my attention started to wander. But I kept a wary eye on them, and when Patsy reached for her parasol and Eve for her knitting needles (and not to knit with, this time) I felt it was time to intervene.

'Hey, hey. Calm down, the two of you.'

'Cold-hearted materialist!' Eve hissed.

'Man-crazy fool!' Patsy growled back.

I figured neither of them meant me.

'Relax,' I told Eve. 'It won't matter if we're in jail on Monday or not. We'd never be able to get good seats for the wedding anyhow.' As I said it, I realized how true the words were. And I was surprised to feel a twinge of disappointment at the fact. 'I mean, it's not going to be in some big church, but in the Chapel Royal at St James's Palace. Crowds won't fit in there. To get in, you'd have to be royalty, or obscenely rich and important.'

'True.' Eve pulled a face. 'Dang!'

'Psht!' Flora, who had reappeared from behind her hands, held a finger to her lips. 'Look! He's back!'

We looked and saw his Lordship, Justice of the Peace Winston Montgomery Murgatroyd, enter the room, a grave expression on his face – so grave, you could practically read the letters on the headstone. Seating himself behind the judge's desk, he took a deep, rattling breath, angled his wobbly chin into the most impressive pose and proclaimed, 'I have thought long and hard on this matter. It is no easy decision to make. Taking into account the accused's young age, I considered leniency–'

Flora sat up straight, her wide, open eyes shining with hope.

'–but with morals slipping everywhere in our society, such an outrageous exhibition of misconduct as we have witnessed today cannot go unpunished.'

The magistrate sent a dark look our way, and Flora withered.

'Thus, I have decided on a suitably harsh punishment, which will hopefully deter these wicked individuals from breaking the cherished moral laws of the realm in the future.' The gavel rose, and fell with a deafening thud. 'For the grievous crimes of indecent exposure and disturbing the Queen's peace, I hereby sentence you to a fine of five shillings each. May God have mercy on your souls.'

~~**~*~*

'Thieves! Marauders!' Patsy swung her fist at the courthouse, a moment before the door slammed shut into her face. 'Five shillings! Can you believe it? Five shillings!'

'Well, now, Patsy,' Flora dared to remark, 'it is not that bad. Five shillings isn't that much.'

This earned her one of Patsy's looks. You know, the ones that could make a sergeant major quake in his boots? 'It's the principle of the thing! We did nothing wrong, so we shouldn't be punished if there were any justice in the world for women. Besides, five shillings might not be that much for you or me - our families are well off! But what about poor Lilly?'

'Her uncle has money, too.'

'But he's as stingy as a Scotsman with a stick up his arse! For all intents and purposes, Lilly hasn't got more money than a church mouse. And five shillings is five times what most people make in an entire month - if they have a job, which none of us do!'

'It's all right,' I began. 'I can–'

'It's simply not fair!' Patsy continued, without paying particular attention to the fact that her best friend, i.e. me, had just tried to say something. 'Men are allowed to earn money - why not we women? It's all right if you're rich, of course, but if you're poor, like Lilly–'

'Hey, girls,' I tried once more. 'It's no problem, I–'

'–then there's simply nothing you can do! What do you think will happen when the bailiff comes knocking to collect the fine? Do you honestly think her uncle will pay? Oh no, it's prison time for our friend! And all that just because of the tyrannical, thick-headed chauvinism of one small-minded London magistrate!'

I cleared my throat. 'Patsy, I–'

'You're right,' Flora agreed, her eyes darting to me with warmth and kindness. I could practically feel her heart going out to me. 'How thoughtless of me! We have to do something! We can't have Lilly go to prison, with all those thieves and murderers and rakes and lechers!'

'Actually,' Eve mused, 'the last two don't sound quite so bad. Don't you think that, maybe–'

'Eve!'

'All right, all right!' Sliding her hand into her handbag with a sigh, Eve held out a few coins. 'Here's my share.'

'I have mine, too, here, somewhere,' Flora murmured, searching her pockets. 'Where did I put my money again...'

'Girls! Girls, will you listen? Or no, don't listen, just look!' And with those words, I pulled a shiny golden sovereign[2] out of my pocket. My friends froze and stared. Patsy's mouth actually fell open.

'Where did you get that?' she demanded.

'From the same place I got this,' I answered, pulling two more coins out to join the first. 'Out of my pocket.'

The astonishment in Eve's gaze slowly morphed into admiration. 'Lilly – you didn't rob a bank, did you?'

'No! Of course not!'

'Oh.' Eve seemed slightly disappointed. But then she brightened again. 'But you must have done *something* horrible to get your hands on that much money.'

A smile tugged at the corners of my mouth. 'You have no idea.'

'How?' Patsy demanded. 'How did you get it? And...now that I think of it, how did you get the money for your bicycle? Eve, Flora and I could afford ours, but you? And don't tell me your uncle has suddenly developed a generous and giving nature, because that I won't believe!'

'No, he's still the same stingy old sock as ever.'

'Then what?'

I winked. 'Let's just say...there's another man in my life who slips me a bit of cash now and again.'

A round of scandalised gasps greeted my announcement.

'Lilly, you...' Flora began, her face terrified.

'...you little vixen!' Eve finished, a broad grin spreading over her features. 'Tell us all! We want details, understood? Details! Who is he? Where is he? What is he? How rich is he? Is he ugly, pretty, tall, tiny, terrible, terrific, tolerable? Is he under sixty? Oh, please tell me he's not some old geezer who – oh, of course he isn't! This is *you* who we're talking about! You wouldn't give a nasty old bastard like that the time of day! Is he handsome? Please, tell me he's handsome! And rich! And wonderful and kind and good and–'

'Sorry, girls.' Hopping down from the stairs, I swung myself onto my pride and joy: my new, gleaming, girlishly gorgeous velocipede. 'I've got places to be!'

'Stop!' Patsy dashed forward, an indignant expression on her face. 'You can't leave us like this! We simply have to–'

The rest of her sentence was lost in the whirr of my bicycle wheels as I whizzed off towards Leadenhall Street. Empire House, 322 Leadenhall Street, to be exact.

I hadn't lied to my friends. I did indeed have a man who gave me money at regular intervals. A gorgeous, powerful, disgustingly chauvinistic man who

---

[2] A one-pound coin, called so because of the picture of the country's sovereign on it.

looked like someone was pulling a tooth from his brain every time he had no choice but to hand me a pay cheque.

I grinned.

It's time to go to work.

NICE SURPRISE

'You're late, Mr Linton!'

The warm greeting of my dear employer immediately made me feel at home. His cold glare, and the arctic waves of disapproval radiating off of him completed the congenial working atmosphere.

'Yes,' I cheerfully agreed, dropped my briefcase on the desk and flopped into my chair. 'One hour, fifteen minutes and....' Quickly, I slipped my hand into my pocket and pulled out my very own watch that I had purchased from my first pay cheque, '...thirty-two seconds.'

Letting the watch snap shut again, I stowed it away.

'Admirable, how exactly you keep an eye on the time of day, Mr Linton.'

'Thank you, Sir.'

'It would be even more admirable, however,' he added with a glare, stepping from the shadowy doorway of his office, where he had been standing, fully into mine, 'if you would devote the same amount of attention to the time of day when you are supposed to appear for work. Punctually!'

I fought to ignore the shiver that went down my back as our eyes met. Mr Rikkard Ambrose was an overpowering personality under any circumstances, but if you had experienced those eyes of his looking into yours from only a few inches away, if you had felt those long, elegant fingers capturing your face while his lips captured other parts of you...

Let me put it this way: it gave a whole new meaning to the word 'powerful'.

'Indeed it would, Sir.'

'Why exactly are you late, Mr Linton?'

'I got arrested.'

He stood there for a moment, his arms folded, his posture stiff as a stone statue. His eyes narrowed infinitesimally, but other than that, he showed not the slightest sign of any emotion whatsoever. The temperature in the room dropped thirty degrees.

'Ordinarily, this would surprise me, Mr Linton. But, coming from you, it does not. Why do you think that is?'

'Because you know I'm a little demon from hell?' I suggested cheerfully, and pulled open a desk drawer. As expected, I found the correspondence of the day there, which Mr Stone from the lobby had left for me. Pulling it out, I started busily sorting through the envelopes.

'A pertinent point, Mr Linton.'

'Thank you, Sir.'

'The time lost will be deducted from your wages.'

9

'Of course it will, Sir.'

There was a pause. No, not a pause. A *silence*. A negative opposite of noise that seemed to stretch, tickle my ears and send a cold shiver through me. Nobody could say nothing like Mr Ambrose. There was a question in that silence. A question he wanted me to answer without having to actually waste his words on asking it.

Ha! Fat chance.

Opening one of the envelopes, I grinned, hiding my face behind the letter. Not a word crossed my lips.

Silence.

More silence.

And a pinch more silence, with a bit of reticence and stillness thrown in.

Finally, he forced himself to say: 'So...'

'Yes, Sir?'

'Why, Mr Linton?'

My grin widened, and I held the letter closer to my face, just in case the grin was so broad it peeked out at either end. 'Why what, Sir?'

'Don't play dumb with me! Why were you arrested?'

'Oh...' I tugged at my ear thoughtfully. 'I don't remember, exactly...'

'Theft? Manslaughter?'

'My, my, you do think rather highly of me, don't you, Mr Ambrose, Sir?'

'Answer the question, Mr Linton!'

'Well, as I said, I don't remember exactly, but one of the accusations was disturbing the Queen's peace, I believe.'

I heard a sigh from beyond the letter. 'Oh. Well, that is not so ba–'

'Oh, and yes!' I snapped my fingers. 'The other was indecent exposure.'

From beyond the letter, I heard a gagging noise. 'Indecent.... *Mr Linton?*'

'Yes, Sir?' I managed to say without keeling over from silent laughter. 'Is something the matter?'

'What did you do?'

'Why, I just took these letters out of the desk, and now I'm looking through them, just like every morning. There's one from the Bank of England, and one from–'

'Mr Linton!'

'Yes, Mr Ambrose, Sir?'

'Are you toying with me?'

'I wouldn't dare, Sir.'

'Then tell me: What did you do to get arrested? What did you do to get accused of...something like *that?*'

I shrugged. 'Nothing really special. I just climbed up the stairs of St Paul's Cathedral and showed my naked butt to passers-by, that's all.'

The noise that now came from the direction of Mr Ambrose could definitely not be described as gagging. Oh no. Not unless you'd want to apply the adjective 'gagging' to the growl of a lion.

'Mr Linton?'

'Yes, Sir, Mr Ambrose, Sir?'

'Are you trying to make fun of me?'

'I wouldn't dream of it, Sir.'

'But reality is another matter, I presume.'

'I don't know what you could possibly mean, Mr Ambrose, Sir.'

'Of course not, Mr Linton.'

There was another moment of Silence – Mr Ambrose's silence. Then, his footsteps started to move away. I peeked out from behind my letter and saw him pulling open the door to his office. Just before he vanished into his hermitage, he paused. The sight of his tall, lean black figure against the fiery morning light streaming in through the window did things to me, deep inside.

'When you are done with those letters, Mr Linton, come into my office. I have work for you.'

The door slammed shut behind him.

~~**~*~*

My darling office tyrant had not promised too much. He had a wonderful surprise waiting for me when I entered his office: the checking of the balance of all his accounts. All of them. In one day. Apparently, he didn't particularly trust his accountants – no great surprise, since he didn't trust God, the saints, himself, the Queen or Father Christmas – and was determined to discover any who might be cheating him and squash them like bugs. And guess what? I had been declared his assistant bug-squasher. That was why I, Miss Lilly Linton, sat on a perfectly good Friday afternoon, going through balance sheet after balance sheet.

If I had been working for a normal man, going through a few balance sheets might not have been so bad. But I was working for Mr Rikkard Ambrose, a man who had to continually keep opening new banks because the old ones got stuffed full with his money so quickly. The day wore on and on. The numbers piled up in endless rows and columns, and soon, my brain was a labyrinth of zeroes, fives and sevens. Where the rest of the numbers went I had no idea. I wasn't a born mathematician.

When the sun began to set, Mr Ambrose threw down his ledger.

'This isn't going the way it ought to. At this rate, we'll never be finished today. How far are you, Mr Linton?'

'Seven plus seven makes...hm...fifteen, minus twelve, makes–'

'Mr Linton!'

'Hm...? What?'

'How far along are you?'

'Two thirds of the way to Limbo, Sir.'

'With the accounts, Mr Linton!'

'Oh. Um, well, I think about halfway through.'

The noise Mr Ambrose made in the back of his throat then was pure disapproval. An old lady who held her teacup with her little finger jutting out couldn't have done it better if a dog had peed on her carpet.

'This won't do. We'll have to postpone the remainder of the work until to-morrow.'

I sat up, my face brightening. 'We will?'

'Yes. We'll have to work on something else this evening.'

The brightened expression drained from my face. 'Oh. We will, will we?'

'Yes! Get out my calendar. Take down my schedule for next week.'

'Yes, Sir. As you wish, Sir.'

I dug the calendar out of my pocket and started to flip through it on the lookout for the appropriate page.

'We'll start with Friday, Mr Linton, and work our way back through the week, understood?'

'Yes, Sir.'

'Adequate. On Friday, at eight o'clock...'

He started to rattle off dates at a machine gun pace, and I tried my best to take all of them down in a script I would later be able to decipher. But, sooner rather than later, my eyes strayed away from the calendar in my hand to the window, beyond which lay a stunning view of the City of London, bathed in fiery evening sunlight. I could be doing anything right now! Instead, I was stuck in this office with a cold, stone-hearted tyrant who couldn't even appreciate subtle jokes about indecent exposure.

I sighed. I could be out riding on my new bicycle right now! Or choosing a nice suit to wear for the Royal Wedding on Monday – or a dress, if I was in a girlish mood. But no, what I had told Eve had been the truth: none of us had the power or the prestige necessary to get good seats, or indeed any kind of seats.

'Mr Linton!'

'Hm?'

'Mr Linton, I don't pay you to daydream!'

'What a pity.'

'Pay attention! We were at Wednesday.'

'Yes, Sir. Of course, Sir.'

'At five pm on Wednesday, I have an appointment with Mr Schenkelbräuer from Rothschild & Sons. Then I have to pay a visit to the Bank of England to talk with Mr Carson.'

'Yes, Sir. Just as you say, Sir.'

It is such a lovely evening outside. Even if you might not want to risk cycling in Green Park again so soon after being dragged in front of the magistrate, you could take a nice little walk, feed bread to the ducks and solid chocolate to yourself. There's no such thing as a bad time for solid chocolate.

'On Wednesday, I have to visit my factory in Whitechapel. Production there has fallen under the maximum, and I have to fire a few people.'

'Um...surely you mean "under the minimum", Sir?'

'Do I usually say things I don't mean, Mr Linton?'

'No Sir! How long will that take, Sir?'

Or you could be sitting at home, fantasising with your little sister Ella about what it would be like to attend a real royal wedding. For once, there would actually be a subject about which you and your favourite sibling could both get excited. Or you could just sit and dream about what it would be like to be queen, and to be able to command men to do anything you like.

'Two to three hours, depending on how many fools I have to sack. Then, after that, we return to the office and work on the balance sheets.'

'How wonderful, Sir. I really look forward to it. But why not do it on Monday?'

Or you could simply spend this evening in front of the mirror, imagining what you would wear to the Royal Wedding if you ever had the opportunity to go...

'Because for Monday I already have an appointment which will last all day.'

'Yes, Sir.'

Hm...maybe blue silk...or perhaps...

'And I will need you, Mr Linton, to come in an hour early that day, and come in your very best attire. As a personal guest of the Queen, I do not need my secretary to embarrass me at her Majesty's wedding.'

'Yes, Si– Wait, *what did you say?*'

BIG DAY

'No, not here, and not here either, damn and blast it! Where...ah – No! That's not it either! Damn it all to hell!'

Trousers, shoes and shawls were flying through the air in a confusing caco-fashiony of clothes. And yes, blast, I knew that wasn't a real word! Right now, I didn't care!

My sister Ella stood beside me, watching, mouth agape, as I disembowelled my wardrobe. I ignored her. Right now, I didn't have time for her.

'Blast, blast, blast! Where is it? I know I have it here somewhere!'

'Um...Lill?' Ella asked, cautiously.

'Is it...No! Damn! That's too dark! That can't be it!'

'Er...Lill? I was just wondering...Why do you have that many clothes in your wardrobe?'

'Where did I put it? I know I put it somewhere, only where?'

'It's just, Lill, Uncle Buford only ever bought us two dresses each, and now you open your wardrobe and it's full of clothes and, um, well, I don't know how to put this delicately, but most of them look an awful lot like men's clothes.'

'Damn and blast! It isn't in the wash, is it?' I pulled my head out of the wardrobe, strode past Ella and was just about to pull open the door of the room we had shared ever since we were little, when a realisation struck me. 'No, it can't be in the wash. Aunt Brank would have found it, and then Hell would have broken loose. It has to be here somewhere!'

'Lill? Did you hear what I said? There are *men's clothes* in your wardrobe!'

'Maybe I put it in the chest,' I mused, tugging at my ear, lost in thought. 'Or I could have stuffed it in the dresser...'

'There's not a man in there, too, is there?'

'Or maybe I folded it and put it in one of the boxes up on the wardrobe...'

'Oh God! Tell me there's no man in there, Lill, please!' Cautiously, Ella crept towards the wardrobe and peeked inside. All that greeted her was a tangled web of clothes. No lechers and rakes were hiding in my wardrobe, or if there were, they were hiding very, very well. But Ella seemed only partially relieved. Turning back toward me, she gestured at the trousers and hats strewn all over my bed. 'What's this? Why do you have them? Where did you get them? And most importantly, what do you do with them? They're *men's* clothes, Lill! *Men's clothes!*'

'I've noticed,' I murmured, striding back to the wardrobe and starting to rummage again. In some part of my mind I realised Ella had been asking me some questions, but I didn't have the time or patience to answer right now. I was on a mission.

'Lill, did you hear me? Lilly, this is important! You have to answer me...and...tell...me...'

Ella's voice slowly drained away as I pulled something from the back of the wardrobe and held it up, triumphantly. The very something I had been searching for.

'Aha! I knew I had it here somewhere! Didn't I tell you? I knew!'

'Goodness gracious!' Ella's eyes were wide, staring up at the thing in my hands with awe and wonder. The men's shirts, top hats and even the trousers were forgotten. 'Where did you get *that*?'

~~**~*~*

I climbed out of the cab and handed the driver his money.

'Here you go.'

'Thanks, Miss.'

He nodded, and drove off. I stood for a moment, looking after him. Ordinarily, I would not have driven to work in a coach. Ordinarily, I didn't waste my money on things like that when it wasn't far, especially not if you were the proud owner of a brand-new velocipede. But in this case...

Smiling, I turned and marched towards the front doors of Empire House. It wasn't quite as easy to march in my current attire as it usually was when I got to work, but nevertheless, I managed it.

Mr Ambrose was standing before the front doors, facing away from me. He seemed to be having a spirited discussion with Karim, who was standing beside the miserable little chaise and irritable grey horse that were Mr Ambrose's preferred means of transportation.

'...and I tell you, *Sahib*, you cannot do this,' Karim was just saying when I came into earshot. 'This is a wedding of Royals! Kings and queens, and other people with long arms and short tempers! You cannot ride to a Wedding of Royals in this coach!'

'And why not?' Mr Ambrose demanded. 'What's wrong with this coach?'

'It's...' Karim began – and then he caught sight of me. His mouth dropped open.

'There! You see?' Mr Ambrose sounded as satisfied as it was possible for him to be. 'You can't think of a single argument.'

'*Sahib*! There! She...she...'

'What do you mean, *she*? The Queen? What's the matter with the Queen?'

'No! Not Queen, *Sahib*! She!' He raised a trembling arm to point in my direction. Mr Ambrose turned to face me – and froze.

Another man might have cursed or jumped. Mr Ambrose did neither. He just froze. His face became stonier than stone, his eyes icier than ice. They raked over me, taking me in from head to foot, and not just me, but particularly what I was wearing.

I twirled, showing off every aspect of the swirling dress. It was magnificent, if I do say myself. I would *have* to say so myself, because Mr Ambrose certainly wasn't going to. Coloured in dark red and mocha, it perfectly complemented my chocolate brown hair and eyes.

'What,' Mr Ambrose demanded, his voice as cold as the nose of a dead polar bear, 'is this, Mr Linton?'

'You'll have to refrain from calling me "Mr" while I wear this,' I advised him, cordially. 'People might look at you oddly if they hear.'

'Answer my question!' With a harsh swipe of his hand, he gestured at the masterpiece of haute couture which somehow actually managed to make it appear as if I was halfway well-endowed upstairs, and not so much at the backdoor. The miracles of modern fashion... 'What is this supposed to be?'

I blinked up at him innocently. 'Why, it's called a dress. You might not have heard of them, Sir, they're a sort of clothing a group of people commonly known as "women" usually wear–'

'Don't play dumb with me, Mr Linton! Why are you wearing...*this*?'

'You told me to come in my best clothes. This is it.' Smiling, I did another twirl. Under normal circumstances, I would have rather eaten dead rats than twirled for a man, but these weren't normal circumstances. The non-expression on Mr Ambrose's face was worth every bit of the twirl! 'I purchased it a while ago, intending to save it for a special occasion, and...well, this *is* a royal wedding.'

'I pay you to appear in men's clothes, Mr Linton!'

'During office hours.' I gestured at the street behind me, where hundreds of people were walking, riding and cycling, all in one direction: towards the wedding. 'Does this look like the office to you? In fact, as the Queen's wedding day, isn't this an official holiday?'

Mr Ambrose looked at me for a moment, doing his best to freeze me with his gaze. But I had been in his employ for some time now and had grown amazingly freeze-resistant.

'Well?' I raised an eyebrow. 'Is it?'

One more moment of silence, then: 'It is.'

Oh, I just loved it when his voice sounded like frostbite.

'Very well, then.' With a smile, I offered him my arm. 'Shall we go?'

He stood there for another moment, struggling with himself. With my outstretched arm, I nudged him in the ribs. 'Come on. It'll be like old times.'

'I have no idea what you mean, Mr Linton.'

Really? How about a certain trip to Egypt last year during which you had me pretend to be your wife, danced with me in the fanciest hotel in Alexandria and then took me up to my room and started tearing my clothes off?

'Of course not, Sir.'

'But we shall go.' He took my arm and steered me towards the chaise. 'We have wasted enough time already.'

'Ah, yes. But before we go...' I turned my eyes on Mr Ambrose's massive bodyguard. 'Karim?'

The bearded mountain looked stunned that the atrociously female creature in front of him had actually dared to address him. Finally, he managed a 'Yes?'

'Get rid of that puny little chaise and call us a real coach, will you?' I gave them both a smile. 'After all, you wouldn't want to show up at the Queen's Wedding in that old thing when you have a beautiful lady on your arm, would you?'

~~**~*~*

By the time we reached our destination, my mood wasn't quite as sunny anymore, for a very good reason.

'Ah.' Stepping outside, Mr Ambrose gazed around the square. 'The perfect day for a royal wedding.'

I followed him outside and immediately was engulfed by a torrent of icy rain. Even when I had managed to open my parasol, it offered scant protection against the downpour. Thunder rolled in the distance.

'Y-you have a d-damn f-funny idea of the p-perfect wedding d-day,' I chattered.

'Indeed?'

'Bloody hell, yes, indeed! What is so perfect about everyone getting soaked?'

'Simple: everyone hurries up to get home and not too much valuable time is wasted on a superfluous ceremony.'

'S-superfluous? What's superfluous about a wedding?'

'If two people decide it would be enjoyable to be chained to one another for the rest of their lives, that's their affair. But I do not see why they have to bother me with it and make such a fuss.'

Ignoring the rain as if it weren't there, Mr Ambrose strode off across the square. 'Are you coming, Mr Linton, or do you intend to laze about here all day?'

'C-coming, Sir!'

Even through the torrential rain, I could clearly see the multitudes of people that had gathered outside of St James's Palace. The fact that they were being drenched didn't seem to quench their enthusiasm the least little bit. They were chanting the Queen's name, and that of her bridegroom, although I heard at least a dozen versions of his funny-sounding German last name, none of which were probably correct.

I don't know how we would have gotten through there if it hadn't been for Karim. The huge Mohammedan strode ahead, one hand on his sabre, and as soon as people caught sight of him, they stumbled out of the way. Even the

Queen's guards retreated so fast they nearly lost their giant fur caps. Only one remembered his duty to Queen and country and dared to step in the way of the bearded mountain.

'Name, Sir?'

Karim gave him his most sinister look, which, if it comes from a seven-foot man whose black eyes and crooked nose are practically the only thing you can see of his face because of all the beard growing everywhere, is pretty sinister indeed, let me tell you. But when it still proved insufficient to make the guard retreat, he growled: 'Karim.'

'And are you invited, Sir?'

'No.' Karim pointed over his shoulder. 'But the *Sahib* is.'

'The *Sahib*? Who... Oh.'

The guard caught sight of Mr Ambrose striding towards him. What little was visible of his face beneath the fur cap paled significantly.

'Mr. Ambrose, Sir. So you could come after all.' He gave a salute. 'We are honoured, Sir.'

'Yes, you are.' Mr Ambrose strode past the guard without giving him a glance. Divesting himself of his wet coat, he thrust it at a butler waiting in the entry hall. 'Let's get this over with. Where is the Queen?'

'Um...Her Majesty is preparing herself, I believe, Sir.'

'What does she need to prepare herself for? She's had three months of engagement time for that.'

The butler cleared his throat delicately. 'I couldn't say, Sir.'

'Well, where is this whole thing going to happen?'

'In the Chapel Royal, Sir, but – Wait! Wait, Sir! You can't go in there yet!'

'Don't bother.' In passing I patted the butler on the shoulder. 'It's not worth even trying.'

The poor man stared at me, his eyes widening in shock – then his gaze snapped back from me to Mr Ambrose. He looked back at me again, once more at Mr Ambrose, and again at me.

His mouth dropped open.

'Yes,' I answered his unspoken question. 'I really am with him. Poor taste, I know.'

He flushed. 'Miss...I...um...I didn't mean to appear inappropriate. I'm sorry, if...'

'Don't worry about it. Only, could you perhaps find me a towel?' I shook myself, sending droplets flying in all directions. 'I don't think it would be very appropriate to be wet all the way through a royal wedding.'

'Yes, Miss. Of course, Miss. And...'

'Yes?'

'May I ask your name, Miss?'

'Linton. Miss Lillian Linton.'

'Welcome to St James's Palace, Miss Linton.' The butler sent a dubious glance after Mr Ambrose's rapidly retreating back. 'And, um...the best of luck.'

I smiled at him. 'A towel would do.'

'Coming immediately, Miss.'

The butler bustled off, and I rushed across the entry hall, after Mr Rikkard Ambrose, dripping rainwater on the red carpet.

Yes, you heard correctly. Red carpet. In the *entry hall*. That wasn't the only thing that was red: the walls were too, and gold besides. The ceiling was the only white surface anywhere within fifty feet. Crystal chandeliers hung from above, glittering in the light of hundreds upon hundreds of candles. The serious faces of late monarchs, Royal Navy admirals and various archbishops stared down at us disapprovingly. And Mr Rikkard Ambrose strode through all that splendour as if it weren't even there. His strides were so long even Karim had trouble keeping up. I had to run to catch up to them.

'Where are we going?' I demanded.

'The Chapel Royal, Mr Linton.'

'Um...are we allowed to simply go in there?'

'I don't believe so, no.'

'But you're going to do it anyway, aren't you?'

'Yes.'

We were marching through a long corridor now. At the end of it, a set of double doors awaited us. Mr Ambrose pushed them open and strode inside as if he owned the place. Maybe he did. How was I to know if the British monarchy was in debt or not?

Beyond the doors lay not a church, nor a cathedral – the modest name 'chapel' was clearly well deserved. But although the room wasn't very large, its sumptuous décor, high, arched windows and dark, partly painted, partly wood-panelled walls told everyone who saw it that this was a place only for royalty.

To my relief, we weren't the first ones to enter. A small crowd of people, including an elderly man in black and white robes who was clearly a priest, were already gathered beneath the windows at one end of the room.

'Ah. Welcome, welcome!' Catching sight of us, the priest strode towards us, arms outstretched. 'Come in, Sir, Miss. What a joyous occasion. Such a happy day deserves to be celebrated, does it not?'

'No, it does not.' Taking off his top hat, Mr Ambrose clamped it under his arm. 'But I presume it is going to happen anyway.'

'Err...well...'

The poor priest looked as if he had been thrown a little off track. Taking pity on him, I smiled and curtsied. He hurriedly bowed back to me.

'Please!' He turned to the other people in the room. 'Is there someone present who can introduce me to this lovely lady and her, um, formidable companion?'

'Allow me.' A portly admiral stepped forward, and the introductions began. By the time everyone in the room had met everyone, my head was buzzing with names. It wasn't buzzing loudly enough, however, to keep me from noticing the fact that whenever we came to the part where Mr Ambrose said, 'And this is Miss Lillian Linton', and another person realized that I was in fact not there alone, but that I was Mr Rikkard Ambrose's date for the evening, the looks I received went from shock to utter incredulity and instant loathing. The latter expression was particularly prevalent on the faces of a few young ladies in the room, and most of the mothers with unmarried daughters.

Shortly after, a servant appeared with my promised towel, and I started to rub my hair vigorously, determined to squeeze out every little bit of moisture. I saw a few of the other ladies eyeing my towel. I wasn't the only one whom the rain falling outside had taken by surprise. So when I was finished, I held out the towel to a particularly wet old French duchess.

'Would you like to have it?'

She looked at me for a moment or two as if I had mouldy spaghetti growing out of my nose. Then she made a noise like 'Pfuit!' and turned away.

'What's wrong with the towel?' I demanded of the empty air. 'It still has some dry patches! And my hair doesn't smell that bad.'

'I presume it is not the towel of which she does not approve,' came Mr Ambrose's cool voice from right next to me. 'But the idea of rubbing her hair into haystack style in the middle of the Chapel Royal.'

'Haystack st...! You really know how to compliment a lady, you know.'

'Yes, I know. Do you have a comb with you?'

'Why on earth would I bring a comb to a royal wedding?'

'I thought so. Well, no matter. Hold still.'

'Hold still? Why...'

My voice drained away as I suddenly felt fingers sliding through my damp hair. Gentle, firm fingers, straightening strands with disturbing ease. I tried to say something, tried to tell him to get his hands off my hair – but my voice suddenly didn't seem to want to work anymore. It lounged in a beach chair somewhere on a sunny shore on the Cote d'Azur, sipping a fruity drink, accompanied by my higher brain functions and sense of propriety.

His fingers slid through my hair with a surety and confidence that made my spine tingle and my knees want to give out. It reminded me too much of other times he had touched me – times on that mad, passionate trip to Egypt when our carefully erected boundaries had broken down and I had done things with him that no feminist should ever do with any man – particularly not with a cold-hearted chauvinist bastard such as Rikkard Ambrose.

Those memories had better stay where they were: in the past, firmly locked away. Mr Ambrose was my path to freedom and a regular pay cheque. I could literally not afford seeing him as anything else.

'There you go.' With a swipe of his forefinger, sliding a stray lock of hair behind my ear, he finished. 'Much less faeneumerial.'

'Faene*what*?'

'Haystackish.'

'Ha, ha.'

'Attention please!' The voice calling from the door did indeed catch the attention of everyone in the room. It was the kind of voice designed to catch attention: deep and carrying, with a slight burr in it. The little man it belonged to wasn't nearly as impressive, but his uniform made up for it. From all the bright crests and golden tresses, I guessed he was some kind of Royal Herald.

'Attention, everybody. The Royal Couple is approaching. Please take your places.'

HAPPILY EVER AFTER WITH WHISKERS

'Come.'

Mr Ambrose offered his arm to me, and I slipped mine into it almost without thinking. We retreated to the first row of chairs, but when I started to sit down, Mr Ambrose gripped my arm tighter.

'No!'

'But...that man said for us to take our places.'

'Yes. *Standing.* You don't sit in the presence of royalty.'

'But...that's stupid!'

'Yes, it is. But until and unless someone successfully explains this to the reigning monarch, we stay upright.' His free hand reached up and, gently, with the back of his knuckles, graced my hair. 'Understood, Miss Linton?'

The way he said 'Miss Linton' sent a delicious shiver down my spine. I hadn't heard him say this in months, and it touched some spot deep inside me I hadn't even known existed.

I swallowed, trying to get out of my throat the lump that was suddenly lodged there.

'Yes, Sir.'

'Adequate.'

The Royal Herald pounded the floor with his staff. 'His Highness, Prince Francis Albert Augustus Charles Emmanuel of Saxe-Coburg and Gotha, Duke of Saxony!'

I leaned over towards Mr Ambrose. 'Is that two people he just announced, or three?'

'One! Be quiet, Mr Linton!'

'*Miss* Linton to you, Sir.'

'Be quiet!'

A man entered the room. Except for the splendidly impressive scarlet uniform with golden tresses, he didn't look much like a prince. He had a round face, and a rather silly little moustache perched on his upper lip. When he bowed and spoke to some duke or other, one could clearly hear the traces of a German accent, and his smile seemed just as silly as the moustache one floor above.

I leaned over to Mr Ambrose.

'Why would anyone want to marry *that*?'

'Miss Linton?'

'Yes, Sir?'

'Shut up!'

'Yes, Sir. Right away, Sir.'

Finally, the Prince of Saxe-So-and-so had worked himself through all the people present with a series of bows, nods and silly smiles, and had reached the front of the crowd where Mr Ambrose and I stood.

'Follow my lead,' Mr Ambrose hissed into my ear. 'Do exactly what I am going to do!'

'What? Stare at him icily?'

'Just do what I do!'

'Yes, Sir.'

Mr Ambrose pulled me towards the Prince – and smiled.

I am not joking.

A bright, broad, shining smile spread across the face of the man whose facial muscles ordinarily seemed to be made out of granite. In my entire life, I had only seen Mr Ambrose smile like that once before, and I remembered very well what had happened that day.

Poor Prince Albert...

'Your Highness!' Mr Ambrose gave a sweeping bow. 'I am so delighted that you were so kind as to invite me to your special day.'

The silly smile on the Prince's face broadened. 'You are welcome, Herr...'

Mr Ambrose waved his hand. 'We've only met once before. I doubt Your Highness would see fit to remember me.'

'But of course I do! Herr Rikkard Ambrose, isn't it?'

'Yes! You honour me, Your Highness.'

'Not at all!' Reaching out, Prince Albert grasped Mr Ambrose's hand and shook it energetically. 'After your generous contribution to the orphanages in my home city, how could I not remember? Thank you, Herr Ambrose. *Ich danke Ihnen von ganzem Herzen.* You are a truly good and generous man.'

I had just about managed to keep my mouth closed when Mr Ambrose had started to smile. But now, my jaw dropped open.

Mr Ambrose had *donated money*?

Of his *own free will*?

To a *good cause*?

Was he sick? Should I check his temperature?

'It was my pleasure, Your Highness,' Mr Ambrose said, looking deeply and earnestly into the Prince's eyes. 'How could I stand idly by and let little children suffer when it was in my power to help? After all, what are a few thousand pounds sterling?'

A strangled noise erupted from my throat. Mr Ambrose glanced over at me, still smiling. 'Something wrong, my darling?'

A few thousand pounds sterling...!

'N-no. Nothing at all.'

'Wonderful.' Taking me by the arm, Mr Ambrose led me a step closer towards the Prince. 'Your Highness, please allow me to introduce my lovely companion for today: Miss Lillian Linton.'

The Prince performed a deep bow. 'How do you do, *Fräulein* Linton?'

I curtsied in my best courtly fashion. If Aunt Brank had seen me, she would have been proud. Well, actually, if Aunt Brank had seen me, considering where

I was and who I was talking to, she would have passed out. But, after she had woken up again, she would have been very proud, I'm sure.

'When I invited you, I had no idea that you would appear in such charming company,' the Prince added towards Mr Ambrose.

For a moment, the smile on Mr Ambrose's face flickered. 'Neither had I.' His grip on my arm tightened. 'But the Fates play with the string of one's life as they please, sometimes.'

I couldn't manage to completely hide my self-satisfied grin. Fates my foot!

'But not even Miss Linton can hope to outshine your bride on her big day.' Reaching out, Mr Ambrose grasped the Prince's hand. 'May I congratulate you, Your Highness, on your good fortune, and wish you perfect happiness in marriage? There is nothing as important in life as finding a good woman to love, and you have found the best of noble blood in the whole wide world.'

My poor jaw! I had just managed to pull it up again, and – wham! – it came slamming open again.

What did he just say?

'Thank you!' The Prince almost looked as if he had tears in his eyes. 'You don't know what this means to me, *Herr* Ambrose, coming from a man like you. I truly hope that once the bustle of the wedding is over, you will come visit me and my bride at Buckingham Palace?'

'I should like nothing better.'

'Attention, please!' All eyes went to the herald again. 'I have just received word that Her Majesty is approaching. Would everyone return to their places, please?'

Mr Ambrose squeezed the Prince's hand one more time, then let go and, still smiling as if he had lockjaw, steered me away. He had to steer me because I was too busy staring suspiciously at the grin on his face to think of moving my feet.

'What is this?' I demanded in a low voice. 'What's wrong with your face?'

'Miss Linton?'

'Yes?'

'Shut up!'

'I won't shut up! I want to know what... Hey!'

Ignoring my protest, Mr Ambrose manoeuvred me into a corner and only stopped when we were firmly situated at the left end of the front row of guests.

'What is the matter with you?' I pressed. 'Three thousand pounds sterling? You gave three thousand pounds sterling to an orphanage? Did someone knock you over the head with an iron bar?'

He turned that radiant smile on me – that smile that sent a shiver of danger down my spine.

'Is it so unbelievable that I would do a generous deed out of the goodness of my heart?'

I eyed him for a moment. 'Frankly – yes!'

'I see you've come to know me well, Mr. Linton.'

'I have, unfortunately. And that's *Miss* Linton to you, Mr Ambrose, Sir.'

'Miss. As you wish.'

'Why did you give away three thousand pounds?'

'You cannot catch fish without bait on the hook, Miss Linton.'

I didn't really know what he meant by that. But I would have eaten a pot full of pus before admitting that to him.

'Three thousand pounds is a pretty big bait.'

That smile flashed again, and this time I saw what I hadn't seen the first time he had pulled this trick on me: the underlying ice behind the smile, and the calculating coldness in his eyes.

'Oh, the three thousand pounds aren't the bait, Miss Linton.' Half-turning, Mr Ambrose nodded towards Prince Albert. 'He is.'

My eyebrows shot up. 'Then you have to be catching a fish with pretty strange tastes!'

'Indeed. There she is.'

I followed the stiff nod of his head just in time to see a figure in white appear at the door. My eyes shot back to Mr Ambrose. He couldn't be serious! Could he?

Mr Ambrose saw me looking and gave me the tiniest of nods.

Yes. He could.

My eyes went back to the door, just as the herald pounded his staff onto the floor. 'Her Majesty Alexandrina Victoria, Queen of the United Kingdom of Great Britain and Ireland!'

The Queen smiled shyly and nodded at the assembled crowed, who all bowed deeply. With her pale, moon-shaped face and too small mouth, she wasn't really much better-looking than her husband-to-be. But when her eyes met Albert's, a smile lit up her face, a real, live smile, and an answering smile spread over the Prince's features. Suddenly, he didn't look quite so silly anymore.

'Tell me why you think of the Queen of England as a fish?' I whispered to Mr Ambrose.

'Later, Miss Linton.'

'But–'

'Later!'

I gave up my protests. To be honest, I was too caught up in watching the couple. Music had started playing in the background, and Victoria was walking towards the altar, suddenly seeming much taller and more royal than before. When the bride and bridegroom stood beside each other, a light appeared to shine out of their eyes that was brighter than the sun. No great achievement on a rainy day like this, but still...the looks on their faces stirred something deep within me.

I glanced over at Mr Ambrose. He was standing stock-still, not looking at me. The moment the couple turned towards the altar, away from him, the bright smile bled from his face, leaving only cold stone in its place.

For some reason, it made me happy.

The priest cleared his throat.

'Dearly beloved, we are gathered together here in the sight of God, and in the face–'

At the word, my eyes were inexplicably drawn back to Mr Ambrose's face. Why? Why did I, now of all times, feel an irresistible urge to drink in the sight of him? Yes, he was the most breathtakingly handsome man imaginable. Yes, he looked a thousand times more like a king than poor Prince Albert ever would. But he was a chauvinist miser, a tyrannical, ruthless opportunist. Exactly the kind of man I most despised!

Or at least I *should* most despise.

With great effort, I tore my eyes away from his face.

'*...of this congregation, to join together this man and this woman in holy matrimony.*'

They jumped right back, unable to look away. Blast them! A girl should be able to rely on her own visual organs to do what she wants, shouldn't she?

Suddenly, looking at him standing beside me, I realized something: he had shifted. Only slightly, very slightly. But as finely attuned as I was to detecting minimal changes in his stony features, it took me only moments to spot that his right hand had made an almost imperceptible movement – towards me!

Ha! You're probably just imagining it. Or maybe he just shifted a bit. So what? People shift all the time when they have to stand around..

People, yes. But Mr Ambrose? Mr Rikkard I'm-made-of-granite-harder-than-your-chisel Ambrose?

All right, maybe you didn't imagine – There! Look, he did it again!

Yes. He had indeed. His hand had moved a fraction of an inch closer to mine. And, to my horror, I felt my own hand starting to move. What was this? After my eyes, was I now losing control over my hands, too? This was intolerable!

But my hand didn't seem to care about my feelings. It stubbornly inched closer towards those long, elegant fingers. Fingers chiselled from cool, smooth stone.

'*...which is an honourable estate, instituted of God in the time of man's innocency, signifying unto us the mystical union...*'

My hand shifted another inch closer. Damn! Why did that bloody priest have to use all those words like 'join together' and 'union'? Couldn't he say 'division' instead, damn him?

'*...that is betwixt Christ and his Church...*'

Oh. Well, I suppose not. A mystical division between Christ and his church would not be convenient, from a religious point of view.

Mr Ambrose's hand moved another fraction of an inch closer.

I glanced up at his face. It showed no emotion whatsoever.

'*...which holy estate Christ adorned and beautified with his presence, and first miracle that he wrought, in Cana of Galilee; and is commended of Saint Paul to be honourable among all men: and therefore is not by any to be enterprised, nor taken in hand, unadvisedly, lightly, or wantonly, to satisfy men's carnal lusts...*'

At that very moment, both our hands twitched towards each other two whole inches. My cheeks started to burn, and I didn't know why. I didn't even know why our hands were doing this...this moving towards each other! Why was this happening? How was it happening? And what did it bloody mean?

I've got a better question, said that little voice in the back of my mind. *Why are you still thinking about the phrase 'carnal lusts'?*

'Shut up!' I growled, too low for anybody to hear.

'...and appetites, like brute beasts that have no understanding; but reverently, discreetly, advisedly, soberly, and in the fear of God; duly considering the causes for which Matrimony was ordained. First, It was ordained for the procreation of children...'

Why, in God's name, why, were my eyes once more drawn to his face at those words? Why was I suddenly imagining what he had looked like as a child? What a child of his would look like?

Forget about what it would look like! That annoying little voice inside me cut in. *Imagine what a nasty little bloody tyrant it would be!*

I wrenched my eyes away from his face again and tried my best to pull my fingers away, too – but to no avail. Once more, they inched closer.

'...to be brought up in the fear and nurture of the Lord, and to the praise of his holy Name. Secondly, It was ordained for a remedy against sin, and to avoid fornication...'

Blast, blast, blast! Why couldn't I stop blushing? Blast!

'...that such persons as have not the gift of continency might marry, and keep themselves undefiled members of Christ's body.'

Right now I didn't feel like an undefiled member of Christ's body. I didn't even feel as if I wanted to be undefiled, thank you very much. Cautiously, I sneaked a peek at Mr Ambrose again, to see if he was in the mood for some defiling.

'Thirdly, It was ordained for the mutual society, help, and comfort, that the one ought to have of the other, both in prosperity and adversity.'

I felt a sudden tugging in my chest. The desire that made my cheeks flame was still there, but over it, enveloping, overshadowing it, was another much more frightening feeling. A feeling that made me want to cross the rest of the distance between Mr Ambrose's hand and mine. Not to feel how his smooth skin curved over the muscles of his hand and arm, but simply to hold his hand in mine and feel the warmth emanating from it.

'...Into which holy estate these two persons present come now to be joined.'

Our hands moved again. Now they were only fractions of an inch apart. Still, Mr Ambrose had not looked at me. He kept staring ahead, his face as unmoving, hard and perfect as that of an Ancient Greek statue. I honestly couldn't say what my own face showed in that moment. I didn't understand half of the emotions roiling in my chest.

'Therefore if any man can shew any just cause why they may not lawfully be joined together, let him now speak, or else hereafter forevermore be silent.'

And Mr Ambrose was silent. He was silent as stone as he moved his fingers the last few millimetres and interlaced them with mine. Around us, tumultuous cheers exploded and a choir started singing with angels' voices. I heard nothing – only Silence. The silence of Mr Rikkard Ambrose. And among all the cheering faces, I saw only his.

And inside of me, a voice kept chanting: *What is going on? What is going on? What the bloody hell is going on here?*

'Wilt thou have this Woman to thy wedded Wife, to live together after God's ordinance in the holy estate of Matrimony? Wilt thou love her, comfort her, honour, and keep her in sickness and in health; and, forsaking all others, keep thee only unto her, so long as ye both shall live?'

Ah, yes! A wedding was going on here. And *not* mine. I had to remember that, in spite of the wonderfully strong hand gripping my fingers. In spite of the tingling feeling dancing up my arm, temping me to step closer towards him.

The voice of the bridegroom rang out through the entire chapel, clear for all to hear: 'I will!'

Mr Ambrose's hand squeezed mine, tightly, and mine squeezed back without asking my brain for permission. My heart pounded, and suddenly, my chest felt indescribably warm.

Help! What's happening to me?

BEHIND THE SMILE

'Well, that went rather well, Mr Linton.'

'Huh?'

I blinked. I was in a coach? How had I ended up in a coach? I could have sworn I was in a chapel a moment ago, holding the hand of–

'Mr Linton? Mr Linton, are you listening to me?'

'Eerr...well...'

Slowly, I raised my head, looking up into the face of Mr Rikkard Ambrose. It was emotionless as ever, hard and cold. No trace of what we had shared just a moment ago was visible in his features.

What you shared? You shared a bit of skin contact! He probably just did it to look good in front of Prince Albert, for whatever sinister plan he has cooked up in that ice-cold head of his!

Yes, that was undeniably the most logical explanation. But then...why did my hand continue to tingle as if it had spent an hour in a jar filled with enchanted fairy dust?

'Mr Linton!'

I jerked my eyes away from my hand and up to him again. 'Yes, Sir? What is it, Sir?' Belatedly, I remembered that I was still wearing a dress. 'And it's *Miss* Linton to you,' I added.

'Not anymore. The wedding is over.'

'*What?* You are going to call me Mr, even while I'm wearing a dress?'

'Most certainly.'

'You...!'

'If you want to spend time insulting me, Mr Linton, do it after hours. We have work to do.'

And with that, he tapped his cane against the roof of the coach. 'Driver? Back to Empire House!'

I glowered at him the whole way back to the office, asking myself how I could ever have let him hold my hand. Right now, my hand was itching to make contact with another part of his body, and not quite so gently.

But there were questions I needed answered. And from what I had learned so far of male psychology, he was unlikely to tell me anything I wanted if I slapped him across the face first. With great effort, I managed to keep my hands at my sides. I even managed to restrain myself when, instead of stopping in front of the front entrance, we drove around to the back and through the gates into the courtyard, in spite of the fact that, deep down, I knew the reason why. My eyes flashed like a cutthroat's favourite razorblades. 'Why are we going in the back? Is it because you don't wish to be seen with a female by your staff?'

'Exactly, Mr Linton. Impressively perceptive, for your standards. Now strip.'

My eyes went wide. Did he just...?

Yes. He did.

Don't! I told my right hand, which was twitching and aching to begin its swift journey up to his face. *Don't! It's not worth it!*

Amazingly, unlike during the wedding, it actually did what I said.

'I hate to break it to you, Mr Ambrose, Sir, but if I divest myself of my dress, it's going to be rather more obvious that I am female, not less.'

'Correct.' Reaching under the seat, he pulled out a bundle of clothes. 'Which is why you will put these on before you leave the coach.'

Open-mouthed, I stared at the clothes. Not because they were anything to write home about. A plain black hat, black trousers and tailcoat. The vest was the only thing fancy. No, it wasn't the fact that the clothes were special which had me gaping. It was the fact that they were mine! *Bloody mine!* Paid for *with my own money!*

'How did you get your hands on those?'

Your hands that have held mine...

I squashed down the thought.

'Karim gave them to me,' Mr Ambrose told me, unconcernedly.

'And how did Karim get his oversized paws on my clothes?'

'He took them from your uncle's garden shed at my instruction.'

My jaw wanted to drop – then remembered it was already wide open. Blast!

'You had Karim break into my uncle's garden shed?'

'Karim has broken into at least seven British-Indian forts, two palaces and three prisons while in my employ. Believe me, your uncle's garden's shed did not present a problem to him.'

'I don't doubt it! My incredulity was related to the fact that he broke British law by committing breaking and entering.'

'Ah. Well, that does not present a problem to him either.'

I took a deep breath.

Calm, I told myself. *If he can stay calm, so can you.*

'And how, if I may ask, Sir, did you know that I had an emergency set of clothes stashed in my uncle's garden shed?'

'You may not.'

'Excuse me?'

'You may not ask. Get dressed.'

And, dumping the pile of clothes into my lap, he climbed out of the coach, firmly shutting the door behind him.

For a moment, one blissful, feminist, rebellious moment, I considered going after him and fulfilling my homicidal fantasies. Then I remembered that he was the man signing my pay cheque at the end of each month, and without that signature, my agenda for independence would go down the drain faster than you could say 'Not fair!' Pulling down the blinds with a muttered curse, I started the arduous process of squirming out of a dress.

Fifteen minutes later I emerged from the coach, quite literally a new man. Stopping two feet in front of Mr Ambrose, I gave a mock salute.

'Mr Victor Linton reporting for duty, Sir!'

'You took your time.'

'Would you have preferred it if I took yours?'

'Wit is not something I pay you for, Mr Linton.'

'Unfortunately, Sir.'

I suppressed a grin as I saw his left little finger twitch. 'We have work to do. Follow me!'

'Yes, Sir!'

We left the yard and entered through large double doors into the main hall. All eyes snapped to us the moment we entered, and let me tell you, there were a lot of them. Eyes, I mean. Clerks, accountants and messengers were hurrying hither and thither, and probably also fither and lither, making absolutely sure that they had performed every minutest task to Mr Ambrose's perfect satisfaction. The moment the great master himself entered the hall, a hush fell over the hurrying crowd, and though they did not dare to slow down, they veered off to the left and right, avoiding Mr Ambrose like panicking chickens as he strode through the hall, me following in his wake. The instant we vanished into the stairwell, an audible sigh of relief sounded from the hall behind us.

Mr Ambrose was the first and last person I had ever met who had mastered the art of marching up a staircase. I guarantee you, even if trained soldiers tried this, they'd break their neck at the second step. But Mr Ambrose did it as if there were nothing to it, and was quicker than I when I was flat-out running. He was at the top long before I was.

Did he wait for me?

I'll give you three guesses.

Thud!

The sound of his office door slamming shut greeted me as I reached the top landing, panting and out of breath.

'Good morning, Mr Linton,' Mr Stone, the receptionist, greeted me with a timid smile. 'In a good mood today, is he?'

'Excellent!' I panted. 'We've just come from the Royal Wedding.'

'Ah. That explains it. Here.' Mr Stone bent to retrieve something from a drawer, and when he came up again, held out a stack of letters to me. 'The correspondence of the day.'

Immediately, a large, scented pink envelope with a coat of arms stamped on it caught my eye. Mr Stone, who had noticed the direction, nodded.

'Yes. One of those again.'

'They've been coming more frequently, lately, haven't they?'

'Almost every day.'

'Hm.' Taking the envelopes, I studied the pink intruder carefully.

'What do you do with them, if I may ask, Mr Linton?' Mr Stone enquired shyly.

'What can I do? It's not as though *he* wants to see them. I stuff them in the lowest drawer of my desk. It's full to the brim already. I wonder how I'm going to fit this one in.'

'Well, in case you need space, I still have one or two free corners in my drawers.'

'Thanks.' I was about to reach out for the doorknob and follow Mr Ambrose into the office, when I hesitated. 'You don't happen to have any idea whom they're from, do you?'

'What?' Mr Stone popped a breath mint into his mouth and reached for a pile of documents on his desk. 'The pink letters?'

'Yes. Does he have a wife? A friend overseas with a strange predilection for pink? A mistress whose services he didn't pay for because she didn't perform to his satisfaction?'

Mr Stone coughed and, with a *ping*, the breath mint ricocheted off his paperweight and disappeared somewhere in the labyrinth of papers on his desk.

'Err...um...well, Mr Linton, I wouldn't know anything about that. I'm afraid you'll have to ask Mr Ambrose. Though I'm sure that all of Mr Ambrose's connections are perfectly respectable and proper.'

'Are you? Well, good for you.'

Tucking the stack of envelopes under my arm, I followed my perfectly respectable and proper employer into his office, where he was busy studying the plans for a new, improved steam engine his men had managed to steal from the offices of his main rival, Lord Dalgliesh, only a few days ago.

'Ah, Mr Linton, there you are. What have you got there?'

'Letters, Sir.' Hurriedly, I covered the pink one with my arm. 'Nothing to be worried about. I'll sort through them later.'

'Acceptable.' Reaching over, Mr Ambrose pulled a bell pull and, a few moments later, a panting messenger boy appeared at the door.

'Send this down to Mr Maddison in the technical department.'

'Yes, Sir, Mr Ambrose, Sir!'

'Tell him the valves still need a little bit of work, but otherwise, the prototype seems sufficient.'

'Yes! Right away, Sir!'

And he was off.

I raised an eyebrow. 'So, you are involving the young and innocent in your nefarious deals now?'

Mr Ambrose took a seat behind his desk and fixed me with his cool gaze over steepled fingers. 'I do not know what you mean, Mr Linton.'

I closed the door behind me. 'Don't play the innocent with me! I'm your personal secretary. Your closest confidante. I always know what you are really up to.'

'Oh, really?' Behind his desk, Mr Ambrose cocked his head. 'Then pray, enlighten me, what was I doing at the wedding ceremony? Why was I wasting my time on a German princeling with too big a head and too small a moustache?'

I opened my mouth – and closed it again.

'All right,' I admitted grudgingly. 'Maybe I don't *always* know what you're up to.'

'Indeed you don't.'

'So tell me!' I took a step forward. 'What was that all about? You...' I hardly managed to bring the word over my lips, the idea was so outlandish! 'You...*smiled.*'

'Indeed. I am reliably informed that contortion of facial musculature is customary at nuptials.'

'It is customary in everyday life, too. But that didn't mean you saw fit to make use of it.'

'True.'

'And you gave three thousand pounds to charity!'

'True.'

'*Why?*'

In answer, instead of saying anything, Mr Ambrose bent down and retrieved something from a drawer within his desk. With a whisper of air, a large sheet of paper landed in front of me on the desktop.

'Read,' he ordered.

DEAR DIARY

I picked up the paper, and read.

'*Her Majesty Victoria, Queen of the United Kingdom of Great Britain and Ireland, in Her gracious consideration for the chiefs and people of New Zealand, and her desire to preserve to them their land and to maintain peace and order amongst them, has been pleased to appoint an officer to treat with them for the cession of the Sovereignty of their country and of the islands...*'

My voice faded away. With narrowed eyes, I looked up at Mr Ambrose and waved the paper.

'What is this?'

He met my gaze with his cold one. 'I do not need to explain myself to you, Mr Linton. I will tell you what I plan in this case only because I shall need your assistance at a later point.'

'Understood, Sir. So...what is it?'

'What you are holding is a copy of the so-called Treaty of Waitangi, signed four days ago by representatives of the British Crown and forty-four Maori chiefs at Waitangi, New Zealand. It establishes British Sovereignty over all of New Zealand.'

My eyes narrowed a bit further.

'I've read about sea journeys. A journey to New Zealand would take at least sixty days.'

'Seventy-five, to be exact. But, depending on the weather, it can last as long as one hundred and twenty.'

'If this was signed just four days ago, how do you have a copy of it now?'

'By acquiring one before the original was shipped, of course.'

'Of course.' I rolled my eyes. 'And what has this Treaty of Waikiki-'

'Waitangi.'

'-Waitangi got to do with you?'

'Simple. With British sovereignty established over the islands, it will be much easier to exploit their natural resources. I am opening up new avenues of business.'

'And what about these Maori you mentioned? What will they say to these new avenues of yours?'

'Every avenue needs paving stones, doesn't it?'

I decided it was best not to think too deeply about what exactly he meant by that. In any case, I still had plenty of other things to think about.

'And what does all of this have to do with the Queen?'

'I have already exerted considerable influence on the British Parliament to grant me economic benefits in New Zealand. Unlike India, Dalgliesh has not been able to sink his fangs into those lands yet, and I plan to make him pay for his negligence. I am going to get this land under my control.'

'No matter the cost?'

'Don't be ridiculous, Mr Linton.' He gave me a censuring look. 'The cost always matters. One simply has to make sure that it is outweighed by profit.'

That wasn't exactly what I had meant. But I knew it would be useless trying to explain to him that I had been referring to the natives. So I simply asked: 'The Queen?'

'The Queen is the last cornerstone in my plan. True, she has little actual political power, but she serves as an important figurehead. With her blessing for my ventures, rival offers will likely be looked upon with disfavour by Parliament. That is why I decided to win over her husband. Considering the way things stand, if I have Albert on my side, I have Victoria.'

'Why?' I asked, frowning. 'Most royal marriages are arranged for the sake of convenience, or for an alliance. Usually, there's no more regard between the husband and his wife than between a pin and its pincushion. Why would you think this case is any different?'

In answer, Mr Ambrose pulled something else out of a drawer of his desk. This time, it was a few smaller sheets of paper, filled with neat handwriting. Mr Ambrose cleared his throat.

'*At about half past, I sent for Albert; he came to the Closet where I was alone, and after a few minutes I said to him, that I thought he must be aware why I wished them to come here, and that it would make me too happy if he would consent to what I wished (to marry me)...*'

My mouth dropped open. He couldn't be reading what I thought he was reading, could he?

'*...we embraced each other over and over again, and he was so kind, so affectionate; oh! to feel I was, and am, loved by such an Angel as Albert-*'

'Mr Ambrose!'

He glanced up. 'Yes?'

'Mr Ambrose! This isn't...You can't be–'

'If you would let me continue, Mr Linton? The pertinent part is still to come.' He raised the papers to his eyes again. *'To feel I was, and am, loved by such an Angel as Albert was too great delight to describe! He is perfection; perfection in every way, in beauty – in everything! I told him I was quite unworthy of him and kissed his dear hand...'*

'Mr Ambrose! This...how...how in God's name–'

'Will you be quiet, Mr Linton? If you keep interrupting me, this will take all day.' He gave me another one of his cool looks, then returned to his reading. *'He said he would be very happy, "das Leben mit dir zu zubringen", and was so kind, and seemed so happy, that I really felt it was the happiest brightest moment in my life, which made up for all that I had suffered and endured. Oh! How I adore and love him, I cannot say!'*

Lifting his eyes from the paper, Mr Ambrose regarded me for a moment. 'This material would support the theory that their marriage was in fact not simply a marriage of convenience, wouldn't you say, Mr Linton?'

'Um...well...'

'This entry is from Tuesday, October 15, 1839. But if this is insufficient evidence to convince you, let me read you a passage from November 9.'

He turned over a few pages, and then began to read aloud in his cool, distant voice once more, while I listened with my mouth hanging open. Part of me knew that I should stuff my ears, but I didn't. I couldn't.

'He looked down into my face, with such an angelic expression in his dear beautiful face. I laid my head on his chest, and he wiped away my tears with his hand and took me and pressed me in his arms, and kissed me so often, as I did him. We then sat on the sofa together, and dearest Albert put his arm round my waist, and leant quite close to me, and kissed my neck and head, and–'[3]

'All right, all right!' I held up both hands protectively. 'I get the picture!'

'Satisfactory.' He leaned back and stowed away the papers, not noticing the glare I was directing at him.

'Tell me you didn't!' I demanded.

'Didn't what, Mr Linton?'

'Tell me you didn't just read me passages from the Queen of England's private diary!'

'I didn't.'

I sagged with relief. 'Oh, thank God! I thought–'

'I read you passages from the *transcript* of the Queen of England's private diary with which my agents provided me.'

'*What?*'

'The transcript. Meaning an exact reproduction of material originally presented in another medium. From Latin *transcribere*.'

'I know what a transcript is, thank you very much! I've only made about two hundred of them for you since starting this infernal job!'

'Two hundred and thirty-seven.'

---

[3] In case you are wondering, these passages are actual quotes from the diary of Queen Victoria. This is not made up.

'Let's get back to the subject, shall we? You stole the Queen of England's private diary?'

'No. I had it copied. People would have noticed it was stolen.'

'*How?*'

'Apparently, the staff at Buckingham Palace is not particularly reliable. When I sent a few of my people over with excellent, albeit fake, references, the housekeeper nearly kissed their feet, she was so happy to hire them.'[4]

'And...and you had them copy out the Queen's private diary?'

'Yes.'

'How could you?!'

'By paying them enough to motivate them.' Abruptly, Mr Ambrose rose from behind his desk. 'It was worth the investment. When Prince Albert looks at our Queen with - what was it again?' he leafed through the transcript. 'Ah, yes. When he looks at the queen with an *"angelic expression in his dear beautiful face"* and suggests to her that I should be granted economic benefits, I hazard she will not be able to resist him.'

I sent him the most disapproving stare I was capable of. To judge by the stony cast of his face, he didn't even notice. 'And what now?' I demanded. 'Why did you tell me all this? It seems you have everything already planned out to the last detail.'

'Indeed I have.' Marching over to a secretary in the corner (unlike me, a wooden one), he pulled a blank sheet of paper out of a stack and returned to his desk. 'But not every step has been put into practice yet. It will not suffice to approach the Prince - I will have to attack the couple from both sides. To that end, I intend to send the Queen a letter. A letter consisting of ridiculously exaggerated compliments for dear, angelic Albert. In her present state of temporary, romance-induced insanity, it is exactly the kind of thing that will influence her to do what I wish.'

I stared at him. 'You? You know how to write compliments?'

'No.' He put quill and paper down on the desk in front of me. 'Which is why you are going to write them for me.'

~~**~*~*

About half an hour later, I emerged from my office and approached Mr Ambrose's desk. He was deeply engrossed in the study of mining revenues from Sub-Saharan Africa, and didn't notice my approach. I cleared my throat.

'Yes, Mr Linton?' He didn't look up.

I thrust the paper at him. 'Here!'

He took it, and, turning, I started to tiptoe away.

'Wait!'

His voice froze me in place. Slowly, I turned back to face him again.

---

[4] There is quite a bit of historical fact in this. Prince Albert waged a small war against the servants of Buckingham Palace because they apparently weren't very good at their jobs.

'Yes, Sir?

'You will remain while I review your work.'

Blast! 'Yes, Sir. As you wish, Sir.'

He placed the paper of scrawled notes on his desk and began to study it. After a few minutes, he bent forward, his eyes narrowing infinitesimally. He remained like this for a few more moments – then he picked up the paper and raised it to his eyes until his perfectly carved, straight nose almost touched the paper.

With one, long, elegant finger he tapped the beginning of my notes. 'Really, Mr Linton?'

I nodded, bravely, my cheeks burning with embarrassment. 'Yes, really, Sir.'

'Hm.'

His eyes wandered further down the paper. Just about in the middle he stopped abruptly, and it almost seemed as if his eyebrows rose half a millimetre. Slowly, he looked up at me.

'Somewhat...extreme, don't you think, Mr Linton?'

My cheeks got even hotter. Bloody hell, was I glad I was too tanned for it to really show! 'No, Sir! It is absolutely essential, Sir.'

'But that part, where you say his d–'

'Yes, Sir!' I interrupted him, hurriedly. 'Trust me. I have five sisters. I know what girls want to hear.'

'Hm.' Mr Ambrose lowered his gaze to the paper again. 'I see, Mr Linton.'

He was just finishing the last paragraph when footsteps sounded outside in the hallway. A moment later, a knock came at the door.

'Enter!'

At Mr Ambrose's cool command, the door opened, and a willowy young man with glasses on his nose and a folder under his arm stuck his head inside. 'Um, please forgive the disturbance, Sir, but I thought you would like to know. A messenger from Miss Brand, the palace maid, just arrived, and it appears that–'

It was just then that the young man caught sight of me and nearly swallowed his tongue. He coughed. 'Sorry, Sir. I didn't know you had company. What I meant to say is that so far, operation RWN is progressing satisfactorily.'

'RWN?' I enquired, eyebrows raised.

The young man reddened, and desperately looked from Mr Ambrose to me and back again. Mr Ambrose waved a hand. 'Tell him. Mr Linton is my private secretary, and knows all about RWN.'

The young man cleared his throat. 'Royal wedding night,' he explained with a sheepish look on his face. 'Um...I've just remembered, there's somewhere I should be.'

'Take this.' Mr Ambrose handed him my paper with suggestions. 'Have Plaskett write it up in appropriately elegant handwriting and send it up for me to sign.'

'Yes, Sir.' The young man bowed hurriedly. I wasn't looking at him, though. I was staring at Mr Ambrose, my mouth agape.

The door closed with a click behind the young man, and I was still staring.

'Operation RWN?' I demanded, my voice sounding a little bit weaker than I would have liked.

Mr Ambrose cocked his head and gave me a look. One of *those* looks. 'Do you still wonder how I knew about the clothes in your garden shed?'

ROYAL EXAMPLE

When I got home that evening, I was still thinking about Mr Ambrose's report on operation RWN. That's the only way I can explain my not noticing the calculating looks my aunt threw me all through dinner. Only when my sister Ella nudged me and whispered: 'Why is Aunt Brank looking at you like that?' did I glance up and see her.

Hurriedly, she looked away, trying to make it appear as if there were nothing more interesting in the world to her than the plate of mushy boiled potatoes in front of her. But it was too late. I had already seen the look on her face: concentrated, cool and calculating – as if she were judging a slice of beef in the meat market. I knew that look all too well.

'Bloody hell, no!' I groaned.

'Lill!' Ella gasped. 'Watch your language!'

'Sorry.'

'What is the matter? What has upset you?'

'Upset me? You want to know what has upset me?' Leaning closer, I jabbed my fork in my aunt's direction, and whispered: 'She's found another you-know-what for me!'

'No!' Ella covered her mouth with one delicate pale hand. 'Surely not!'

'Surely yes! I know that look on her face. You can bet on it.'

'But...so soon?'

'Yes.'

'After you, um, grabbed the last one by the...err....and did...that thing to him?'

'Yes.'

'How would she be able to find someone willing?'

'Trust me, Aunt can get inventive when she wants something. And she wants us out of the house, married to the richest men she can lay her greedy paws on.'

'Now, really, Lill!' Ella shook her head. 'I can't believe that. Aunt may be a bit, well, forceful in trying to find matrimonial arrangements for us, but I'm sure she only wants our happiness.'

I looked at my little sister, one eyebrow raised. 'You think that do you?' I patted her head. 'Bless you.'

She gifted me with one of her radiant smiles that lit up the whole room. 'So you agree with me?'

'Not in a million years! But I'm sure it's very noble of you to be so ridiculously trusting.'

After dinner, I slipped out of the dining room before my aunt could catch me and drag me off to her latest you-know-what. Grabbing my favourite book from where I had hidden it from Aunt Brank, at the very back of the small library's lowest shelf, I made my way into the garden, behind my favourite bush, where no dogs ever peed and no aunts ever disturbed me.

Sighing with contentment, I flicked open *Some Reflections upon Marriage*. I didn't even have to leaf through it. I knew the book so well, it fell open just at the passage I was looking for.

But, alas! What poor Woman is ever taught that she should have a higher Design than to get her a Husband? Heaven will fall in, of course; and if she makes but an Obedient and Dutiful Wife, she cannot miss of it. A Husband, indeed, is thought by both Sexes so very valuable, that scarce a Man who can keep himself clean and make a bow, but thinks he is good enough to pretend to any Woman!

I gave another contented sigh. How wonderful it was to have found someone with whom I was completely and utterly of one mind – even if she had already been dead for over a hundred years.

I was so lost in Mary Astell's witty treatise that I nearly missed the light patter of feet passing my bush. Nearly, but not quite – because some part of my mind had been waiting for that sound all along. Raising my head, I saw a flash of white between the branches of the bush, and knew I had been right. It was she!

Closing my book and slipping it into my pocket, I peeked around the bush – and there she was! My little sister, Ella, hurrying towards the barrier between our garden and the neighbours'. And there, on the other side, was *he* – Edmund, the piano tuner's son, who, for the last year had been romancing my little sister, and whom, in my magnificent mercy, I had not yet decided to eviscerate.

They rushed towards each other like Pyramus and Thisbe, separated by an impenetrable barrier. Only where the two characters from Greek mythology had had to make do with a solid wall, fate had bestowed dozens of gaps between the poles of a fence on this happy pair.

'Ella, my love!'

'Edmund, my love!'

'My everything!'

'My sunshine!'

I glanced up at the sky, wondering idly if either of them had noticed it was already nighttime, and the moon was standing high. Probably not.

'Oh, Ella! Words cannot express how much I love you! The hours away from you have been torture!'

'So have mine! So have mine, Edmund! The entire day I was writhing in pain until I could see you again!'

Really? I cocked my head. *I didn't particularly notice that when you asked me to pass you the salt at dinner, little sister.*

'Oh, Ella!'

'Oh, Edmund!'

'Oh, my Ella!'

'Oh, my Edmund!'

'I love you so!'

'And I love you even more!'

'Impossible! Nobody could possibly love anybody more than I love you!'

'Except me!'

'No!'

'Yes!'

'Definitely not!'

'Definitely yes! I love you!'

'And I love you more!'

Sighing, I sank back behind the bush. The conversation of the two hadn't exactly gotten any more interesting in the last few months. I admit, in the beginning, it had been mildly entertaining – like a romantic comedy playing out in my own back garden. But a girl could only stomach so many 'I love you's before she felt an intense desire to hurl into the bushes. And since the bushes were my favourite reading spot, hurling was to be avoided at all costs.

I lost myself in the words of Mary Astell once more. But I had hardly been at it for five minutes, when a gasp from beyond the bush brought me to attention.

'What? Edmund! What did you say?'

My head darted forward, and my eyes found the piano tuner's son. He was leaning forward, against the fence, an intense expression on his face.

'It has been a year and a day since we first confessed our love to each other. I think it is time!'

Ella was as pale as a sheet. 'B-but...'

'I know it is a big step. But we love each other. Why wait?'

'But...Edmund...before marriage? It is not right! I couldn't...I wouldn't...'

He leaned forward even more, until his face was almost touching hers through one of the gaps in the fence. 'Don't you love me, Ella? Don't you want me?'

Ooh la la, this was a new tune! No more I-love-you-I-love-you-too. To judge from the look on the face of the piano tuner's son, he was ready to get down to business. Slowly, he reached out through the fence to touch Ella's face. Not quite so slowly, I reached out and grabbed a stout walking stick with a heavy iron knob I had stashed out here in the garden, just in case Edmund's head would ever need to be introduced to Mr Metal.

'Ella,' he murmured in a low voice that was probably meant to be seductive. Judging from my little sister's expression, she was by no means as immune to it as I was. 'Please. I love you. I need to feel you so badly.'

'I need you too, Edmund,' my little sister whispered back, giving me a renewed urge to hurl. I fought against it bravely.

'Then come to me. Let me touch you. Let me feel you. We have loved each other for over a year. The time is right to take the next step – now!'

All right! That's it, my friend!

Grabbing Mr Metal in both hands, I started forward and was about to step out from behind the bush when Ella stumbled back, breathing heavily.

'Give me some time!' she begged. 'Just a little time to...I...well...a little time, that's all! Please!'

And with that she whirled around, and dashed back towards the house.

~~**~*~*

By the time Ella arrived in our shared bedroom, I was already lying in bed, breathing very, very regularly. A ladder at the window can work real wonders, sometimes.

The room was dark. I could only see the pale silhouette of my little sister in the moonlight. Wordlessly, she slid out of her dress, into her nightgown and under the covers. We lay there for a while in companionable silence.

'Lill?'

Her voice was soft, but not really quiet.

'How did you know I was awake?'

'I always know, Lill.'

'Because of the special bond we share as siblings?'

'Because you snore when you sleep.'

A pillow flew out of my bed and barely missed the small hill under the blankets that was Ella.

'I don't snore!'

'Yes, you do. But in a very nice, ladylike way.'

'Oh, really? Thanks so much for the compliment.'

There was a pause.

'Lill?'

'Yes, Ella?'

'What would you do if a man asked you to...*you know*...before you were married?'

I remained very still.

'I'd chop his head off! Or better yet, I'd turn him over to Patsy!'

Ella gasped. 'That? Just for a kiss?'

My head whipped around. It was even darker in the room by now. I couldn't see enough of her face to see if she was making fun of me. But, knowing Ella, I highly doubted it.

'A kiss? Only a *kiss*?'

'Well...yes.' Now Ella sounded puzzled. 'What did you think we were talking about?'

My silence was answer enough. Or at least it would have been, for anyone whose mind was not as blissfully innocent as that of my little sister Ella.

'Well?' she persisted.

I cleared my throat. 'I was referring to, um, congress.'

I could practically hear Ella's frown. 'Isn't that some assembly of delegates in America?'

I cleared my throat again. '*Amorous* congress.'[5]

---

[5] Yes, it really is true: during the Victorian Era, the official polite term for sex was 'congress'. I bet you are never going to see a congressional debate with the same eyes after this.

The gasp that came out of the darkness was pure horror.

'Lill!'

'Um...sorry. But it's true.'

'How could you think...I would never...I couldn't...I wouldn't!'

'Yes, of course not. Sorry.'

I had to apologise half a dozen more times before Ella had calmed down enough to speak in complete sentences again. When she was finally lucid once more, she said: 'I certainly did not want to ask your advice about *that*.'

'No, of course not.'

'Because, of course, you wouldn't know anything more about *that* than I do. You're just as innocent as me.'

In that moment, I was fervently glad that the room was pitch black. I wouldn't have liked Ella seeing my ears turn red.

A hard body grinding against mine, pressing me into the mattress, buttons popping, hands moving, lips meeting in a frenzied dance-

'What I wanted to ask you,' Ella continued, blessedly interrupting the torrent of my memories, 'is about, um...well...kissing.'

She somehow managed to endow the word with the forbidden lust of original sin.

'Yes?' I prompted.

'Well...do you think there should be any of *that* before marriage?'

'Kissing where exactly? The hand?'

'Well...no.'

'The cheek?'

'Not really, no.' Ella's voice was nothing more than a soft squeak by now, hardly audible out of the darkness. 'I was thinking more of on the...you know...'

'No, I don't actually.'

'On the l...li...lips.'

'Ah.'

'Not that I intend to do anything of the sort, Lill! I mean, haha, who would I do it with? I mean, I don't know any young men, and certainly not well enough to go around kissing them or letting them kiss me, even if I wanted to, which I don't. It's merely hypothetical, you understand? Completely hypothetical. I would never contemplate doing something like that in real life! Never, for one moment!'

Up until that moment, I had never been a great fan of Shakespeare. But I had to admit that with his phrase 'The lady doth protest too much, methinks', he had pretty much hit the nail on the head.

'So, as a purely academic exercise,' I enquired, 'you would like my opinion on whether or not a hypothetical lady should give a theoretical kiss to her imaginary lover before they enter into a stochastic marriage?'

'Yes!' Ella breathed a sigh of relief. 'Exactly!'

'Well...'

'Yes? Yes?'

'I have no experience on the subject myself, of course,' I lied.

'Of course.'

'And I would never consider marrying, myself, of course.'

'Of course.'

'But...'

'Yes?'

'I heard that the Queen kissed Prince Albert before their marriage.'

Ella's first gasp had been nothing in comparison to the one that escaped her now. It was the queen bee of all gasps. 'No!'

'Oh yes.'

'Really? Pinky swear?'[6]

'Pinky swear with bells on!'

'How do you know this? How would you know anything about Queen Victoria?'

'Trust me,' I told her, 'I have it from a good source.'

Ella was silent for a while.

Then: 'The Queen.'

'Yes, Ella.'

'The Queen kissed Prince Albert before they were married.'

'Yes, Ella.'

'So...there can't really be anything terribly wrong with it, can there?'

'I suppose not.'

Another moment of silence. It wasn't the same silence that always emanated from Mr Ambrose, though. This silence was much less icy, and much, much more thoughtful.

'Lill?'

'Yes, Ella?'

'Would you mind terribly...well...what I meant...what I mean to say...'

'Spit it out.'

'Would you mind if I stepped out for a moment or two? I forgot there's something I have to do tonight.'

I bet you do.

'Of course not. Go ahead.'

Ella was out of bed and at the door before I could blink.

'Thanks!'

And she was gone.

---

[6] The tradition of the pinky swear did indeed already exist in Victorian times, as attested by this mid-19th-century rhyme:

Pinky, pinky bow-bell,

Whoever tells a lie

Will sink down to the bad place

And never rise up again

The origins of the practise are unclear, but some sources point to Japan, where the tradition usually involved having your pinky cut off if you broke the promise. For some reason, the rather more squeamish Western cultures did not include this aspect of the custom when they adopted it, however.

THE YOU-KNOW-WHAT OF HORROR

Ella didn't even wait to put her dress on. She was out before I could move a muscle.

Hm... where could she be going? You have three guesses, Lilly.

I only really needed one.

Sighing, I rolled out of bed, threw on a robe against the cold of the night and went to the window, where I had let the ladder stand, just in case. Down in the house, I could hear the pitter-patter of Ella's swift, light feet. I, for my part, climbed leisurely out of the window and down the ladder. By the time the back door exploded outward and Ella rushed into the garden, one hundred percent the delectable damsel in her white nightgown, I was sitting behind my usual bush, trying to count the daisies on the ground in the moonlight.

'Edmund!'

Ella's cry faded away unheard. Instead of pining at the fence, her lover had apparently done the sensible thing and gone to bed. Ella didn't seem to realise or care, though. She rushed towards the fence.

'Edmund!'

Once again, no answer. Gripping the poles of the fence, Ella pressed her face between the bars and called, so loudly that I was worried she might wake up our aunt up in the house: 'Edmund, my love!'

However, Edmund my love – or rather *her* love, thank God – didn't respond.

Ella then said a very, very bad word. A word that made me raise my eyebrows and raise my opinion of my little sister's vocabulary a notch or two. Turning, she stomped over to the garden shed. For a moment I didn't realise what she was after – until, that is, she reached out her arms and with both hands grabbed the ladder leaning against the shed. The ladder I had used to climb out of the window. The ladder which had rested against the garden shed for over a year without the lovers once getting the idea of using it to climb over the fence.

I sucked in a breath!

This was a historic moment! I was almost sorry I didn't have a professional painter here to record it for posterity. I was still in a daze by the time Ella had reached the top of the ladder. Not hesitating a second, she swung her legs over the fence.

'Mpf! Ouch!'

There was a dull thud as my little sister hit the ground. It shook me out of my paralysis, and I rose to peek over the bush. Was she hurt?

But Ella was rising to her feet, dusting earth and bits of grass off her formerly white dress. Without hesitation, she marched off towards the Conways' house

And I?

Why the heck was I still standing here?

Giving myself a mental kick, I surged forward, grabbing the ladder and starting upwards. Ella was so focused on her goal that she didn't notice me, not even when I dropped down behind her, emitting a considerably louder *thud* than she had.

'Edmund!' she called, softly, advancing towards the back of the Conways' home. I could only hope that Mrs Conway didn't have a lighter sleep than her son Edmund, or we'd be in big trouble. Grabbing Mr Metal in both hands, just to be sure, I ducked behind the nearest bush. It didn't feel comfortable. It wasn't *my* bush, my little fortress of feminism where I felt like nothing in the world could touch me. It was a strange bush, with funny-smelling leaves. Plus, a cat left me a little sweet-smelling present there.

'Edmund!'

My grip around Mr Metal tightened. *Shut up!* I mentally yelled at my little sister. *Do you want to wake up the whole neighbourhood?*

But Ella's plans apparently were more tightly focused on one particular neighbour. Grabbing a handful of gravel from the path behind the house, she pulled back her arm and let it fly. I had to admit, I was impressed. My little sister had a better arm than I had suspected. The gravel sailed through the air and hit Edmund's window on the first floor with an audible clatter. Maybe I should take her out to play squash or tennis some time.

'Edmund!'

Another load of gravel hit the window. A yelp came from inside the house, and footsteps could be heard from within. A moment later, the window slid upwards, and a rather dishevelled-looking Edmund Conway stuck his head outside. His face was sleepy and confused – but the sleepiness vanished the moment he caught sight of Ella.

'Ella, my love! What are you doi – '

'Come down here!' Ella ordered.

'But I – '

'I said come down!'

'But we can't just–'

'Now, Edmund!'

He blinked, stared at her for a moment – then withdrew his head. A moment later, he emerged feet-first, and soon dangled from the windowsill. I wondered for a moment how he thought he was going to get in without his dear parents finding out about his midnight rendezvous. But apparently, lovesick minds don't think that far.

'Umpf!'

With a *thud* – which, I noticed with satisfaction, was louder than both mine and Ella's, even though he had his mother's rosebushes to cushion his impact – he hit the ground feet-first and fell over. Ella rushed forward. 'Edmund! Did you hurt yourself?'

'No, no.' Shaking his head, he attempted to rise – and promptly sank back to his knees. 'I'm t-totally f-fine.'

'Oh my darling! Don't do anything so dangerous ever again, do you hear me?' She hugged him fiercely, conveniently forgetting for the moment that it was she who had asked him to come down to her in the first place.

'I'm fine, really. Why did you want me to come outside?'

Ella sank down onto her knees, until she was on Edmund's level. They were only inches apart. I experimentally swung Mr Metal, wondering how hard Edmund's head would be. If he made one wrong move towards her, we would find out.

'Well...I have been thinking,' Ella breathed. 'And I...I wanted to give you something.'

'Give me something?' He looked puzzled. 'I don't understand. What could you possibly want to give me at this hour of the night? What are doing here?'

'This.' And, grabbing him by the collar, she pulled him towards her, crushing her lips to his.

I weighed Mr Metal in my hands, thoughtfully. Could that be counted as him making a wrong move? True, technically he hadn't moved. But in relation to her he had. If a train hit a pedestrian, was it really the train who was at fault, or the pedestrian?

Ella continued to maul Edmund for at least half a minute. When she finally broke away, gasping for air, his face was as red as a wagonload of tomatoes.

'Ella, I...I don't know...'

Ella apparently knew, though. She pulled him forward again, moulding her lips to his as if she had been doing nothing her whole life except seducing the sons of piano tuners. Maybe she had? What did I know? I should have paid more attention when we were younger to what she was up to when she was off alone.

'Ella! Whatmmmpff...'

Edmund shut up then, relaxing against her. It apparently was becoming clear to him what exactly Ella was doing here, and that she wasn't planning to stop any time soon. Slowly, the two of them sank to the ground, until Edmund was nothing more than a prone body, helpless under Ella's ravenous lips.

I had to admit, I was thoroughly impressed. This was a side to my little sister I hadn't seen before, and I liked it. I liked it a lot. This was much more fun to watch than the gooey 'I love you's I normally was subjected to. Smiling, I sat Mr Metal against a tree and sank down onto the grass for a nice, long, late-night entertainment.

~~**~*~*

I blame Ella. I blame her completely and absolutely. If she hadn't spent hours out in the garden doing lip-gymnastics with the piano tuner's son, obligating me to watch out for her, I might not have been as tired the next morning. And if I hadn't been tired the next morning, I might have been awake enough to withstand my aunt's attack.

'Up! Up with you! Out of bed! The early bird gets the worm! Early to bed and early to rise, makes a man healthy, wealthy and wise!'

'I'm not a bird!' I moaned, pulling the pillow over my head. 'And I'm certainly no man!'

'No, you remind me more of the worm, to be honest. But that can't be helped. Out of bed, Lillian!'

Pillow and covers were stolen from me with one cruel, powerful tug, and I was left helpless and undefended. Moaning, I raised my hands to shield my eyes from the stabbing spears of morning sunlight.

'Can't I sleep a little bit longer?'

'No! Get out of bed, now! And get dressed! We have a visitor coming for breakfast. Someone I want you to meet.'

If I had been any more awake than a marmot in hibernation, this comment would have made me instantly suspicious. But alas, I was far too marmotty. I was so marmotty that I didn't even realise that marmotty isn't really a word. With another moan, I staggered out of bed, and, after trying several times to slip into the bedside lamp, I found my dress and slipped into it instead. By the time I had struggled into my clothes, I had managed to get my eyes at least half open.

'Good morning, sleepyhead!' Ella skipped into the room, her cheeks rosy, her eyes gleaming with life. 'Isn't it a wonderful morning?'

I eyed her bright smile grumpily. 'I suppose that depends on the kind of night you had.'

'I had a wonderful night, Lill! Slept the whole night through, and had the most wonderful dreams.'

'I'm sure you did. Now, would you please help me button up this darn dress? I can't reach all the way to the back.'

Five minutes later, after Ella had helped straighten me out and splashed my face with cold water to keep me from starting to snore, we started downstairs towards the dining room. I was feeling moderately more awake and exponentially more worried.

'Ella?'

'Yes, Lill?' she sighed, her eyes gazing dreamily off into the distance.

'Do you know who it is that Aunt Brank has invited for breakfast?'

'No idea,' she trilled, dancing ahead of me, twirling her arms. 'Oh Lill! Isn't this a wonderful day? Simply extraordinarily beautifully perfect?'

I wasn't too sure about that. Aunt Brank had invited someone for breakfast. And, considering my aunt's preferences, this could only mean one thing: a you-know-what!

Please! I prayed. *Please, let me be wrong! Let it be anything but a you-know-what! Anything else!*

The door to the dining room opened, and Ella danced in, still humming a joyful melody. I followed, hackles raised. But when I saw *him*, it still nearly knocked me off my feet.

He was small.

He was balding.

He had a round, cheerful face and a broad smile. In other words: he was the incarnation of the devil.

'Ah, there you are, girls.' My aunt, a vulturous expression on her face, rose and pointed to the man sitting beside her, next to an empty chair clearly reserved for me. 'Lilly, there's someone I'd like you to meet. Mr Fitzgerald, this is my niece, Lillian Linton.'

I stared at Mr Fitzgerald, who rose to his feet and made a bobbing little bow. There he was. The nightmare of nightmares. The terror of terrors. The you-know-what which I feared more than anything else on this earth:

The suitor.

I HATE YOU, OR MAYBE NOT, OR…OH, TO HELL WITH IT!

Blast, blast, blast! How the heck had this happened? How had I ended up here?

This shouldn't have happened! I remembered it all distinctly: I remembered sitting down for breakfast. I membered Mr Fitzgerald asking whether we were going to the dance at Lady Abercrombie's this evening, and I remembered saying no. *Five times.* But apparently that had not been as expressive or significant as the one time my aunt had said yes.

How she was able to finagle an invitation to the ball out of stuffy, old Lady Abercrombie was a mystery to me. The old owl sent out invitations to her balls four weeks in advance, and was mortally insulted if you didn't reply by next morning at ten o'clock at the latest. But somehow, my aunt had managed it. Her desire to rid herself of her nieces really knew no bounds.

And that was how I came to be walking towards the large double-doors of Lady Abercrombie's palatial town house, while on my one side, my little sister Ella danced along, totally oblivious, lost in memories of last night's romantic escapades, while on my other side, my aunt hissed all the reasons into my ear why it would be oh-so-advantageous to marry Mr Fitzgerald.

'…a large house here in town, and although he's not of noble blood, he has a considerable estate in the country. He has an income of at least twelve thousand a year – '

'Pounds? Pence? Or dead rats?'

'Don't use that tone with me, young lady! You could be a lot worse off, you know.'

I gave her a long, long, significant look. 'Oh, I know.'

'Don't you dare act superior, missy! Your uncle and I have been the epitome of generosity! We took you in, clothed you, fed you–'

'–and tried to marry me off half a dozen times.'

'Of course! A penniless girl like you should be happy that we would exert ourselves to help you find a husband.' She let her gaze sweep up and down my figure. 'God knows, you'd never find one on your own!'

From behind me, I heard a giggle, but I didn't turn around to look. I knew who it had come from anyway.

'Well, unlike *some* people,' I told the evening air, 'I've never been particularly eager to chain myself to a man.' Glancing back over my shoulder, I smiled at my twin sisters, Anne and Maria. 'But it seems that even people who are desperately looking for a rich husband don't always find one as quickly as they say they will. Isn't that true, Anne? Maria?'

The death-glares they sent me in reply were answer enough.

We had reached the Abercrombie townhouse by now. My aunt swept through the open door. Servants bowed everywhere around us, taking our hats, shawls, coats and whatever else they thought superfluous. At the door to the ballroom, Lady Abercrombie awaited us, her haggard face somehow managing to radiate even more haughty disapproval than my aunt's when she looked at me. I almost clapped, so impressed was I by the achievement.

'My Lady.' My aunt curtsied as deeply as her stiff neck would allow. 'So gracious of you to invite us. We are overwhelmed by your kindness.'

'Hrumph!' Lady Abercrombie said.

'Quite right, Your Ladyship!' my aunt simpered. 'You're so right!' She turned to us. 'Doesn't her ladyship express herself with inimitable eloquence, girls?'

'She didn't say anything,' I pointed out.

My aunt sent me a glare that could have blasted the walls of Windsor Castle. Old Lady Abercrombie on the other hand raised an eyebrow, and beckoned me closer. 'Come here, girl!'

My aunt's glare intensified tenfold, but there was also a certain vindictive triumph in her eyes. They clearly said: 'Now you've done it! We'll see how you'll get yourself out of this one!'

'The rest of you,' the old lady commanded, 'amuse yourselves! I'm sure there's plenty of food to eat and drinks to drink at my expense, and since I'm not going to invite any of you to another ball in the foreseeable future, you had better make the most of it.'

'Um, yes, Your Ladyship. Of course, Your Ladyship.'

My siblings in tow, Aunt Brank retreated, and I was left behind alone with the dragon of this sparkling cave. Around us, people chatted, laughed and nibbled at delicacies. Beside me, old Lady Abercrombie just stood, watching everything with sharp eyes, not saying anything.

She was trying to wear me down with silence. But I had been trained by the best. Lady Abercrombie might have been a tough old shoe to chew, but her cold silence was nothing in comparison to that of Mr Rikkard Ambrose.

Finally, she gave it up.

'Tell me, girl – why is your aunt here?'

'Because Your Ladyship invited her.'

She gave me a piercing stare.

'And,' I added, 'because she wants to marry me off. The man she has her eye on is here tonight.'

'Indeed?' That seemed to catch her ladyship's interest. 'Who is it?'

'A Mister Fitzgerald.'

Lady Abercrombie's eyes widened. '*Morton Marmeduke* Fitzgerald?'

'How many Fitzgeralds are here tonight?'

'Two. But the other one is a ninety-year-old.'

'That's not him.'

'Good God!' Lady Abercrombie smiled. 'Morton Marmeduke as Romeo. I wouldn't have thought it of him!'

'If it is all right with you,' I murmured with a shudder, 'I would prefer not to think of him that way, either. So, if we could please talk about something else...?'

'Ah. That way, is it?'

'Yes. It is.'

'I can't really say I'm surprised. Morton is a nice enough fellow, but...well.'

'Exactly, Your Ladyship.'

Out of the corner of my eye, I spotted a familiar figure approaching. Instinctively, I took a step backwards.

'Your Ladyship...this place doesn't happen to have a back exit, does it?'

Following my gaze, she spotted the round-cheeked, smiling man approaching us, and shook her head. 'Sorry, girl. You're going to have to fight this one out on your own.'

My hands clenched into fists. 'I thought so.'

'But I'll be watching.' The old lady winked at me, and started away. 'It'll be interesting to see who emerges as the victor.'

I took another step back. But it was too late. He was already upon me.

'Miss Linton!' There was a radiant smile on Morton Marmeduke Fitzgerald's face as he beamed up at me. Yes, *up* at me. Have I neglected to mention that, besides being round and balding, he's about half a head shorter than me? And he was smiling as if I were Father Christmas, the Easter bunny and Venus the love goddess all rolled into one. 'I'm so happy to see you were able to come!'

Before I could tell him 'Well, I'm not', he grasped my hand and bowed deeply. 'May I ask you for the honour of the next dance?'

I was just about to tell him to go bugger himself, when, over his head, I caught a glimpse of my aunt giving me one of her special looks. I cleared my throat.

'Um...of course, Mr Fitzgerald. I'd be delighted.'

What was one dance, after all? I could use it to demonstrate exactly why he would not like to marry me. Experimentally, I clacked my heels against the ballroom floor. As luck would have it, I was wearing good, stout shoes. Exactly the wrong kind of shoes for dancing. Excellent!

'Thank you, Miss Linton!' Beaming like a cherub on cloud nine, he took a tighter hold of my hand and led me onto the dance floor. The musicians struck up the tones of a waltz. 'These,' he told me, his round face shining, 'will be the happiest minutes of my life.'

Oh, Mister...You've got that so wrong. Just wait and see. Or rather - feel.

Tam-ta-tam, tam-ta-tam...

The melody of the waltz picked up, and we started circling. I waited until the press of bodies around us brought us a little bit closer, then – *wham!* – my foot struck out.

'And?' I asked with a bright smile. 'How are you enjoying the dance so far?'

He smiled back up at me. 'Very much, Miss Linton.'

What? Had I heard correctly? Maybe I had missed. Although I could have sworn I heard the distinctive crunch of leather under my foot.

'Really?' My smile widened. 'How fascinating.'

I raised a foot again.

Wham!

'You don't think that my dancing style might be a little bit out of step?'

Wham! Wham!

'Of course not, Miss Linton! Whyever would I think that?'

Oh, I don't know...Maybe because I'm stepping on your feet, you moron?

'In fact, I think you are a lovely dancer,' he added and – horror of horrors – pulled me closer! 'And a lovely girl, too.'

I shoved him away as gently as possible, then slammed my heel on his foot again. No reaction. Well, except for a contented sigh.

'Truly,' he murmured, his eyes half-closed in bliss. 'A wonderful dancer.'

'Mr Fitzgerald?'

Wham!

'Yes, Miss Linton?'

Wham! Wham! Come on...!

'Are you feeling all right?'

'Yes, quite well, thank you.'

Wham!

'There's not per chance anything wrong with your feet, is there?'

'My feet? They are flying, inspired by your beauty."

I ground my teeth.

'How kind of you.'

Wham!

Still nothing. Not the slightest reaction. What was wrong with this man?

'Tell me, have you danced with many girls in your life?'

He blushed, bringing a rosy hue to his round cheeks that made him look like a ripe apple. But that didn't mean in the least that I had an urge to gobble him up. Oh no, not at all!

'Not really, Miss Linton.' He glanced down, then peeked up again. 'You see, I'm a rather shy and withdrawn sort of person. I spend most of my time on my country estate, overseeing my tenant's farms. Your aunt and I were not very well acquainted. We had only met once before. I was quite pleasantly surprised when she invited me to breakfast at your lovely home.'

Well, I wasn't!

I lifted my foot once more. I had never been a quitter.

Wham!

'I don't get out much, you see,' Mr Fitzgerald added, shyly. 'I don't know why, but people – ladies in particular – don't really seem to respond well to me.'

'Oh, really?'

Well, you're not responding very well to what I'm trying to do either!

Wham!

Nothing. Simply no reaction. Bloody hell! Did this fellow have toes at all?

He sighed. 'Yes, it is, unfortunately.'

'I'm sorry to hear that, Mr Fitzgerald. I can't imagine why that is. You're such a charming–'

Wham!

'–caring, kind man.'

He gave another small sigh.

'I suppose it's because I'm not a particularly manly man, you know. I inherited my estate, and never have been really motivated to expand it or do anything except keep the land in good shape and the tenants happy. So most of my life has been spent in idle luxury. I've never really had to learn how to stand on my own two feet.'

'Indeed?' *Wham! Wham!* 'Well, personally, I think you are doing extremely well at the feet thing.'

He beamed. 'Thank you, Miss Linton! That's the nicest thing anyone has ever said to me!'

After that, it was pretty much a lost cause. The man smiled at me as if he were a puppy and I his long-lost owner. He danced three more dances with me, and afterwards kissed my hand and said he would count the seconds till our paths crossed again. I'm not joking! *Count the seconds!* Seriously!

Something had to be done.

If my usual tactic of toe-destruction wouldn't help in this case, I had to come up with something else.

Hm...

How could you signal to a man that you couldn't stand him and didn't want to have anything to do with him?

Several options occurred to me immediately.

A) Dump a bucket of horse dung over his head

B) Kick him in the derriere

C) Strangle him

But none of these options could easily be accomplished in a ballroom, and particularly not under the watchful vulture eyes of my aunt. No, I had to come up with something more subtle, something more discreet.

'Ah! That's it!' Snapping my fingers in sudden realisation, I plunged my hand into the pocket of my dress. There it was: after the parasol, the most dreaded weapon of any girl worth her salt. With a contented sigh, I pulled out the fan and let it snap open.

Now for the tricky part.

At the insistence of my aunt, I had spent weeks learning the secret language of the fan that, according to her, sophisticated ladies used to converse with their lovers, memorising the correct gestures for messages such as 'kiss me', 'follow me', and 'I want to get engaged!' Only, what my aunt didn't know was that I had also spent considerable time in secret, learning other kinds of messages to communicate with a fan. Messages which I deemed much more useful.

I turned in the direction where I had last seen Mr Morton Marmeduke Fitzgerald. The little half-bald man was just busy nibbling on some delicacy and conversing with a man in glasses. He caught my eye and smiled. I smiled back, holding his gaze.

Carefully and distinctly, I drew the fan across my cheek.

I-H-A-T-E-Y-O-U-I-H-A-T-E-Y-O-U-I-R-E-A-L-L-Y-H-A-T-E-Y-O-U!

With a snap, I let the fan slam shut, opened it again, and repeated the motion.

P-I-S-S-O-F-F-Y-O-U-B-A-S-T-A-R-D-P-I-S-S-O-F-F-Y-O-U-B-A-S-T-A-R-D-P-I-S-S-O-F-F-N-O-W!

And, just to be absolutely sure I brought my message across, I placed the handle of the fan to my lips.

Y-O-U-A-R-E-T-H-E-S-P-A-W-N-O-F-A-W-A-R-T-H-O-G!-A-R-E-A-L-L-Y-U-G-L-Y-W-A-R-T-H-O-G!-G-E-T-A-W-A-Y-F-R-O-M-M-E-O-R-I-L-L-D-U-M-P-A-B-U-C-K-E-T-O-F-C-R-A-P-O-V-E-R-Y-O-U-R-H-E-A-D!

Well, the last message hadn't been listed exactly like this in *Mrs Flower's Guide to the Fan Language for Proper Young Ladies*. I might have had to improvise a bit, but still, I had surely gotten the message across.

Mr Fitzgerald held my gaze for a moment – then nodded. Ah! Thank God! He had gotten the message. Sighing with relief, I turned away, and went in search of a waiter. I needed some stress relief. I headed towards the first man with a tray of canapés I spotted and tapped him on the shoulder.

'Excuse me?'

'Yes, Miss?'

'Do you have solid chocolate?'

Five minutes later, I was leaning against a column, my eyes closed and my mouth filled with the ambrosia and nectar that was solid chocolate melting slowly, when someone cleared his throat right in front of me. Unwilling to descend from my own personal heaven, I opened my eyes, and there, right in front of me, stood Morton Marmeduke Fitzgerald, his round face full of emotion.

'Miss Linton?'

'Yuff?' I managed. Then I hurriedly swallowed, coughed, and repeated, in a tone that conveyed how not happy I was about having had to swallow my solid chocolate early: '*Yes?* What do you want?'

'I saw your charming display of the fan language earlier.' Mr Fitzgerald's round eyes were shimmering. Were those *tears* threatening to spill over? Actual tears? 'And I just wanted to say: I feel exactly the same!'

'You do?'

Then why are you standing right here in front of me instead of at the opposite end of the ballroom? Or better yet, at the opposite end of England?

'Yes. When you drew your fan over your cheek so delicately, with such exquisite feminine grace, signalling to me that there are feelings of love for me burgeoning inside your heart...'

Whoa! Hold your horses! Have what burgeoning inside what?

'...it touched something deep inside me, Miss Linton. It really did. I did not have the courage before to approach you, but when you made your feelings known to me, it changed everything.'

I made my feelings known to you all right, you moron! I told you I hate your guts, and the rest of you, too!

Or...was that actually signalled by drawing the fan across the cheek? Wasn't it by drawing it through the hand?

No! It was the cheek! I'm sure!

Well...almost.

Mr Fitzgerald took a step closer, his eyes now definitely shining with tears. 'At first I wasn't sure. At first I couldn't imagine how a girl like you could love a man like me, who is so obviously not worthy of her–'

You got that right, Mister!

'...but then I thought: Love crosses all boundaries!'

What? No it doesn't! Definitely not the very definite boundaries between you and me!

'Still, I remained in doubt. Had I really seen what I'd thought I'd seen? Had you really sent me the signal I had hoped for? It was agonising, not knowing for certain. But then I saw your next gesture.'

'My...next gesture?'

OhpleaseGodletmehavegottenthatonerightpleasepleaseplease!

'Yes! That delicate snap of the fan that told me you wanted to speak with me–'

Ohnonononononononooooo!

'–and then, the final sign.' He closed his eyes in rapture, and a shudder went through him. 'The final signal that made it clear to me that you wished to know me as more than just a friend. Placing your fan onto your lips like that – asking me to kiss you.'

What?

'But please, rest assured,' he added hurriedly, seeing the horrified expression on my face. 'I am not a man to take advantage of young ladies. I will not kiss you until we are engaged to be married.'

'Thanks,' I croaked. 'You have no idea how relieved I am to hear that.'

'Oh, I can imagine.' Gently, he reached out and placed his hand over mine. 'A gentle young lady such as yourself, a delicate flower, must not be mistreated. Please rest assured that when we are married, I will always purport myself with the utmost propriety.'

'Wonderful. That sounds just...wonderful.'

'May I ask you to accompany me out onto the terrace, Miss Linton? I would like to have a talk with you in private.'

I was so dazed by the shock I had received, and so desperately in need of fresh air, that I let myself be led outside before I realised why exactly he probably wanted to 'have a talk with me'.

Oh God! No!

The terrace doors closed behind us. They were pretty, glittering glass doors – but to me, they looked an awful lot like the gates of hell.

'Miss Lillian Linton.' Mr Fitzgerald turned to me with an earnest, adoring expression on his face. It made me feel woozy. 'I know we have only known each other for quite a short time – '

'One day, to be exact.'

'Yes. As I said, quite a short time. But...do you believe in love at first sight?'

'No. Not really,'

'Oh.' He blinked. It was obvious he had been hoping for a different answer, and I had messed up his script.

'Um...well, *I* do. And when I first saw you at your aunt's breakfast table, you took my breath away!'

'That probably was the garlic Leadfield, the butler, serves with the boiled potatoes. It can have that effect.'

'No!' The little man took a step forward, his round face glowing with adoration. 'It was you! Your feminine grace–'

What?

'–your beauty, your kindness, your angelic aura–'

Was this fellow on opium?

'–it all convinced me instantly that there was not, that there could never be, any other woman in the world for me!'

'Um...are you sure you have looked everywhere? The world is pretty big, you know.'

'Yes!' Stepping forward, he grasped my hands and, before I could wrench them from his grasp, lifted them to his lips and kissed them.

Eww!

He was still holding my hands in his. I tugged at them, but he didn't get the hint.

'Miss Linton! I cannot suppress my feelings any longer. You must allow me to tell you how ardently I admire and love you!'

'Must I really?'

He seemed not to have heard that.

'My feelings for you are hot and glowing like the sun, and yet soft and blooming like rose petals opening in summer!'

'Gosh. You don't say.'

'My heart thrums at the very sound of your name! Your eyes shine like the coat of my finest thoroughbred. When you laugh, the bells of heaven sound in my ears.'

'You could try earplugs.'

I tugged at my hands again. But they seemed to be fixed to his with glue.

'I love you, Miss Linton – no, I love you, *Lillian*! I love you passionately! And I know you love me, too!'

'You do, do you?'

Tug! Tug!

Blast it! Did this little fellow have adhesive sweat?

'Oh yes!' Still not letting go, he sank onto his knees in front of me.

Oh, no, no, nonononono! Not that! Please not that!

'Please, Lillian, I beg of you: make me the happiest man in the world! Give me the answer I am hoping, no, I am living for. Will you marry me?'

I tugged at my hands again – and in the effort to get them free, I might have lowered my head the tiniest little bit, tensing my neck muscles. Mr Fitzgerald chose to interpret it for the gesture commonly referred to as 'nodding'.

'That is all the answer I need! You are speechless with joy, aren't you? So am I! Oh, Lillian my darling, come into my arms!'

Jumping up, he dashed forward, ready to embrace me.

And I?

Well, what was a girl to do in a situation like that? What could I do when a man had just bared his heart to me?

I did the only thing I could do. I stabbed him in the eye with my fan.

'Ouch!'

At least that was one item of the fan language that couldn't possibly be misinterpreted. Instinctively, marvellously, blessedly, he let go of my hands and I jumped back with the agility of a mountain goat. And I bet no mountain goat was ever that agile while wearing a ballgown with a huge crinoline! Whirling around, I ran down along the terrace, my only thought to get as far away from Mr Fitzgerald and his lovesick puppy-dog eyes as I possibly could.

'Lillian, my love! Wait!'

But I didn't wait. Oh, no! I sped up. I've always been a pretty fast runner, if I do say so myself. I was out of the light spilling from the terrace door in a flash, and in the moonlight, I could already see my escape not far ahead: the corner of the house! Behind that, there would be gardens, with lots of bushes to hide behind, and no ball guests to throw impromptu love confessions into my face.

Sucking in a big gulp of air for my dash to freedom, I sped up, swerved around the corner of the house – and ran smack into someone.

A tall, very solid, very male someone.

Staggering back, I looked up, a catalogue of expletives on my tongue – but they all died on my lips as soon as I caught sight of the man in front of me.

'Well, well...good Evening, Miss.'

I had been wrong.

There *were* ball guests behind the house. At least one of them.

Mouth agape, eyes wide open, I stared up into the regal, aquiline face of Lord Daniel Eugene Dalgliesh.

THE HALF HAPPY COUPLE

'Miss?' Lord Dalgliesh stepped forward, extending his hands to steady me. I felt his long, aristocratic fingers grip my shoulders. 'Miss, are you all right?'

How to answer that truthfully?

Scratch that. There was no way to answer that truthfully. If I did, he'd know that I was far from all right. And he'd know it was because of him. Because I knew who and what he was.

'I...I'm just a little taken aback,' I murmured, casting my eyes down. *Please don't let him recognise me. Please!* 'I didn't expect to literally run into somebody like that.'

He smiled. It was a harmless smile. A friendly smile. It was a lie.

'I can understand that. I am sorry to have distressed you. May I escort you somewhere?'

'No, it's all right, I'm–'

My voice cut off when I felt his grip suddenly tighten on my arm.

'Miss?' His voice suddenly didn't sound quite so harmless anymore. Still friendly, but not harmless at all. 'Miss, have we met before? I could swear...'

A barrage of images flashed through my mind in an instant.

Lord Dalgliesh and Mr Ambrose facing off across a ballroom, their eyes glittering like ice.

Lord Dalgliesh's men charging us in the dark alleys of the East End, knives drawn.

Lord Dalgliesh and Mr Ambrose shaking hands like they wanted to break each other's bones.

Lord Dalgliesh standing in his secret hideout, under the red cross and golden lion banner of the East India Company, shipping off illegal goods and stolen secrets to God-only-knew-where.

Lord Dalgliesh's guards shooting at us, ready to kill.

Had I met Lord Dalgliesh before?

Oh yes, I had. And I had no wish to repeat the experience.

Luckily, half the times we met (the ones where guns and knives had been involved) I had been in men's dress. But even so, if he recognised my female incarnation, it would not bode well for me.

'No, I don't believe so,' I managed in a reasonably calm tone and tried to step back. His grip tightened still more.

'But I do.' His eyes, sharp as steel over his aquiline nose, narrowed. 'Yes. We have met somewhere before. At a ball. I saw you with–'

'Let go!'

But it was too late. I saw his eyes widen, and his lips silently form the word *Ambrose*.

'Miss Linton.' Suddenly, he was smiling again. This time, it looked neither harmless nor friendly. 'So good to see you again. I always wondered what became of you after that night. Why don't you step over here for a moment? We haven't come across each other in a long time, and I would love to discuss a mutual acquaintance of ours.'

'Sorry. I don't really have the time right now.'

I tugged to free my shoulders from his grip – to no avail. His hands were like steel clamps. And he was still smiling.

'I insist. Please follow me, Miss Linton. We are going to have a good, long talk, where nobody else can hear and–'

'Lillian! Lillian, my love!'

Let me tell you, when that shout came from behind me, it was the last thing I expected. I still could hardly believe it when a moment later, Morton Marmeduke Fitzgerald stumbled around the corner, huffing and puffing on his short legs. He was the most unlikely guardian angel I had ever set eyes on, and the first suitor ever in my life I was actually glad to see.

Lord Dalgliesh apparently was just as surprised to see Mr Fitzgerald as I was. Good.

'Morton!' Tearing myself out of Lord Dalgliesh's loosened grip, I hurled myself at Mr Fitzgerald, crushing him against me. 'I'm so happy to see you!'

'Um...you are?'

'Yes, of course, my dear!'

Morton blinked. 'Are you sure?'

'Of course, silly! We just got engaged, remember?' Half-turning, I threw a very significant look at Lord Dalgliesh. 'I'm so happy! Morton is such a good man, and important, too. There would be such an outcry *if anything were to happen to him.*'

'Indeed?' Lord Dalgliesh sized me up for a moment – then his gaze slid to Mr Fitzgerald, and he gave a 'Well, you can't judge a book by its cover'-shrug. His eyes found mine again, and they were steel-blue slits. 'I'll take your word for it, Miss Linton. Although I think, of the two of you, you are far more important.'

Half-turning, he gave a sharp nod. 'Until we meet again, Miss Linton.'

And he strode away into the darkness.

'Who was that, darling?' Mr Morton asked, beaming up at me.

'No one of consequence,' I lied. 'Shall we go inside?'

'Yes! Wait until everybody hears the news! They'll all be so excited! Especially your aunt!'

I shuddered. 'Oh yes, I'll bet she'll be.'

Taking a deep breath, I let myself be led back into the house of Lady Abercrombie. Now I had two big problems facing me. Namely, in rising order of importance:

How was I going to get away from this party alive without Dalgliesh getting his hands on me?

And, much more importantly:

How the hell was I going to get rid of my new fiancé?

~~**~*~*

I could describe the reaction with which my aunt greeted the announcement of our engagement when I and Morton – or Morty, as he asked me to call him – came back into the ballroom. I definitely could. However, I don't really want to. If you had been hurled into the darkest pit of hell with gleeful harpies cackling above, you wouldn't be particularly eager to talk about it either, trust me.

Suffice it to say that it took her only three minutes and twenty-seven seconds to spread the news through the whole ballroom, and when she was done, she sat happily in the middle of a circle of congratulatory well-wishers, as if she were the happy bride-to-be, smiling at everybody, while in her head counting the social and monetary advantage this would bring. To judge by the breadth of her smile, they both were considerable.

'Lillian, my love! Shall we dance?'

I tried to manage a smile at the man I refused to think of as my future husband. 'Um...of course, err...Morty. I'd be delighted to.'

When hell freezes over!

He pulled me onto the dance floor, and I let him. The dance began. Half-heartedly, I tried to smash his feet, but I hadn't really counted on it working. His feet appeared to be nearly as hard as Mr Ambrose's head. He would be nearly impossible to get rid of.

And do you know what the worst of it was?

Part of me *liked* Morty!

He seemed to be – wonder of wonders – a decent man, a nice man even, who cared about his tenants and just wanted to live a quiet life in the country. If I had to pick a man with whom to spend a nice, quiet evening and discuss the benefits of sheep dung as crop fertiliser, I would probably have picked him. But that didn't mean I wasn't going to stab him in a dark alley with my parasol rather than marrying him!

After three more dances, tradition demanded that the happy couple – thank God! – split up to dance with other people. I lost sight of Morty, but I always took care to stay in the centre of the crowd, far away from any dark corners. Once or twice I spotted Lord Dalgliesh, and from the way he looked at me I could tell he had not given up.

'Miss Linton!'

I whirled at the sound of someone calling my name – but it wasn't Dalgliesh. It wasn't Morty, either.

'Captain Carter!'

The British Army captain gave me his favourite cheeky grin, and did a little bow that was anything but respectful. He was one of the few males on this planet that I could actually tolerate.

'Miss Linton. What a pleasure to see you. And how is your aunt? Still happily nasty, I trust?'

And remarks like this were the reason for my tolerance.

'Nastier than ever before, thank you. Avoid her at all costs.'

'I shall do my best.'

'How is our mutual friend, Sir Philip?'

Captain Carter pointed over to where a tall, lanky figure with oversized ears and a rather impressive nose was dancing with a wispy blonde, his eye dazed with adoration. 'In love. How else?'

'That makes how many times this month? Four?'

'Five.'

'My, my, he is in good form.'

'It's the spring air, I'm sure.'

Behind us, the musicians struck up the tune of a lively dance. Captain Carter extended his hand. 'Well, Miss Linton? Would you like to dance?'

I breathed a sigh of relief. 'Yes!'

Unlike the torture sessions on the dance floor with other members of the male species, I actually liked dancing with Captain Carter. He was one of the few men I had met whose hands didn't wander, and who truly seemed to enjoy the dance itself, not the groping. He helped me enjoy it, too, a thing I would not have believed possible before I'd met him.

Plus, while I was dancing in the middle of the ballroom in the hard, muscled arms of a British Army captain with a shiny sabre at his side, the chances of my being forcibly abducted by Lord Dalgliesh seemed relatively slim.

The first dance started. It was a quadrille – definitely not my favourite, but Captain Carter made it bearable. He never pushed me around, never took his eyes off my face, and didn't even mind when my foot occasionally landed on his, which, in this case, happened purely by accident, I swear. After two rounds through the ballroom, just when I was starting to get comfortable, the captain nodded sideways to somewhere out of my field of vision.

'Dear me. I think I have a rival for your affections.'

I gaped at him. '*What?*'

'Look over there.'

Turning with the music, I followed his nod with my eyes and what I saw drove the captain's words right out of my mind. There, in the shadow of a column, stood Lord Daniel Eugene Dalgliesh.

I had been doubtful before as to whether Lord Dalgliesh would permit me to leave. But looking at him, standing there like that, staring at me, I knew. I could see the bleak truth in his eyes.

'That man has been staring at you ever since we started dancing,' the captain's voice drifted to my ears from far, far away. 'Any idea who he is?'

'No,' I lied. 'No idea at all.'

The dance drifted to a close around us. Halting our moves, Captain Carter dismissed Dalgliesh with a shrug and smiled down at me. 'Well, I can't blame him for staring.'

I stomped on his foot. This time, it wasn't by accident.

'Ouch!' His grin widened. 'Not in a good mood tonight, are we?'

'No! Definitely not.'

'Would you like another dance?'

'Yes! Definitely yes!'

'All right. Hold on. I think this one is going to be a bit livelier.'

He was right. The notes of a polka started whirling through the air. We danced this dance, too, and another after that, and it was still not enough. I knew that soon enough, the worries of the world would come crashing down on me again, but just for the moment I wanted to shove them in a corner, hang a blanket over them and pretend they didn't exist. For one waltz and one blissfully mad polka, I forgot all about Lord Dalgliesh and my...

Ew! There really was no other way to say it: my *engagement*.

Two blessed dances. But the bliss didn't last long after we stepped off the dance floor.

'Captain Carter!' My sister Maria advanced on us, giving me a bright, cheerful I'll-gut-you-like-a-fish smile. She was leading someone forward. A small, roundish someone. 'How wonderful to see you here. Have you met Lillian's *fiancé*? Mr Morton Marmeduke Fitzgerald.'

The captain's eyebrows shot up like Chinese fireworks. He stared at Morty – who thankfully didn't notice because he was busy bowing and mumbling greetings – and then glanced over at me.

'Fiancé?' he whispered.

'Temporary!' I whispered back.

'Since when is there such a thing as a temporary fiancé?'

'Since I invented it! Now shut up!'

'Yes, Miss Linton.'

'And don't smirk like that! This isn't funny!'

'Of course not, Miss Linton.'

And, of course, he didn't stop smirking.

But what he didn't know was: this really *wasn't* funny. Because it was about much more than my getting an unwanted fiancé. Over Morty's head, I caught another glimpse of Lord Dalgliesh, his golden hair shining in the chandelier's light. He wasn't alone, now. Reinforcements had arrived: several officers in uniforms of the presidency armies surrounded him. Huzzah! Lord Dalgliesh's personal pack of bloodhounds had arrived.

I had to get out of there. And I had to do it fast.

'Lilly!' Maria sent me another bone-chilling smile. 'Why don't you tell Captain Carter exactly how you and Mr Fitzgerald met? I think he'd just love to hear such a romantic story.'

'I'd love to, I really would, but, um...I've just remembered I have to go to the powder room. Please excuse me.'

And before my sister could grab me and think of any more tortures for me, I ducked behind a portly Dame of the Empire and vanished into the crowd. I hadn't been lying. I really had to get to the powder room. Just not to powder anything, or to pee. Pushing people aside right and left, leaving a trail of 'Ouff!'s and 'Pardon me!'s behind me, I made my way to the discreetly marked door. Grabbing a nearby waiter by the arm, I pulled him behind a vase filled with flowers.

'Miss?' He looked taken aback. 'Um... how may I help you?'

'Well...I'm not sure...' I cleared my throat. 'It's a bit delicate.'

He smiled. 'Don't worry, Miss. I'm sure there's something I can do.'

'Oh, would you?' I gazed up at him with wide, adoring eyes, doing my best imitation of my little sister Ella. 'The thing is...oh, I hardly know how to say it!'

'You can trust me, Miss.'

'I can see that.' Shyly, I touched his arm. 'You seem like such a kind man. You see...a friend of mine – a younger cousin – spilled wine on his tailcoat and trousers. And, you know, he is here to make a good impression on old Lady Abercrombie, and she can be, rather...particular.'

The servant shuddered. 'No need to say more, Miss.'

'I just need someone to slip out and get him a fresh tailcoat and trousers,' I pleaded, making my eyes even bigger. 'Please? They don't have to be new, just presentable. I'll pay, of course. Here you are, two shillings. You may keep the rest.'

The man's face lit up. 'Miss! That's very generous!'

Depends on how you look at it, Mister. My life is worth two shillings.

'Just hurry, will you?' I pleaded. 'My young cousin is hiding right now, but sooner or later Lady Abercrombie is going to notice he's gone, and then–'

'I understand. What size is your cousin?'

'About the same size as me. Hurry! And thank you for doing this!'

The waiter flashed a smile. 'No need to thank me, Miss. I'll be back in a moment.'

I spent hours – or at least it felt like hours – in agony, pretending to chat and laugh with the people around me. Every now and again someone would appear and say:

'Miss Linton? Congratulations on your engagement!'

And I would have to resist the urge to vomit into a vase. Every moment, I expected Dalgliesh to appear and try to grab me. But when someone suddenly appeared behind me, it was not Dalgliesh.

'Miss?'

'There you are!' I whirled and grabbed the clothes from the waiter, not even glancing at what they were. 'Thank you! Thank you so much! I, um, will bring them to my cousin right away!'

And I slipped into the powder room. To heck with the waiter if he'd find that strange. I was never going to set a foot in this house again anyway!

One wrestling match with a hoopskirt later, I stepped out of the powder room, my own man once again, even if only in pretence. Keeping my head down, and especially doing my best to avoid any eye contact with my family, I made my way towards the exit. I was a little bit sorry about leaving Ella behind to fend for herself, but she was still in such a state of bliss from last night that I doubted she would even notice.

'Lillian? Lillian, my love!'

Damn and blast! *He* would definitely notice, though. I glanced up just long enough to catch a glimpse of Morty, his eyes shining, looking around to find his beloved.

Well, his beloved was out of here, pronto!

Pushing past my dear betrothed, I made my way towards the doors of the ballroom. A servant bowed as I passed.

'Would you like me to call you a cab, Sir?'

Wonderful, Lilly! He didn't call you 'Miss'!

'No, thank you.'

I'd be glad enough if I could get out of the house alive.

They were waiting for me in a niche near the exit. Lord Dalgliesh and one of his henchmen, this one not in uniform. They were hidden from sight, behind a curtain that normally hid unsightly boots and umbrellas from the eyes of visitors. I would never have noticed them if I had not been looking for them. The curtain twitched as I approached, and immediately, I stopped to listen.

For a moment or two, there was nothing. Then:

'Where is she, My Lord?'

'This is her engagement party. She is not going to come out quickly. Especially not if she suspects we're lying in wait for her. She will leave in the middle of a crowd of her friends. We'll have to be quick and decisive. Do you have the syringe?'

'Yes, my Lord.'

'Good.'

A pause.

'I know it's not my place to ask, my Lord, but...why do you want her? She seems to be a nobody. Just another silly little girl wanting to get married. And this is a very public place. The risk of exposure–'

'Bryant?'

'Yes, my Lord?'

'Don't ever question my orders again. Do you understand?'

There was another pause. I could practically feel the tension crackling in the air.

'Yes, my Lord.'

'But...'

'Yes?

'Since you are going to be in charge of questioning Miss Linton, I might as well tell you now. I want her because she has information. Whatever is visible on the surface, she is more than she seems to be. She appears to be acquainted with Mr Rikkard Ambrose.'

Another pause.

'Oh.'

'Indeed.'

'I'm sorry, my Lord. I did not know that.'

'Now you do. See that you keep it to yourself, or your days are numbered.'

Taking a deep breath, I started forward, and at the sound of my footsteps the whispering voices cut off. But I could feel them, behind the curtain, ahead of me – a dark force, waiting to reach out and grab me. Would they? Would they recognize me? Maybe I should have told the waiter to bring me a false moustache, too. Although that might have made him slightly more suspicious.

The curtain fluttered without a breeze. Sucking in a deep breath of air, I hastened my steps – and prepared to run.

Come on, Lilly! Just a few more steps, and you're past the curtain!

Three, to be exact.

Two.

One...

THE BLISS OF LOVE

Zero.

Minus one.

Minus two.

Minus three.

Hey! I was counting negative numbers, and still walking! That meant they hadn't jumped out to grab me! *Yay!* I was alive and free to rail against the injustice of patriarchy for another day! Huzzah!

Out of the corner of my eye, I had just caught a glimpse of them behind the curtain in passing: Dalgliesh's golden hair, and the face of the other man, angular and darkened by sunlight. Obviously, they had not caught me looking. By now, I was nearly at the front door, and the curtain behind me did not rustle. No footsteps announced any unwelcome pursuers.

Except for two, that is.

'Where can she have gone?'

'I have no idea, Mrs Brank! One moment, she was there, right beside me, as happy as could be, and the next one she was gone!'

Oh, no, no, no! Please, God, not those two!

As usual, God had his ears stuffed with beeswax. The voices of my aunt and fiancé approached from behind at the speed of two galloping horses.

'Oh, Mr Fitzgerald! I am so sorry! I should have known something like this was going to happen. Lilly has always been such a wilful child!'

'Surely, Mrs Brank, you do not think she left by choice? I just announced our engagement, and she was clearly bursting with joy! Why would she wish to leave?'

Just then, the two of them brushed past me. I could see the expression on my aunt's face. No matter her faults, my aunt knew me well. In answer to Mr Fitzgerald's words, she gave only a tactful silence.

The exit wasn't far ahead now. Only a few steps. I started counting positive numbers again.

Ten steps.

Nine.

Eight.

My aunt and Mr Fitzgerald reached the exit. I ached to catch up to them, to go faster, to run like the wind – but I knew that I couldn't. I could still feel the steely gazes from behind the curtain on my neck and knew that the moment I started to move faster than average, they would see through my disguise, and grab me.

Nice and slow, Lilly. Nice and slow.

Seven steps.

Six.

Five.

Four.

It would be over soon. I just had to hold out a little longer. A tiny little bit longer. Outside, I could hear my aunt and my fiancé discussing my mysterious disappearance. In an effort to keep myself from breaking into a run, I focused on their voices.

'I can't believe she went out on her own, Mrs Brank – not considering the way I know she feels about me! Something must have happened, someone must have taken her! I should never have left her alone. As her betrothed, her safety is my responsibility!'

'Um…yes.' There was hesitation in my aunt's voice. I could see she probably found the idea of my having to be forcibly dragged from Morty's side because of my mad, passionate love for him not quite convincing, but thought it impolitic to point this out to him. 'You are probably right. Maybe you should look for her.'

Three.

Two.

One.

'You are right, Mrs Brank. I will!'

Out!

I blinked in the darkness of the night for a moment. When my eyes slowly became used to the gloom, I could make out the stocky form of Morty a little way away, gazing left and right in search of his lost future bride. My aunt was standing a bit closer to the door, only feet away from me.

Quickly, I turned to the left and headed down the street, away from the house.

Don't let them see me, don't let them see me, don't let them see me...

'Where could she have gone?'

'I don't know, Mr Fitzgerald.'

'I can't see anyo – oh, excuse me! Sir! Sir, have you seen a girl? About your height, with shoulder-long brown hair, and–'

I broke into a run.

~~**~*~*

If I'd had any hope that a night of searching through the wet alleys of London might cool Morty's passion, that hope vanished the moment he showed up at our house the next morning. And by morning, I mean six o'clock. *Ante* meridiem.

I mean, honestly! *Six am!* Just because he thought the woman he loved had been kidnapped and ravished by a rake? The nerve of the man! I had to work, after all.

Of course, he wasn't actually aware of that little fact, so from a purely logical standpoint I couldn't really blame him for it. Still, at six in the morning, with my sleep-deprived eyes only half open and my hair a mess of brown lianas on my head, I wasn't inclined to be particularly logical – or polite. As I stumbled to the door, still in my nightgown, cursing whoever was standing outside, ringing the doorbell like a madman, I was contemplating the use of brute force to shut them up.

'Yes?' I yanked the door open. 'Who is it and why are you making such a rack–'

I got no further. An instant later, I was engulfed in a crushing hug. Something small and cuddly had thrown itself at me. Did we have a monkey waiting outside the door?

'Oh my God! Thank you! You are safe, Lillian my love! You are safe and well!'

No. It wasn't a monkey. It was a Morty.

He tried to kiss me, and I ducked to the left. He tried to kiss me from the other direction, and I ducked to the right. Some distant part of my mind that

62

wasn't completely sleep-deprived had time to admire how quick my reflexes were at six in the morning.

'Oh Lillian, my love! I was so worried! So terribly worried! I'd like to hold you and never let go again!'

'Yes, Morty, I can feel that. Say...you wouldn't mind loosening your grip a little, would you?'

'What?'

'Loosen. Your. Grip!'

'Oh. If you think I should. I...' Morty's eyes went wide. Only now did he seem to register that I was wearing nothing but a nightshirt, and he, to put it delicately, was hugging me very, very closely. He let go as if he'd been burned and jumped back at least three feet.

'Oh. Um... I'm so sorry, Lillian, my love! So terribly sorry! It won't ever...I mean...I will never again...I didn't mean to...'

His stuttering went on until my aunt made her way down the stairs and shooed me off into mine and Ella's room to dress. Knowing that my aunt would be up to drag me down by my hair if I didn't hurry, I enlisted Ella's help in squeezing into my dress and was back downstairs in a couple of minutes.

The good news was: Morty was so embarrassed by having hugged a girl in her nightdress that he kept his hands off me during the entire breakfast. The bad news was: he definitely had not changed his mind about the engagement. Between the embarrassed looks he sent my way, there still were at least a dozen hot looks of passionate longing. There really was no way around it: the man was head over heels in love with me. He was so happy to see me safe and well, he didn't even ask where I had disappeared to last night.

My aunt, however, had no such inhibitions.

'Lillian?' Leaning over to me, she spoke in a low but unmistakably no-nonsense voice. 'Where did you disappear to last night?'

Having Mr Ambrose for an employer really had been enormously educational. It had taught me the value of the world's most underestimated rhetorical device.

Silence.

'Lillian? Answer me!'

And more silence.

'Answer me now!'

And just a little bit more to annoy her. Ha! I knew how to be silent. I had learned from the master of masters.

'Very well.' The gaze my aunt shot me through narrowed eyes told me she didn't particularly appreciate Ambrosian rhetorical tactics. 'Be a stubborn little girl about last night, if you will. But today you will behave like a lady, understood? Mr Fitzgerald will expect you to spend the day with him – and that you will do! No buts, understood?'

'Yes, Aunt.'

I would give her no buts – however, that didn't mean I was going to do what she said. I was an excellent liar. Always had been. What can I say, it's a natural talent.

Besides, I really had to get to work. So, just before breakfast ended, I excused myself, saying I had to go to the powder room. My aunt threw me a suspicious look. But what could she do? She could hardly demand to go with me in front of her future nephew-in-law.

I was thorough. I went down the corridor to the powder room, banged the door in an audible manner, and only then snuck back up the corridor and out the back door into the garden. Minutes later I emerged from the garden shed and, stepping out onto the street, started on my way towards Empire House, 322 Leadenhall Street.

Work that day was nothing to write home about. Not that Mr Ambrose would have granted me time off to write home about it even if it had been. I slaved all day on those balance sheets of his, and when the day drew to a close, he wanted me to take the rest home, to work through in my free time.

'Not on your sweet life!' I shook my head, retreating a few steps. 'I sweat all day for you in the office! I'm not going to do it at home!'

'It would show an admirable work ethic,' he pointed out coolly.

'But you wouldn't pay me extra, would you?'

'Of course not. That's why it would be admirable.'

'You can take your admirable work ethic and stuff it up your–'

And I said a word that made him send me a very frosty look.

'Language, Mr Linton!'

'Yes, Sir.'

'Will you do the work at home or not?'

'No, Sir. Besides, I could not, even if I wanted to. I have a situation at home.'

'Oh?'

'I...'

I hesitated for a moment. For some reason I didn't want to tell him.

'Out with it, Mr Linton!'

'I...am engaged.'

'Indeed?'

'To a *man*!'

'How shocking.'

'Don't laugh at me!'

'Do I look like I'm laughing?'

No, of course he didn't! Damn him!

Mr Ambrose cocked his head. 'Off with you, then. Enjoy your time with your fiancé.'

Rikkard Ambrose really was a cold bastard. He knew how to inflict a maximum of icy dread into my day with just a few simple words.

~~**~*~*

Morty was in love. Really, madly in love. With me.

I hadn't counted on how much more difficult this would make things. My previous suitors had wanted me for my family's good reputation, or had just been after a woman with two legs, two arms and a hole for popping children out of at regular intervals. Having to deal with a man who wanted *me*, and me only, was another kettle of fish altogether. I didn't know how all those romance heroines stood it! Why didn't they start to vomit in the first chapter?

Men in love, it appears, are a whole lot more difficult to get rid of than greedy or lusty men. In the latter case, a good stomp on the foot will probably do the trick. Men like that leave you alone and go off in search of easier prey. But a man in love – he won't notice how many times you tread on his foot. He just thinks what he's feeling down there is displaced heartache.

I didn't realize how bad it had gotten until I received the first letter. I was sitting with my siblings at breakfast one morning, and was in a marginally better mood than usual: in a rare exception, neither my aunt nor Morty had made an appearance. I was just digging into my gruel with unusual gusto when Leadfield limped into the room. It took him about a decade to shuffle from the door to the table, but finally he managed it and presented me with a silver tray on which lay one single, solitary letter.

'For you, Miss.'

'For me?' Frowning, I picked the mysterious object up. No one ever wrote me letters.

'Yes, Miss.'

'Hmm.' Picking up a knife from the table I sliced open the missive. The moment I did, the scent of violets assaulted my nose. I coughed and ripped the letter open the rest of the way. What the hell...?

My dearest Lillian,

It tears at my heart that today I cannot join you at the breakfast table. The time away from you is like torture. Urgent business matters have called me away, and with every mile that I put between me and you, I curse the puny affairs that have made my absence from your side a necessity. I promise, the moment they are concluded, I will hurry back to you, my love. This evening, I shall be back at your side, ready to weep on your bosom from the joy of your presence and...

It went on like that for a good three pages. I didn't read it, though. I'd had more than enough by the time I had reached 'weep on your bosom'.

Weep on my bosom?

I wasn't even exactly sure whether I had a bosom. Chest, maybe, but bosom? I had never been particularly well-stocked in the upstairs department, if you get my meaning. But whether or not I had a bosom, no man on this earth was ever going to get the chance to *weep* on it! *Yuck!*

Mr Fitzgerald returned that evening, and though I managed to keep him from either weeping on or kissing me, he used such fiery language to assure me of his everlasting love that it was almost as horrible as ending up tear-soaked. Over the next few days, it got increasingly difficult to escape his loving clutches to get to work on time, and the looks Mr Ambrose threw me when I walked into the office grew increasingly colder.

Finally, I decided something had to be done.

'Morty?'

'Yes, Lillian my darling?'

We were strolling through Green Park. Or rather, he was strolling. I was stamping, grinding my parasol into the ground with every step.

'I'm not your darling!'

'Pardon, Lillian my darling?'

'Or at least I don't want to be!'

He smiled and nodded, gazing adoringly at my face. He hadn't heard a word I'd said.

'Morty, listen to me! This engagement was a mistake! I don't love you!'

He laughed.

I'm not joking. He laughed.

'Lillian, my love! You do make the most amusing jokes!'

'I'm serious, Morty! I don't love you! I don't want to marry you! I don't want to marry anybody! I'm perfectly fine by myself, thank you very much!'

He laughed again. 'Getting pre-wedding jitters, are we? Don't worry, Lillian, my darling.' Leaning over, he pressed a kiss on my cheek. 'I know you love me. I'll be strong enough for the both of us, and soon we'll be a happy family.'

'How...wonderful.'

Waste Disposal Squad in Action

How am I going to get rid of him? How am I going to get rid of him? How the hell am I going to get rid of him?

This was the only thought running through my head, again and again, when I made my way to work on Friday. I was getting desperate. I mean, I suppose I could always let myself be led to the altar, and when the priest asked me, 'Wilt thou have this Man to thy wedded Husband, to live together after God's ordinance in the holy estate of Matrimony?' answer with a big, fat, resounding: *'No!'*

But to be honest, I didn't know whether anyone would listen to me. I was still a minor. My aunt and uncle could decide practically everything for me. Could they decide whom I was to marry, too?

Part of me was afraid that, yes, they could.

I had to find a way to get rid of Morty! I simply had to! I had no intention of marrying any man. And if I did, it certainly wouldn't be a man like him. It would be a man like –

I cut that thought off before it could go any further. Now wasn't the time for silliness. Now was the time for deep thought.

'Lillian, my love!'

Correction: Now was the time for *running!* The voice from behind me froze the blood in my veins and set my heart hammering. He was behind me! If he caught up to me, I'd never get to work! And then...well, I wasn't quite sure if Mr Ambrose would 'fire' me, because I wasn't sure you could apply such a hot word to Mr Rikkard Ambrose. But he would definitely freeze me.

I hastened my steps. I just had to get around that corner! Maybe...

'Lillian, my darling! Stop! It's me, Mor-oomph!'

I was halfway to the street corner before I realized that Morty's footsteps were no longer following me. His voice, too, had cut off abruptly. Knowing I might regret it, I stopped to listen.

No 'Lillian, my love!'

No 'Lillian, hand over your bosom so I can cry tears of happiness on it!'

No nothing.

Slowly, very slowly, I turned. In the whole street, there was no sign of Morty. There wasn't any sign of anyone. And yet, in the moments before Morty's voice had cut off, I could have sworn I had heard a second, heavier pair of footsteps.

Out of the corner of my eye, I caught a motion, and whirled. But the mouth of the alley I whirled towards was empty. Strange. For one moment I thought I had seen a shadow moving into it. No...not moving, exactly. Being dragged.

An involuntary shiver ran down my spine.

Stop imagining things! I told myself. *And get to work!*

Mr Ambrose did not freeze me. But he wasn't very warm and chummy, either. We still hadn't worked through the balance sheets, and his mood was getting icier with every penny of taxes that was added to the total. That day, I went home exhausted and thoroughly depressed at the thought of the weekend ahead. True, my dear employer worked me like a carthorse, but at least he wasn't prone to frequent and flowery confessions of love. I shuddered at the thought of having no office to escape to for two whole days. I knew what awaited me instead: forty-eight hours of Morty around the clock.

Only...

When Saturday morning dawned and we all sat down to breakfast, Morty didn't show up. Neither did he show up for lunch, or our usual stroll in the park to which my aunt in her cruelty had condemned me. When, after an hour of feeding the ducks, he still hadn't put in an appearance, I shrugged and returned home.

'What are you doing back here so early?' my aunt snapped. 'And where is Mr Fitzgerald?'

I shrugged again. 'He wasn't there.'

'What do you mean, he wasn't there?'

'I mean that he was in absentia. Skiving off. Not present.'

'Don't take that tone with me, young lady! Go dress for dinner! He must be here for dinner, and I'm sure he'll explain everything then.'

But he didn't appear for dinner either. I didn't dare to hope yet when I went to bed that evening, but when Sunday morning came and there still was no sign of him, hope would no longer be denied and fought her way into my consciousness.

Is it possible? Can he really be...gone? Simply vanished? But how?

I didn't want to believe it yet. Believing it would make it real – and that would make the disappointment when Morty finally walked through the door only all the more crushing. But he didn't walk through the door all day, nor climb through the window nor come down the chimney.

It can't be possible! He can't be gone! He can't! I can't be this lucky!

I tried telling myself that again and again as I lay in bed that night, trying to fall asleep. But the ridiculous grin on my face just wouldn't die down, and neither would the hope blossoming in my non-bosomy chest. I suppose I should have felt a bit worried about what might have happened to poor Morty – but I was too blissful at the prospect of not becoming Mrs Morton Marmeduke Fitzgerald to bloody care!

This happy prospect became exponentially more likely when, by next morning, Morty still hadn't put in an appearance. Ignoring my aunt's sour face, which could have been used to make enough pickled eggs to supply London for a whole year, I danced out of the house, threw on my men's clothes and dashed off to work, running twice as fast as I normally did. By the time I arrived at 322 Leadenhall Street, I was barely out of breath. I danced into Mr Ambrose's office, hardly able to suppress my urge to sing.

'Isn't it a wonderful morning, Sir?' I sighed, twirling like a ballerina in the middle of the office.

Mr Ambrose didn't raise his cool gaze from the paper he was reading.

'Any particular reason for your unnecessary exuberance, Mr Linton?'

'Yes, oh yes! A man has disappeared! Maybe he's sick, or he's been pressed into the Navy, or –' I did another pirouette, '– he might even be *dead!*'

'And that is cause for joy why, exactly?'

'Because he's the bloody man who wanted to marry me, that's why!'

He cocked his head. 'I see. My congratulatory condolences, Mr Linton.'

'Thanks!'

'How did this fortunate event take place, if I may ask?'

I frowned. It wasn't like Mr Ambrose to ask questions. And he had a funny lack of a look on his face. Somehow a bit different from the usual absence of expression that usually reigned on his stony visage.

'No idea. But now that you mention it...'

'Yes, Mr Linton?'

'It's strange...'

'What is?'

'He isn't the first suitor who has disappeared without a trace. The last one disappeared just like that, suddenly, without the slightest explanation.' I bit my lip, thinking – then shrugged, and skipped over to my desk with a grin. 'But as long as they're gone, why should I care about the how? Maybe I have a guardian angel.'

Abruptly, he turned around, and marched back to the door. 'Doubtful. I cannot imagine a divine entity would waste its time guarding you.'

'Thank you for the compliment, Sir!'

'Get out the balance sheets, Mr Linton. We're going to get through with them today, understood?'

'Yes, Sir!'

We didn't get through with them. There were lots and lots of the blasted things, and this was going to take longer than Mr Ambrose had anticipated. Either he hadn't known how rich he was, which I doubted very much, or he hadn't anticipated how big of a bite the government was planning to take out of his profits. In that case, I pitied the poor tax collector who would come around trying to collect. There truly were fates worth than death, and I didn't wish them on anybody. Not even tax collectors.

I toiled from morning until (almost) night. Mr Ambrose continued to crack the figurative whip until thirty-seven seconds before eight pm, when he finally admitted that we might actually not manage to finish the work tonight.

'Put away the balance sheets,' he ordered. 'In all probability, we will not be able to finish our work today, after all.'

I glanced at my pocket watch. Twenty-five seconds to closing time. Yes, I'd say that it was probable, too.

Grabbing stack after stack, I stored away several months' worth of bookkeeping. The only thing I had on my mind was getting out of the office extra quickly to enjoy my newfound freedom – but when I removed the last stack of financial papers from Mr Ambrose's desk, something beneath caught my eye: a slim black folder, lying conspicuously alone at the corner of the desk.

I hadn't put it there. Usually, all the files on Mr Ambrose's desk were put there by me. But this one? No. The thing just lay there, dark and mysterious, sending a shiver down my spine. It sparked a dim memory in my mind. Months ago, shortly after I had first started working for Mr Ambrose...

Haven't I seen something similar?

But no. I was Mr Ambrose's secretary. What possible reason would he have to keep any files secret from me? Still, even the inscription on the file seemed familiar: *M.M.F.. from L.L. Waste Disposal.*

What could that possibly mean?

'Sir?' Picking up the file, I held it out to him. 'What am I supposed to do with this?'

He looked at me for a moment – a strange look that sent another shiver down my spine. Bloody hell! I had to set up a shiver blockade somewhere back there.

'Well, Sir?' Mr Ambrose was still gazing at me, unspeaking. I glanced down at the file. What in God's name was so familiar about it?

I looked back at my employer, and he cocked his head. 'File it under "success", Mr Linton.'

'Yes, Sir. As you wish, Sir.'

~~**~*~*

Free!
Free!
Free!
I was *free!*
Free as a bird!

No, actually much freer than a bird! A bird had to build a nest and fill it with ugly, quarrelsome baby birds and then spend all his time stuffing their greedy little beaks with earthworms. I didn't have to stuff anybody with anything. I could just tell them to get stuffed!

My aunt was in a sour mood, of course, but since this was sort of her natural state, I wasn't particularly worried about it. As for Morty – I wished him all the best, wherever he was. The happier he was in his current place of residence, the less likely he was to come back to me. And when a little pinch of guilt overcame me now and again for not worrying more about the fate of my fiancé, I had only to resort to the pages of the *Times* to recover my earlier sense of exalted relief at not being faced by the prospect of marriage:

QUARRELSOME WIVES

It has come to the attention of the Editor of this paper that recently, a number of cantankerous women have gone so far beyond the boundaries of propriety as to take their husbands, the very men to whom they swore a vow of loyalty in front of God, to court. Why, one may ask, did they feel the need to accuse the men who should be dearest to their hearts? Was it because they were murderers? Thieves? Traitors to the Crown?

Far from it! It was mere, petty dissatisfaction – rebellion against the way in which God made the world. Forgetting their vow of obedience, they dared to contradict the master of the house and then, when faced with the just punishment for their quarrelsome ways, they dared to call upon the law of England to defend their breaking of their wedding vows.

Can such behaviour be tolerated?

Just as God did not tolerate Eve's sin, we must not tolerate these latest offences of women against the divine order of things. When a man desires to punish his wife, this is his business, and his alone. Only women without an ounce of proper feeling in them would protest anything to the contrary. It is well-known that those women who object to their husband's castigating have been led astray by influences from outside the home. Working women, those are the ones who are protesting against their just punishment. If we want to put an end to the quarrelsome nature of many wives, we must put an end to women's employment. Undoubtedly, it is the predominant cause of wife beating, and completely contrary to the purposes for which woman was given to man. Woman's purpose is to be the angel in the house, not the devil outside of it.

Thus, I call upon every right-thinking man in Great Britain to not give work to women, or associate with so-called 'ladies' who have reached an unbecoming degree of independence by practising a profession. If we all recall the divine order of the world and return to what is proper and right, it may not yet be too late to save Great Britain from the terrible fate that is threatening.

Charles Marcus Earl

The Editor[7]

Do you understand why I might be a teensy-weensy bit anxious about getting married?

Yep. I thought so.

'Lillian!'

My aunt's voice tore me from my delicious fantasies of strangling the editor of the Times. Lowering the paper, I glanced up just in time to see her rushing

---

[7] These views did not spring from my imagination. An article in the Hull Packet, only a few years after this story takes place, asserted practically the exact same message. Several phrases are actually quoted from this article.

into the room. I was expecting her to make some cutting remark about how unfeminine of me it was to read the paper, and had already prepared a mollifying response – but I didn't need it.

'Oh Lillian! Lillian, how wonderful!' My aunt rushed towards to me. There was a radiant smile on her face. My guard went up immediately. 'Simply wonderful! Oh, Lillian, I am so glad that that awful Mr Fitzgerald has disappeared!'

Cocking my head, I lifted one eyebrow. 'Well...so am I. But I must admit, I'm rather surprised you feel that way.'

'Oh, don't be silly!' She pulled me up out of the chair and hugged – actually *hugged* – me to her. 'Of course I'm glad he's gone! You deserve much better!'

With those words, my good mood evaporated, and a thrill of apprehension shot through me.

'Better?' I demanded. 'Better like *whom*, exactly?'

PINK LETTER LADY

A baronet! She had actually managed to find a blasted baronet! And as if baronets weren't rare enough in the United Kingdom of Great Britain and Ireland, she had found one who apparently wanted to *marry me!* And even worse: an hour spent in my company had not been enough to change the man's mind!

What the bloody hell was I going to do? Aunt Brank had been eager enough for me to get married before, but now? When there was a noble title involved? She would move heaven, earth and hell to pull this wedding off. If need be, she would drag me to the altar by my hair. The only way I would be able to escape was if I fled England!

'Good morning, Mr Linton,' Mr Stone greeted me cheerfully as I stomped down the hallway on my way to my office.

Then he caught sight of my face.

I threw him a glare. 'Who said anything about *good*?'

'Um...' He swallowed. 'My mistake. Mr Ambrose is waiting for you.'

I bet he is! But right now, that doesn't matter! I have to think up a way to get out of town, a way to get away from my aunt. I don't have time for Mr High and Mighty Ambro-

My thoughts cut off abruptly as an idea struck me. It wasn't gentle about striking me, either. It gave me a hefty wallop in the head.

Mr Ambrose! That was it. The last two times I had left England – the only two times, in fact – it had been in the company of Mr Ambrose, to take care of problems presented by the many and varied business interests that he possessed all over the globe. The two of us had invaded the secret headquarters of Lord Dalgliesh, had sailed to France, traversed the deserts of Egypt and fought robbers and hired killers together! Surely he could come up with some more robbers to kill in some desolate corner of the earth, preferably more than five hundred miles away from my dear aunt?

'Mr Linton, I can hear you breathing out there!' a familiar cold voice cut through the door of Mr Ambrose's office. 'Get in here! You are already twenty-seven seconds late.'

'Work calls,' I informed Mr Stone and, pushing the door open, sauntered into the office with a broad smile on my face. 'Good morning, Sir! It is a wonderful morning, is it not?'

Cold silence greeted me.

I don't know whether you've ever been greeted by cold silence before. In case you haven't, let me tell you – it doesn't make for a great welcome party.

'The perfect weather for a walk in the park,' I added, trying to keep the bright smile on my face. 'Or a trip to the country. Or maybe, I don't know...even a longer journey?'

A pair of dark, sea-coloured eyes found my face. 'Get the balance sheets, Mr Linton!'

Not a very promising start, I had to admit to myself as I hurried to do his bidding. I would have preferred 'Of course, Mr Linton! Let's go to Honolulu!' But if Mr Ambrose ever made things easy, he wouldn't be Mr Ambrose – or would have stopped breathing. Though, on second thought, I wouldn't put it past his corpse to try and order me around.

'You know,' I mused, putting down the balance sheets in front of him, 'You look a little pale, Sir.'

Those dark eyes met mine. 'Your point being, Mr Linton?'

'A journey to sunnier climes would do you a world of good,' I said encouragingly.

'I'll take this half. And you–' Mr Ambrose lifted half of the balance sheets off the stack and slammed them down in front of me on the desk, 'take this.'

'France is very beautiful at this time of year, I hear.'

'I expect you to be finished in no more than two hours.'

'So is Italy. I've heard that in the Toscanan–'

'Mr Linton?'

'Yes, Sir?'

'What are you going to do now?'

'Work through balance sheets, Sir.'

'And what are you *not* going to do?'

I thought for a moment. 'Waste time talking about Italy, Sir?'

'Exactly. Get to work.'

And I got to work.

Half an hour later I was through about one fifth of the pile and hoping sincerely that Mr Ambrose's accountants had done their job properly. I had leafed through the balance sheets, but I hadn't exactly read anything while leafing. Well, how could I? How could anyone? If you were being threatened by a marriage to a rich British nobleman, you would have been just as crazy with worry as poor little me!

My mind was frantically going through possible ways of trying to get Mr Ambrose to leave the country and take me with him.

Inventing an imaginary business conference in Belgium?

Forget it! He'd see through it in an instant!

Just asking him politely, with a nice 'please' at the end?

Are you crazy?

Telling him I loved him passionately and wanted to elope with him to Gretna Green?

You really are crazy if you think that'll work!

There really was only one thing I could do to get him to take me out of town: get him to make a trip that would be financially profitable. Profit was Mr Ambrose's god and patron saint. For profit, he'd walk a thousand miles, or probably even sacrifice his firstborn son, if he had one.

Clearing my throat, I glanced over at Mr Ambrose – who was already finished with about twice as many papers as my good self.

'Mr Ambrose, Sir?'

He didn't look up. 'Yes, Mr Linton?'

'I've been thinking...'

'What an astounding feat.'

'I was thinking about–'

'Let me guess. Italy?'

'As a matter of fact, no, Sir.'

I waited for him to ask what I had been thinking about, if not Italy. He didn't.

'Don't you want to know what I was thinking about, Sir?'

'Not particularly, Mr Linton.'

'Well, I'm going to tell you anyway!'

'Indeed.'

'I was thinking about whether we might be taking another trip soon.' Now he did glance up at me. The temperature of his gaze was enough to cause frostbite on the tip of my nose. 'Not a pleasure trip,' I explained hurriedly. 'Strictly business, of course! It would be an absolute strictly one hundred per cent business trip!'

'I see. And what, Mr Linton, would be the purpose of this absolute strictly one hundred per cent business trip?'

'Um, well...business. Making money. Lots and lots of money. Stuff like that.'

'And how had you envisioned making lots and lots of money on a trip the destination of which you do not seem to know yet yourself?'

'Err...I don't know, Sir.'

'I thought not.'

He sent me another nose-freezing look. 'There is no reason to leave the metropole at the current moment. All my business operations around the globe are running smoothly.'

'Are they?' *Bloody, stinking hell!* 'I'm so happy to hear that, Sir.'

'Indeed?' Spearing me with a gaze that was far too perceptive for my liking, Mr Ambrose lifted a fresh pile of balance sheets. 'According to my new calculations, we will still need three days to finish with these. If we are not interrupted, that is. We will not leave London in the near future. The closest scheduled business trip is in a month.'

Damn! That wasn't nearly quick enough. If everything went the way Aunt Brank wanted it, I'd be married and have five squalling brats by then. No matter how biologically unlikely, if I stayed in London, she'd manage it somehow!

'We've wasted enough time. Get back to work, Mr Linton!'

'Yes, Sir. Immediately, Sir.'

I threw myself mindlessly back into work. My mind was off calculating contingency plans. Was there some way I could possibly prevent this marriage? Puke on my fiancé? Proclaim to be an anarchist and mass-murderer? Drug my husband-to-be with opium and ship him off to the East Indies?

No. Nothing would work. Aunt Brank would make me clean up the vomit. She already knew I was an anarchist, and if I shipped a baronet off to the East Indies, the British Government was sure to take exception.

I had to get out! And I had to do it *now*. Mr Ambrose was my only hope.

Crap.

Abruptly, I rose to my feet. 'Excuse me, please, Sir. I have to get new ink.'

All I received in reply was a curt nod. Quickly, I turned and dashed out of the room – but not to refill my inkwell. In moments, I was through the door from his office into mine and had started pulling down files from the shelves. In a frenzy, I started leafing through them, desperate to discover something, anything that would help me! These were the pages where Mr Ambrose had recorded all his ventures and adventures, all his profitable journeys all around the world. There had to be something in some remote corner of the earth that could still spit out enough money to arouse Mr Ambrose's interest! There simply had to be! Had to! Had to...

Ah!

~~**~*~*

'Mr Ambrose?'

Silence.

'Mr Ambrose, Sir?'

More silence. Freezing silence.

'Mr Ambrose, Sir, I've been thinking...'

'*Again?*'

'Yes, Sir. Indeed I have, Sir.'

'Try to control the urge, Mr Linton.'

I tried to control the urge all right – the urge to kick him where the sun doesn't shine! It was only with great effort that I remained seated and continued leafing through the balance sheets, feigning a casual attitude.

'Of course,' I assured him. 'I'm sorry, Sir. I'll be quiet. I just thought you'd maybe like to know about...well, let's forget it. I'm sure the gold will be found by somebody sooner or later.'

The last sentence hung in the air, the word 'gold' thrumming ominously in the silence. In my head, I counted the seconds.

Three...

Two...

One...

'Gold? What gold, Mr Linton?'

Bingo!

'Oh, nothing.' Not looking up from the balance sheets, I waved my hand dismissively. 'Just something I thought you would be interested in – but no matter. You said leaving town is out of the question, so it doesn't signify.'

'*What gold, Mr Linton?* Tell me, *now!*'

I tried my best to hide my smile behind a page full of banana sales proceeds. 'Well, there's this thing I found among your old files – just a little business opportunity that you might want to reconsider taking on. But if you're too busy here in London...'

'*I'll* decide when I'm too busy, Mr Linton!'

'Yes, Sir!'

'Give me that file! Now!'

'Of course, Sir! Right away, Sir!'

Approximately half a second later I had whipped out the file in question and was over at his desk, proudly presenting the result of my ceaseless searching. With bated breath I waited as Mr Ambrose opened the file and started to study the contents. This was it! My chance to get out of the country and out of the clutches of my aunt, the apocalyptic monster of marriage.

Please, God! Please, I'm not sure whether the heck you exist or not, but please just let him fall for this!

'What do you think?' I demanded proudly. 'Isn't that an excellent business opportunity?'

He continued to study the file for a few moments. Then, slowly, very slowly, he raised his head and gave me a look. One of *those* looks.

'A South American ruin, a seventeenth-century manuscript with coded directions leading to a lost civilization and a hidden treasure in the jungle? Mr Linton, this does not particularly sound like a business opportunity to me – more like the synopsis of a cheap adventure novel.'

'It is business!' I protested. 'And there's nothing cheap about adventure novels! I should know! I buy at least three every week!'

'I never would have guessed.'

'Don't you like gold and treasure?'

'I do. Almost as much as I like obedient employees.'

'So can we go?'

'No.'

'But–'

'What did I just say about obedient employees, Mr Linton?'

'But think of the opportunity, Sir! The wealth, the profit–'

'And the opportunity for you to get out of town?'

My ears started to burn. Quickly, I snatched the file back out of his hand. 'I have no idea what you mean, Sir!'

Blast, blast, blast! How does he know? How the hell can he possibly know?

'I'm sure you don't, Mr Linton.'

He can't know! He's just bluffing!

Well, maybe he was. But if there was one man on earth who had a better poker face than a marble statue, it was Mr Rikkard Ambrose.

I gave it one last try. 'Are you sure about not wanting to do this? Just think of all the gold! And it won't be difficult to get at all! I mean, South America is only a few thousand miles away–'

His cold gaze stopped me cold. No pun intended.

'I have no time to waste on foolish adventure quests into the South American jungle, Mr Linton! I deal in real business, not fantasy!'

'Yes, Mr Ambrose, Sir!'

'Now, get me the next round of balance sheets!'

'Yes, Sir! Immediately, Sir!'

I rushed out of the room before I could succumb to my irresistible buttkicking urges. I was just returning with the requested documents, when a cautious knock came from the direction of the door.

'Mr Ambrose, Sir?' I heard Mr Stone's voice from outside.

'Enter!' Mr Ambrose commanded, snatching the balance sheets away from me before I had a chance to put them down. Mr Stone tiptoed into the room, and held out a small stack of envelopes to Mr Ambrose.

'These just arrived from the Bank of England, Sir. Quite urgent, I am given to understand.'

'Hm.' Grabbing the letters, Mr Ambrose sliced the first one open with a finger and pulled out the paper inside. His eyes flicked across the page in *prestissimo*. Then he glanced up at me.

'Urgent indeed. I will have to take care of these myself, Mr Linton. Go to your office and make sure I am not disturbed under any circumstances, understood?'

'Yes, Sir! Just as you say, Sir!'

'And, Mr Linton?'

I was already at the door when his call made me turn around. He held out a pile of balance sheets to me.

'Take these with you. I'll expect you to be through with at least half when I'm finished.'

My shoulders slumped. 'Yes, Sir. Of course, Sir.'

'Adequate. Close the door behind you, and do not open it again until I say so.'

'Yes, Sir.'

I walked out and heard the door shut with a click, behind me.

Settling down at my desk and staring miserably at the balance sheets, I thought: *I'm going to be a baronet's wife.*

Was there ever a more depressing thought?

Once or twice, I had glanced into the romance novels that were bread and butter to my younger sisters, Anne and Maria. The heroines of these romances seemed to want nothing more than to marry a rakish lord and spend the rest of their days in delirious lovy-dovyness, popping out babies every nine months, or every six, if they could manage. The noblemen in these books were always tall, dark and handsome and, after initially appearing to be total bastards, they revealed themselves to actually be – surprise, surprise! – kind, loving husbands.

Well, let me just tell you what's wrong with that picture: the average English nobleman is built like a bent beanpole, with oversized ears and nose. While he is capable of great love and passion, they are generally reserved for racehorses, not wives. And in ninety-nine per cent of the cases, if the nobleman in question appears to be a total bastard, he in the end turns out to be a really absolutely total bastard.

Except to racehorses, of course.

'I'll be damned if I let myself be sold off to one of those blue-blooded nincompoops!' I growled, furiously digging through the pile of documents in front of me, hardly noticing the numbers flying by. 'No matter what Aunt Brank thinks she'll be getting out of it! I'll kill myself first! Or better yet, I'll kill him! Or burn down the church! Or–'

'Um…Mr Linton?'

A tentative knock came from the door, and Mr Stone stuck his head in.

'Yes?' I barked. He flinched.

'Um…there's a lady out here.'

'Lucky you! Enjoy the company, but don't make too much noise. I'm working.'

I returned to my numbers, but Mr Stone cleared his throat, and I had to look up again, my eyes narrowed. '*Yes?*'

'Err…this lady out here…She has come to see Mr Ambrose.'

'Mr Ambrose gave orders that he doesn't wish to be disturbed!'

'I've told her that.'

'And even if he hadn't given those orders, it'd be more likely that he wanted to see a rotten pile of seaweed than a member of the female sex.'

'I told her that too, Mr Linton. In, um, slightly more diplomatic phrasing.'

'How very kind of you. And?'

'And she still insists on seeing him. So I thought…'

'…that you could dump her into my lap?'

Mr Stone's cheek flamed. 'Well, um, Mr Linton, I wouldn't exactly say it like that, I…' His voice trailed off, and he looked at me, desperately.

I rolled my eyes. 'All right. Send her in!'

'Thank you, Mr Linton!'

He vanished. Moments later, another knock sounded at the door. I was surprised, for I had expected the hammering of a matron with a temper to rival that of my friend Patsy. I would have thought it would have taken a true gorgon to get past two front desks and penetrate this far into the lair of Mr Rikkard Ambrose. But the sound that came from the door was an almost apologetic little, gentle tapping, like a baby woodpecker trying his beak out for the very first time.

'Come in!'

The door slowly swung open, and a woman entered. No – not a woman, a *lady*. Definitely. She was older, in her late fifties or early sixties maybe, with a wrinkled little face that showed the lines of both much joy, and much sorrow. Clad in a pink dress and with a pink parasol clutched anxiously in her hands, she looked so harmless and lost that even in my present mood, I couldn't help but soften towards her a little. This fragile little thing wanted to see Mr Rikkard Ambrose? The poor dear had no idea what she was in for.

'I-is this the office of...' she gulped.

She couldn't even say his name! Apparently, she did have *some* idea what she was in for. But she didn't *really* understand. Not completely. She couldn't have. If she did, she would be on a ship bound for the Colonies right now, thanking God for escaping her terrible fate.

'Yes?' I probed, cautiously.

'Is this the office of Mr Rikkard Ambrose?'

'Yes, it is.' *And it's not too late, yet. You can leave before he gets hold of you.*

The lady swallowed, her little hands clenching around the handle of her parasol. 'I would like to see him.'

'Are you sure about that?'

'Yes.'

'I see. Well...I'm afraid Mr Ambrose is busy at the moment.'

The lady swallowed again, and raised her chin. 'I would still like to see him.'

Oh-la-la! This little lady had more mettle in her than I'd suspected at first sight – or at second, to be honest.

'Are you acquainted with Mr Ambrose?' I asked, cautiously.

You can't be. You haven't been frozen solid by his ice-cold gaze.

An expression flitted over her face. It might have been a smile – but it might just as well have been a painful wince. 'Yes. I know...knew Mr Ambrose.'

What? From where? Where??

'I've never seen you here.'

'I've never been here before.' One corner of her mouth moved up into a tremulous half-smile. 'You have probably received some of my correspondence, however.'

It took me a moment to catch on. Then my eyes went wide, and I stared at her, really seeing her for the first time: pink dress, pink parasol, a pink bonnet on her head...

No.

It couldn't be.

'No...!'

I didn't realize for a moment that I had uttered the word aloud. She had noticed though, and her smile broadened a little bit.

'I see you realize what correspondence I'm speaking of?'

I realized all right. This lady, standing right in front of me – it had to be her! The one I had wracked my brain about all those past months! The one whose letters filled nearly every drawer of my desk by now! The mysterious figure from Mr Ambrose's past:

The pink letter lady!

But...but this can't be her!

I stared at the old lady, combining her image in my mind with the theories I had developed as to the identity of the writer of the pink letters.

A friend overseas?

No! She's bloody well right here, isn't she?

A mistress?

As if! Mr Ambrose wouldn't willingly spend a penny on anything, least of all a woman! Besides, isn't she a little...well...you know!

A wife?

No! No, no, no, nonononononoooooooooo!

It simply couldn't be her. I refused to believe that *this* was the *femme fatale* from Mr Ambrose's past. She looked like Britain's favourite granny in training, for heaven's sake! It had to be someone different who had been sending him letters! Maybe one of the many ladies asking for charity, whose letters I had been depositing in the paper container (not the bin, because Mr Ambrose insisted on not wasting paper and wrote his notes on the back of the charity requests he refused to answer) over the last few months. Yes! That had to be it!

'If you're here collecting for a charity, I'm afraid I'll have to disappoint you.' I gave her an apologetic smile. 'Mr Ambrose has many excellent qualities–' *Although I can't think of any right now.* '–but generosity is not one of them.'

'I know.' The woman's answering smile was sad. 'I'm not here collecting for a charity. I'm here to see my son.'

THE BLESSINGS OF MOTHERLY LOVE

I felt the floor sway under my feet. Her words rocked me to the very core of my being.

Mother?

She was his *mother?*

Apparently she was. And do you know what was the only thought that my extraordinary, profound and intelligent mind could come up with as a reaction to this profound revelation?

NothiswifenothiswifenothiswifeYesYesYesYes! Andnothismisstresseither! Yesyesyesyipee!

I am really profound, right?

'Your...son?' It was more of a croak than a question.

The woman nodded, slightly bending in the knees. It was not quite a curtsy – it was a far more regal gesture of greeting.

'My name is Samantha Genevieve Ambrose.'

'Linton,' I mumbled, automatically bowing my head in return. My eyes were fastened on the little woman in front of me, while I tried desperately to imagine Mr Ambrose having fit inside her once. It was quite absolutely impossible. 'Mr Victor Linton. Delighted to make your acquaintance.'

'How do you do, Mr Linton. And may I ask what position you occupy under my son?'

Immediately, my mind flashed back several months, to a dark hotel room in Egypt, the messy double bed, and all the positions I had occupied under Mr Rikkard Ambrose. Thank God that my face was too tanned to really blush. Still, I could feel my ears burning.

'I, err, am Mr Ambrose's private secretary.'

Very private, on occasion.

'I see.'

'And you...' I still couldn't stop staring. 'You really are his mother? Are you sure?'

A small smile tugged at the corners of her mouth. 'I was there at the birth, you know. Yes, I'm quite sure.'

If my ears had been burning before, they felt about ready to explode now. 'Sorry! I didn't mean...! It's just, Mr Ambrose always seems as if he were chiselled out of some mountain, not made out of flesh and bone.'

'Yes.' The proud light shining in her eyes undeniably confirmed her words. She really was his mother. Or she was crazy enough to think she was. I still wasn't sure which was more likely. 'He has grown into a strapping young man, hasn't he?'

That's putting it mildly.

'That's not the only reason why I was surprised,' I dared to say. 'I've been with Mr Ambrose for quite a while now, and he has never mentioned a mother. Now that I think about it, he's never mentioned any family.'

Pain shot across her face like a bolt of lightning. She concealed it fast, but it was there, and it was real. This was no imposter or madwoman. This was a mother in agony.

Oh crap! What am I going to do?

'Never?' she asked in a whisper.

'Never.'

She closed her eyes for a moment. 'Well...no. I imagine he wouldn't.'

When she opened her eyes again, they were moist. But she had not let the threatening tears spill over. And, to judge by the stubborn set of her chin, she wasn't going to.

'I still want to see him.'

Blast, blast, blast! This isn't fair!

No secretary should have to deal with something like this! Blustering bankers? No problem. Stinking beggars? Send them my way! Striking employees? I'm your girl! But nearly weeping mothers? He didn't pay me nearly enough for this!

I cleared my throat.

'I am afraid Mr Ambrose doesn't want to be disturbed.'

There! Problem solved. Now she has to go away, right?

'I still want to see him, Mr Linton.'

Damn!

'He really, really doesn't want to be disturbed,' I hedged.

'I really, really want to see him. P–'

Don'tSayItDon'tSayItDon'tSayIt!

'–lease.'

Bloody hell!

'Please, Mr Linton!'

Why does she have to sound so damn desperate? And those big, sea-coloured eyes of hers! They look so helpless, and at the same time, so much like his.

'Please.' She took a step towards me.

I sank down in my chair, as if my desk would be enough to protect me from her desperate motherly feelings.

'Mr Linton, I can see that you're a man of feeling– '

You're wrong about that, Lady!

'–and surely you can sympathize with me.'

Not if I want to keep my job, I can't!

'Why don't you come back some other time?' I suggested desperately. 'He might not be so busy then.'

A sound escaped her throat. It was half-laugh, half-sob. 'Another time? You have no idea of what you speak! Do you know how many times I've tried to see him since the catas– since he left home? That was after I found out he was still alive, of course! God! Mr Linton, I haven't seen him in ten years! Please! Just please...'

Damn you Rikkard Ambrose! Damn you!

I swallowed, hard. 'I'm sorry, my Lady, but he left explicit instructions. No one is to disturb him. And I believe that includes you.'

Her shoulders sagged.

'Does my son hate me this much, then?' she wanted to know, the pain evident in her voice. 'What did he tell you to do with all my letters? Destroy them?'

Yes. He did.

'No! No, he didn't.'

Wait! What did you just say, Lilly?

'He wouldn't have any of them destroyed! He told me to keep them all safe.'

Stop lying! Stop lying right now! Tell her right now that you've been stockpiling them against his express orders!

But I had to give the poor woman something to cling on to, hadn't I? I couldn't just destroy every last bit of hope she had!

'Here, you see?' Bending down, I ripped open the lowest drawer of my desk and held up a whole pile of pink letters as evidence.

'They're unopened.' Her voice was trembling. 'He hasn't read them?'

'I think it's too painful for him.'

Poppycock! Stop lying, Lilly!

'The expression on his face when he looks at the letters is so tender and painful–'

...or maybe rather cold and disdainful? Stop lying right this minute!

'–I can't imagine the feelings that must be tearing through him.'

She closed her eyes again for a moment. Opening them once more, she stepped forward, and placed a hand over mine, lightly squeezing.

'Thank you, Mr Linton. You are a good man.'

Not really. Trust me. I checked last time I took a bath.

'And as a good man–'

Oh God! Here it comes...

'...I ask you to hear a mother's plea. Please. I've tried to stay away. I've tried to respect his wishes. But I can't let him do this to himself and his family any longer. I *have* to see my son.' Her eyes bored into mine. Bloody hell, if they just didn't look so much like his! I felt my defences crumble. And then came her last cannon shot: 'Please.'

That's it. I'm fired.

I took a deep breath. 'You know...'

'Yes?'

'I think I've been mistaken. I just remembered that Mr Ambrose didn't say he *doesn't* want to be disturbed. He said he *wants* to be disturbed. As much as possible, at every opportunity. Especially by mothers, and any other relatives that happen to pass by. So, by all means, go in.'

The smile that spread across her face was reward enough. I just hoped I'd still think so in three weeks when I had to fend for myself, out of work and without a penny in my pocket.

'Thank you, Mr Linton! Thank you so much!' She squeezed my hand again, then let go and slowly moved towards the door of Mr Ambrose's office. 'I won't forget this.'

Oh, neither will I. He won't let me.

Turning to face the office door, she raised her hand and knocked.

'I said I didn't want to be disturbed, Mr Linton!' came a familiar, cutting and cold voice from inside. 'What is it?'

She opened the door.

'Hello, son.'

There was deafening silence.

She stepped inside, and the door fell shut behind her.

Half an hour had passed before the door opened again. She hurried out, a gleam in her eyes that I had only ever seen on the faces of mothers and deranged opium addicts. Nodding to me in passing, she left my office.

Silence reigned.

Long silence.

Then, Mr Ambrose stepped out of his office, his face as cold as the Antarctic in winter after an invasion by Nordic frost giants. His eyes snapped to me.

'Tell me, Mr Linton,' he demanded, his voice deceptively calm. 'Did you listen in at the keyhole?'

My eyes widened innocently. 'Me? Of course not!'

His eyes narrowed infinitesimally. 'You had better not be lying to me, Mr Linton!'

'I'm not! I swear on women's right to vote!'

'Women *don't have* the right to vote.'

'But they will have, soon!'

In a flash, Mr Ambrose had crossed the distance between us. His hands slammed down on my desk, and he leaned forward until my nose was only inches away from his clenched, rock-hard jaw.

'If I ever find out that you have listened at the keyhole,' he breathed, a thunderstorm roiling in his dark eyes, 'you will be very, very sorry. Understood, Mr Linton?'

'Yes, Sir!'

And I did understand. Completely. Absolutely. Why would I listen at the keyhole, when there were so many better options available?

~~**~*~*

The door closed behind her. With ravenous curiosity, my eyes fastened on the closed door. Suddenly, I knew exactly how Pandora must have felt when she rattled that box, trying to find out what was inside. Mr Ambrose's mother! Good God! What secrets I could discover here! She must have known him before he turned into a block of stone - back when he had actually been a human being!

In front of my inner eye passed the seal on the pink envelopes that I had seen so many, many times: undoubtedly the coat of arms of a noble family. And yet, Mr Ambrose used no title. Not duke, not baronet, not lord, not even 'the right honourable so-and-so'. He was just 'Mister'. Cold. Hard. Short. Efficient. And strangely, a hundred times more alluring and powerful than any noble title would have been.

Where had he come from? Why would he deny his noble roots? Especially if there was money to inherit? Why had he spent years and years in the Colonies? Why was there enmity between him and Lord Dalgliesh? A thousand questions - and the woman behind that door probably held the answers to all of them!

And the best thing was: I wouldn't even have to ask her!

Quickly, I jumped to my feet and rushed over to the door. All right, I admit it! I hadn't let her in out of the goodness of my heart! I had completely selfish motives! That didn't mean my heart wasn't still good, a tiny little bit. But 'g' came after 'c' in the alphabet, just like goodness came after curiosity.

Falling to my knees in front of the door, I was about to press my ear to the keyhole, when I hesitated.

What was I doing?

Why listen at the keyhole? After all, Mr Ambrose had kindly provided me with my own surveillance equipment. Rushing back to my desk, I snatched up a horn that was connected by a tube to the wall. Ordinarily, it was used by Mr Ambrose to bark orders at me or any of his other employees that happened to be unlucky enough to catch his attention. Today, it would be used for a different purpose.

Taking a deep breath to calm my breathing, I lifted the horn to my ear. For a few moments, there was absolute silence. Then -

'Mother?'

I hardly recognized Mr Ambrose's voice. For one moment, it almost sounded as if there were actual emotion in it.

I shook my head. It probably was just the distorting effect of the long rubber tube. The first time I had listened to him speaking through it, he'd sounded like a deranged nightingale with a severe speech problem.

'Ricky.'

I nearly bit my tongue off. Ricky? Ricky?!

The thought of anyone referring to my employer by that name made me feel faint. I suppose, on some level, I knew that his mother probably hadn't referred to him as 'Mr Ambrose' or 'Sir' while he'd been growing up, but it was still a shock.

'W-what are you doing here?'

Had I heard right? Had he just stuttered? Mr Rikkard 'don't-use-unnecessary-time-wasting- syllables' Ambrose?

It had to be a trick of the bad connection.

'I came to see you, son.'

'How did you get in here?'

Oh, bugger!

'That nice young secretary of yours let me in.'

'Did he, now?'

Blast, blast, blast and double blast!

There was a rustle of papers from the other end of the tube. I could just imagine Mr Ambrose building up a wall of important documents between himself and the unwanted visitor.

'Why did you wish to see me?' *His voice was suddenly back to the cold, calculated tone I knew and lo- Well, the tone I knew and had gotten really used to, anyway.* 'I am a busy man, Mother.'

'I know, Ricky. I just...I had to see you, son. It's been so long...'

'Not long enough.'

There was a noise - it sounded like an anteater blowing its nose. Or maybe it was a mother in pain.

'Is that really how you feel, son?'

'I don't feel. I know.'

'But after all those years...can't you forgive? Even a little bit?'

'Do you know what happened to me during those years, Mother?'

'No.'

'I thought not. If you did, you wouldn't have dared to ask that question.'

The soft clicking of her heels sounded through the tube. She had taken two uncertain steps forwards.

'Won't you return home, Ricky? Please?'

'Why should I return to someone who did not stand by me?'

'I tried! I really did! I - '

'Don't lie to me! You know what happened! You were there. And you never said a word!'

Silence.

Silence more deadly than any I had heard before.

Finally, Mr Ambrose spoke again, his voice as cold as an arctic grave: 'No. I will not come back for your sake.'

'Then don't do it for me. Do it for Adaira.'

I stiffened. Adaira? Who the hell was Adaira?

'Don't you dare bring her into this!' *There was a threat in Mr Ambrose's voice now - real danger, maybe even for his mother.*

She didn't seem to care.

'Oh yes, I will *bring her into this!* She misses you, Ricky! She has missed you ever since you left!'

Bloody hell! Mention who she is already, will you?

But nobody seemed inclined to grant my silent wishes.

'She loves you, son. If you don't believe that I love you after what has happened, believe in her.'

Love him? Love him? Who the heck was this little witch?

'Is there anything else you wanted to say, Mother?' I could feel the ice crystals growing on Mr Ambrose's voice all the way through the tube. 'I have important business to attend to.'

'More important than your family?'

'Undoubtedly.'

'Even Adaira?'

Silence.

But I didn't mind. I had gotten my answer: family! She was family!

'Your father is holding a celebration next week at–'

'I do not care!' He cut her off like an executioner the head of a condemned man. 'I will not attend any celebration of his!'

'It is Adaira's birthday.'

Silence.

This time, it wasn't cold, though. I could feel a definite atmospheric thawing from the other end of the tube.

'She'll be introduced into society, Ricky. I want you to be there.'

'I don't care what you want!'

A pause. Then:

'She wants you to be there, too.'

Another pause.

'Ricky?'

Silence.

'Ricky? Will you do this for her?'

More silence. Quite extraordinarily silent silence. Original, inimitable Ambrose Silence.

'Ricky, please, I...'

'Where?'

His voice was like a freshly sharpened blade of ice.

'At the hall.'

'Of course!' The ice-blade flashed with dark danger. 'Of course, it would have to be there!'

'Thanks to you, it can be. Without you, we–'

'Don't!' Now, the ice-blade lay at her throat, ready to strike. 'Don't thank me! Don't you dare!'

'But I have to! Without your generosity–'

I took my ear away from the tube, stuck a finger inside, turned it in the hope to remove dirt, and reapplied the ear. Had I heard right just now? Generosity?

'–without your kindness, we would never have–'

85

Apparently, my ears still weren't working properly. Kindness? Mr Masterfully Merciless Ambrose?

'Silence, woman!'

And there was silence. I didn't know many men who could silence their mothers with a single command. In fact, I probably didn't know any. But Rikkard Ambrose managed without the slightest problem. The silence that echoed on the other end of the tube was absolute. It was the silence of unspoken secrets, deep hurts and dark deeds in a long-buried past.

It was she who finally broke it.

'Please.' Just that one word. 'Please, Rikky.'

'Don't! Don't ask this of me!'

'If Adaira hears you didn't want to come, she will be heartbroken.'

'Heartbroken? She will be spitting fire!'

'True.' For the first time since the conversation had begun, there was the tiniest smile in Lady Samantha's voice. 'But she will also be heartbroken. Please - don't make me tell her you didn't want to come.'

Silence. And then:

'I'll come-'

'Oh, thank you! Thank - '

'-if there is no important business detaining me! I will not put everything on hold merely to gratify the foolish wishes of a silly young girl, mother! I will come only if I have no reason to be elsewhere! More than likely, something will come up. If I don't appear, don't be surprised.'

I could feel Lady Samantha wanting to argue, but she and I both knew that this was the best offer she was going to get.

'All right. If that is how you wish it...'

'It is. And now get out, woman! I have work to do.'

'Yes, of course. I shall tell Adaira to expect you.'

'Only if nothing important comes up, Mother. Only then!'

~~**~*~*

'Oh no,' I confirmed once more, smiling up at Mr Ambrose. 'I definitely didn't listen at the keyhole.'

He stared at me for a few moments more, his dark, sea-coloured eyes boring into me with an intensity that made me shiver. Finally, he righted himself and nodded.

'I see.'

Whirling around, he marched towards the window and planted himself there, tall and erect, his hands clasped behind his back. He stared out over the City of London. The light of the slowly sinking sun that flooded in through the windows cast a fiery halo around him, and he almost looked like an avenging angel.

Which was ridiculous, of course. Mr Ambrose would never work for anyone - not even for God. And most certainly not for free.

I don't know how long he stood there. I didn't dare move or make a sound. There was a tension in the air that went far beyond the normal deadly hostility radiating from him. Finally, when I had started to believe that he would continue standing like this until kingdom come, he said:

'Mr Linton?'

'Yes, Sir?'

'Pack your things! I shall await you ready to depart at St Katherine's Docks at 6 am tomorrow morning.'

I stared at his broad, rock-hard back. Maybe my ears still weren't working correctly?

'E-excuse me, Sir?'

'I don't excuse anything or anyone, Mr Linton. Most especially not you.'

'But I don't understand, Mr Ambrose, Sir! Why St Katherine's Docks? Why tomorrow at six? Are we leaving?'

He turned around then, fixing me with his ice-cold gaze.

'Don't you remember, Mr Linton? We have an urgent business trip to go on.'

'We have?'

'Oh yes. Or, to be more precise, a treasure hunt. You had better pack thoroughly. We won't be able to get anything we need in the jungle. South America awaits!'

SNEAKING AWAY

Late at night, long after I had come home from work, and long after I should have gone to bed, considering what awaited me tomorrow morning, I snuck up the stairs towards a very special room in our house. My only light was a solitary candle, throwing flickering shadows on the wall. In its faint glow, I could see the thick layer of dust on the wooden steps, broken only by a few solitary footprints.

God, Lilly...What are you going to do if he's not up at this hour? Or worse, if he says no?

A stair creaked under my foot, and I froze. Except for me and the one I was going to visit, the entire family was deep asleep. Aunt Brank had no idea that I was up this late. If she had known, and if she'd had any idea what I was going to do, she would have been spitting fire.

You can only hope that he receives your plans better than she would.

It was probably a vain hope. But I had to try, at least.

Cautiously, I continued up the stairs and, at the top, continued down the hallway until I reached the solitary door that was my destination. Raising my hand, I knocked twice, softy.

'Uncle Bufford?'

There was a moment of hesitation from behind the door, like the moment you would expect to pass if a vampire found someone knocking at the door of his coffin looking for blood donations. Then, a gruff, weary voice from inside called: 'Enter.'

And I did.

It was dark inside the room. Only a single candle, burned down to a stump, illuminated Uncle Bufford's study. He was sitting bent over his ledgers behind his massive oak desk, a frown on his face and a pipe jammed into the corner of his mouth. I knew that there wasn't anything in the pipe. Uncle Bufford would die before spending a penny on anything as frivolous as tobacco. But the pipe was an heirloom from his great-grandfather, and it provided a convenient barrier that kept him from constantly gnashing his teeth together.

Just as he was trying to do now.

'*You?*'

He pronounced the word as if London's most wanted lecher and murderer had just entered his study.

'Yes.' I gave my best imitation of a demure curtsy. 'Me.'

'Put your candle out! Have you any idea how much candles cost, nowadays? One candle in the room is more than enough light!'

'Yes, Uncle.' Immediately, I moistened my fingers and extinguished the candle, giving him a look-how-obedient-I-am smile.

He narrowed his eyes. 'You want something.'

Damn!

'Why would you think that?' I almost managed to make my voice sound injured.

'Because people only ever come to see me when they want something. Usually money.'

'Last time I saw you, I refused your money,' I reminded him.

'True.' The frown on his gnarled old face loosened a little. 'So – what is it that you want?'

I decided that it was no use beating around the bush. Uncle Bufford, like Mr Ambrose, was not an admirer of wasted time.

'I'm going away on a trip, Uncle.'

'Are you, now?'

'I might be away for a while.'

'Is that so?'

'Yes.'

For a few moments, silence reigned. Then he asked a question I would never have expected.

'Will you be safe on this trip?'

I had to work hard to keep my jaw from dropping. *Uncle Bufford? Concerned?* I hesitated. What to say? Finally, I settled on the truth. 'Probably not.'

'But you're still going.'

'Yes.'

Uncle Bufford took his pipe out of his mouth and tapped it against his jaw. 'Well, what did you come to see me for, then? Seems like your mind is already made up.'

'I came because of Aunt Brank. I thought that maybe you could keep her from completely losing her mind over this.'

He raised one bushy eyebrow. 'Your aunt lost her mind decades ago. Why would I waste my time trying to do anything about it now?'

'Err...all right. Point taken.'

'You don't want me to pay you an allowance for this trip, do you?'

'No.'

'Good. Because you're not getting one.'

'Don't worry. I've got all the money I could want.'

'Do you, now?' He gave me a penetrating look. But, to my immense relief, he didn't ask why or from where. Those simply weren't the kind of questions Uncle Bufford would ask. Where money was concerned, he tended to focus on questions like 'How much?' and 'How soon?' – but only if he was going to get a share.

'Your aunt isn't the only reason you're here, are you?'

Damn! I had forgotten how astute the old buzzard was.

'No. She isn't.'

'So, who is the other one?'

Who. Not *what.* Bloody hell, he really was too astute for my liking.

'Ella.'

'Ah.' He nodded, sliding the pipe back into his mouth.

'Will you keep an eye on her while I'm gone?'

'I never leave this room. You know that. I don't tolerate company – especially the company of women.'

I raised an eyebrow. '*I* am a woman. You haven't thrown me out yet.'

'You are going away for an extended period, and you don't want money from me. I am feeling slightly more lenient towards you at the moment.'

Was that a smile playing around one corner of his mouth? His bloody beard was too thick to tell! I narrowed my eyes at him.

'We've strayed from the subject, Uncle.'

'Have we?'

'Yes, we have. We were talking about Ella.'

'You were talking. I was waiting for you to get to the point.'

'The point is that I can't leave without knowing that Ella will be taken care of. With the kind of marrymania Aunt is in right now, she might strike on the idea of offering Ella to this baronet as a replacement when she can't get hold of me.'

Uncle Bufford nodded, thoughtfully. 'Exchanging one unit for a newer and more elegant model – that's a deal I wouldn't say no to.'

I sent him a death-glare but didn't follow it through with bodily violence. 'I need someone to watch over her while I'm gone.'

He raised one bushy eyebrow. 'And you immediately thought of me?' If I hadn't known better I would have sworn there was amusement in his eyes.

'Not really. In fact, I thought of thirty-seven other candidates first.'

'Only thirty-seven? I'm flattered.'

'But they all lacked one essential quality.'

'I'm intrigued. What is this special quality that makes me so unique?'

I took a step forward and fixed him with my best imitation-Ambrose stare. 'The power to make decisions.'

He gave another, slower nod. There was understanding in his eyes. Understanding and...respect? 'That is true.'

'You have the ultimate power to decide Ella's future.'

'Also true.'

'So, what I am asking you is: don't.'

'You want me to never give your sister a chance at marriage? At a different life? A future of her own?'

'No. I want you to not make any rash decisions. Wait until I am back before you decide anything. Give me a chance to speak with my sister.'

His eyebrow rose a fraction of an inch further. 'Really? And why can your sister not speak for herself?'

'Because, although Ella is as beautiful as the Goddess of the Morning and as sweet as honey, she can be a bit of an idiot, sometimes.'

Uncle Bufford considered this for a few moments. 'True.'

I regarded him warily. 'So...will you do as I ask? Will you wait until I return?'

'If a good marriage prospect presents itself–'

'Even then! *Especially* then. Please, Uncle Bufford. This is important.'

He grunted and looked down at his ledgers again. 'I won't start parenting at my age!'

I had already opened my mouth to argue, when he added, gruffly: 'But I won't let her do anything foolish. I cannot abide foolishness.'

My shoulders sagged in relief.

'Thank you.'

'I also cannot abide women! Including you!'

I smiled a secret little smile. 'Yes, Uncle.'

'They're nothing but work and needless expense!'

'Of course, Uncle.'

I gave a curtsy and started to leave the room. I was already at the door when, from behind me, I heard a gruff voice murmur: 'Be careful, will you?'

~~**~*~*

When I arrived the next morning at St Katherine's Docks, Mr Ambrose was already there, overseeing a group of men loading crates and barrels on board his favourite vessel, the *Mammon*. The men looked exhausted. Mr Ambrose looked as fresh as frozen daisies.

I saluted. 'Good morning, Sir! Here I am, present and correct.'

'And late.' Fishing his watch out of his pocket, he let it snap open. 'You should have been here twenty-one seconds ago, Mr Linton.'

'Not according to my watch, Sir.'

'Then your watch is slow. Correct that fault, Mr Linton.'

'Yes, Sir!' I promised, secretly vowing to myself to pinch his watch sometime soon and put it back twenty-one seconds. Curiously, I let my gaze drift over all the men who were hard at work lugging stuff onto the ship – a lot more than

90

any sensible man would need for a journey, let alone someone as frugal as Mr Ambrose. Besides, most of what they carried weren't travel bags or trunks. They were crates and barrels.

'What's all this?' I gestured to the men and their burdens.

'Items.'

I rolled my eyes. 'I had already noticed that, Sir. Items for what?'

'For sale. Since we are going all the way to South America, we might as well take some wares to trade. No reason not to make a little profit on this trip. It will probably be the only money we will make on this foolish excursion.'

'Where will we be selling?'

'In Argentina. I am expanding my business there. There is a lot of wealth in the country, but little industry. An ideal market for industrial goods.'

The last few crates were carried on board. A sailor appeared at the railing and waved to get our attention.

'Mr Ambrose? Mr Ambrose, Sir? We're ready to cast off!'

Mr Ambrose gave the man a curt nod, and he disappeared. Half turning towards me, my employer cocked his head. 'You have the file with the English translation of the seventeenth-century manuscript?'

I padded my pocket. 'All here, Sir.'

'Adequate. I put you in charge of deciphering the directions, Mr Linton. I will have enough to do planning the sale of the wares and commanding the ship.'

'Commanding the... Do you mean to say you plan to be at the helm yourself?'

'Of course!' He turned away and marched off towards the ship. 'You don't think I'd waste money on a captain, do you?'

'No, Sir. Of course not, Sir.'

'Hurry, Mr Linton! We haven't got a minute to lose.'

'I thought a sea journey like this takes weeks and weeks, Sir?'

'All the more reason not to waste any time now!'

'Yes, Sir!'

The moment we stepped on board, he called: 'Haul in the gangplank!'

Never in my life had I seen any captain's orders being obeyed that fast. In a matter of minutes, the sails were set, and we were moving towards the exit of the dock, the Thames awaiting us ahead. When we had just slipped out of the dock, I noticed two vessels veering off and following us.

'What are those?' I demanded, pointing.

Oh God! Please don't let it be Lord Dalgliesh!

Mr Ambrose didn't seem concerned, to judge by his expression. But, he being Mr Ambrose, his expression didn't really mean much of anything. It wasn't until he spoke that I was put at ease.

'The *Midas* and the *Croesus*, Mr Linton. They will be accompanying us to Argentina.'

Midas? Croesus? With names like these, it wasn't very hard to figure out who those ships belonged to. I stared at Mr Ambrose.

'You own more than one ship? You have *three*?'

He returned my gaze, coolly. 'I have a fleet of ships, Mr Linton. These are by no means the largest – although, after the *Mammon*, they are the fastest.'

I swallowed. Sometimes, I tended to forget the kind of wealth he commanded. I glanced back at the *Midas* and the *Croesus*, and couldn't help notice that, for merchant vessels, they were unusually well armed.

'Do you expect any trouble with pirates?'

'No. No pirates.'

I had become quite skilled by now at interpreting the things Mr Ambrose *didn't* say.

'But you *are* expecting another kind of trouble?' *The kind that requires cannons and guns to survive?*

All I got in answer was silence, and the lapping of the waves against the bow. I waited. Nothing came. Mr Ambrose stood on deck, so stiff and hard you might have suspected him of wanting to become the *Mammon*'s figurehead.

Oh, well... Why should I care if he didn't want to talk? Whatever trouble awaited us in South America couldn't possibly be worse than a gaggle of suitors and potential grooms, right?

No.

Wrong. So very wrong. But I didn't know that back then.

WELCOME TO ARGENTINA

The sun burned down on my face with an intensity that made it very clear I was no longer in England, or anywhere near its shores. And what was I doing? Lying in a hammock, enjoying the warmth on my skin?

Not bloody likely!

'Faster, Mr Linton! Haven't you ever tied a stopper knot before?'

'Much as it might surprise you, Sir,' I grunted, tugging at my hand with all the force I could muster, trying desperately to free it from the tangle of rope around my fingers, 'sailing knots are not considered an essential part of the education of an eligible young London lady!'

'You don't say.'

'Will you just keep standing there annoying me, or are you going to bloody help?'

'I thought I was going to just focus on the annoying. But since you evidently won't get the work done alone...'

Letting his words trail off, he stepped forward and gripped the entangled knot of rope and fingers that held my hands captive. Strong, elegant, long fingers closed over mine. I wanted to shout a warning, wanted to threaten him with bodily harm if he accidentally ripped one of my fingers off – but before I could get a word out, the knotted rope fell apart and slipped to the ground.

I stared at my freed hands.

'How did you do that?'

'Practice, Mr Linton. Try again.'

'Why do I have to? You have plenty of sailors on board.'

'Yes. But if you know how to sail, I will have to pay one less crew member on our next voyage.'

I threw him a disgruntled look. 'You really are the most abominably stingy skinflint in the history of mankind, aren't you?'

If there had been such a thing as expressions on the stone face of Mr Rikkard Ambrose, one might almost have said he looked pleased.

'Yes.'

'That wasn't a compliment!'

'Indeed, Mr Linton?'

'Indeed, Sir!'

'Why haven't you started tying knots yet, Mr Linton?'

Grumbling something I hoped was too low for him to hear, I grabbed the nearest rope.

That was how much of the days passed: during the day, I was on deck, drudging like a peasant under Louis XVI just before the Revolution, while during most of the night I had to work on deciphering the manuscript. The only difference was that, unlike Louis's poor peasants, I wasn't going to rebel. After a while, I found that I actually enjoyed working on the ship. I was doing something useful for a change, and learning things in the process. Mr Ambrose was right. London ladies *should* learn how to tie sailing knots. Not that I'd ever admit as much to his face, of course!

I was busy scrubbing the planks of the poop deck (which, thank God, didn't really deserve its name) when I heard the shout of the lookout, far, far above me:

'Ships ahoy!'

Jumping up, I whirled around, scanning the sea. The water was of such a bright blue here that it almost hurt my eyes to look at it. But with a bit of squinting I could just manage to look, and after a few moments, I saw them: three dark spots on the horizon. Slowly, my eyes became used to the light, and the vague shapes solidified into ships. One small boat, one two-master, and one sizeable three-master that moved just a little bit faster than the other two.

They all were heading straight towards us.

I whirled again and spotted Mr Ambrose standing a few dozen feet away, straight as a rod of iron, his hands clasped behind his back, looking out over the ocean. I started towards him, pointing to the ships that were closing in on us.

'I thought you said there would be no pirates!'

'Those?' Mr Ambrose jerked his hand at the vessels dismissively. 'Those aren't pirates. Do you not see the flags, Mr Linton? Those are vessels of the Argentine Republic.'

'Oh, thank God!' I relaxed against the railing. 'I thought we were in trouble! Thank God we're sa—'

The thunderous *boom* of a cannon shot cut me short. Stumbling back, I was nearly hurled backwards onto the deck. Instead, I slammed into something hard – very hard. Two strong arms wrapped around me.

'You do not have very good sea legs, Mr Linton, do you?'

'Why the bloody hell are they firing at us?'

'They aren't firing at us.'

'It damn well sounded like firing to me!'

'Language, Mr Linton! That was just a warning shot. They want us to stop us, inspect our wares and collect tariffs.'

His arms were still around me, for some reason. I cleared my throat, feeling my ears start to heat. 'Oh. If that's all...'

'They're not going to start really firing until they figure out we aren't going to stop.'

'*What?*'

'I do not like to repeat myself, Mr Linton.'

'I don't give a flying fig what you do or don't like!' Wrenching myself out of his grip, I whirled around, eyes blazing. He didn't seem particularly impressed. He continued to look out over the ocean, ignoring me, so I planted myself right in his face to get his attention. 'What the heck do you mean, *we're not going to stop?* Do you mean to say you want to sell your goods without paying one penny of taxes?'

He didn't even raise an eyebrow. 'Did I forget to mention that detail before?'

'Bloody hell, yes, you forgot to mention it!'

'I see. Well, you seem to have deduced it on your own.'

Another thunderous cannon shot sounded in the distance. Another warning shot, but one that went by no means as wide as the first one. A fountain spewed up next to the *Mammon*, splattering us with saltwater. Something that felt like a small fish bounced off my head. I stumbled back, sputtering and cursing. Mr Ambrose didn't move one inch, not seeming to notice the rivulets of water dripping from his top hat. I glared at him.

'It's not very hard to deduce at the moment, *Sir!*'

'Correct.'

He still hadn't deemed to look at me, but stood on deck, a wet and chiselled statue, his arms crossed and his face showing not a hint of worry or anxiety. I wondered if throttling the captain was acceptable nautical behaviour. Probably not.

Damn!

'You can't bloody sell goods without paying taxes!'

'Why not, Mr Linton? It's the preferable way of selling goods. It generates maximum profit.'

'But that means we're smuggling!'

'No, Mr Linton. We are defending one of the inviolate rights of man: the principle of free trade.'

'Which is?'

'I can sell whatever I want, whenever I want, wherever I want.'

I took a moment to translate this from Ambrosian speech into normal language. 'In other words: you smuggle.'

'Of course not! There's a vast difference between free trade and smuggling.'

'Indeed, Sir?'

'Indeed, Mr Linton. Brave defenders of free trade such as ourselves have the armed power of the British Empire behind them. Smugglers don't.'

'But... it's still illegal.'

'Technically not.'

'Oh, really? Care to explain?'

He deemed to glance at me then. 'The Argentinians closed their borders a few years ago. Now, trade is weighed down by heavy tariffs, and restricted to a few large ports controlled by the government. It is illegal to sell goods anywhere else on Argentinian soil.'

'And?'

'And we are not going to sell goods on Argentinian soil. With brand-new steam engines made in Britain, we can sail up Argentinian rivers, and sell our goods along the river. If the customers come aboard, they will in fact be on *water*, not on Argentinian *soil*. Therefore, our selling goods is not illegal.'

I stared at him.

'Are you serious?'

He turned the full force of his cold, sea-coloured eyes on me. 'Do I look like I am joking?'

'That's splitting hairs!'

'Very profitable hairs. They are well worth splitting.'

'And the Argentinians? Do you think they agree with your creative ideas on the legality of free trade?'

Mr Ambrose considered for a moment, gazing at the ships and smoking cannons in the distance, tapping his lip. A thunderclap ripped apart the air as a third, and probably final, warning shot sounded.

'Probably not,' he conceded.

I used a very colourful expression I had learned from Patsy, who, in turn, had gotten it from her father's drunken old coach driver.

'Language, Mr Linton!'

'I'll use any damn language I damn well want! We're being shot at!'

'I am aware of that fact, Mr Linton.'

'Well, don't you think we should bloody do something about that?'

'Yes. It is time now.'

I sighed. Well, thank heavens! Finally, he had seen sense! We were going to stop and pay our taxes, and then we could go on our way like good little sailors.

'*Sahib!*' Karim came striding over to us, his beard flying like a flag in the sea breeze. 'The Argentinians are signalling us! They want us to take in our sails and prepare to be boarded. What do you wish us to send in reply?'

Mr Ambrose took a step forward, clasping the railing with both hands. If possible, his face became even harder. Hard as bedrock.

'A broadside.'

'Yes, *Sahib*.'

For a few moments, I wasn't sure I had heard correctly. Then, commands were being shouted across the deck, and the ship began to turn. I stared at Mr Rikkard Ambrose, wide-eyed.

'You can't mean to...Oh God! You're going to attack the Navy of Argentina?'

'No. *I* am not going to attack. *They* were the ones to fire the first shots.'

'They were warning shots! You said so yourself! They were just threatening us!'

'Indeed.' For a moment, Mr Ambrose took his eyes off the sea, and met mine, sending an ice-cold shiver down my back. 'I don't take kindly to being threatened, Mr Linton.'

Oh dear...we were in trouble. Big trouble.

But not as big as the Argentinians were in.

The ship was nearly turned by now. Mr Ambrose marched along the deck, taking up a position at the centre of the ship, facing the Argentinians. They had slowed down. They obviously thought we were stopping to be boarded.

'Ready?' Mr Ambrose asked.

Karim glanced at the first mate, who nodded.

'Ready, *Sahib*.'

Holy Mother of...! This can't be happening! It simply can't!

'Fire!'

It can't be happening! It can't be happening! It ca–

BOOM!

BURNING WATERS

BOOM! Bo-boom! Boom!

The cacophony of explosions nearly threw me off my feet. Fire spewed from the side of the ship. Smoke billowed out, and the water below was driven away from the ship in a mighty wave. For a moment, it looked as though the jaws of the ocean had opened beneath us. Then, the jaws suddenly clamped shut again. The ship rocked back into the opposite direction, and I stumbled forward, nearly flying over the side.

A strong pair of hands gripped me around the waist and pulled me back.

'Where do you think you are going, Mr Linton?'

'I'm perfectly fine! Let go of me. There's no need to shout man overboard.'

Mr Ambrose pulled me back against him. I realised how very closely he was holding me. I also realised that we were both still thoroughly wet. Through the sodden fabric, I could feel hard muscle press into my much, much softer flesh.

'Under the circumstances,' Mr Ambrose's cool voice caressed my ear, leaving frostbite in its wake, 'the expression "man overboard" would not be entirely appropriate. Wouldn't you agree, *Mr* Linton?'

I swallowed hard. 'Let go of me.'

Yes, please let go before I turn around and pull you closer, and start to...

'Are you sure you can stand on your own? I won't waste my time jumping in after you. I have a battle to fight.'

Images flashed through my mind of the battles we fought during our time in Egypt: hot battles under the desert sun that, more often than not, ended with both of us losing – losing most of our clothing.

Damn! Get a grip, Lilly!

'I said *let go!*'

Silently, he released me and stepped back. I felt the sudden urge to whirl around and throw myself into his arms. But a moment later, I heard his cold, calculated voice right behind me.

'Ready, Karim?'

Those two little words brought me right back to reality. Bloody hell! We were in the middle of our own little war!

'Yes, *Sahib.*'

'Adequate. Let us proceed.'

Mr Ambrose's eyes focused on the distant Argentinian ships. Smoke was rising from one of the ships, and I could hear confused shouts over the waves.

'Um, Mr Ambrose,' I began, 'are you sure it's a wise decision to–'

'Silence! Prepare the guns!'

All right, I guess that was an answer.

'Load cartridge!"

All over the ship, powder boys lifted gunpowder cartridges and shoved them into cannons. It was a perfectly synchronised movement of deadly precision. Almost unwillingly, I smiled to myself. Of course it was! This was Mr Ambrose's ship.

'Ram cartridge!'

The powder boys jumped aside, and the rammers shoved the powder charge all the way back to the breech end of the barrel.

'Load round!"

Cannonballs were lifted to the mouth of the cannons. On the Argentinian ships, a flurry of movement ensued as the crews tried to turn in time to evade the shot. But they had no chance. Mr Ambrose's commands fell from his granite lips in a fast, merciless staccato.

'Ram round!'

The cannonballs were shoved into the barrel.

'Run out!'

Dozens of cannons rolled forward as one, pointing their deadly mouths out of the side of the ship.

'Fire!'[8]

I grabbed the railing, just in time to keep myself from being thrown overboard by the force of the recoil. The deafening roar of cannons slammed into my ears and the bright fire burned my eyes, but at least I remained on my feet. That was more than you could say for most of the crew of the biggest Argentinian ship.

Even over all the distance, I thought I could hear shouts and bellowed, panicked orders – then the cannonballs slammed into the ship's hull, tearing through wood, tar and metal as if it were crepe paper. One cannonball ripped through a sail, and the mast it was attached to groaned in agony.

---

[8] This procedure is highly historically accurate, including the job names of the different crew members and every action they perform. Loading a cannon was a complicated business that involved lots of people with different tasks to do.

But the other two ships had caught on to what was happening by now. They were turning fast, their crews bustling over the decks like ants. Cannons appeared out of the side of one of the ships.

'Err...Mr Ambrose?' I began. 'I think they are going to–'

Before I could finish, Mr Ambrose was beside me, and suddenly, my body was encased in an iron grip, shoving me to the planks.

'Down!'

Boom!

Even lessened by the distance, the explosion was still ear-splitting. The wind screamed as missiles ripped through the air, and next I was expecting to hear the crunch of wood being crushed under the weight of cannonballs. But instead, I heard a strange ripping noise. Above me, Mr Ambrose snorted.

'I don't see anything remotely amusing about this situation!' I hissed.

'I am not amused, Mr Linton. On the contrary.' He pushed himself to his feet, pulling me up behind him as if I weighed no more than a feather, which, let me assure you, was *not* the case. 'If anything, I am contemptuous. They're using chain shots. They're destroying our rigging.'

'Rigg– What? *My knots?* They're shooting at *my knots?*'

'Indeed they are.'

Frantically, I whipped my head up to the sails – or rather, to where the sails had once hung. All that was left now were stained rags.

'Bloody hell!'

'Don't excite yourself, Mr Linton.'

'Don't excite myself? We're never going to escape now!'

'That's where you're wrong.' Striding to the railing, Mr Ambrose raised one arm. An officer at the other side of the ship snapped to attention. Mr Ambrose's arm came down, in a signal. 'Full steam ahead!'

The officer turned to a trap door in the deck of the ship, and repeated the shout: 'Full steam ahead!'

Only moments later, the ship rumbled to life like a volcano before a big eruption. It shot forward, against the wind, out of the firing range of the enemy ships. Watching, awestruck, my heart hammering in my chest, I saw the *Midas* and the *Croesus* follow suit. Clouds of steam rose from amidst their masts.

'They're steamships,' I breathed. 'They're all steamships!'

'Of course they are.' Mr Ambrose was still standing at the railing, arms crossed, his back to me. 'Did you think I would go into battle unprepared, Mr Linton?'

My eyes narrowed. 'I didn't even know we were going into battle, *Sir!* I thought this was a trading expedition!'

'You should know me better than that by now, Mr Linton. Wherever I go, I go into battle.'

He raised his hand again in another signal, a silent one this time. The ship swerved. Looking around, I noticed that we were not moving away from the enemy ships. On the contrary. We were moving around and towards them.

'Err...Mr Ambrose?'

He didn't pay any attention to me.

'Mr Ambrose, Sir?'

He motioned to the men again, and everyone who had been taking cover because of the enemy fire re-emerged, returning to their positions at the cannons.

'Mr Ambrose? We *are* going to escape, aren't we, Sir? We are going to sail away? After all, with the steam engines, we are bound to be faster than they are!'

Instead of answering, he parted his marble lips and called out. The shout rang out over the entire ship: 'Prepare the guns!'

Oh-oh...

'Load cartridge! Ram cartridge!'

'Mr Ambrose, you can't seriously be planning to go after them! Those are government troops!'

'Not *my* government, Mr Linton. Load round! Ram round!'

With a resounding *thunk* the cannonballs hit the back of the barrels.

'Run out!'

The cannons rolled forward again. On the Argentinian flagship, which was now pointed completely the wrong way to even get one shot in, panicked activity broke out – but too late.

'Fire!'

The next round of cannonballs erupted into the sky. We weren't the only ones who had fired this time: the *Midas* and the *Croesus* had followed suit. The barrage of cannonballs hit one enemy ship so hard it nearly capsized. Splinters of wood flew in all directions, water gushed into the ships, and it seemed a miracle to me that, somehow, both managed to stay above water.

'Why don't they sink?'

'Watertight bulkheads,' Mr Ambrose said, without taking his eyes off the distant ships. 'Vertical walls separate the ship into compartments and keep the water from spreading, even if the hull is breached. But we'll soon smash those into splinters.'

'Oh, um...good.'

Though not so good for the Argentinians, maybe.

Mr Ambrose raised his hand. 'Prepare the guns!'

As if they had heard him over the distance, the Argeninians fell into frantic motion. Someone on their ship shouted a command, and slowly, it began to turn. Not towards us, though – no. Away.

'They're running away!' I watched, in horrified fascination. 'You're chasing away the navy of a sovereign nation!'

'Yes. And?'

He sounded as if he did things like this every other day.

But then, maybe he did. What did I know? I hadn't been in his service that long. Yet, already the things I had seen were enough to send shivers down my back – both the pleasant and the unpleasant kind.

'Load cartridge!' Mr Ambrose's command rang out over the deck of the *Mammon*. 'Ram cartridge!'

The enemy was definitely running now. Their sails were flapping helplessly, only half-filled with wind. I almost pitied them. Almost. After all, they *had* shot at my knots.

'Run out, and...fire!'

The cannonballs flew higher, this time. I thought for a moment that Mr Ambrose had made some kind of navigation mistake – but I should have known better. He was Mr Rikkard Ambrose, after all. The crack of the mast told me that he hadn't made a mistake. Not at all.

My eyes focused on the leftmost of the ships just in time to see the huge mast splinter and break off near the deck. Slowly, it began to keel over, gathering speed – and then suddenly everything went very quickly. Screams rose up from the Argentinian vessel, and the mast smashed not just into the deck of this ship, but into the rigging of the one beside it. Both vessels shuddered, nearly capsizing. They clung to each other, connected by the mast, swaying through the waves like drunken lovers.

Well, maybe not *exactly* like drunken lovers. They didn't try to snog each other or recite *A Red, Red Rose* by Robert Burns, for example.

Karim stepped up beside Mr Ambrose. The wind grabbed his beard, flinging it up into his face, and he snatched it, holding it in one hand with a growl.

'Shall we pursue them, *Sahib*?' he enquired. 'Do you wish us to continue to fire?'

'Are you mad, Karim? Do you know how much one round of cannon ammunition costs?'

'No, *Sahib*.'

'Too much to be shot after fleeing fools, that's how much! Give the order to turn about, back to our original route. We're heading for Argentina.'

'As you wish, *Sahib*.'

'And if we do not arrive before those three bad excuses for battleships, I shall be very displeased.'

'Of course, *Sahib*.'

Slowly, the *Mammon, Midas* and *Croesus* turned around and headed away from the smoking semi-wreckage that had once been three vessels of the Argentinian Navy. I glanced back, nervously.

'So...what now?' I wanted to know. 'Have we just started a war between the British Empire and Argentina?'

'Nonsense, Mr Linton! I may have the British Empire's support behind me, but I am not the British Empire. I am a private individual.'

One corner of my mouth quirked up. 'So, what have we started? A war between Argentina and the Ambrosian Empire?'

'I doubt it. States don't declare wars on private individuals. For some unfathomable reason, they consider it beneath their dignity.'

I raised an eyebrow at him. 'And if they should happen to make an exception in this case?'

He met my eyes. A shiver ran down my back at the expression in those sea-coloured orbs. 'Then I pity Argentina. I would not wish to be in the shoes of anyone who has to fight a war against me.'

Without another word, he turned, and walked away.

He was serious. Perfectly serious.

This was going to be an interesting journey.

A Friendly Message from Home

We anchored in a picturesque Argentinian harbour that would have made a wonderful motif for any postcard. It was attached to a small town with little stone houses overgrown by ivy – the sort of place that didn't look as if it got visitors often. The people cheered and greeted us with warm smiles when we went ashore, and they eagerly perused the list of goods Mr Ambrose had brought from faraway England. Their smiles quickly disappeared, however, when they heard the prices Mr Ambrose was asking.

Fortunately, I didn't speak a single word of Spanish and didn't have to participate in the haggling. Instead, I could lie in the sun and watch as Mr Ambrose waged a fierce battle around every single *peso*.[9] Of course, he won most of them.

'If you keep this up all the way, we're not going to be very popular in Argentina by the time we leave the country.'

He sent me a cool look, which was actually quite welcome in the blistering heat. I would have to get him to give me cool looks more often. 'What gave you the notion that I desire to be popular, Mr Linton?'

A smile quirked up one corner of my mouth. 'No idea. Forget I said anything.'

We didn't stay long in the harbour. When we left again, the townspeople clearly expected us to take the route down the coast. It was quite a lot of fun to watch their flabbergasted faces when we fired up the steam engine and, with steam puffing out of the *Mammon*'s steel smokestack, started up the nearby river into the interior of the country.

Even more amusing to see were the faces of the crews of the boats we passed on our way upriver. With the river overflowing with water, and the current too strong to fight with oars or sails, every single vessel, except ours, was sailing with the current, down the river. I soon started to make a hobby out of sitting on deck and waving to the startled captains as we puffed our way past them, towards the jungle and the mountains. Unfortunately, I could never engage in this amusing pastime for long: every time Mr Ambrose caught me at it, he chased me back to work.

Finally, we arrived at a large city situated at the junction of two rivers. I was a city girl at heart, and breathed easier at the sight of tall, elegant stone houses and paved streets.

'At last! I was getting really tired of those endless hours spent below deck trying to decipher that bloody manuscript!'

'It is your job. It doesn't matter if you get tired of it.'

---

[9] The currency of Argentina.

'You can't make me work all the time, you know! A person could get daft from trying to work all day.'

'Which would differ from your current level of intelligence how, exactly?'

I threw him a dark look, which he completely ignored.

We were standing at the pointy end of the ship, which by now I had learned was called 'prow'. I was gazing admiringly at the beautiful city that stretched out in front of us. Mr Ambrose was staring coldly at his crew, directing our landing with curt gestures of his hands. A small crowd was already gathering at the docks.

'What is this place called?' I wanted to know.

'Santa Fe de la Vera Cruz. It's the provincial capital.'

Capital, eh? Even in such a large, important city, it appeared, people weren't expecting much traffic to come up the strong-flowing river, and they were delighted to see us. Some people in the waiting crowd even cheered or threw their hats into the air. I let them have their happy delusions. They'd stop cheering soon enough, when Mr Ambrose pulled out his price list.

Behind the docks and the cheering crowd, a palatial building rose, the Argentinian flag fluttering from its highest pinnacle. I saw Mr Ambrose eyeing it with cool calculation.

'Forget about it,' I told him.

He threw me a look. One of *those* looks. 'How can you know what I was thinking, Mr Linton?'

'I don't know. I just know that whatever you're thinking is a bad idea from the look in your eyes.'

'Indeed, Mr Linton?'

'Indeed, Sir.'

Silence.

'Well?'

'Well, what, Mr Linton?'

'Well, what were you thinking about?'

'If you must know, Mr Linton, I was considering charging the Argentinian government for the damage done to the *Mammon*'s sails by their Navy's cannons.'

I almost choked. 'You can't be serious!'

'You would advise against it, Mr Linton?'

'Considering that you are in Argentina, and the damage to your sails was incurred because you fired on Argentinian ships? Yes, Mr Ambrose, Sir, I would.'

'Hm. You may be correct, Mr Linton. States can be strangely sensitive when it comes to attacking their army or navy.'

It wasn't long before we had landed, and the cheers of the crowd, as I had suspected, ceased rather abruptly. In no time at all, Mr Ambrose had set up an impromptu stall beside the gangway and, from behind a collapsible table, was haggling with the natives like nobody's business. Or like Rikkard Ambrose's business, to be exact. I didn't understand a single word of the half-heated (the natives) half ice-cold (Mr Ambrose) business proceedings. But a few expressions like 'Avaro!' or 'Maleducado!' were muttered in a tone that left little doubt about their meaning. Still, I noticed that people always waited until they were well away from Mr Ambrose and the giant figure of Karim towering behind him before muttering such words.

The day wore on. I continued working on deciphering the manuscript for some time, but my head could only deal with so many illegible scribbles, and I soon returned to watching Mr Ambrose more or less legally rob the inhabitants of Santa Fe. If I had ever wondered before about how he got so abominably stinking rich, now I knew. He could haggle the kilt off a Scotsman. I continued to watch, a smile playing around my lips each time one of the Argentinians walked by me, muttering expletives.

When one of Mr Ambrose's sailors came down the gangplank, balancing a small barrel on one shoulder, I leaned towards him.

'What does 'Avaro' mean?'

'Skinflint. Why?'

'Oh, nothing. I'm just improving my Spanish.'

Within another hour, I had learned the Spanish words for 'bastard', 'blaggard' and 'monkey's arse'. I was watching the crowd, keeping an eye open for new and interesting sources to expand my vocabulary, when I first saw *him*.

At first I only noticed him because his skin tone was lighter than that of the natives. Not pale by any means, no, but not the same gleaming, polished bronze that generally prevailed here, either. His was a white face, although darkened by continued exposure to sunlight. The man to whom the face belonged was moving through the crowd like a shark through water, heading straight towards us.

I could see his face more clearly now. Rather dark for a white man, dark and angular. I frowned. Where had I seen that face before? I could swear that I...

The man reached into his pocket. Suddenly, I remembered – just a moment before the man withdrew his hand from his pocket and I saw the harsh glint of sunlight on metal. Pushing away from the ship, I jerked upright.

'Mr Ambrose! Look out!'

The words had hardly left my lips when a massive dark shadow streaked past me. With a guttural battle cry, Karim hurled himself onto the stranger, grabbing the arm that held the gun and twisting it skyward. There was a thunderous report, and the flash of a gun sent people staggering backwards, terrified. Cries in Spanish rose up all around, and everyone fought to get away as fast as their legs would carry them.

No. Not *everyone*. Two men were moving forward, out of the crowd, straight towards us, also pulling guns.

'Look! There! Get them!'

But my shout went unheard. There was no one to get them. All the sailors were on board the ship and Karim was still wrestling with the first shooter. Mr Ambrose was alone. The first of the two men raised his weapon.

In a move so fast I could hardly follow it, Mr Ambrose gripped the table and pushed. The heavy monstrosity turned over, crashing to the cobblestones with a unhealthy *crack*. Mr Ambrose flung himself down, and a moment later, a bullet whizzed through the air where he had just stood. The next one thudded into the table with a dull *crunch*.

Not wasting a moment, Mr Ambrose leapt over the table. He was on the first shooter in the blink of an eye, and in the next blink, his fist made contact with the man's eye. The bastard went down like a felled tree. But the other one was finished reloading. He raised his gun and–

–and stumbled backwards as I threw my arms around his neck from behind, jumping onto his back.

'Grrgl!'

'Take that, you blighter!'

Now, I'd be the first to admit that I wasn't exactly a wrestling champion, or a professional streetfighter. But I had managed to stay alive in a household with five female siblings and an aunt for over ten years. You can't do something like that without learning a few tricks.

Grabbing a pencil from my pocket, I jabbed it into the shooter's midriff. When he opened his mouth to yelp, I stuffed a dirty, ink-stained rag inside and gave him a good whack on the head. He gurgled and collapsed to his knees, which I took as an invitation to tighten my stranglehold.

'There! How does that feel you bastard?'

He groaned in reply, and I jammed my pencil into his side again.

Hey, nobody said growing up with five sisters is easy.

But apparently, the guy I was clinging onto had had some pretty tough siblings, too. Whirling around with me still clutching his neck, he staggered backwards into a wall. Unfortunately, the wall was not made out of rubber or soft satin cushions. The breath was knocked out of me brutally, and my ribs protested in a flare of pain. My grip loosened, and with a violent jerk, the shooter shook me off, sending me flying. Landing face-first in a puddle of mud-water, I rolled around to come nose to nose with the barrel of a gun.

'Say goodbye, lad!' the shooter growled, taking aim.

My eyes widened. I stared at the man – and then my eyes slowly moved further, behind him, to the fast-approaching shadow.

'Goodbye,' Mr Ambrose hissed, and whacked the man over the head with his cane so hard that I heard the crunch of bones. He crumpled to the ground in a heap, and then there was silence.

Well, except for the distant cries of Argentinians running from the crazy Englishmen, and the gurgling sound made by the man still in Karim's clutches. Growling some guttural expletive into his beard, the Mohammedan rose, holding up his prize with one hand by the scruff of the neck.

'Here, *Sahib*. I thought maybe you might want him alive.'

Bending to pick up one of the fallen guns, Mr Ambrose checked to see if it was loaded. Then, without even blinking, he raised it to eye level and shot the assassin through the head.

'You were wrong,' he informed Karim. 'Let's go. I don't think the people here want to purchase any more of our goods.'

'As you wish, *Sahib*.' With a half-bow, the mountainous bodyguard chucked the corpse into the harbour. It disappeared into the water with an ominous splash. Then he turned, picked up the fallen table and the bag of money as if they weighed no more than a feather, and followed Mr Ambrose aboard the ship.

'Mr Linton?' Mr Ambrose's voice came down from the deck. 'What are you waiting for? Don't stand there, gawking! Move!'

I blinked, then stared up at him. 'Well, excuse me if I'm not used to seeing people get shot in the head!'

'You are excused,' Mr Ambrose granted graciously. 'But only this once. See that you control yourself better in the future.'

And with that, he turned and marched away.

'You're welcome!' I shouted after him. 'For saving your life, you know! I'm so glad you're still as alive and chipper as ever!'

'Get moving, Mr Linton!

~~**~*~*

We continued up the river at a quick pace. If there were any pursuers on our metaphorical heels, they had no chance of catching us. The river was a raging torrent, and even with the steam engine, we sometimes had trouble making our way.

One night, a few days after the fight on the docks at Santa Fe, I was just about to cuddle up under the blanket on my bunk, when I heard a creak from overhead. Who would still be up at this hour? We were anchoring at the shore for the night, and while there were guards posted, they were on land, and not on the deck above me. Curious, I went up to investigate.

When I stuck my head out of the door, I saw a dark figure standing on the poop deck, black coat tails fluttering in the wind. Sighing, I stepped out and closed the door behind me.

'Trying to repeat your no-sleep-experiment, Sir?'

He didn't turn.

'No, Mr Linton. I'm thinking.'

'At this hour? It's barely twenty minutes to midnight.'

'You don't say.'

I climbed up on the deck and positioned myself beside him, leaning on the railing. He threw me a cool look.

'I prefer to think alone, Mr Linton.'

A smile tugged at the corner of my mouth. 'You don't say.'

A pause. Then:

'You know those men were sent by Dalgliesh, don't you, Sir?'

'Yes, I know.' Cocking his head, he regarded me shrewdly. 'What I want to know is how *you* know, Mr Linton.'

I smiled winningly at him. 'Female intuition?'

My winning smile didn't quite seem to work, to judge by the look he sent back at me out of the corner of his eyes. 'Mr Linton...!'

I shrugged. 'Or I *might* have seen one of those goons and Dalgliesh at a ball together.'

His head whipped around, his dark eyes boring into me with unsettling intensity. 'You met Dalgliesh at a ball? *When?*'

'Oh, a few weeks ago, back in London.'

At the ball where my engagement was announced.

I didn't mention the last part to Mr Ambrose, though. For some unfathomable reason, he seemed to be rather easily aggravated when it came to any suitors I might have. He probably thought I would slack off at work if someone managed to wrestle a ring on my finger. Not that that would ever happen!

'*Weeks* ago?'

Oh-oh...I could practically hear the frost growing on Mr Ambrose's voice. He fully turned to face me, concentrating all the considerable force of his dark, penetrating eyes on me. 'And you didn't see fit to mention this to me until now?'

Actually, I hoped I could avoid telling you altogether...

'Well, you know, you're a busy man, and I thought–'

I didn't get any farther than that. To my utter shock, I was suddenly engulfed in a vice-like grip, clutching me to a chest as hard as stone.

'I do not pay you to think, Mr Linton!' I heard his ice-cold voice at my ear. 'Understood?'

'Yes, Sir. I only wanted to–'

The rest of the sentence ended in a wheeze as his grip tightened even more. Then, before I could really grasp what happening, he was gone, and I could breathe again. Panting, I grabbed the railing to steady myself, and stared up at the dark, towering figure beside me gazing out onto the river as if I didn't exist.

Had this really just happened? Had Mr Ambrose, Mr *Rikkard Ambrose*, just *hugged* me?

After weighing all the scientific evidence and making a careful probability calculation, I decided that, no, on the whole, it hadn't happened. It was simply incredible. Things like that didn't happen in real life.

But they might happen on a romantic journey into the interior of South America, a little voice in my head said.

I snorted. Sure! Next thing, I'd be taken captive by a rakishly handsome pirate lord! Shaking my head at my own foolishness, I returned to my own cabin to get a good night's sleep.

About two hours later, the river pirates attacked.

NIBBLING AT PIRATES' BOTTOMS

If anyone was hoping for me to awaken in the arms of a handsome pirate, I have to disappoint them. Instead, I was awakened by gunshots and curses mingled with Spanish battle cries. Most were pretty incomprehensible, but I did catch something about cutting off balls. Apparently, my self-taught Spanish lessons were paying off.

Dragging my behind out of bed, I quickly pulled on the first scraps of clothing I could find, grabbed a knife from the table, and hurried up on deck.

Torches lit the night like angry dragons' eyes. From up the river, another boat was approaching, men with guns and sabres bustling on deck, shouting enchantingly filthy curses. Our men were rushing to the railing, no less armed to the teeth. Their faces were grim, but determined. Seeing a mountainous figure tower up out of all the confusion, I hurried over to him.

'Karim! What is going on?'

'A pirate attack,' he told me, his face unmoving as a gnarled old oak.

'I can see that for myself, blast you! What are we doing about it?'

'Waiting.'

I was getting fed up with the bodyguard's lack of conversational skills and was about to tell him so, when an iron grip closed around my arm.

'What,' demanded an ice-cold voice right next to my ear, 'are you doing up on deck?'

I held up my knife which, this morning, I had used to dismantle a particularly stubborn crust of bread into chewable portions. 'I came to fight! We're under attack, aren't we?'

'Yes!' His grip didn't loosen. On the contrary, it tightened. 'And that means that you have no business being here! Go and–'

'Sahib!'

Karim's warning shout came not a moment too soon. I could see the flash of gunfire from the enemy ship out of the corner of my eyes, and a moment later I was flying, crashing onto the deck, a heavy weight slamming on top of me.

'Oomph!'

'Stay down!' Mr Ambrose hissed into my ear. 'And don't move!'

I can't say I found my first pirate raid particularly exciting. It is rather hard to see all the exciting stuff that's going on while you're being squashed to the floor with a heavy, hard and determined Rikkard Ambrose on top of you. I pointed this out to him several times, but he must not have heard me over the gunfire, or he would surely have been so considerate as to get off me and help me to my feet, right?

Yes, *of course*!

The story – as later told by Karim, with an annoyingly self-satisfied smirk on his face – went thus: the pirates had been travelling downriver, probably on the trail of one of the merchant ships we had encountered on our way up. How they must have cheered when – lo and behold – instead of having to chase some vessel miles downriver, they found us anchoring at the shore, practically defenceless. Like all self-respecting pirates would, they of course immediately agreed to rob us, gut us and throw our limp corpses in the river. What a golden opportunity, right?

Wrong.

The pirates were somewhat surprised, to say the least, when, upon opening fire on the defenceless merchant ship, hidden hatches had opened in the side of said merchant ship, revealing a nice collection of pristinely polished cannons, pointed straight at them. Their surprise was still more intense when the defenceless merchant ship opened fire, destroying the rigging of their boat and bringing down both masts with one salvo.

The biggest surprise, however, came when the captain of the helpless merchant ship sent out his men to the wrecked pirate boat, led by a mountain-high, sabre-swinging maniac in a turban, who made short work of the fearsome pirates, shooting most and chaining the rest with their own chains. It wasn't long before the ragged remnants of the brave pirate crew were arrayed on the deck of the *Mammon*, looking rather dazed.

'Well?' I demanded, trying to scrape dirt off my beloved peacock vest, which had gotten a bit stained and ruffled on the deck of the ship. I threw a morose look at Mr Ambrose, wondering whether he would foot the cleaner's bill. Probably not. 'What now? What are we going to do with them?'

Mr Ambrose was walking down the line of stunned pirates, examining each as if he were a bug under a microscope. 'Well, they meant to rob us. Why don't we return like with like, as the Good Book recommends?'

'*You* take advice from the Bible?'

'From the rare parts of it that are sensible.' Mr Ambrose nodded to Karim. 'All right. Take everything of value they have, sink their boat and throw them overboard.'

The pirates were still so much in shock that the first one of them landed in the water with a splash before they realized what was happening. My head cocked in contemplation, I watched the protesting pirates being swept away by the current.

'Mr Ambrose, Sir? Aren't there flesh-eating fish in these waters?'

'They only attack humans when there is blood in the water, Mr Linton.'

'Um...there *is* blood in the water, Sir. Quite a lot, in fact.'

'You don't say.'

~~**~*~*

Leaving behind a lot of happy piranhas, we crossed the border into Brazil a few days later. We encountered no more trouble, until we reached a small village on the edge of a cliff jutting out into the river. Mr Ambrose spent a few hours haggling the natives' ears off, selling them a lot of overpriced things they didn't need but suddenly realised they desperately wanted. We were just about to depart again, when an old man approached the ship and called out to us in Portuguese.

Karim started forward to intercept the stranger, but I shook my head. 'No. Don't. Let him speak.'

Karim gave me a look that could have scared the feathers off a chicken. 'I do not take orders from you, woman-that-is-worse-than-*ifrit*! Why should I listen to an old fool's prattle?'

'Anybody who's brave enough to approach Mr Ambrose of his own free will deserves a chance to speak, in my opinion.'

Karim grumbled, but had to finally admit a certain truth in that statement. We let the man pass, and he continued on to where Mr Ambrose was overseeing the loading of the ship with new supplies. We watched him stop next to the tall, dark figure of our employer and start to talk. From where we stood, we couldn't hear what was being said, and reading something from Mr Ambrose's expression (or lack thereof) was a skill beyond my meagre abilities. But the old man left soon, and Mr Ambrose came over, his fingers tapping a staccato on the head of his cane.

'What is it, *Sahib*?' Karim wanted to know, just as I opened my mouth to ask the very same question. 'What did the old man have to say?'

Mr Ambrose's gaze slid over to us. 'He says that there is fighting upriver. I thought the Brazilian Empire had squashed the rebellion by now, but apparently they're still trying to stamp out the *farrapos*.'

'Ah.' Karim nodded, grimly.

I nodded grimly, too, and tried my best not to let show I had no idea what the heck *farrapos* were. Still...they didn't sound particularly nice.

'Do you think we should take another route?' I suggested. 'Try and circumvent the trouble?'

He met my eyes, coolly. 'Circumvent? That would take weeks! Who do you take me for, Mr Linton? We have work to do, and I'll be damned if I let myself be put off by a couple of peasants complaining about high taxes on their salted beef.'

That didn't sound like very dangerous rebels. So I shrugged it off and thought no more of it. At least until the next morning, when, stepping out onto the deck, I saw smoke rising in the distance.

'What's that?' I demanded. 'Another town?'

Mr Ambrose glanced in the direction. 'No. Too much smoke. Probably the remnants of one.'

It took a moment for the full meaning of his words to sink in. And even then I didn't really understand until, a couple of hours later, we rounded a bend in the river and in front of us appeared the smoking ruins of what must once have been a peaceful settlement.

I stared. Then my eyes slowly slid to Mr Ambrose.

'*A couple of peasants complaining about high taxes on salted beef?*'

He shrugged. 'Peasants can get quite unnecessarily emotional about salted beef.'

The governor of the town himself came down to the docks to greet us and gawk at the stupid Englishmen who wanted to sail right into a warzone.

'I cannot allow you to go,' he told us firmly, standing on the dock, a dozen of his guards behind him, several wearing bloody bandages. Mr Ambrose watched from the railing, no emotion on his face. 'No, no, I simply cannot. It would be suicide! Besides, General Lima e Silva himself has declared the country beyond this town a forbidden zone! No one may enter without risk to their lives. I cannot allow you to proceed!'

'You make fair points, Governor,' Mr Ambrose told him. 'There's only one thing you forgot.'

'Indeed? And that is?'

'I did not ask for your permission. Karim – full steam ahead!'

Soon, the yells and protests of the governor and his escort had dwindled into nothing behind us. I stood beside Mr Ambrose at the railing, watching as the smoking ruins of the town slowly disappeared beyond the horizon.

'Mr Ambrose, Sir?'

'Yes, Mr Linton?'

'You are very brave.'

'I know.'

'And you never let anyone stand in your way.'

'No, I don't.'

'And you're tenacious, and determined, and...well, altogether the toughest man I have ever met.'

'I know, Mr Linton.'

'And I really admire all those qualities.'

'Indeed, Mr Linton?'

'But...'

'But?'

'But sometimes I really think you need to have your head examined.'

~~**~*~*

Mr Ambrose wasn't quite as reckless as I had at first assumed. From that day onward, we didn't travel by day anymore, but anchored at the shore during daylight hours and went on the move when the sun went down. Also, we travelled on half steam, reducing the noise of the engine to a level where, over the constant din of the jungle around us, it could hardly be heard. Lights were strictly forbidden, and all conversations had to be kept to whispers. To my surprise, the tactic actually worked. Now and again, we heard distant explosions and screams, or saw smoke rising over the trees. But, apart from that, we saw nothing of the two armies wrestling for control over the land. I almost felt safe – until we reached a narrow bend in the river, with rocks jutting out from the bottom. It was clear for anyone to see that from here on out, the river was too shallow for us to continue by boat.

'What now?' I wanted to know, my gaze drifting anxiously between the river and the shore.

Mr Ambrose gave a shrug. 'We knew from the beginning that we could only travel part of the way by boat. We'll have to continue on foot from here on out.'

My gaze became glued to the shore. Just at that moment, a distant explosion echoed across the water.

'Through...through the jungle?'

'Naturally, Mr Linton. Unless you see a convenient road anywhere near.'

'No, Sir! Of course not, Sir!'

'What about the manuscript? Have you concluded your efforts to decipher it?'

I opened my mouth to say 'I think so' – then remembered that this wasn't the kind of answer Mr Ambrose would appreciate. 'Yes, Sir! I have, Sir.'

'Adequate. Let's get a move on, then.'

Everything was well-prepared. It didn't take long for our supplies to be un-loaded and the ship to be ready for departure. I was somewhat surprised, however, when I realised that, apart from me and the packhorses, only Karim would accompany Mr Ambrose into the jungle.

'Why not take a few more people along?' I wanted to know. 'If we truly find gold–'

'If we find gold,' Mr Ambrose cut me off, 'I only want people along with me whom I can trust.'

He marched off to oversee the ship's departure, leaving me behind, slightly stunned at the magnitude of what he had just implied. Without knowing exactly why, I suddenly felt a lump in my throat.

The ship sailed off only a few minutes later, now without smoke curling from its funnels, carried swiftly downriver by the current. I stood, gazing after it, until a sharp command from Mr Ambrose made me turn.

'No sense in wasting our time here! Mr Linton, you have our directions?'

'Yes, Sir. We are to head northwest, until we come to another river. According to the manuscript's directions, that will be our next point of reference.'

'Very well. Lead on.'

I turned away from the water to gaze up at the wall of tangled green that was the jungle. Funny – from the boat it had seemed much smaller. Now, stand-ing on the bank, and without the reassuring puffing of the steam engine that was a comfortable link to civilisation, it dawned on me for the first time how very, very big those trees were, and how very small I was in comparison.

'What are you waiting for, Mr Linton? Knowledge is–'

'–power is time is money.' I raised my chin, and stood straighter, facing the forest head-on. 'Yes, I know.'

'You actually listened to me.' He sounded slightly surprised. I glanced over at him.

'You speak little enough. When you do, it's usually worth listening to.'

And with that, I started forward and let myself be swallowed up by the jun-gle.

The heat was like a fist, hitting me in the face the moment I stepped into the shadows of the trees. Don't get me wrong, it had been hot out on the river, too. But there had been a bit of a breeze blowing there, especially when we had still been on the fast-moving ship. Now, however, we were about to enter a gigantic green beast that seemed to feast only on the heat that it stored in its big, moist belly. The first trickles of sweat started running down my forehead, tickling all the way. With every step further into the gloom, the heat intensified.

Next came the noise. It wasn't actually that loud – but it was always there, echoing in strange, archaic tones that seemed not of this world. A bizarre ca-cophony of screeches, chattering and catcalls surrounded us, most so far above my head that I couldn't hope to make out their origin. Looking up, I saw only slivers of light through a shadowy canopy of leaves. A shiver went down my back.

This was another world we were entering. A strange and dangerous one.

Mr Ambrose marched past me, his face stoic, his strides determined.

'Stop dawdling!' he called, not bothering to turn his head. 'What are you afraid of? Trees?'

Afraid? *Me?*

I had caught up with him in three seconds and was sprinting ahead, panting hard. To hell with the strange and dangerous world! I was an independent woman! I could do anything!

The trees enveloped me and with Mr Ambrose and Karim close behind, I delved into the depths of the jungle.

~~**~*~*

We did a good bit of delving that day. Mr Ambrose had no intention of adjusting his pace to the gruelling surroundings. We marched through the Brazilian jungle as if it were St. James's Square, the only difference being the sweat that poured from every pore in copious amounts. Sometimes, we heard gunfire in the distance, but it never came close to us, and I was beginning to believe we had successfully avoided drawing attention to ourselves. However, we all were aware of the lingering danger. Nobody spoke a word, and no matter how hard it might be, we kept our footfalls light and silent.

Hours passed in mute marching. Night was beginning to fall, and I was more than ready to fall along with it, and never get up again. Every muscle in my body ached, except for those in my mouth and stomach, and they were the ones that actually could do with a bit of exercise. We had only stopped once for a quick break, and what we'd had to eat then might be considered a decent meal according to rabbits' standards, but not to mine.

Blinking sweat out of my eyes, I stared up ahead, at the silent figure of Mr Ambrose. He had long ago taken the lead and was still marching with the same long, determined strides as he had when we had set out, not even slowing to take out his compass and check our direction. Some part of me ached to catch up and kick him in the backside for being so insufferably tough, but that part of me didn't ache half as much as the rest of my body. I was ready to collapse.

However, I'd die before I admitted that out loud!

I'm a strong, independent woman! I can do this!

True, I was. However, I much preferred being a strong, independent woman in London without a twenty-pound knapsack on my back. Clenching my teeth, I got a firmer grip on the leather straps of my burden and continued on, setting one foot in front of the other.

Only when the shadows of the trees had almost completely swallowed us up and we could hardly see our own feet anymore did Mr Ambrose decide it was time to make camp.

'Stop!'

Unfortunately, the command came a little too late for me. Not being able to see my feet, I was most certainly not able to see his, or the hand he was probably holding up to indicate it was time for us to halt.

'Ouch!'

'Oomph!'

'Watch where you are going, Mr Linton!'

'Same to you, Sir! And remove your hand from *there*, pronto!'

Mr Ambrose cleared his throat. 'Pardon, Mr Linton. In the dark, I didn't see–'

'But you most certainly *felt*! Fingers off, got it?'

'Watch your tone, Mr Linton!'

'I can't watch anything right now. It's too bloody dark! Can't we light a fire?'

There was a motion in the gloom right in front of me. It might have been a headshake. 'No, Mr Linton. It would draw too much attention.'

'Without a fire, how will we keep predators away?'

'Karim will keep watch.'

'Keep watch?' I looked around, seeing only vague shapes and shadows. 'How, exactly?'

'I am well accustomed to conditions like these,' the Mohammedan's gruff voice came out of the darkness. 'We have jungle in the country of my birth, very much like this, and I have the ears of a bat and the eyes of a panther. I will know if someone approaches well before they come close enough to do harm, and we will be able to– *Wait!* What was that?'

There was a noise, as if from a twig snapping. It was followed instantly by a silken noise that I knew all too well by now – Karim, drawing his sabre out of its sheath.

'We have to move! There is someone–'

'*Don't move!*'

The voice cut through the hot night air like a whiplash. A voice of command. A stranger's voice. Lights flared up all around us, sending a flash of fear through me. Blinking, I shielded my eyes from the sudden brightness. When, after a few seconds, I had grown a little more accustomed to the light and lowered my hands, I saw that from the trees all around us, men were emerging. Men in brightly coloured uniforms, similar to those of the governor's guard at the last town we had passed.

There was one man in particular I noticed. He was tall and gaunt, with high, aristocratic cheekbones and a curl to his lips that made me think he didn't just have power, but enjoyed using it, too. He had a high forehead, intense yellowish brown eyes and a rifle levelled at Mr Ambrose.

'Well, well...' he drawled, in nearly perfect, only slightly accented English. 'Who have we here? Two Englishmen, and an Indian, if I am not mistaken. What are you doing so far from home? Speak, and speak quickly if you want to have a chance at surviving this unscathed!'

Speak?

He wanted *Mr Ambrose* to speak? Under *threat*?

Oh dear. Whoever this was, he was in for a disappointment.

'Well? Open your mouth!' The officer – for officer he was, no doubt – jabbed Mr Ambrose in the chest with his bayonet. Mr Ambrose didn't even flinch. 'Get on with it! I have a war to fight!'

Mr Ambrose wasn't impressed. He stared down the length of the rifle, his eyes glinting ten times as cold as any steel could. He said not a word.

'A stubborn one, eh? Very well. Barros! Costa! Bind them, take five other men and get them back to headquarters! The general will decide their fate.'

I AM HORRIFICALLY TORTURED

'*I am well accustomed to conditions like these,*' I mimicked as we were marched along, pulling a wooden face reminiscent of a certain inept bodyguard. '*We have jungle in the country of my birth, very much like this, and I have the ears of a bat and the eyes of a panther.*'

'Be quiet!' Karim growled from behind me.

'*I will know if someone approaches well before they come close enough to do harm.*'

'I said–'

'Silence, both of you!' Mr Ambrose's hissed command was enough to make us shut up. 'This is no time for senseless bickering!'

Well, he was right about that. Our situation was about as dire as it could be. Despite having discovered Mr Ambrose's papers in his knapsack, the mysterious commander into whose hands we had fallen seemed disinclined to believe that we were simply harmless subjects of the British Empire, in the wrong place at the wrong time. To judge by the cold, calculating glances he sent our way, he was imagining a far more sinister explanation. Thanks to Mr Ambrose, I was an expert at deciphering cold, calculating glances. And these, trust me, were not boding well.

Tied together by thick, unyielding rope, we were being led off through the jungle towards the soldiers' headquarters and this mysterious general who would decide our fate. I didn't like the idea of having my fate decided by any man, let alone a general. In my experience, they were more used to aiming cannons at other people than trying to understand their point of view.

'What are we going to do?' I whispered, shuffling a bit closer to Mr Ambrose, just as much as the rope allowed.

'We are going to behave like model prisoners, Mr Linton. We will be quiet and well-behaved. Do you understand? *Quiet.*'

Oh, I understood all right. He didn't want these military types to know about the treasure. I quite agreed. Whether rebel or government officer – the man in charge of these soldiers had a cold sparkle in his eyes that made me think not much was beyond him, theft and murder included.

'And then?' I asked, lowering my voice even further.

'Then, if fate is on our side, we will find a chance to continue on our way.'

Translation: I will mud-wrestle fate until she is agreeable.

I smiled. Sometimes, it really was a pleasure to work for Rikkard Ambrose.

Storm lanterns lighting up the way ahead, we continued our march through the jungle. There was no path visible anywhere, and without a compass, there was no way of telling which way we were going. Even had I had the skill to read the direction from the stars, the thick tangle of branches overhead prevented anyone from getting their bearings.

Anyone except our captors, that is. They obviously knew where they were going. After only ten minutes march or so, the thick jumble of vines and leaves around us thinned, the trees began to stand farther and farther apart, and finally, the jungle receded and we marched out into the open.

In the dark, I couldn't see much of what lay ahead. But there was a feeling of freedom, of clear space and skies above, that made me think we were not just in a clearing, but a much wider open space. I felt a faint breeze rustle my hair and breathed in, feeling like I had real air in my lungs for the first time all day.

'*Alto! Quem vem aí?*'[10]

Men stepped out of the darkness, armed with sabres and rifles. They had their hands on the hilts of their weapons, but the moment they recognised the soldiers ushering us forward, they relaxed.

'*Olá, Costa! O que você tem aí?*'[11]

'*Prisioneiros. O Coronel quer levá-los para a cela.*'[12]

'What are they saying?' I whispered to Mr Ambrose.

'He asked who we were, and the other told him we were prisoners.'

'*Pobre então bastardo.*' The soldier who had stepped in our way glanced at us, shaking his head. '*A sua vida não vale uma merda agora.*'[13]

'And now?'

Mr Ambrose threw me a look. 'He's saying that we look like decent folk and should be treated well.'

'Oh, indeed?'

I didn't know much Portuguese, but the word 'bastardo' hardly required translation.

'Indeed, Mr Linton.'

'Well, thank you so much for reassuring me, Mr Ambrose, Sir. I feel much better now.'

'Go on!' Costa ordered in broken English, grabbing me by the scruff of the neck. 'To cells with you! *Adiante!*'

I had been right – we were on a wide, open plain. And not far from the edge of the jungle, buildings rose into the sky. Ruins, from what I could see of them by starlight, some still smoking. But there were a few left intact, and to one of those we were now being herded. The rope that bound us together was cut, the ones around our wrists remaining. Someone grabbed me and began to drag me away. Only then did I realise they meant to separate us. I started to struggle, trying to reach out to Mr Ambrose – but the next moment, something very hard and painful hit my head, and everything sank into blackness.

Well, was my last thought before I drifted off into oblivion, *at least now I'll be getting a good night's sleep.*

˷˷**˷*˷*

---

[10] Halt! Who goes there?
[11] Hey, Costa! Who have you got there?
[12] Prisoners. The colonel told us to take them to the cells.
[13] Poor bastards. Their lives ain't worth shit now.

115

When I awoke, I found that the hospitality of the Brazilians went beyond all my wildest dreams. My kind hosts had not only tied me to a chair, no, they had set up that chair under a mould-riddled, leaky ceiling from which an impressive amount of foul-smelling liquid dropped onto my head. The walls weren't mere wood or concrete, no, they were ancient masonry with vintage rusty iron rings set into the stone, in which one could just picture a slowly rotting skeleton. There were decorous cobwebs in the corners of the windowless room, and by the light of the torch set into a wall bracket, I could see a ballet of rats performing for me on the floor. This wasn't just a measly little cell, like the ones I had sometimes occupied back home in London. No, this was a genuine, bona fide *dungeon*! I had to admit, I was impressed. These Brazilians really knew how to treat tourists. Now, all that was missing was a torturer.

From somewhere, I could hear footsteps approaching. Craning my neck, I was just able to glimpse a door out of the corner of my eye. Keys rustled. The door swung open, and in stepped a heavyset man wearing a uniform, a ferocious scowl, and bloodstained gloves on his hands.

'Ah.' I nodded. 'There you are.'

'Eh?' The man's scowl grew even more ferocious. 'What's this *bastardo* babbling about?'

The door opened wider, and my old friend, the officer, stepped inside, his eyes sparkling with the same cold, calculating malice. 'Isn't it obvious? Our friend here has been expecting us.'

I raised my chin and tried to stare down at my captor with cool composure. Considering I was tied to a chair, the staring-down part turned out to be rather difficult to accomplish.

'Indeed I have.'

'I wouldn't have expected any less.' Sketching a bow, the officer raked me with his calculating gaze. 'Colonel Alberto Silveira, officer of the armed forces of the Empire of Brazil, at your service.' He smiled. 'I would not advise you to take this civility too literally.'

'I wasn't planning to.'

'An intelligent young man. Very well, then. Let's cut straight to the chase, shall we? I have had a talk with the general, and he fully agrees with my assessment of the situation. You three are rebel spies sent to spy on our troop movements, or possibly even saboteurs. And you will tell me everything about your mission objectives, what you have learned so far and what kind of sabotage you still have planned!'

I stared at the man – then looked down at myself. Tailcoat, shiny waistcoat, pocket watch, striped trousers... I had lost my bowler hat somewhere and was somewhat less than perfectly clean, but apart from that you could have plucked me straight from the streets of London.

'Is this what a rebel spy usually looks like?' I asked, raising an eyebrow.

Colonel Silveira didn't seem impressed by my argument. 'Disguise! Bah! I do not know why a rebel might feel the need to appear like a ridiculous, fat little Englishman–'

'Hey! Just a minute! Who are you calling fat?'

'–but if you think you can throw me, Colonel Alberto Silveira, off the scent with a trick like that, you must be mad!'

'I told you, we are no spies! We are travellers from England! Citizens of the British Empire! That is all!'

The colonel made a dismissive noise. 'No Englishman would be crazy enough in his head to go into a warzone!'

'You obviously haven't met Rikkard Ambrose!'

'The tall, dark one?' Silveira took a step closer, his eyes narrowing. 'Oh, please! He may look like a leader, but I know better. We have searched your luggage. We found his papers, and the Mohammedan's – but of yours there is no trace!'

Small wonder, since technically, I don't exist in trousers.

'There is only one explanation.'

That I am a reckless crossdresser risking her neck in a bid for independence?

'You are the head of the whole outfit! You are the chief spy, in charge of this whole operation, whose identity is so secret even his companions must not know it!'

Golly. I had no idea I am that impressive.

'So, tell me, young man…' The colonel took another step closer, his thin lips curling. 'What should I call you?'

'Linton. Mr Victor Linton.'

'Ah.' He nodded, thoughtfully. 'An alias, of course?'

'Of course.' *At least the first half.*

'It will do for now.' The curl in his lips spread, until it had grown into a full-grown smile. It wasn't one of the nicest smiles I had ever seen. 'We shall have the truth out of you in due course.'

I raised my head still a little more, in defiance. 'Oh, you will, will you?'

'Oh yes.' Stepping back, the colonel beckoned to the man with the bloody gloves, who in turn stepped forward, holding out a knife. The colonel took it, lovingly running his index finger along the blade. 'Perfect,' he whispered. Then he turned to me.

'You see, Mr Linton, there are a myriad of ways of extracting information from prisoners. A thousand refined methods exist to cause the human body a maximum of pain. Dozens of experts have written treatises upon the subject, and infinite variations have been developed to suit any and every situation.'

His finger reached the tip of the dagger, and gently pricked it, until a single drop of blood ran down the blade.

'However, I have always found all this energy invested into the subject to be not really necessary. Above all others, there is one single method which is guaranteed to break any man. Attacking both his body, his mind, and, much more important, his hope for the future, it is the single most effective method for dealing with stubborn prisoners. Whether spy, soldier, or simple criminal, not a single man has fallen into my clutches who has not succumbed to it sooner or later.'

Lowering the knife, he slid it down over the front of my tailcoat, down over my belt and between my thighs, until he reached a point, where, for realism's sake, I had stuffed a pair of my uncle Bufford's old socks.

'Try to guess of what I speak,' he hissed with deliberate menace.

'Good God! You don't mean...?'

'Yes!'

I tried to think of something appropriate to say.

'Um...you blaggard!' I tried tentatively. 'Have you no mercy?'

'Tell me who you really are! Tell me what you are doing here, and I shall spare you! Otherwise...!'

He pressed the tip of the knife down.

'Argh, no, please don't,' I said with as much gusto as I could manage. It was rather hard when I had to focus all my energy on not bursting out laughing.

'Will you tell me what I want to know?'

I bit my lip, considering. 'Hm...let me think...no!'

'Very well.' His eyes narrowed. 'You are a brave man, Mr Linton.'

'Not really.'

'You leave me no choice! Fidel!'

'Yes, Sir?' The torturer snapped to attention.

'I have other business to take care of. You are in charge of interrogating the prisoner. You know what to do?'

'Yes, Sir!'

'Do not damage any other part of him as yet, Fidel. I want him to be able to talk and walk. As for his ability to father children...*that* I am not interested in. Do we understand each other?'

'Perfectly, Sir!'

'Very good.' Hilt first, Silveira handed the knife back to his henchman. Giving me a sharp, glittering smile, he turned on his heels and marched out of the room. 'Until later, Mr Linton. I look forward to hearing all you have to tell us.'

The door closed behind him with an ominous *click*. Fidel the fabulous torturer smiled a gap-filled smile at me, and stepped closer.

'Well, well, little man,' he growled, sliding the dagger along my ribcage.

'Can you please not do that? That tickles.'

'I'll do a damn sight more than tickle you soon!' The blade of the dagger came to a halt on a certain padded area. 'Speak! Speak now, or suffer the consequences!'

For a moment, I chewed on my lip, thoughtfully. 'Hm...I think I'd rather suffer the consequences.'

'Very well! You have been warned! You shall suffer like no man in this dungeon before you!'

He drew back the knife with a snarl and stabbed it down.

'Argh, argh,' I said, dutifully. 'Please, no, that hurts so much.'

His eyes went wide. They flicked up to stare at me – then he stabbed again!

'Aaaargh,' I informed him courteously. 'Cruel man! Have you no mercy! Cease this agony! I beg of you, I cannot stand it any longer, et cetera et cetera blah blah.'

And again!

'No!' I yawned. 'You are the most merciless man alive. You are the devil himself. How can you be so cruel as to inflict this torture on a poor, innocent young man who has done nothing to you? Can't you see how I am writhing in pain? Argh, Argh, Argh, and so on, and so on.'

And again! And again!

'Please! Have mercy on me! You are destroying my manhood! How will I ever be able to look another man in the eye after this, deedle-de-dum de-dum de-dum.'

Stab! Stab! Stab!

'And you're also destroying my trousers, by the way. Have you any idea how expensive a pair of trousers is in London nowadays? Especially with a skinflint for an employer?'

'Shut up! Shut up, shut up!' The torturer was sweating by now, madly stabbing away at the considerable bulge at the juncture of my thighs. At the time, I had thought I'd been a bit generous for polite society, but now it was proving enormously beneficial. Goes to show that what they say isn't true after all – size *does* matter.

'If you go on like that,' I politely informed my captor, 'there won't be enough for mincemeat left down there. Don't you want to take a little break? Maybe sharpen your knife?'

'I said shut up!'

'All right, all right! It was only a suggestion. No need to get your knickers in a twist. You're doing a good enough job with mine already.'

The only response to this was a garbled string of curses in Portuguese which, despite my best efforts, I was unable to decipher.

'Could you repeat that with translation, please?' I enquired. 'Some of those sounded really interesting! I'd love to share them with my friends at home. They could come in really handy at tea parties.'

'Keep your mouth shut, you bastard son of a bitch!'

'Ah, I see. And what was the corresponding Portuguese, again?'

In answer, the dagger was slammed so hard in between my legs that it dug right through the trousers and buried itself in the wood of the chair underneath. With another Portuguese profanity, the fabulous Fidel tugged at his torture instrument of choice, and it was suddenly yanked from the chair, flying from his hand and sailing through the air, to fall to the stone floor a few feet away. Fidel staggered back, staring at the juncture of my thighs. It wasn't the first time in my life that a man was staring at this particular point of my anatomy, but usually they did it a bit more discreetly and with less abject horror on their faces.

'What are you?' Fidel whispered, his voice ragged.

I gave him back a winning smile. 'Didn't you know? I'm unique. Like a snowflake.'

The poor torturer stumbled back a few more steps. 'W-what I do now? Heavens, what I do now?'

I nodded at the door. 'Your boss went that way. Why don't you go and ask him?'

Fidel looked right, then left, as if desperately looking for a solution – then turned, and ran out of the dungeon, conveniently leaving the door open, and the knife lying on the floor. Too bad he hadn't also untied me before he ran.

'Oh well.' I sighed, and began to rock in my chair, gently but steadily pushing it towards the gleaming blade on the ground. 'You're an independent girl, Lilly! You can't expect men to do everything for you.'

I was rather fortunate that there were no guards in the vicinity. They would probably have heard the crash of the overturning chair, not to mention the barrage of English and – I'm proud to say – Spanish and Portuguese curses that followed soon after. A minute or two later and only a few bruises richer, I hurried out of my cell, brushing the last cut remnants of rope and splinters of wood off my dirty tailcoat.

All right. What now?

I looked around. From down the corridor, on my left, I could hear low voices mumbling and laughing in Portuguese. Light shimmered on that side, whereas in the other direction, there was only darkness. Darkness and more dungeon cells.

I would have to get past the guards. And to get past the guards, it would be very helpful to have someone along who actually knew how to load and fire a gun – like Karim, or Mr Ambrose. Don't get me wrong. I wasn't planning on becoming a damsel in distress. But I was definitely a damsel under stress. I mean, I was trying to escape from a military prison, for heaven's sake! Nobody, not even my inner feminist, could expect me to do that without help. Besides, if I left Mr Ambrose behind to rot in a dungeon, who would sign my next pay cheque? And if I left Karim behind to rot in a dungeon, I would never get the opportunity to remind him sweetly every day that I had saved his butt, his beard and everything in between.

I turned and hurried off down the corridor, deeper into the bowels of the prison. There were little barred windows set into every cell door, probably to allow the wardens to leer at the prisoners inside, or to spit at them if they were in a really good mood. Ducking low, I glanced in through each and every opening. In the first few cells, there only were a few scraggly individuals who looked about as similar to Mr Ambrose as a grizzly bear to a statue of King Richard the Lionheart. Then there came one with a decorous pile of bones. And then–

'Ah! There you are!'

Mr Ambrose looked up from where he had been kneeling on the floor, grinding the ropes that bound his hands against a sharp shard of clay. When he caught sight of me, his eyes widened infinitesimally – then narrowed.

'Mr Linton!'

I gave him a winning smile. 'Good morning, Sir. Do you still have your balls?'

Mr Linton to the Rescue

There was a moment of silence within Mr Ambrose's cell. I wasn't sure whether it was a pregnant silence, yet. That depended very much on how much attention Colonel Silveira had paid to my dear employer's nether regions.

'I was just about to enquire how you managed to escape from your cell so quickly. However–' Mr Ambrose's dark eyes focused on me, boring into me, '–now, a slightly different question is on my mind. *Why do you wish to know about the status of my reproductive organs?*'

'Call it personal curiosity.'

'See to it that your curiosity becomes somewhat less personal, Mr Linton.'

'Yes, Sir! Immediately, Sir!'

'Can you open this door?'

I looked down, and got a pleasant surprise. The door didn't actually have a lock. Apparently, Colonel Silveira never had to face the possibility of a prison break before. If he had, he'd probably have installed something a little more complex than simple bolts on the outside of his cell doors.

'One escape coming right up, Sir!' I hollered through the door and slid the bolt aside. A moment later I stuck my head in through the door. 'You haven't told me whether you still have your balls, yet.'

'And I am not going to. Come help me untie this, *now*.'

He was still rubbing away at his bonds with the pottery shard. Clearing my throat, I stepped closer and held out the knife. 'How about using this, instead?'

'Wha–oh.'

'Yes.'

'Give that to me.'

'What's the magic word?'

'Now!'

I looked at Mr Ambrose, and he looked right back, his dark eyes glittering dangerously in the half-light. They sent a shiver down my back that had nothing to do with the cold air down here in the dungeons. For him, that probably was the magic word. I couldn't imagine it ever not having worked. Particularly not if the person he was talking to was of the female variety.

Blast!

I handed him the knife. Mr Ambrose snatched it up in both hands and started sawing away at the rope that bound him.

'Where did you get the knife?' he demanded.

'From my jailor. A very pleasant fellow named Fidel.'

'*What?* And how did you get out of the cell?'

'Fidel left the door open for me.'

One of Mr Ambrose's eyebrows moved up about a quarter of a millimetre. 'This Fidel sounds like a very accommodating jailor.'

'Oh yes, he's a great chap! He cursed a lot and tried to stab me about a dozen times.'

'Indeed?'

'Indeed, Sir.'

'Hm. We will have to discuss this at some later point in greater detail, Mr Linton. But for now, let us leave this inhospitable place.'

'Yes, Sir! Right you are, Sir!'

His bonds falling to the floor, Mr Ambrose rose to his feet. 'Do you know where Karim is? And our luggage, and horses?'

'Karim is probably farther down the corridor. If I was the colonel, I'd want him locked up in the safest cell I had, behind three doors.'

'All right. Let's go.'

My conjecture proved justified. We found Karim several cells farther down the corridor, behind an additional door, this one with a real lock, which Mr Ambrose opened using some fiddly little metal thing he pulled from his sleeve. When we reached the second door, the one with a bolt, we heard gagging noises from inside.

'Karim?' Mr Ambrose called. 'Are you in there?'

The Mohammedan's huge beard appeared in front of the opening, replaced by his face a moment later when he bent his knees. '*Sahib?*'

'Yes.'

'I knew you would escape! Nothing is beyond you, *Sahib*.'

I cleared my throat, delicately, and tucked a lock of hair behind my ear. 'Actually, it wasn't he who escaped. It was me.'

There was a moment of silence in the cell, this one definitely pregnant. With ugly quadruplets.

'*Sahib*? Is this true?'

Mr Ambrose didn't look at me. He stared straight ahead, his expression ten times as unreadable as ever. 'Unfortunately, it is.'

Another moment of silence.

'Well,' Karim's gruff voice finally came from beyond the door, 'it can't have been very difficult. I am sure anyone could manage it.'

'Indeed?' My voice was as sweet as solid chocolate with honey and nougat inside. 'I notice that *you* are still in your cell.'

The bodyguard muttered an unintelligible curse. I was pretty good at Spanish profanities by now, and I was beginning to understand Portuguese ones, but whatever language Karim cursed in, it was none I had heard of before. It was, however, adoringly abominable.

'I was just in the process of breaking out,' Karim growled, clearly holding onto his temper by the skin of his teeth.

'Indeed? And how exactly were you planning to do that?'

'Why don't you ask him?' There was a *thud*, and suddenly, a pale, bluish face was thrust against the bars. Not Karim. Most certainly not. This man was a lot smaller, and a lot more being suffocated. The gagging noises I had heard earlier now made sense.

'Just out of curiosity,' I enquired. 'Who is the man you're strangling to death?'

'I would be interested in that information as well,' came Mr Ambrose's cool voice from behind me.

'This little *haramjada* is one of their torturers. The insolent imp came in here with his knives, thinking to deprive me of my manhood!'

'Oh. Did he succeed?' I asked hopefully. It would be an interesting experience to hear Karim sing soprano.

'Bah! Of course not! I tore my bonds, overpowered him and told him to open the door. But he would not. He said they were bolted from the outside. So I decided to apply a little pressure.'

The face of the jailor had turned a nice shade of violet by now, and the gagging noises sounded suspiciously like the beginnings of a death rattle.

'Yes, I can see that.' Mr Ambrose nodded. 'The problem is, he's telling the truth. There really is a bolt on the door.'

'Oh.'

'But not for long.' Stepping forward, my dear employer grabbed the bolt and rammed it back. I grabbed the doorknob and pulled the door wide open. Karim ducked through, without releasing his grip on the jailor.

'You're welcome,' I told him with a sweet smile, which he returned with a deadly glower. Ah, friendship between colleagues was such a wonderful thing...

'Should I kill him, *Sahib*?' the Mohammedan enquired, shaking his prisoner like a ragdoll.

'Not quite yet.' Mr Ambrose stepped in front of the violet-faced jailor. 'My employee is going to relax his grip on your throat now. If you try to scream, you'll be dead before you have time to draw a breath. Understood?'

A gurgle came from the jailor's throat which, with a lot of imagination, could be interpreted as a 'Yes'.

'Adequate. Let go, Karim.'

With a grunt, the bodyguard released the man's throat. Before the choking chap could topple to the floor, however, he caught him around the middle, twisting his arms behind his back in a manner that made me wince just from looking at it.

'Our horses. Our provisions. Where are they?' Mr Ambrose's voice was as hard as the stone walls around us, and considerably colder. The jailor recognised the tone of a ruthless man when he heard it.

'Provisions...three cells down,' he gasped. 'Horses...in stables. Outside. I...show you.'

'Adequate.'

'Please...no kill me.'

'Don't worry. We won't.'

My eyes darted over to Mr Ambrose, staring. What? We wouldn't?

Karim seemed just as taken aback.

'Gag him, Karim, and throw him in the cell.'

'But, *Sahib*–'

'Do as I say! Now!'

Not even Karim had the power to resist Mr Ambrose's magical word. Ripping two strips of cloth from the jailor's uniform, he stuffed one into his mouth and tied the second around his head, so his mouth was covered. With the remnants of his own bonds, he tied the man's hands, and then solicitously placed him right on a stain of smelly mould in the corner of the cell.

'What now?' he demanded, stepping out of the cell and bolting the door behind him.

'Now we get our provisions and our horses. And then we ride northeast, as planned. Let's go!'

'Northeast? But I thought–'

'Silence! Let's go!'

It took me five minutes, but by the time we had recovered our provisions and were sneaking down the corridor towards the exit, it had clicked.

'You did that on purpose, didn't you?' I whispered, staring at Mr Ambrose's back in front of me with something I'd never have let him see if we were face to face. Something suspiciously close to admiration. 'You let that guard live, and fed him false information about the direction we were going. When the others find him, he'll tell them everything he heard, and they will lead the chase for us into empty jungle.'

'Quite so, Mr Linton.'

'You, Sir, are a devious son of a bachelor.'

'I prefer the term "seasoned tactician", Mr Linton.'

'Of course you do.'

'Silence! We're approaching the gate.'

The front door was standing open about five inches or so. Squinting, I could make out the forms of three men standing outside, their backs to us, chatting and laughing. Clearly, if they expected an attack, it wasn't from the inside.

'I take the one on the left,' Mr Ambrose commanded in a whisper. 'Karim takes the two on the right.'

'And me?' I demanded.

'You take this.' And he dumped three knapsacks full of provisions onto me. Staggering under the weight, I barely managed to remain upright. By the time I had gotten enough breath back to curse, Karim and Mr Ambrose were already outside, and I could hear the noises of a struggle. It didn't last long. When I staggered out of the door, two men were lying limp on the ground, and Mr Ambrose had the third in a headlock, the man's own knife at his throat.

'You have two choices now,' Mr Ambrose informed the wide-eyed young soldier coolly. 'You can show us where the stables are, or you can die with a knife in your throat. Which do you prefer?'

It didn't take the young man long to decide. He was a most intelligent fellow and directed us to the stables without once trying to run or even screaming for help. Having reached the stables, Mr Ambrose repeated his ruse from inside the prison, leaving his prisoner bound and gagged, with erroneous directions.

'Time to go.' Bending over, Mr Ambrose peeked out through a gap between two of the wooden boards of the stable wall. Outside, the sun was just beginning to rise, and first spears of light were stabbing through the gaps in the wood. If we hurried, we might still be able to slip away under cover of semi-darkness.

'Anyone out there?' I demanded.

'A patrol just passed. I listened to the rhythm of patrols from my cell. If they don't suddenly change the pattern for some reason, we should have five to six minutes to reach the edge of the jungle.' Pulling his packhorse behind him, Mr Ambrose marched out of the stable with a stride so arrogant you might think he was in charge of this place. 'Let's go!'

We started to cross the open ground in a northeastern direction, in keeping with Mr Ambrose's ruse. With every step we took, I sent a prayer to heaven. *Please, God, ignore the fact that I don't really believe in you and help us survive this! Please!*

God apparently wasn't feeling very charitable that day. We had just stepped into the shadow of the trees when we heard a shout behind us.

'*Ei! Você aí! Pare!*'

'I guess those aren't wishes for a happy journey in Portuguese?' I asked, glancing around to see several soldiers come running from the stables.

'No! Run!'

REVOLTING REBELS

We ran straight on into the jungle, the sounds of pursuit on our heels, until we reached a little stream winding between the trees. Then, Mr Ambrose had us turn and follow the stream southwest, concealing our tracks. As soon as we reached a rocky patch of shore where our footprints wouldn't remain frozen in mud, we left the stream and changed direction again, heading northwest this time.

'That will throw them off our scent for now.' Mr Ambrose breathed, supporting himself against a nearby tree. We had been running so hard, even he looked a little less than perfectly cool and composed right now.

'For now?' Slumping onto a big rock, I glanced the way we had come. 'Why should they bother to follow us at all? Surely they have more important things to do. There's a war on, after all.'

'Yes. And do you know what both sides in a war always need, desperately?'

'A decent general? Provisions other than dead rats and rotten cabbage?'

'That, too. But most of all, Mr Linton, they need gold. More and more gold with every second of the war that passes. War is a monster that devours gold and shits death at the other end.'

'How poetic, Sir. So what does that have to do with us?'

Mr Ambrose directed his dark, sea-coloured gaze at me.

'When we picked up our luggage, didn't you notice anything strange about it?'

'No. Why?'

'Because it had been tampered with. The drawstring on your knapsack was loose, and the manuscript wasn't where we stashed it last.'

'Blast! You mean they–'

'Yes. They took a good look at it. Maybe good enough to figure out what it is. I don't think they believed it was genuine. But that might well change once they learn in what direction we're going – the same direction in which the manuscript says a great treasure lies waiting.'

I took a deep breath, trying to slow my still-hammering heart. I hadn't run that hard in years, not since I was nine and Uncle Bufford had caught me painting a smiley face on the bottom of his freshly washed trousers. Right now, in the gloomy jungle, with the birds overhead calling out ominous warnings, I almost wished myself back there.

Then I remembered the glorious adventure ahead, and my bottom remembered the spanking I had received for the smiley incident. Swiftly, I changed my opinion.

'So, what should we do now?'

'Continue on, of course!' Righting himself, Mr Ambrose got a firm hold on the reins of his packhorse. 'What else can we do?'

'Well,' said a strange voice from behind me, 'for a start, you can surrender.'

'What the he–'

That was all I managed to get out before something very hard and painful hit me in the head, and I felt my knees give way.

Bloody hell! was my last thought before I plummeted into oblivion. *Not again! This is getting embarrassing!*

~~*~**~*~*

When I woke up, I was tied to a chair in a smelly underground dungeon. Huzzah! It's always so cheering and comforting to find yourself in familiar circumstances, don't you think?

Similarities notwithstanding, however, this was not the same dungeon as the one I had been in before. The mould on the floor was in a different pattern. There were a lot more spiderwebs in the corners, and instead of being infested with rats, this little underground Eden was home to a clan of cockroaches.

It wasn't long before I heard footsteps from outside. Two pairs of footsteps. When the door opened, two men in army uniforms stepped in. One was clearly an officer, the other a common soldier who wore – surprise surprise! – blood-stained gloves.

'Finally. I thought you were never going to show up.'

The officer raised one eyebrow. 'You've been expecting us?'

'Naturally.'

'You seem very calm for a man in your position.'

I gave him a charming smile. 'What can I say – practice makes perfect.'

The officer stepped forward. He was a little man with a sharp nose and quick eyes. Not as intimidating as Silveira, not by any means. But I knew better than to judge people by their appearance. After all, I didn't look particularly impressive myself, and I was the most incredible person I had ever had the pleasure to meet.

'Let me introduce myself.' His quick eyes sweeping over me in a flash, the little man stepped forward, bowing. 'I am Lieutenant Louis de Alvarez of the glorious Army of the Piratini Republic. At your service.'

'Of course you are. Although I probably shouldn't expect that the services you're ready to render include letting me go, right?'

'Indeed not. I see we've caught ourselves an intelligent man. Very well, then. Let's cut straight to the chase, shall we?'

'That would be wonderful. For some inexplicable reason, I feel somewhat bored by our conversation.'

'Trust me, you won't be for long! I've had a talk with the–'

'...general?'

Alvarez's eyes narrowed. 'No. The major, actually. The general is away on business. Why?'

'Oh, just a guess. Do go on, please.'

'I have had a talk with the major, and he fully agrees with my assessment of the situation.' His sharp little eyes bored into me. 'You three are spies sent by the imperialist oppressors of the central government to discover our troop movements, or possibly even sabotage our efforts.'

'Are we, now?'

'Yes!'

'How interesting.'

'And you will tell me everything about your mission objectives, what you have learned so far and what kind of sabotage you still have planned, understood? Everything!'

'I suppose it wouldn't do any good to point out that we're just visitors from England?'

'England? Bah! No Englishman would be crazy enough in his head to go into a war zone!'

'Just checking.'

'Trust me – you're not the first imperial spy I have caught in my net! I know the look! Small, slimy, greasy-looking fellows with shifty eyes and–'

'Hey!' I had to admit this fellow was getting my dander up. Being called fat was one thing. But this? This was below the belt! 'No need for that! Why don't you just start and torture me already?'

Come to think of it, that would also happen below the belt. But what the heck! I'd better get it over with.

The officer took a step closer, his eyes burning with patriotic zeal. 'You won't feel so cocky once we're through with you!'

'Oh yes?'

'Oh yes, indeed!' Stepping back again, the colonel beckoned to the man with the bloody gloves, who in turn stepped forward, holding out a – wonder of wonders – knife. The colonel took it, lovingly running his index finger along the blade. 'Excellent,' he whispered. Then he turned to me.

'You see, my friend, there are a myriad of ways of extracting information from prisoners. A thousand refined methods exist to cause the human body a maximum of pain. Dozens of experts have written treatises upon the subject, and infinite variations have been developed to suit any and every situation.'

'You don't say.'

'However, there is one method which, above all others, will ensure that a man spills every last one of his secrets. A method that tortures not only a man's body, but also his pride, and hope for the future.'

Lowering the knife, he slid it down over the front of my tailcoat, down over my belt and between my legs, until he reached a certain point between my thighs, where my trousers had already been severely mistreated.

'Try to guess of what I speak,' he hissed with diabolical menace.

'Oh, I think somehow I've got a pretty good idea.'

'Ha! Then cower in fear, for I have no mercy for spies and other vermin!'

Cocking my head, I looked up at him. 'You know...you rebel fellows should try working out that little tiff you have with the government. If you'd got to know each other, I think you'd find you are a lot more alike than you probably believe.'

'Ha! I am impervious to your imperialist propaganda!'

'How nice for you.'

'Speak, or suffer the consequences of your actions, royalist scum!'

He pressed the tip of the knife down.

'Ahrgl arghl argh,' I said, dutifully.

'Ha! Now that you feel the pain, you're not so cocky anymore, are you?'

I smiled up at him. 'I'm not quite sure. Could you let me feel a little more?'

The man's face grew grim, but there was a glint of respect in his eyes. 'You are a brave man!'

'Dear me. I have no idea why everyone seems to be labouring under this misapprehension.'

'But no matter how brave a man is, he cannot live through this! We will break you yet! Carlos!'

'Yes, Sir?' The man with the bloody gloves saluted.

'Take over from here! I must go to the refectory and see what the men have found in their baggage. Maybe that will give us a clue as to what these spies are after. I shall expect a full report when I return.'

'You may rely on me, Sir!'

'Excellent.' Hilt first, Alvarez handed the knife back to his underling. Cracking his knuckles menacingly, he turned on his heels and marched towards the door. 'Until later, my friend. Say goodbye to any dreams you've ever had of fathering children.'

The door closed.

'Oddly enough,' I remarked to the room at large, 'fathering children has never really been part of my expectations in life.'

My gaze drifted to the torturer, who was twirling the knife between his fingers, an evil, yellowish grin on his face. I sighed.

'I suppose we had better get on with it, right?' I spread my legs as far as my bonds would allow. 'Stab away!'

~~**~*~*

About five minutes later, I stepped out of the cell, whistling and twirling a knife in one hand. This torturer had had an even more interesting reaction than the last one. When he had thoroughly perforated my self-made manhood, getting no more reaction from me than some mild comments about the weather, he had more or less lost it and started digging around with his hands, trying to find out what the hell was the matter with me.

The sight – and smell! – of Uncle Bufford's old socks must have been too much for him. He had very obligingly stumbled back, slipped, and hit his head on the stone floor. From there, it was a more or less simple matter to overturn the chair, grab the fallen knife and cut myself loose. True, I was a few bruises richer once more, but what was that compared to the knowledge of having done a good job? Nothing!

Plus, I had carried one additional piece of booty off with me.

'Hello, there, Sir!' Grinning, I bent to look through the opening in the cell door. 'How are you?'

'Mr Linton? Is that you?'

'In the flesh.'

'And in a lot more besides! Where did you lay hands on that getup?'

Glancing down at the uniform I was wearing, I flattened a few creases. 'Oh, this old thing? That's nothing. I got it from my jailor – along with a knife, and these keys.' I held up a ring of keys, proudly.

'Your jailors seem to be uncommonly accommodating, Mr Linton.'

'What can I say? Charm. It's all down to charm.'

'Then why don't you charm us out of here?' came Karim's growl from a few doors down.

'I suppose if I ask what's the magic word, I won't get a "please" out of you, will I?'

'Get a move on!'

'Well, since you ask so nicely...'

Two minutes later we were sneaking down the corridor of whatever hellhole we'd been thrown into this time. Mr Ambrose's face was unreadable as ever, but Karim's expression was expressive enough for both of them. Having his neck saved by a woman twice in one day was clearly going down like vinegar with pus and snail slime.

'I heard Lieutenant Alvarez talking,' I whispered, as we sneaked up the corridor, one ear open for any sudden noises.

'Who?'

'The charming gentleman who knocked me over the head and locked us all in here.'

'Ah. And what did he have to say for himself?'

'That he wanted to search our belongings, and that they were in the refectory, whatever that means. I have no idea what kind of place this is.'

'I do.' Mr Ambrose pointed to a stain on the wall opposite. I squinted trying to make anything out, but...

And suddenly it was clear! That was no stain! The image of the man was faded, and hardly recognisable, but the halo over his head was still pretty clear, and was ample clue to the identity of the individual.

'A church, maybe,' Mr Ambrose murmured. 'Or more likely, an abandoned monastery. You said he used the term "refectory"?'

'Yes, but I don't know what that mean–'

'I do. Come along.'

On our way to our destination, we had some more friendly encounters with rebels. By the time we reached the refectory, both Mr Ambrose and Karim had acquired uniforms of the Piratini Republic, although Karim somewhat spoiled the effect by refusing to take off his turban.

'It's not so bad,' I tried to forestall an argument. 'Maybe they'll think he's part of the Republic's East Indian detachment.'

Mr Ambrose threw me a dark look, and Karim mumbled something about needing help from a female.

'Hey, I was only trying to be helpful. I–'

'Quiet!'

Raising one finger to his lips, Mr Ambrose slowly approached a large door at the end of the corridor. Reaching out, he pushed against the door, gently, almost tenderly. It moved, slowly, opening just a crack.

'I don't see him in there,' Mr Ambrose whispered. 'But there are three soldiers – and one of them has the manuscript.' He glanced over at us. 'We have to get it back. Without it, we might as well turn around and go home.'

His face said clearly that this wasn't an option.

'Leave it to me.' Karim stepped forward, cracking his knuckles. 'I've been ambushed two times too many this day. I have scores to settle!'

Before either of us could move a muscle, he had drawn his sabre and slipped into the room, silent as a gagged shadow that had taken a vow of silence. A moment later, we heard two thuds out of the refectory, followed by an 'Ouff!' – and then nothing.

The door swung open, and Karim stepped out, carrying the manuscript in one big hand, and all our three backpacks in the other.

'Do you have everything?' Mr Ambrose demanded.

'Yes, *Sahib.*'

'Then let's get out of here,' I hissed. 'Before they–' I jutted my finger towards the refectory door, '–wake up!'

The Mohammedan gave me a level look. 'They won't.'

'Oh. You mean you, um...'

'Yes.'

'In that case, I think we should get out of here even faster. I haven't gotten to know the dear Lieutenant Alvarez very well, but he doesn't seem to me like a man who appreciates having his soldiers' throats cut.'

'For once Mr Linton,' Mr Ambrose said, grabbing his knapsack, 'I am in agreement. Let's go!'

Apparently, the glorious Army of the Piratini Republic wasn't quite as well-staffed as the forces of imperialist oppression. They had only one guard outside the prison, and he was snoring, with a pipe hanging out the side of his mouth. Mr Ambrose didn't even bother to knock him over the head.

'Why waste time knocking him out and tying him up?' Kicking open the stable door, he grabbed his packhorse by the bridle and pulled. 'Now, if anyone comes along, he'll report that he was watchful as an eagle the entire time, and didn't see a single soul leave. Much more convenient for our purposes.'

He dragged his horse to the stable door, then returned and gazed through a crack in the wall out over the open land.

'Hm. There is a guard right between us and the jungle. Maybe, we could just get past him. We have their uniforms. Karim, if you were to take off your turban...?'

'No, *Sahib*.'

There was a moment of silence – this one so pregnant it would probably end in a disastrous miscarriage. 'No' was not a word in Mr Ambrose's vocabulary. The moment stretched...and stretched...and maybe we would need a C-section after all.

'I see.' Mr Ambrose straightened. 'Then keep behind us as much as possible. And...'

'Yes?'

'Try to appear small.'

I looked at the enormous, muscle-bound Mohammedan. If Mr Ambrose had asked he appear as a purple goblin with adorable little horns, that would have been more likely to succeed.

'Yes, *Sahib*.'

Leaving the stables, we began to move around the outbuildings, towards the jungle. Karim kept low, behind one of the horses, and for a giant mountain of muscle did a pretty good job of appearing not to exist. Only the occasional glimpse of the top of his turban over the packs on the horse's back gave away his presence.

We approached the guard with measured steps. He didn't seem particularly suspicious. But then, I probably didn't *seem* particularly nervous. But I was! Like hell I was! The sweat trickling down my forehead didn't just come from the heat.

'When we reach him, let me do the talking,' Mr Ambrose whispered.

'Why? Because you're the *man in charge*?'

'No! Because I know more Portuguese than the words for "stinking bastard" and "son of a goat"!'

Undeniably true. But it still chafed, being told to keep my mouth shut.

As we came closer, the guard's brow furrowed, and he shouted something, pointing to the horses. Damn! Had he recognised them? If we had stumbled across one of the party who had taken us, we were finished.

'Sim, são os cavalos dos presos. Você pensou que eles iam ficar por aí parados? Disseram-nos para levá-los para o batalhão do leste.'[14]

---

[14] Yes, they're the prisoners' horses. Do you think they'd just be left to stand around idle? We've been told to bring them to the battalion out east.

The soldier's frown deepened.

'Mas não há batalhão para o les-'

Mr Ambrose struck. He leapt forward so suddenly I didn't even manage to blink before he had his knife at the guard's throat.

'Silêncio!' he hissed.

All right, even I understood that.

The guard's eyes were as wide as saucers. *'Imperialistas!'*

Hey – another word I'd understood! I was getting really good at Portuguese.

Roughly, Mr Ambrose pulled the guard towards him, the dagger digging into the man's skin. *'Não é bem assim. Mas se você mover um músculo ou dizer uma única palavra, você é um homem morto!'*

All right...maybe I still had a little bit to learn before I mastered the language.

'What did you just say to him?' I hissed.

'I told him to shut his face! And I'd advise you to do the same, if you want us to stay alive. Hand me that rope!'

We made quick work of binding and gagging the man, leaving him among the tall grass, out of sight. Mr Ambrose made a point of mentioning to Karim, in distinctly audible Portuguese, that we were going east. Hopefully, this time, the ploy would work. We could only hope that there wasn't a third or a fourth warring faction in this crazy jungle into whose hands we could fall.

'Let's go!' Taking hold of his horse's reins again, Mr Ambrose dashed forward. 'We've wasted enough time!'

As fast as we could without actually running, we made our way towards the trees. I was convinced I could feel the eyes of patrols digging into my neck. If they spotted Karim between the horses, our disguise wouldn't be worth a farthing! At every moment, I expected shouts to echo over the open space behind us, expected shots to ring out – but nothing came.

When the shadow of the forest swallowed us, I could hardly believe it. Could it really be true? Could we actually have made it?

Slipping into a gap between two giants of trees, I felt the imaginary eyes of the patrols behind us leave my neck. I let out a breath I hadn't known I was holding.

Yes! Huzzah! We're safe!

Or at least that's what I thought at the time.

I hadn't really factored in that the 'safe place' we were running into was the deepest darkest heart of the Amazonian Jungle.

REALLY HOT JUNGLE HEAT

Tell me, what do you think the jungle is like? Do you imagine monkeys swinging cheerfully from branch to branch, bananas and pineapples hanging plentifully from every branch that happens not to be occupied by swinging monkeys, and the majestic ruins of ancient heathen civilisations rising out of the misty tangle of trees?

Well, if you think that, you're completely barmy.

The jungle is dirty. The jungle is moist. But there's one thing the jungle is most of all. This aspect of the jungle is so absolutely jungle-ish that all experienced junglers will confirm its essential jungleness. Above all else, the jungle is utterly, completely and totally hot.

I mean *really* hot.

Put-the-pot-on-Lucifer,-I-want-to-boil-some-souls-in-hell hot.

Don't get me wrong. It had been hot out on the river, and during our first day of travel through the jungle. Besides, I had travelled through the deserts of Egypt, so I was by no means unused to hot temperatures.

However, I was unused to being boiled alive.

'Bloody hell!' panting heavily, I raised my hand to wipe the sweat off my forehead – only to have more pour down out of the wild tangle that had once been my hair. 'And I mean that literally! How can it be this hot in here? I thought the desert was supposed to be hot!'

'High humidity,' Mr Ambrose's curt voice explained. He was marching in front, and Karim behind. I would have objected to being squashed in the middle like a little girl between her guardians, if I had any energy left to argue with. 'The higher the humidity, the hotter human senses perceive it to be.'

'Perceive it to be? You mean it's not really this hot?'

'Exactly. Your body is a fallible animal. Simply ignore its false information.'

'Oh, thanks so much! That's a great help!'

'You are welcome, Mr Linton.'

I managed to go on for about a dozen yards more before I collapsed. Through the haze that lay over my vision, I saw Mr Ambrose stop and turn.

'In case there was a miscommunication, Mr Linton,' a voice informed me which, even in this climate, somehow, miraculously managed to be cold as ice, 'we are not stopping for the night yet. Because, as you might have noticed, it isn't night yet. Get up!'

'Pfft...!' I said.

'Mr Linton!'

'Ffff...fff...Pfft...!'

'Am I to infer from your excessive panting that you do not have the where-withal to continue?'

'Pff...pff...'

Cold eyes swept over me, sending a much-needed chill down my back. Oooh..... wonderful! Bloody wonderful! Mr Ambrose was better than an ice pack! Somehow, I found the strength to raise my head and look at him, standing above me in all his perfect, untouchable glory. There was hardly a hint of sweat on his face, damn him! There was probably enough ice in his heart to keep him nice and cool.

'I'm not weak, darn you! This is inhuman! Nobody can manage this!'

'Indeed?' He cocked his head, the hard planes of his chiselled face casting shadows in the twilight. 'I seem to be managing. And so, believe me, do the numerous native tribes living in this jungle.'

'There are people *living* in this hell? Of their own free will?'

'Indeed there are.'

'How do they stand it?'

He shrugged, and turned away. 'Unlike you, they are resilient. And I believe they wear somewhat less clothing than you or I. Now, are you going to get up, or will I have to drag you up?'

I opened my mouth to throw an expletive at him – but before I could, *it* came. The idea.

The inspiration.

I had no clue where it had come from. This certainly wasn't the best climate for creative thought. But it had come, and it was a whopper. Without doubt the best, most brilliant idea I had ever had in my entire life. Better than painting a smiley on the butt of my uncle's trousers. Better than fighting for women's rights. Better even than trying solid chocolate.

I smiled.

'All right. I'll get up.'

And I'll get you for this! Drag me up indeed! Ha! You just wait! Revenge is on its way...!

Grabbing a nearby sapling, I managed to haul myself to my own two feet. They didn't really feel like my own anymore, rather like random appendages some not-particularly-talented craftsman had stuck to my legs. Every muscle in my body was aching now, even those I should, technically, not be using for walking. But somehow, I got myself vertical again and, calling on all my feminist fortitude, started setting one foot before the other.

You can do this! You can show him – in the literal sense of the word!

And so I trudged along, biding my time. I waited until Karim had stopped grumbling. I waited until Mr Ambrose was fully concentrated on the path ahead again. For almost half an hour I walked and waited – then I put my plan into action!

The first sign the two of them got that something was out of the ordinary, was the subtle noise of cloth sliding over cloth. Mr Ambrose didn't bother to look around. But Karim, ever the attentive watchdog, looked up sharply and–

He made a strangled noise in his throat.

I smiled.

Mr Ambrose must have either heard the noise or sensed my smile, because he turned around and, when his gaze fell on me, stiffened like a rod of iron.

'What do you think you are doing, Mr Linton?'

'Why, removing some unnecessary clothing, of course, Sir.' Smiling, I slid the rest of the way out of my tailcoat and let it hang loosely from one hand, swinging back and forth. 'Thanks so much for giving me the idea, by the way.'

'I? I did nothing of the sort!'

'Of course you did. Don't you remember?.' Stowing the tailcoat away in my backpack, I drew in a deep breath of air. Ah! Much better! Now, the only thing I was wearing over my clingy, sweat-soaked linen shirt was my peacock vest – a fact that Mr Ambrose seemed to be noticing, too. 'You said the natives do it, didn't you?'

'True.' Cold and hard as opals, Mr Ambrose's eyes slowly rose where they had been lingering on the shirt clinging to my body. 'But there are two important differences between you and a native of South America, Mr Linton.'

'Indeed, Sir?'

He took a step towards me. 'Yes, indeed, Mr Linton! Firstly: you are English!'

'You don't say.'

Another step. His dark eyes bored into mine – and then flicked, so fast I almost didn't catch it, to the rest of me, taking everything in. 'And secondly: *they don't work for me.*'

'How disappointing for you. Haven't you opened a branch down here yet?'

A noise erupted from his throat, somewhere between a growl and the grinding of stone on stone. He looked at me for a moment, his eyes narrowing infinitesimally – then whirled around, and gave a curt shrug. 'Fine! If you wish to run around the jungle without your tailcoat, Mr Linton, be my guest. But be warned that such improper attire will not be tolerated in my office.'

'Of course not, Sir.' I purred.

We continued on. I gave him a little time to recuperate, to lull him into a false sense of security. It wasn't until noon that day that I put the next part of my plan into action. Again, there was the sound of rustling cloth. Approximately two point five seconds later, Karim cleared his throat.

'Um...*Sahib? Sahib!*'

'What is it, Karim? Is there a problem? Did you see something suspicious?'

'Err...in a manner of speaking, *Sahib*, yes! *Sahib*, she–'

Mr Ambrose turned, just in time to witness my trousers slipping to the ground.

'Aahh!' Pulling in another deep, luxurious breath, I stretched my thighs. 'Much more refreshing like this, don't you think?'

'I...cannot...agree,' Karim managed to get out between clenched teeth. I glanced over. The poor man managed to be red in the face, even under a tan as brown as mahogany. He was holding one hand clamped over his eyes, and the other outstretched towards me, as if to ward off evil. 'Put those back on *now!*'

'Oh, I don't know.' Making a little pirouette, I surveyed my new attire. 'I like it like this. Nice and breezy.'

'You...you...*ifrit!* Temptress! Demon in human form!'

'How would you know? You haven't taken a good look at my form yet.'

In answer to this, Karim only muttered a string of highly incomprehensible, and highly impressive, curses. Choosing to ignore him for now, I turned to Mr Ambrose with a sweet smile on my face.

'And you, Sir? What do you think?'

Silence.

A very, very silent silence.

Yet was it a pregnant one?

Well, to judge by the way Mr Ambrose was looking at my legs, it very soon would be.

Slowly, very slowly, he raised his eyes to meet mine.

'What in the name of all that is properly attired do you think you are doing, Mr Linton?'

I gave him a smile, as sweet as solid chocolate. 'Why, simply adjusting to the climate, Sir, as you suggested.'

'I didn't suggest for you to run around displaying your unmentionables to the world!'

'The world?' I raised an innocent eyebrow. 'But it's the middle of the jungle. There's no one here except Karim–' A groan came from behind me. I ignored it. '–me, and of course.... you, Sir.' I gave him another sweet smile.

'You can't have anything against seeing my legs, now, can you? After all...' I stepped towards him until our bodies were nearly touching. Leaning closer to his perfectly still, chiselled face, I whispered: 'It wouldn't be the first time, would it?'

Out of the corner of my eyes, I saw his left little finger twitch.

Yay!

'Are you going to continue with this lunacy?' he growled. 'Or are you going to remember what behoves a decent young English lady and give up now?'

'I don't really think wearing these–' I pointed out, holding up my trousers '– is what most people think behoves a decent young English lady, Sir – but I'm doing it anyway. Besides...' A wide grin stretched my face. 'Have you ever known me to give up?'

His little finger twitched again.

'Karim!' he barked.

'Yes, *Sahib*?'

The bodyguard snapped to attention, his hand still firmly clamped over his eyes.

'Take your paw away from your face, man, and get to the front! I'll be guarding the back from now on.'

'Oh *Sahib*! A thousand blessings upon you! Thank you! May your soul be saved and find its way to the Garden of Eternal–'

'Yes, yes! Move!'

Thumping against a few trees in the process, Karim made his way around me. Only when he was certain he was well ahead and out of the femininity danger zone did he lower his hand.

'Well, now I know what to do if I ever want to get the better of you.' I grinned at the Mohammedan's broad back. 'I'll just have to drop my trousers, and that'll be it.'

A growl from behind me suggested that Mr Rikkard Ambrose did not think very much of this idea.

'Very well.' I bent to retrieve my knapsack from where I had dropped it on the ground, taking care to waggle my behind, only covered by the end of a shirt and a thin chemise, at Mr Ambrose in the process. Although I had been wearing men's clothing for a long time, I had never really been interested in wearing men's underwear – a fact that was coming in very handy right now. 'Shall we go? Or were you two planning on lazing around here all day?'

Whistling, I set out northeastwards, Karim fleeing before me like Napoleon before Wellington at Waterloo. And Mr Ambrose – he followed me like…

Like Mr Rikkard Ambrose.

There simply was no comparison to describe him. Especially not the way his gaze drilled from behind into my neck and, well, other parts of me. As hard as I tried (and it wasn't very hard, if I was being honest) I couldn't keep an impish smile from my face.

Hm…how many more pieces of clothing did I have left?

I decided I had better start and find out soon.

INTERESTING IDEAS

The sun was setting beyond the horizon, the only hint at a sunset being the glorious solitary rays of golden light streaming in through the trees ahead, when I reached up and, pulling off my hat, shook out the long, tangled strands of my hair. From behind me, I heard a noise like a stone statue being choked to death.

I smiled.

Bloody hell, this is fun! So…what next?

I was just reaching up to find some nice buttons to open when from behind me abruptly came a voice: 'Stop! I…ehem. I mean we'll stop here for the night.'

'Already, *Sahib*?' Karim asked, and started to turn – until he remembered, and whirled to face away from me again. 'It'll be quite a while till the sun is down yet.'

'Don't question my orders! Do as I say!'

'Yes, *Sahib*. As you wish, *Sahib*.'

Spoilsports! Sighing, I let my fingers drop away from my buttons. Ah, well…tomorrow would be another day. And as for the night…

My devious smile returned.

How exactly did one spend the night in the jungle? On the hot, moist ground, pressed up close against each other in a tangle of–?

My question was abruptly interrupted by something soft hitting me in the back of the head.

'Sling this!' Mr Ambrose commanded me as I whirled to catch the thing. 'Go on, don't laze about!'

Blinking in the twilight, I held up the object. For a moment, I thought it was a vast gown, designed specifically to entrap females and spare the sensitive nerves of men. Then I realised that it was, in fact, a hammock.

Hm…that has possibilities…

'There's one for each of us,' Mr Ambrose told me, as if he had read my mind. Looking up from the tangle of cloth in my hands, I met his eyes and fluttered my lashes.

'Oh, really? Could you maybe help me and show me how to hang one of these up? I'm afraid I've never done it before, and I might do it wrong.'

Come hither, come hither, I'm a helpless little damsel in distress – until I get you in my clutches! Then I'll eat you for dinner!

'If you do it wrong,' Mr Ambrose informed me. 'You'll land on the forest floor. A course of action I would advise against, considering the poisonous snakes.'

With that, he left me standing.

Damn! He was a tough coconut to crack! But, on the other hand, I was in the jungle now. So I was bound to get some experience in the cracking of coconuts.

Deciding to make a strategic retreat and resume the battle on the morrow, I looked for two trees standing close enough so I wouldn't have to stretch the hammock to the length of Loch Ness, and far enough apart for me to not have to fold myself. I finally settled on a pair and began to lash the thing down. The result was less than perfect, but at least provided me with a reasonably dry and soft surface to lie on.

Swinging back and forth, I lay in my hammock, chewing on a piece of dry bread, while Karim and Mr Ambrose sat around a tree stump, discussing our strategy in low voices – or discussing ways to force me to leave the rest of my clothes on. How would I know? Lying in my peaceful little haven, I watched the sun go down and wondered what the morning would bring.

~~**~*~*

By the end of the day, I was definitely starting to have misgivings about my battle plan. Certainly, Mr Ambrose seemed inordinately interested in my increasing lack of clothing. So, however, were the jungle insects. When I woke up next morning, the nasty little beasts had decorated me with a number of angry red stings in places even I didn't think were polite to mention. Perverts!

Karim, at least, hadn't escaped unharmed, either. During breakfast he kept scratching his butt in a manner that, combined with the fact that he had his hand clamped over his eyes the whole time, made it very hard not to snigger. But as for Mr Ambrose – well, whenever I wanted to snigger, I just had to look at him, and the urge would disappear instantly. He didn't scratch himself once. Not a single solitary bleeding time! Was his stone skin impervious to mosquito bites? Or did the stench of too much money keep the hungry little bastards away?

Damn him! How dare he just...sit there, perfectly impervious, while I was itching like the devil? For that offense, he deserved to be eternally tortured!

Well...

Then I would have to see that he got what he deserved.

'Dear oh dear.' Sighing, I rose from the tree root on which I'd been sitting eating my breakfast, and stretched, taking care that my chemise rose up as high as the laws of physics allowed. 'It's really hot this morning, don't you think?'

'No!' Karim barked, almost desperately. 'No, I don't think so at all! In fact, I detect a definite chill in the air this morning! Isn't that right? *Sahib*, you know best! It's chilly, is it not?'

'I concur,' Mr Ambrose said in a voice that could have made the Amazon frost over. 'Positively freezing.'

'Strange. I somehow feel that I'm too hot. You know what? I think I'm wearing too much clothing. I should...'

Karim was out of there before I could say another word. With a curse, he jumped up and, hand still over his eyes, stumbled off to scout ahead.

'That's south!' I shouted after him. 'We're going northeast!'

'I had better be going, too,' Mr Ambrose stated coolly, rising to his feet.

'What?' I glanced around at him and, from under lowered lashes, gave him a challenging look. 'Don't you want to guard my rear today?'

His gaze lowered until it fixed on my barely covered derrière. 'I think your rear will be much safer without me as a guard.'

'Well, that's too bad,' I told him, and whirled around, grabbing my backpack and flitting after Karim. 'I guess I'll just have to live in danger,' I called over my shoulder.

In answer I only received silence.

Well, apart from the monkeys cackling in the distance.

We continued our course northeast, just as yesterday: Karim in front, me in the middle, and Mr Ambrose at the back. I would instantly bet money on the fact that it was not a position he was used to. You just had to glance once at Rikkard Ambrose to know that he was always at the front, always first and best at everything. It made me wonder why, in this case, he was content to march behind me. I had great fun wondering, because, really, there was only one possible answer.

'Are you enjoying the view, Sir?' I asked about half an hour after we had set out. A little small talk couldn't hurt anybody, right?

'I've seen jungles before,' came the brusque reply.

'I wasn't talking about the jungle.'

There were a few moments of pregnant silence, strongly in need of an abortion.

'Mr Linton?'

'Yes, Sir?'

'Be silent!'

'Yes, Sir!'

'And, Mr Linton...'

'Yes?'

'When we return to London, you are buying more underclothes!'

'I don't know, Sir... Underclothes are quite expensive. Will I get a raise?'

'Don't stretch my patience, Mr Linton!'

'Oh well, I'll stretch something else, then.' And, leaning against a tree, I stretched my aching limbs. It felt good! Especially when, from behind me, I heard an indistinct noise coming from Mr Ambrose.

It went on like this for exquisite hour upon exquisite hour. With something to keep my mind – and certain parts of my body – occupied, hiking through the Amazonian jungle didn't feel nearly as difficult as I had feared it would. Not even the stings of mosquitoes could bother me much. After all, to a certain extent I could perfectly well understand how much fun it was to nettle somebody. And my approach seemed to be getting to Mr Ambrose a lot more than the pitiful attempts of the mosquitos.

It was just after we had set out again after stopping for a short lunch that I decided to make my next move. The sun was shining through a small open patch in the roof of leaves above us, highlighting my figure, I was sure, to anyone who walked behind me. The perfect scene! Now all that was missing was action. Slowly, I raised my hands to the buttons of my vest.

'Mr Linton!'

Ignoring the call from behind me, I undid the first button.

'Mr Linton, what are you doing?'

'I'm adjusting my attire. Don't you remember?' Slowing down, I half-turned to glance at him. 'I said this morning that I thought it had gotten even warmer.'

'It hasn't!'

'Really?' I undid another button, revealing the wet, clinging linen of my shirt. 'I feel positively *hot*.'

'Mr Linton, cease that immediately!'

'What?' Reaching for another button, I teased it with my forefinger. 'This?'

'Yes.'

'But why?' The button popped open. Oh, how wonderful I had purchased a vest with this many sparkly little buttons...'They're just buttons.'

'It's not the buttons I'm concerned about,' he bit out. 'It's–'

'Yes?'

'Nothing!'

'Oh, well, if that's the case...'

I let the last button pop open. This time, I didn't slow down, let alone stop. Oh no, I took care to continue walking, accentuating the sway of my hips with every step in a way that back home in England, would have caused shocked gasps, even had I been fully dressed.

But I wasn't.

Not at all.

The vest dropped with a soft, silky noise. Catching it on one finger, I slung it over one shoulder, where it dangled like a hook, waiting for the big fish to bite. But what was much, much more important was behind the hook: the bait. Sweet little me.

I had no illusions about my physical appearance. I was utter perfection, thank you very much. My figure was perfectly slender and elegant and not at all overly padded (despite solid chocolate being my favourite food), my cleavage was enough to rob any man of his senses (probably because he would faint in the senseless effort to find it), and my smile was the most brilliant smile in the city of London (that was reminiscent of a tiger waiting for dinner).

All right, maybe I did have a few little illusions! But I was aware of them, so pretending I didn't know that I was no great beauty was perfectly all right. I had always been content with being beautiful to myself, and never cared much for the opinions of society at large, let alone its male representatives. So it didn't bother me at all if I heard a man murmur that I was fat, or sunburnt or a shrew that should be locked up for public safety. But Mr Rikkard Ambrose...

He was different.

He had never said anything about my looks. He never said anything about anything. But he had done things. Quite a few things, to be exact.

Hard hands holding me captive, lips catching mine with demanding force...dark eyes flashing in the shadows, boring their way into my very soul...

Even in the jungle heat, the memory from Egypt sent a shiver down my back. Oh yes, Rikkard Ambrose had done things to me, with me, and on top of me. Things that showed me exactly how he felt about my body. Even if it weren't for the burning cold gaze I could feel drilling into me from behind at this very moment, I knew that to him, my behind wasn't too generous, my smile not too feisty, and I suspected that with thorough research, he'd even be able to find my non-existent cleavage.

Then why not give him the chance to look?

The thought popped into my head unbidden, but not at all unwelcome. I waited for my inner feminist to screech in protest, to start waving her 'No men allowed!' sign – but nothing happened.

Why protest? Why hesitate? You know he wants you. Besides, with the exception of a few exceptionally hairy specimens dangling from trees somewhere above us, you are the only female within a hundred miles. That's bound to be a point in your favour.

Good God! What was happening to me? Had my inner feminist gone nuts in the heat? Well, I certainly felt hot enough. Even the cold stare drilling into my back didn't cool me down anymore. On the contrary – somehow, incredibly, it seemed to heat me up.

I suddenly realised, with a clarity that had evaded me before, that all that was between me and Mr Rikkard Ambrose was a shirt, a corset and a very, very thin chemise. The hand that held my vest clenched involuntarily, and for a moment, just a moment, I was tempted to pull it back on. But then I remembered the noise Mr Ambrose had made when I had popped that one button, and the dark gaze he had swept over me earlier, and another, much stronger temptation swelled up inside me.

Once again, I smiled.

~~**~*~*

When Mr Rikkard Ambrose awoke in his hammock the next morning and opened his eyes, he found a wet white linen shirt several sizes too small to be his dangling above his head, teasing the tip of his straight, sculpted nose. I watched from where I sat against a tree as he went stiff (well, stiffer than usual), staring up at the offending object above him.

'Mr Linton?'

'Yes, Sir?'

'Remove this item at once!'

'Item? What item, Sir?'

'You know exactly what item I am referring to, Mr Linton. Remove it, and get dressed. We're leaving.'

'Certainly, Sir. There's just one tiny little problem with that...'

'Yes?'

'I am already dressed.'

'*What?*'

Ripping the shirt from the branch above him, Mr Ambrose sat up abruptly and slid out of the hammock. His feet landed on the ground with a resounding *thud*. But he didn't turn towards me – probably because he knew what he would see if he did.

'Do you mean to tell me,' Mr Ambrose said in a very cold, very controlled voice, his magnificent back still towards me, 'that you intend to skip through the jungle with nothing more to cover you than a piece of skimpy lingerie?'

'Oh no, Sir. I still have my corset on.'

'What a tremendous comfort to us all!'

Without turning, Mr Ambrose hurled the shirt at me, and somehow managed to hit me right in the head. I sputtered, pulling wet linen from my face.

'Where's Karim?' my dear employer enquired in a voice so sharp one could have cut stones with it. 'Has he gone to dance tango with the monkeys, or is there at least one person in this group besides me who has not lost their mind yet?'

'He's gone scouting ahead.'

'This early? Why?'

'I, um...' I didn't often manage to blush. But in this heat, and this moment, my cheeks did turn a little redder than their usual tanned colour. 'He woke up just as I was pulling my shirt off. Gave the poor man quite a shock.'

Mr Ambrose, who had just been about to open his knapsack, froze in mid-motion.

'Yes.' His voice was unusually soft. Soft as a panther's fur. Soft as a snake's kiss. 'I would imagine so.'

'I, err...don't think he saw very much.'

'Is that so?'

'He ran off into the jungle as soon as he had untangled his legs from the hammock he dropped out of.'

'I see.'

My heart was beating wildly against my chest. Dragging in a deep breath of humid air, I tried to calm it down and stop my mouth from being so bloody dry! I had to get a grip, and get on top of this game again!

'So...what about you?' Slowly, I rose from my sitting position, taking a step towards him. The air, even hot as it was, tickled coolly over the bare skin of my arms and legs. 'If you see me, are you going to run off into the jungle, too?'

Silence. He didn't turn around to look, but continued to fiddle with his knapsack.

'What's the matter, Sir? Are you afraid?'

It all went so fast I had hardly time to blink. The knapsack landed on the ground, and he was surging through the trees towards me in a black streak, like a sleek, dark jungle cat. The next moment I was flung off my feet and back against the tree I had been leaning against just a moment before, the rough bark digging into my soft flesh.

Rikkard Ambrose towered above me, so close that I could feel the aura of power radiating off him on my skin. Cocking his head, he leaned down to my ear and growled: 'Don't play games with me, Mr Linton!'

'Oh yes? Why not?'

'Because if you do, you might soon find yourself the plaything rather than the player!'

I felt a tingle of temptation travelling down my spine. Raising my eyes to his, I met his implacable gaze – warm chocolate brown colliding with the cold, fathomless depths of the sea.

'Who says I want to play games?' I demanded – and kissed him.

STONE CRACKING OPEN

Or at least I tried.

But I had been right in regard to one thing about Rikkard Ambrose. He always had to be the first at everything. I had just managed to part my lips when he fell on me like a ravenous animal, the pent-up need of days exploding in one hard, fast, heart-wrenching kiss.

The shock of it hit me like a hurricane. Memories came flooding back, of him and me, entangled in ways beyond decency or doubt. Memories from so, so long ago...Oh God! It had been months since I had touched him. I hadn't realised until now, but I had missed his touch as if a part of my heart had vanished. And so, apparently, had he.

Good God...!

The wave of shock only slowly abated, and in its wake came a wave of need ten times its size. My knees almost buckled, and I was left helpless, with no idea what to do. Last time this had happened, on our trip to Egypt, we had been kissing for a reason. We were in disguise, pretending to be man and wife. Thus it was – purely as part of the disguise, of course – perfectly acceptable to engage in public displays of affection.

But now?

Now there were no disguises. We were stripped of all pretence, alone in the jungle. *Very* alone.

Which means nobody will ever know about this Lilly, a little voice at the back of my mind pointed out.

Good point.

I wasn't going to get a chance to think any further upon it, though. In fact, I wasn't going to get a chance to think at all. Catching my chin in the silken vice of his hands, Mr Ambrose forced me to open farther, and I did something I normally never did – I willingly complied. All thoughts disappeared as his tongue invaded my mouth and I took it, took him, took everything he gave me and still wanted more.

And then *he* did something he normally never did. He gave me exactly what I wanted.

He moved, his powerful body pushing forward, his hands sliding away from my face to capture my shoulders. I was pushed back hard against the tree, the plains and ridges of his granite body digging mercilessly, marvellously into me. The aura of unrelenting power in the air around him was so overwhelming, it nearly made my knees buckle. I was trapped between a rock and a hard place – and I didn't mind at all.

Wrenching his mouth free of mine, he skimmed it across my cheek, eliciting a shiver, until he reached my ear.

'What about now, Mr Linton?' he whispered, his voice hard as stone and cold as ice. It made another shiver race down my spine. 'Do you want to play games now?'

'Yes!'

Afterwards, when thinking back on this moment, I wouldn't be entirely sure whether it was actually me who had uttered that single, oh-so important word. But it didn't really matter. It was out there, and Mr Rikkard Ambrose was not a man to hesitate.

His hands started moving, sliding away from my shoulders. For a moment, I was disappointed, wanting to cry out at the loss of his touch – until his hands returned in other places. Places much more interesting than shoulders.

Holy Moly...!

Sliding over curves, caressing every inch, only separated from my skin by a threadbare scrap of a chemise, Mr Ambrose's hands worshipped me as if I were a cheque for a million pounds he had found in the street. His hands were just as hard as his body was, and yet at the same time inexplicably soft and almost...tender?

Oh God, oh dear God...if this is a sin, please change the heavenly rules fast, because I'm not giving this up, no chance in hell!

'Mine!' Mr Ambrose's one-word growl tore me from my delirious state of bliss right into another. His hands left my body to grasp my face again, holding it as if it were the most precious diamond in all the world. As he gazed into my eyes, not kissing, not even really touching much, just looking, I felt something rise inside me more powerful than any emotion I had felt before. I felt hot and cold all over. I felt as if I could conquer the world, and lose it all in one single instant. I felt like a goddess – a goddess who would fall from heaven if he ever stopped looking at me like that.

'Mr Ambrose, Sir?'

It was a question – yet even I didn't know what exactly I was asking. He gave me the best reply I could have wished for: his silence and his hungry lips. A moment or two later, his hands joined in the fun again, sliding over me with effortless grace and tightly leashed power.

But, hey – why were his hands the only ones that were busy? Why the heck was he the only one having fun? I was a feminist, for heaven's sake! I didn't need a man to do things for me! Why were my hands just dangling limply at my side? If I was going to sink into the depths of depravity, I was bloody well going to jump right in and do my part, thank you very much!

Besides...the thought of my hands on that tight, hard body of his...

Enough said.

My hands were already halfway up towards him before I had finished the thought. Even through thick layers of cotton, I could feel the hard muscles of his arms, flexing and contracting as his hands explored my body with shameless demand. I clung on, wanting to feel, wanting to own, but he tore free as easily as a lion from a cobweb, continuing his merciless assault. Gliding to his chest, my hands grabbed fistfuls of his tailcoat, trying to pull it aside, to get at what I wanted, but the damn thing wouldn't budge. I cursed the fact that unlike me, the stupid man hadn't had the foresight to toss away his clothes over the last couple of days. Blast! Did a girl have to do everything by herself nowadays?

I grabbed the buttons of his shirt.

'Mr Linton...' he growled against my throbbing lips. 'What are you doing?'

'I think you can stop calling me "Mr Linton" now,' I breathed.

Pulling away from my mouth, he captured my earlobe with his teeth, making me gasp. For a moment, he held me like that, then let go and, his lips brushing against my ear, whispered: 'Mister Linton!'

'Oh dear. Stubborn, are we?' I felt a smirk spread over my face. 'Well, I guess I'll just have to provide you with proof of my femininity.' I opened the first button. 'After all, we wouldn't want you running around with delusions, now, would we?'

My fingers were flying now. Button after button on his shirt opened, but soon I was interrupted by his tailcoat, and switched to that.

'Mr Linton...!'

There was a note of warning in his tone. I completely ignored it. Opening the last button, I shoved the tailcoat back off his strong, broad shoulders. It fell to the ground with a wet *thud*.

'That tailcoat is almost new, Mr Linton! Only ten years old!'

'Then why don't you get it, Sir?' I whispered, running a finger over his hard cheekbone. 'Why don't you pick it up off the ground?'

'I...'

'Don't want to, do you? Maybe because you see something more interesting?'

'Mr Linton–'

'You know,' I murmured, standing on my tiptoes, straining up towards him until my body was mashed against his, 'you really have to stop calling me that, don't you think? Feel that.' I moved against him with delicious friction, eliciting a growl from the back of his throat. 'Does that feel like a mister to you? Or...' I strained up even further, until my mouth, my tongue, my tickling breath was right next to his ear. '...does it feel feminine?'

The noise he made then was not human. It belonged not in London, England, in the strict, ordered world of Empire House, but right here in the wild depths of the jungle.

At the sound, heat rose inside me like a volcano, and my fingers were back at the buttons of his shirt in an instant. The wet fabric clung to his skin as if it didn't want to let go, but I was a damn sight more determined than his shirt! Button after button, the white linen parted, revealing a marvel of marble with which no ancient Roman statue could compete. When my tentative fingers first touched the hard planes of his chest, a groan rose from the back of his throat.

'Hmm...' Leaning in, I ran my nose along the ridge between his iron-hard pectorals and breathed in his scent. I didn't care that it was indecent. I didn't care that we had been trekking through the jungle for days, and sweating every minute. He smelled of man, money and power, and I loved it! 'Very nice. Very nice indeed.'

Reaching the top of his chest, I placed a soft kiss on his collarbone that made him shudder. His arms closed around me in a vice-tight grip.

'Don't stop!'

Slippery as an eel, I slid out of his hold.

'I said don't stop!'

I smirked up at him. 'Ah, but I had to – I'm for the equality of man and woman, after all.' Sliding one hand down his bare chest in a gentle caress, I placed the other on my own. The thin material of the chemise did little to conceal what lay beneath, and the corset did more aiding and abetting than concealing. 'Wouldn't you like to reciprocate?'

Cocking my head, I leaned back against the tree, offering myself to him.

Mr Ambrose wasn't one to ignore a free offer. His fingers grabbed hold of my corset, racing, searching for a way to open, and making me want to faint in the process.

'Where are the buttons on this thing?' he growled.

I giggled. I couldn't help it.

'Mr Linton!'

'*Mister*, Sir?'

'Just tell me where the damn buttons are!'

Mr Ambrose, swearing? I was hardly able to hold in my laughter. 'It doesn't have buttons! Haven't you ever opened a lady's corset before?'

'That,' he growled, leaning down towards me until his lips brushed my ear in a tantalising threat, 'is not exactly the kind of question a lady should ask a gentleman.'

'Well, from where I'm standing,' I whispered back, running one finger down his hard, half-bare chest, 'you don't particularly look like a gentleman.'

Suddenly serious, I looked up into his eyes. There was true confusion there. Could it be that he hadn't...That he had never before...with any other...

Good God.

I abruptly lowered my eyes again, suddenly abashed. Why? Why the hell was I suddenly feeling so inexplicably shy?

'Really?' I whispered. 'You really don't know? You've never...'

I didn't finish the sentence.

Suddenly, I felt a finger at my chin, taking control, lifting my gaze up to his. Anxious, chocolate brown eyes met his impenetrable sea-coloured orbs.

'Knowledge is power is time is money, Mr Linton, remember? Why would you suppose I would ever waste time on something as frivolous and senseless as that?'

'You're doing it now,' I dared to point out.

Shut up, Lilly, shutupshutupshutup!

But he didn't pull away. Instead he stared at me for an immeasurably long moment, and then nodded. 'Yes. I am.' His arms tightened around me, and he pulled me against his chest in an embrace that was not at all sensual, and yet so much deeper in meaning.

'Why?' I whispered.

'You're my little *Ifrit*.' His voice travelled up to me right through his chest, deep and strong. 'How could I possibly say no?'

I felt something tug at my heart, so hard it was almost wrenched out of my chest and slipped into his.

'But don't you dare think I'll be counting this as work hours!' he growled. 'I will deduct every minute from your pay cheque at the end of the month!'

Moisture pricking at the corner of my eyes, I grinned into his chest. 'Please do.'

The way I was feeling right now, this would be over in two pennies worth of time. And that would be worth it a thousand times over! Inside me was rising a feeling stronger than heat, stronger than need, stronger than all the other emotions boiling inside me. I was his first! His very first and only! I was his little *ifrit*. I would have crowed it from the rooftops – if there had been any rooftops available. Instead, I pressed myself even more closely up against him, my lips finding his ear.

'Want to waste a little time with me, Sir?'

The only answer was an animalistic growl that any tiger would been proud of. His fingers returned to their search, sliding over my corset with unshakable determination.

'At the back,' I breathed. 'Laces!'

'At the back? *Why?*'

'No idea! Just do it! Open!'

We were almost there! Almost! His hands were just sliding around, searching for the laces at the back of my corset – when from the bushes beyond the hammocks a few dozen yards away suddenly a voice came:

'*Sahib? Sahib,* I've scouted ahead, and the way is clear. We can star–nnng! What, by the beard of the–!'

RAMIFICATIONS

Mr Ambrose's hands froze.

There was a moment of silence that really, really wanted to be pregnant, but couldn't be, because I still had too many damn clothes on!

'Karim?'

'Y-yes, *Sahib*?'

'You didn't see anything.'

'N-no, *Sahib*! I didn't see a thing! I swear it! *Al'hā jhūṭha la'ī māfa kara, atē mērē akha dī bēgunāhī nū muṛa kara sakadā hai!*'[15]

'Indeed.'

'I-is it safe to come out now, *Sahib*?'

'Yes.' Mr Ambrose's voice sounded as cool and composed as if he had just been double-checking his accounting. His hand fell from my back, and only I heard the whispered word: 'Moderately.'

I didn't know whether to strangle Karim or laugh out loud. Since the latter was probably much easier to accomplish, I decided on that.

'What is she laughing about?' Karim demanded, still in the bushes. 'Is she taking her clothes off again?'

'No, Karim. You can come out of there now.'

'If you say so, *Sahib*.'

The Mohammedan stepped out of the bushes, but didn't remove his hand from where it was once more firmly clamped over his eyes.

'I need my knapsack, *Sahib*. Where...?'

Mr Ambrose didn't let him finish. Stepping away and leaving me bereft, he grabbed Karim's knapsack from the ground, and a moment later, the massive sack hit the Mohammedan in the chest with a heavy *thud*. Karim didn't so much as flinch, but grabbed the thing and slung it over his shoulder.

'Thank you, *Sahib*. The way ahead is clear. Should we set out now, or do you wish to eat first?'

As if drawn by a magnet, Mr Ambrose's dark eyes slid back to me. 'I must admit, I feel quite hungry,' he admitted, his gaze raking over my curves. 'But I think it's better if, today, we set out anyway.'

And, without one more word, he grabbed his knapsack from the ground, snatched up his hammock and disappeared into the jungle.

~~**~*~*

It took a while for my mind to resurface from the delirious whirlpool of passion it was leisurely bathing in. We had been marching for half a day, and still my mind was splashing around in pleasant daydreams involving Mr Rikkard Ambrose's pectorals. When it cautiously peeked its nose through the surface for the first time and smelled the cold air of reality, it was quite a shock to me.

What had just happened?

What had I done?

Oh my God!

Had I just really rid myself of nearly all my clothes...and then, with him...and he had grabbed me and... with his lips, and his hands, and his...*Oh my God!*

---

[15] May Allah forgive me for the lie and restore the innocence of my eyes!

What if Karim hadn't come when he had? I didn't know much about what went on between a man and a woman, but I did know that the side-effects included bellyswelling and babyproducing. *Me?* Have a *baby?* I shuddered at the very thought. To swell up like a balloon, suffer through incredible pain, and then, as a reward, be saddled with a screeching little monster that demanded all my attention and time? No, thank you! I already had one monster demanding all my time, and he, thankfully, didn't screech!

Not that the idea of having a child didn't somewhat appeal to me, in the abstract. It would be gratifying to have someone to whom I could pass on my beliefs in justice and equality. The problem was that, before we could get to justice and equality, we would have to get through a lot of smelly diapers. And that thought I didn't relish at all.

Besides...what if it were a boy, and he grew up to be just like his father? The idea that I would have to deal with two tyrants at the same time, and they wouldn't even need to pay me for it!

And aren't you forgetting something, Lilly? What about the reaction of your dear aunt and uncle?

My knees nearly buckled under me – and this time, it wasn't from overpowering passion. My aunt, Hester Mahulda Brank, was a social-climbing vulture with the heart of a frost giant and the conscience of a serial killer. Her husband gave even Mr Ambrose a run for his money in how much he detested spending any. Together, they would provide about as much helpful support to a struggling young mother as Judas did to Jesus. Only, they would probably be smart and demand more than thirty pieces of silver.

And as for making it on my own...to do that, I needed a job. One that I doubted very much I would be able to keep once I was six months pregnant. Mr Ambrose was allowing me to work for him in male disguise. I suspected he would be less amenable if I tried to work for him in male disguise with a huge pregnant belly bulging under my peacock vest. That sort of thing tended to hint at femininity.

Maybe you wouldn't have had to work at all. It would have been his child, too, after all. Maybe he would simply have helped you out of the goodness of his heart?

Yep. That would have been so like him.

And if he would have? If he really would have?

Then I would have been in even bigger trouble. Because if Mr Rikkard Ambrose, against all the dictates of his nature, would actually have helped me without expecting anything in return, then that would have meant that there was more to this than the mad passion of two cooked brains in exotic surroundings. Much, much more. In this heat, Mr Ambrose might melt so far as to take advantage of me – but let me take advantage of him? Let someone get at his precious purse? Never!

If he had opened it out of his own free will, just for me...

I couldn't even finish the thought. A shiver ran down my back at the weighty implications of such an action.

And you, Lilly? You keep wondering what he might do for you. But if push came to shove, what would you do for him?

A good question. So good in fact that, at the moment, I didn't have an answer.

But there was one question to which the answer was crystal-clear.

Could I let something like this ever happen again?

No!

No, no, no, nononononono, and again, no!

I thought of the wild, irrational passion I had felt a few hours ago. It seemed very far away now. When logically weighed against all the ramifications, all the problems, the unresolved feelings and unspoken words that awaited us if this repeated itself, it didn't seem like much. No, a few moments of passion definitely were not enough reason to risk my safety, security and future, let alone my self-esteem. Right then and there, I came to a firm resolution that Mr Ambrose and I were finished!

But then I felt Mr Ambrose's gaze on my neck and remembered his hard body pressed up against mine, and I realised that some things might be even firmer than my firm resolution.

~~**~*~*

'That's it,' I said, pointing excitedly ahead. 'That's the river!'

Mr Ambrose appeared beside me in a blink. 'I can hardly see it yet through the trees. Are you sure it's the same one that is mentioned in the manuscript?'

I bloody well hope so, or we'll get hopelessly lost and we'll end up getting eaten by cannibals somewhere in this green stew pot.

'Yes! Absolutely.'

'I see.'

'We follow the river for ten miles, then find our next point of orientation.'

'Acceptable. Lead on, Karim.'

Luckily, we didn't encounter any cannibals along the river. If some were going to make a meal of us, however, they would have to hurry. Our supplies were dwindling rapidly, and our water flasks were almost empty. When I mentioned this to Mr Ambrose, he gave a curt nod.

'Yes, I know, Mr Linton. I would have taken action before, but I wished to get as far ahead as possible of any pursuers first.'

'Taken action? How?'

'You'll see.'

He wouldn't say a word more. That night, when we made camp, Karim, at a nod from his employer, pulled out an axe and started chopping down saplings. Soon, he had four serviceable sticks, cleaned of bark and branches. Ramming them into the ground, he went over to his knapsack.

'What are you doing?' I wanted to know.

The only answer I got was a grunt. These days, Karim didn't even glare at me anymore, due to my lack of clothing. At least he had stopped walking around with his hand in front of his eyes after he had run into a tree for the ninety-seventh time.

Karim returned with a large, folded piece of leather. As he spread it over the sticks, I saw that it had a little hole in the middle, that was now hanging at the lowest point of the construction. A raindrop from above fell on the leather, ran down the slope and slipped through the hole – just in time to drop into the bowl which Karim had placed beneath.

I was so fascinated by the construction that I hadn't even noticed Mr Ambrose's absence. Only when he returned out of the direction of the river, a four-pronged wooden spear in one hand, and a bundle of fish in the other, did I realise he had been just as busy as Karim, if not more so. I took in the sight of him, swallowing. Marching towards me in his tailcoat and tight trousers, carrying spear and fish, he seemed like a strange mix of master of civilisation and caveman. On most men, such a mixed look would have looked ridiculous. But one look at the way Mr Ambrose handled his spear was enough to make clear that this was one hundred per cent real. If civilisation collapsed tomorrow and he would have to make his way in the wilderness, I had no doubt he would be just as much master of the situation as he was in his office at Empire House, 322 Leadenhall Street.

I watched him while he cleaned and skinned the fish with efficient movements. It was fascinating, but also pretty unappetising. I couldn't imagine ever eating something that slimy. But once he had gotten a fire going and the smell of roasting fish was drifting over towards me, water started to run in my mouth.

Good God! I'd had no idea that I was so hungry! Was one of those fishes actually for me?

I pondered the question.

Yes, it probably was. But Mr Ambrose would also probably deduct the cost for it from my wages. And since it had been fished by Britain's richest financier, the cost was bound to be pretty high.

I sighed. There was no help for it. I might like to think of myself as independent, but here in the jungle I wasn't. At least until I got Mr Ambrose to teach me how to make one of those spears. Resigned to my fate, I settled against a tree and closed my eyes to wait. I was in no hurry to find out how much Mr Ambrose would demand for half a roasted fish.

'Here.'

My eyes snapped open.

He was there, in front of me. Mr Rikkard Ambrose, towering above me, his hand extended. And in his hand was a stick, still smoking, with the first two roasted fish.

'W-what?' I blinked up at him, in complete confusion.

He cocked his head. 'Eat.'

And, with a look so dark and intense I was incapable of resisting, he shoved the stick into my hand. His eyes swept over me, from top to bottom, as if he wanted to check that all was still there, then he turned, marched back to the fireside and resumed skinning fish.

I sat there, with the stick in my hand, taking it all in.

Mr Ambrose had just given something to me.

Mr *Rikkard Ambrose*, uncrowned King of the Misers of Great Britain and Ireland, had just given something to me *without demanding anything in return*.

Well, well. Miracles do happen.

Deciding to postpone thinking about the immense theological-philosophical implications of this wondrous event until later, I dug into my fish. The taste hit me like a sledgehammer, and I leaned back, sighing in bliss. I suppose that, to many people, the fish would have tasted a little bland. But to yours truly, who had grown up on a diet of potatoes and dry bread in the household of her generous uncle, they seemed like the sweetest feast heaven could offer. In other words, almost as good as solid chocolate.

We continued along the riverbank, marching almost as fast as during the previous days, but making camp slightly earlier so Karim could set up his rain-water-catching contraption and Mr Ambrose could go fishing. The moment he picked up his spear that second evening, I was at his side, grasping the wooden shaft and halting him in his tracks.

His eyes zeroed in on me.

'What do you want, Mr Linton?'

'One of these.' Meeting his gaze unblinking, I tugged at the spear. 'Teach me how to make them.'

He cocked his head, his gaze growing more intent. 'Indeed?'

'Yes indeed, Sir.'

'What's the magic word, Mr Linton?'

I smirked. 'Now!'

That clearly wasn't what he had been expecting. For one moment, one single little moment, the muscles around his mouth seemed to twitch – almost as if he was tempted to laugh.

'It seems like you've been paying attention, Mr Linton.'

'I always do, Sir.'

He gave a hard tug, and his spear slid from my grasp.

'I see. Well, then let's get down to business. Get the small axe from your pack, a knife and twine.'

'Yes, Sir! Right away, Sir!'

FISHY BUSINESS

Making a fishing spear was astonishingly easy. In essence, it was nothing but a stick split at one end into four prongs that were held apart by twine and pieces of liana. Actually catching a fish with one – that was an entirely different matter.

'Blast, blast, blast! Stay where you are, you bloody slippery little beast!'

'Silence, Mr Linton! I am concentrating.'

Vengefully, I stared over at Mr Ambrose who already had a pile of three nice, fat fish resting beside him. The spot on the bank next to me was still empty. A little farther down the stream, the fish I had been trying to catch sprang out of the water, waggled its tailfin at me in a triumphant manner and disappeared downstream.

'I'll be back for you, you fin-flapping fiend!' I shouted after him. 'You won't escape me!'

Mr Ambrose gave me a look.

'What?' I demanded. 'It's frustrating, not catching anything! And it's so unfair! It's not my fault if you have more luck than I do! It's that stare of yours. It freezes the fish in place, so you can pick them off at your leisure.'

'I highly doubt that the temperature of my vision has anything to do with the matter, Mr Linton.'

'Oh yes? Then why don't I manage to–? Damn! Missed again!'

'It's simply a matter of practice.' The splash of two long strides through the river was all the warning I got before Mr Ambrose's strong arms encircled me. One gripped the spear I was holding, the other went around my waist, pulling me back against him. My breath caught in my throat.

'Come here,' I heard his voice, only inches away from my ear. 'I'll show you how to do it.'

Oh, yes, please! Show me! Show me everything!

Suddenly, my mind wasn't on fish anymore. Not at all.

I could feel the hard muscles of his chest against my back, could feel the tiny movements as he breathed in and out, in and out, in and out. His hand around my waist was holding me firmly against him, leaving me no room to wriggle.

As if I would have wished to move! Ha! Right then, there was no place I would rather be.

'Right, Mr Linton. Now, spread your legs...'

What? Already?

'...to get the better stance. You have to stand firm on your feet to make a catch.'

Oh. Right. Fishing.

Licking my lips, I spread my legs as advised. He was right – it was a firmer stance. But with as little as I was wearing right now, it also left me feeling unexpectedly vulnerable. His hand moved against my belly, and I felt a tingle of temptation race down my spine.

'I suppose you've always made the catch you want,' I asked, my voice breathier than usual for a fishing trip.

His voice in return was hard and implacable. 'Always.'

I swallowed. 'So...how do you do this?'

I would suggest tearing off each other's clothes, falling into the river and engaging in a mad, passionate orgy right there in the hot water.

'I stay still and silent.' He shifted, and through the thin cloth of my chemise, I felt every one of his muscles flex against my derrière. Every. Single. One. 'When a fish comes, I wait until the prey is directly beneath me – then stab!'

Stabbing sounds good. Now, please!

'And what...do I...do?'

God! Why did my voice have to sound like that? Why?

'You? For now, you just follow my lead. I'll show you, and with a bit of practice, you'll be able to do it alone just as well.'

Somehow, I highly doubt that.

'All right.' I dragged in a ragged breath. 'Let's fish.'

When I returned to the camp about an hour later, I had caught three fish –
two with Mr Ambrose's help, one on my own. I had also torn up, incinerated
and discarded my firm resolution to stay away from Mr Ambrose. All right, so I
couldn't let myself go all the way with him. Who cared? I had never been planning to go that far in the first place, right? It was just some fun. The church
might frown on it as sin, and members of polite society would faint at the very
idea, but in my opinion, polite society could stick its judgements where the sun
didn't shine. I was an educated, independent girl! If I wanted to do something,
I would not let any stuffy old social norms that I had had no say in keep me from
doing it!

And I wanted Mr Ambrose. Badly.

So...what to do?

Sliding the first of my roasted fish from the stake, I bit down, smiling.
Well...it had been really hot, recently. Maybe it was time to lose another little
piece of clothing.

~~**~*~*

I made my first move after half a day of marching. Really, I was a bit surprised I hadn't had the idea earlier. You would think, having to hike miles
through the jungle, this abominable thing would be the first thing to remove.
But I had been so used to it that I never thought of it until now. We had just set
out again after our noon meal, when I stretched, and announced to the jungle
at large: 'You know...I'm feeling quite hot today.'

In front of me, Karim stopped abruptly in his tracks. 'Oh no. No, no,
nononono!'

'Besides,' I continued, 'this thing is really uncomfortable. I think I'll loosen
it a bit.'

'No!' With a cry of anguish, Karim darted off into the forest. It was really
amazing how seriously he took his scouting duty.

Reaching behind me, I lazily brushed a few raindrops off my sweaty skin,
and in the process, just happened to loosen one of the laces of my corset. With
a soft noise, it slid open.

From behind me, out of Mr Ambrose's throat, came another noise – one that
definitely wasn't soft.

'Ah.' I sighed. 'Much better.'

Then I walked on without looking back.

It wasn't until half an hour later that I reached back and, with tentative fingers, loosened another lace. This time, the growl from behind me seemed to
shake the trees all around.

Golly, this is fun! Maybe I should do this at home, in the office, too.

Or maybe not – if I valued my life. But out here he couldn't strangle me. I was the one who had the manuscript. I was the only one who knew where the treasure was.

So, with that cheerful thought in mind, I reached back again and loosened another lace.

'Mr Linton?'

The voice from behind me was as cold as ice and as hard as tempered steel.

'Yes, Sir?'

'Cease this immediately!'

My lips curved up into a smile. 'Cease what, Sir?'

Come on! Say it out loud!

There was a pause. 'These...these *things* you are doing.'

My oh my...Was Mr Rikkard Ambrose shy?

I opened another lace, just to find out. The noise he made didn't sound shy at all. It did, however, sound rather strangled.

'Is something wrong, Sir?' I asked solicitously. He was my employer, after all, and if there was something wrong with his health, I should look after him, shouldn't I?

'Yes!'

'Is there something I can do to help?' I asked, casually undoing another lace. Blimey, this thing had a lot of laces!

'If I were you, Mr Linton,' his dark voice drifted over to me, 'I would not ask that question again.'

When we stopped that evening Karim had already set up camp. He must have seen the glint in my eyes when I walked into camp, because he grabbed his hammock and fled into the jungle, in a desperate attempt to protect the innocence of his eyes.

That was fine. He was more than welcome to keep it. Mr Ambrose, however – now, that was another matter entirely.

He was right behind me still. I could sense him there, could feel his gaze on me the same way a gazelle could sense a hunting lion. Only that gazelles didn't usually do what I did then.

Reaching back, I opened the last lace on my corset. The whole thing, which had been precariously perched on my hips for the last few hours, fell to the ground with a soft *thud*. Turning, I stepped out of it, towards Mr Rikkard Ambrose.

The look on Mr Ambrose's face was like nothing words could describe. It was like an iceberg spewing fire, like a volcano frozen in mid-explosion, and yet something entirely other and far, far more. It was completely hard and empty, and yet underneath that...

No. I really couldn't describe it.

It was Mr Ambrose. Pure and simple, and yet incredibly complicated.

I moved towards him, until I was just a foot or two away. With every step, I was incredibly conscious of the fact that now there was nothing between my skin and the outside world but a thin, flowing chemise. Air brushed against parts of me that hadn't been exposed since I was four and my mother had dunked me in the bathtub. And all in all, that had been a very different sort of experience.

Mr Ambrose's coldly burning eyes watched my every step as I approached. When I reached up to touch his face, his hand shot up with incredible speed, trapping my fingers in a vice-tight grip, keeping me from getting any farther. The growl that ripped from his throat was the rumble of a cracking mountain.

'Are you trying to drive me mad?'

I lifted an eyebrow. 'You're still fully clothed in this heat. You are already mad, Sir. I'm just trying to make it a bit more fun.'

Tentatively, I tried to move my hand. His grip tightened, so I simply stepped towards him, into him, and leaned against his chest.

'Hmmm...'

His whole body stiffened – and that's saying something! For Mr Ambrose, it was perfectly normal to walk around as if he had an iron rod up his arse. Now, though, it was as if he himself were the iron rod, or a statue carved from bed-rock.

All the better! If he didn't move, he was all mine to play with.

Standing up on my tiptoes, I leaned in and pressed a soft kiss to the corner of his perfectly sculpted mouth. No matter that he was standing as stiff as a board – the skin there felt soft, and incredibly inviting. I bestowed another kiss, a little closer to the centre, nipping at his lip.

'Mr Linton...!'

His voice was strangled. The movement of his lips against mine was a delicious appetiser.

'You know,' I whispered, 'if I didn't know you, the fact that you want me to dress up in men's clothes and keep calling me "Mister" when I kiss you might give me strange ideas.'

A choked sound of outrage came from the back of his throat, and hurriedly I raised my free hand, placing one finger on his lips.

'Psht. Don't worry. I know better. And if I didn't know your tastes before–' Mashing myself up against him, I pressed myself into his hard body. Hard everywhere. '–I know now.'

His eyes flashed like icebergs in a thunderstorm and, for a moment, I was tempted to reach down and drive home my point. But no. Not yet, anyway. I had decided that if I couldn't go all the way, I was going to take my time, and enjoy every single minute of the journey.

'Would you be so kind as to let go of my hand?' I asked, in what was in my opinion a very sweet voice, considering he was almost crushing my poor fingers.

'That depends,' he growled, 'on what you plan to do with it.'

'Why, to play a little game. Nothing more.'

'In that case,' he told me, his grip tightening even more, 'I think I'd rather keep hold of it!'

Spoilsport! He apparently hadn't had the same epiphany as yours truly yet. He apparently didn't plan to have a little bit of fun. Too bad. I would just have to change his mind for him.

'You won't let go?'

'No.'

'Not under any circumstances?'

'None.'

'A shame. Well...' I sighed. 'Then I'll simply have to use my other hand.'

Before he could do a thing, I had slid my free hand around the back of his neck and pulled myself up until my lips were on a level with his. The kiss was swift, soft, and incredibly exhilarating. It was the first time that I had taken control, the first time *I* had really kissed *him*, not the other way around.

And he kissed me back. The rest of his body stayed hard as iron, but his lips melted underneath mine, allowing me entry into his secret world for just one moment. When that moment ended, we were both left breathless, staring at each other with searing intensity.

'Why?' he rasped.

'Because I want you!'

His eyes grew even more intense.

'*Why?*' he repeated.

'Hell if I know! Do you know why you want me?'

He thought about that for a moment. 'No. Definitely not.'

I tightened my hold on his neck. 'So maybe we should just try it and find out.'

His arms ensnared me, pulling me closer. 'Maybe.'

Our lips brushed tentatively, testing the waters. Oh, and what sweet waters they were. It felt like tasting the fountain of youth, with water from the fountain of unbridled lust mixed in. Our arms and hands were tightly around each other, refusing to let go, but even they didn't hold on as tightly as our eyes.

'You,' he informed me, a storm raging in those sea-coloured orbs of his, 'are a lecherous, wilful, undisciplined little wench with the mouth of a tavern girl!'

'And you,' I told him, 'are a miserly, chauvinistic bastard with a rock for a heart and a stone for a brain!'

There was a moment of silence – then our mouths clashed in a kiss so hard, so fast, that it would have caused a deadly accident on any road. It might still, here, in the middle of the jungle: with his arms tightly around me, I felt about ready to die and go to heaven. When we broke apart, we were both panting.

'There!' I smirked up at him. 'Does that feel like the mouth of a tavern girl?'

'I wouldn't know. When we get back to London, should I do some comparative research?'

'Don't you dare, you...you...!'

His mouth silenced me. And mine did the same to his. I had never before realised how wonderful silence could be. I had always felt the need to speak out, to make myself heard, but right then and there, in Mr Ambrose's arms, I wanted nothing but to silently sink into him. My shy fingers, exploring his chest, his back, the hard muscles of his arms, did all the talking that was needed without having to say a word.

One of my shy fingers, suddenly not so shy anymore, slipped into his tail-coat, traveling up the hard ridges of his abdomen, with only a thin shirt between us, and...

COMING FROM BEHIND

The muscles under my fingers jerked and petrified.

'Mr Linton!'

'What?' My lips teased the corner of his mouth. 'Is something the matter, Sir?'

'What is your hand doing down there?'

Catching one of the buttons of his shirt between two fingers, I started to twirl it around. 'Try to guess.'

'Mr Linton–!'

His voice broke off abruptly when I undid the button and slipped my hand inside.

'Mr Linton!'

'No, no,' I corrected him courteously. '*Miss*, remember? I'm a Miss. But you...' My eyes widened as my fingers explored farther down. 'You are "Mister" all right! Oh, yes, *quite definitely* Mister!'

'You little...!'

Suddenly, I was airborne, my hand ripped from his shirt, my feet off the ground. It took a moment for me to realise that Mr Ambrose had swept me up in his arms and was carrying me towards a giant of a tree, some of its gnarled old roots reaching as high as my knees. With the eye of a man who knew exactly what he wanted, he headed straight for the right root and set me down so my face was level with his. Grasping my face with both hands, he claimed my mouth with hungry ferocity.

'God!' he breathed against my lips. 'I have no idea why I am doing this. It is madness! It is waste and risk and irresponsibility – but I can't stop! I–cannot–stop!'

'Then don't!' I whispered. I didn't want to think about him stopping to kiss me now. I didn't want to think about him ever stopping.

Then something he had said earlier suddenly drifted back into my mind:

When we get back to London, should I do some comparative research?

When we get back to London...

I stiffened in his arms, averting my face when his lips tried to find mine again. Good God! Was I stupid enough for this to occur to me only now? Of course we couldn't keep doing this forever! Of course we would return to London, eventually! And of course we would be back in the office, where I would have to pretend to be a man. This thing...Whatever it was we had between us – would it have to stop when we returned to London? *Could* it stop? Could I?

Somehow, I doubted that jumping on Mr Ambrose and chewing on his lips would be compatible with my male disguise. If people found out – My aunt, my uncle, Ella...Oh God! Ella! She would die of guilt! She would think I had been seduced by a ruthless rake (never mind that it had actually been the other way around) and would torture herself for all eternity for not noticing earlier and putting a stop to it! And as for my friends, Flora, Eve and Patsy...

I swallowed, hard.

Patsy.

Oh dear.

Oh dear oh dear.

I remembered all too clearly the day when Patsy had attempted to hold a suffragist rally in Hyde Park, and had been steamrollered by Mr Rikkard Ambrose's icy eyes and masterful rhetoric. If Patsy found out that I had succumbed to Mr Ambrose's dubious charms...

Well, let's just put it this way: I had better quickly discover a way to survive a stab wound through the heart from a sharpened parasol.

And then, of course, even worse than Patsy, there was the one person who would probably be most horrified if the truth about me and Mr Rikkard Ambrose came to light: Mr Rikkard Ambrose. He had made no secret of his disdain for women, no secret of the fact that if I wanted to work for him, I had to do so disguised as a man. If I were revealed as a woman, and, moreover, a woman with whom he was having an illicit affair, the scandal would be so enormous it would fill the newspapers from London to Kuala Lumpur. My heart picked up the pace. The mere thought of his reaction...!

Taking a deep breath, I fought down the rising panic and got a grip on myself.

No need to fret, Lilly, I told myself. What happens in the jungle, stays in the jungle. Tropical trees and monkey dung are more than enough proof of that. You'll just have to hope that these unfeminist cravings you have are due to tropical fever and will vanish as soon as you set foot on good old English soil.

'What's the matter?' touching my cheek with a gentleness I would never have believed him capable of, Mr Ambrose lifted my face until my gaze met his.

'Nothing,' I told him. 'Kiss me!'

~~**~*~*

'Stop! We've arrived.'

Halting, I looked around. There was nothing but jungle to be seen. No sign of the landmark that was described in the manuscript. And it wasn't really the kind of landmark that could be overlooked.

'Are you sure, Sir?'

He gave me a level gaze.

Of course he was sure. He was Rikkard Ambrose.

'But how do you know? How do you know we've travelled ten miles along the river yet, as it says in the manuscript?'

'Because I counted my steps. A simple trick, if you can keep them steady and regular.'

Which he no doubt could. Regular as clockwork.

'Hm...' I gazed around, searching for the landmark. Oh dear. Maybe this was going to be a bit more difficult than I had imagined.

'You mentioned some kind of landmark earlier,' Karim said, with his customary atrocious timing. 'What is it, anyway?'

I cleared my throat. 'A mountain.'

There was a moment of silence. And, since it emanated from both Mr Ambrose and Karim, I hoped to hell it wasn't pregnant!

'Mr Linton,' my dear employer finally said, his voice cold and controlled, 'in case you have not noticed, we are surrounded by one-hundred-feet-tall trees on all sides. We cannot even see the ground a few yards away, let alone any mountains!'

'I noticed!' I snapped. 'I'm working on it! I'll find a solution!'

'Indeed?'

'Don't act so...so...ice-cold all-knowing arse-like! Do you have any ideas?'

He just looked at me. That cool, hard, look told me everything without words: he did not need to have ideas, because that's what he paid me for.

'We can always climb a tree,' Karim suggested.

'Oh yes?' I arched an eyebrow at him. 'And who would be crazy enough to climb one of those monstrosities?'

This time, it wasn't just one gaze I felt on me. It was two. And they were both extremely calculating.

'Oh no!' I took a step back. 'No, no, nonononono, no, *no*! Forget it! Never in this life or the next!'

~~**~*~*

'Bloody tyrannical, insufferable, domineering bastard!' My hand gripped the branch above me and I pulled myself up, just managing to keep a hold of the slippery, wet wood. 'Curse him to hell and back! *Bastardo! Avaro!*'

Accompanied by a cacophony of Portuguese and Spanish swear words, I slowly made my way up the tree. Now and again, an orangutan would watch me quizzically from a neighbouring tree, probably wondering what this hairless rat on two legs was doing up here. I was wondering the same thing myself.

'Are you there yet?' a familiar cool voice rose up to me from far below.

Halting for a moment, I looked up at the eighty feet or so of slippery tree above me. 'Not quite.'

'Well, get a move on! We don't have all day!'

Clenching my teeth, I bit back the selection of favourites from my collection of international curse words that I would have liked to hurl at him. 'Yes, Sir! Right away, Sir!'

'And don't fall off! A fall from this height would kill you, and I don't want to waste any time on a burial!'

'Very understandable, Sir. I will do my best to spare you the inconvenience...'

...you self-centred son of a bachelor!

I grabbed the next branch.

Do you want to know what was most annoying about all this? You might think that it was the fact that my chemise was torn in more places than I could count, or that I had leaves and twigs tangled everywhere in my hair, or even, oh, I don't know, the fact that I was hovering in a tree fifty yards above the ground, ready to fall to my death at any moment.

But no.

The most annoying thing about all of this was that, while I was climbing this thrice-blasted tree and *he* egged me on from below with his maddening little comments, all I really wanted to do was get down there and shut him up. With my lips.

Yes. That's how far I was gone. That bloody bastard was the one who had sent me up here in the first place, and all I wanted to do when I got down again was throw myself into his arms and kiss him senseless. Now, I ask you, is that a sensible feminist approach to things?

A monkey on the tree next to me offered his opinion on the matter, by turning its back on me and waggling its impressive red bottom in my face.

Even the monkeys thought I was pathetic. Fantastic!

After one hundred and twenty-one more branches, and three hundred seventy-two more are-you-there-yets, I was finally as high as I dared to go. The branch I was sitting on already creaked suspiciously under my generous derrière, and I had a suspicion that the branches farther up would be even less likely to approve of my favourite diet of solid chocolate.

From far below me, out of the nether regions where the devils of hell lived, came a cool voice: 'Are you there yet?'

I counted to ten, then decided even counting to a million wouldn't help to cool my temper down, and simply answered: 'Yes.'

'Adequate. Though you took your time about it! What do you see?'

For the first time since reaching the upper regions of the tree I looked around – and words failed me.

A steaming sea of green velvet stretched in front of me in all directions. We had chosen a tree for my little climbing exercise that was higher than all the others around it, and so I had an excellent view of what people called 'the jungle'. The word didn't do it justice. Something more was needed. Something chaotic and beautiful and infinitely large and breathtaking. A colourful bird rose above a tree in the distance, calling out over the jungle with a mournful cry that tugged at my heart. Far, far away in the distance I could see a sparkling band of water glittering between the majestic trees and–

'Mr Linton!'

–and I had better cut this description short if I wanted to keep my job.

'Yes, Sir! I'm working on it, Sir!'

Ordering my eyes to stop staring in wonder and get back to work, I started searching the distant horizon for a mountain. It didn't take me long. The peak rose high and solitary into the air, covered with luscious trees about halfway up its slopes, then slowly turning sparser until, at the very top, it revealed a jagged, bare stretch of rock. Pulling the compass Mr Ambrose had reluctantly entrusted to me out of its pouch, I let it snap open and levelled it at the distant crest.

'Mr Linton? What are you doing up there!'

'My work! Be quiet! That shouldn't be too difficult for you, now, should it?'

I watched as the compass needle teetered and finally came to a halt. I took a good, long look at the face of the instrument to make sure everything was in order, then nodded to myself.

'All right!' I called down. 'The mountain is to the west! Do you hear? We have to head westwards!'

'Adequate.'

Blast him! Would it kill him to say 'Good work' just once in his bloody life?

Yes, he'd probably choke on it.

'Now come down here Mr Linton, and stop wasting time! This isn't a sightseeing tour!'

'Yes, Sir! Right away, Sir!'

I tucked away the compass and was just about to start sliding down the tree again when something caught my eye. Some way off, in a patch of trees that wasn't quite as thick as the surrounding jungle, a scrap of colour flashed. Freezing, I looked closer. There was movement there. Movement and–

Oh dear.

'Um...Sir?'

'Don't waste time up there, Mr Linton! Get a move on!'

'I will, in a moment, Sir. Just one thing. What colour was the flag of the Brazilian Empire again?'

'Yellow and green, why?'

'Because then I think we have a problem.'

EXOTIC EXERTIONS

There was silence from the bottom of the tree for a moment, while I tried to follow the progress of the Brazilian soldiers through the thick foliage. Then:

'What kind of problem, Mr Linton?'

But I didn't answer. That was because, in another direction, I had caught sight of a different group of coloured specks, moving in the same direction. *Blast!*

'Mr Linton! What kind of problem?'

'The double kind!'

'What are you talking about?'

'Out of the way down there! Secretary incoming!'

As fast as I could, I slid down the trunk of the tree, not caring if I tore my chemise or even my hands. We had more important things on our hands than a little blood!

Karim had stepped well back – probably to avoid glimpsing up my fluttering undergown as I raced towards the ground. Mr Ambrose, however, had no such compunctions. He stood right where I had left him, his face like an ancient Mayan statue, his eyes flashing like icicles.

'Step back!' I yelled, hurtling towards the muddy ground.

He just gave me a look. He didn't even need to open his mouth, and I still understood: *Not a chance in hell!*

Just at the right moment, he stepped forward. His arms came up and closed, tightly. The impact knocked the breath out of me. For a moment, I thought I would have been better off landing in the mud than on his stone-hard form. But then we toppled over, rolling through leaves and over roots, until we finally came to a rest and I ended up, panting heavily, on top of his perfectly sculpted chest, my eyes staring into his, my lips only inches away from his mouth.

Correction: this was a million times better than the ground.

Bad Lilly! Bad! No time for that now! Tell him!

'Soldiers,' I panted, only able to get out the one word right then and there.

'What?'

'Soldiers, Sir! The Brazilian Army. And I think the rebels, too! They're after us, heading our way.'

I had never seen any man get out from under a girl so fast. Well, to be honest, I had never seen any man get out from under a girl at all, but I imagined that most would be pretty reluctant. Not Mr Ambrose. He was out from under me and up on his feet in half a second, leaving me lying in the dirt.

'What are you waiting for, Mr Linton? Up on your feet! Karim, get the horses and take Mr Linton's knapsack for now! We have to move fast!'

'I can bloody well carry my own knap-' I began, but cut off with a yelp when Mr Ambrose grabbed my hand and jerked me to my feet.

'Not now, Mr Linton! Karim, get moving! We're going west!'

~~**~*~*

We marched all day long, and I suspected we would have marched into the night as well, if there hadn't been the danger of getting hopelessly lost in the dark. Mr Ambrose, marching at the back, was like a hellhound on our heels, dictating a pace so gruelling I could almost smell the gruel in the air.

With every step I thanked God that I had thought of removing my corset a few days ago. I should have thought of that days earlier. The freedom of movement without the horrid thing was a blessed relief – or at least to me it was. To Mr Ambrose, whose eyes almost never left me – not so much. Without the tight corset, certain parts of my anatomy that had been constrained before were now, um...how should I put it delicately...? *Free to move.* Yes. Free to move. A movement which Mr Ambrose seemed to find quite fascinating.

By the end of a heavy day's marching, neither of us had enough stamina left to do much besides lie flat on the ground. But even so, the little noises he sometimes made when marching behind me, and the stares he gave me when we both lay in our hammocks, totally exhausted – they drove my blood to the boiling point and made me wish Captain Silveira and his merry men to the devil, along with their rebellious counterparts! No matter that Mr Ambrose remained absolutely silent. His eyes said more than a thousand indecent words.

We kept this up for five days. Five inconceivably long, endless, torturous days. Finally, I'd had enough.

'No more! I can't...! No more..!'

Panting, I fell to my knees in the mud. My hair was plastered to my face in a sweaty tangle. My chemise, once a pretty white, was now a wild mixture of greens and browns. My legs ached as if someone had shoved red hot irons up the soles of my feet, my chest was heaving, desperately seeking for air, and I was hardly able to keep my eyes open.

'Get up, Mr Linton!'

'Can't! Too...much!'

Marching around me, Mr Ambrose planted himself in front of me. 'We have to go on! We can't afford to stop now! If we don't manage to give them...the...slip...'

His voice slowly trailed off.

Raising my tired eyes, I glanced up at him and saw his eyes were fixed somewhat lower than my face, right about where my heaving chest was located.

'Mr Ambrose!'

'Hm?'

'If we don't manage to give them the slip?' I prompted.

'Ah. Yes. Of course.' He shook his head, and his eyes snapped back to my face where they belonged. 'If we don't manage to give them the slip before they catch sight of us, we're lost. If they've come this far to chase us, they won't give up now.'

I tried to rise to my feet – I really did! But to no avail. My legs would not cooperate.

'I'm sorry,' I panted. 'I...can't! I'm not used to this. I've never walked more than a stroll in the park now and again. This is too much.'

I waited for him to snap at me, to make some scathing remark about the weakness of women – but he didn't. Instead he did something that I would never, ever in a million, nine hundred ninety-nine thousand, nine hundred ninety-nine years have expected of him:

He bent down and picked me up.

Picked me up as if I were a feather.

Picked me up as if he were the hero of some cheap romance novel, and I the helpless heroine.

Ha! Fat chance!

'Put me down!' I demanded. 'Put me down this instant!'

He ignored me.

'Karim? You've been scouting ahead as usual, haven't you? Where's the nearest river?'

It took Karim a moment to react. He was too busy staring slack-jawed at his employer clutching a semi-dressed female in his arms.

'Err...um...yes, *Sahib*. Yes, definitely. About half a mile to the northeast.'

'All right. We'll have to try the same river trick to disguise our tracks, and hope that it works better than last time.' He glanced down at me, sharply. 'Can you hold on for that long, Mr Linton?'

'I could, but I won't! You can't carry me for half a mile! I should know – I have to carry myself around all day, every day! I'm damn heavy!'

Most men would have tried to deny it. Most men would have said something like 'Oh no, darling, you're as light as a feather!'

But this was Mr Rikkard Ambrose.

'I won't disagree with you there. What do you stuff yourself with to get like this?'

Did I have enough strength left to strangle him? My arms were already around his neck. It shouldn't take much energy to shift my hands a bit and squeeze. But then – if his neck was as hard as the rest of him, the actual throttling would probably be beyond my meagre strength.

'None of your business!' I growled. 'Now put me down! I'll hide in the bushes! Run! Take the manuscript and get out of here! I'll be all right on my own! I'll–'

I started to loosen my hold around his neck.

He moved so fast I didn't see it coming. One moment I was preparing to let go, determined not to be a millstone around his neck, not to hinder his escape – and the next he was kissing me, his lips fervent and unrelenting. All thought of letting go evaporated. Raising me up in his arms as high as I would go, he clutched me to his chest, kissing the breath out of me, devouring my mouth as if his life depended on tasting me.

When he finally broke away, my body had turned to goo in his arms, and my brain to molten mush. He gazed down at me, and I gazed back up, whatever protests I had been about to make before long vanished from my mind. His perfect, chiselled face was so close, his eyes incredibly dark and intense as they stared into mine.

'What were you saying?' he enquired, cocking his head.

I blinked. 'Wrgsfgl?'

'That sounds about right.' He tightened his grip on me. 'Hold on!' he commanded.

And what did I do?

I nodded like a good little damsel.

'Adequate. Let's go!'

And he marched off into the jungle, the helpless maiden tightly clutched in his arms.

God! If Patsy ever got wind of this, I was never going to live it down!

~~**~*~*

'That is it. We're safe.' Closing his eyes, Mr Ambrose sank against the tree behind him and let himself slide down onto the ground. 'Or at least as safe as we're going to get.'

'Err...good.' I cleared my throat. 'You can let go of me now.'

Yes, everyone, you heard correctly. I was *still* clutched in his arms. He had refused to set me down when we reached the river, wading through the current with me held tight as if it were nothing. Even when I had told him that I was fine now, that I'd rested enough and gotten my strength back, the damn man

165

wouldn't let go of me! Bloody chauvinistic, insufferable, arrogant son of a bachelor! How dare he treat me like some damsel in distress? How dare he care that much about me? How dare he look into my eyes like that and make me feel all warm and gooey inside? That was simply not fair!

Which reminded me...He still had his arms around me.

'I said,' I informed him once more, just in case he hadn't heard me the first thirty-seven times, 'let go. Now!'

'I heard,' he told me, his eyes still closed. It didn't show on his face, but carrying me had taken it out of him.

'Then why won't you let go?'

'Firstly,' he murmured, 'because you are my secretary, not the other way around. And I will never take orders from you.'

'And secondly?'

Slowly, his eyes drifted open – and my breath caught. I had been wrong before. Very wrong. The lazy look he was giving me through half-closed lids was anything but sleepy. It was ravenous.

'Because I don't want to,' he growled.

I swallowed.

'Why?'

Leaning forward, he slowly, casually brushed his lips against my cheek, then moved on to my throat, making me quiver. 'You have to ask that?' he whispered against my skin. 'After I've had you in my arms like this for hours upon hours, moving about, shifting against me in your shift, muttering no end of your little spikey complaints and shooting your tantalising, ear-burning insults at me, you ask why I can't let go?'

A noise erupted from the back of his throat that was like no other I had ever heard.

'Most men,' I whispered, 'wouldn't appreciate being insulted.'

His eyes, cold and hard as steel, met mine. 'Do I look like most men to you?'

'No,' I admitted.

Still clutching me in his arms, he rose to his feet, moving slowly and powerfully. His face was only inches away from mine now, his gaze holding me captive as surely as if he had me in iron fetters. Carefully, he set me down on my feet. But he didn't let go of me. His hands clutched my face as if it were the most precious gem in the world and he had acquired the exclusive mining rights for a hundred miles in either direction.

'Mr Linton– Lillian...'

The sound of my name on his lips was a shock to me. I tried to remember whether he had ever said it before, but couldn't. Maybe once or twice, when he hadn't been completely in his right mind. Was he in his right mind now?

Bloody hell, who cares if he's in his left, bottom or upper one? Grab the chance by the balls, Lilly!

I licked my lips.

'Yes, Sir?'

'Don't ever ask me to leave you behind again!' Pressing his eyes tightly shut, he leaned forward until his rock-hard forehead rested against mine. 'Do you hear me? *Not. Ever.*'

'Y-yes, Sir.'

'I'm not wasting money on an advertisement for a new secretary.'

'No, Sir. Of course not, Sir.'

'And I need you because you are the one who deciphered that damn manuscript.'

'Certainly, Sir. Just as you say, Sir.'

'And...and I need you because...because...'

He opened his mouth – then closed it again. Then opened it once more.

'Yes, Sir?' I enquired, my voice hardly more than a whisper.

His only answer was a tortured growl. A millisecond later, his lips came crashing down, making his point more clearly than the world's most eloquent speech. Pushing me back up against the tree he claimed me, devoured me like a raptor its prey. The exhaustion of the last few days fell off me like dust, shaken from my shoulders. My arms snaked up around his neck, pulling myself against him, hard.

Last time had been too sweet, too gentle to fully appreciate it. But now, with our passions unleashed and burning like the stallions of the sun god before the fall of Icarus, I couldn't help but notice what a difference the missing corset made. Where before there had been a thick, stiff wall between me and Mr Ambrose, there was now next to nothing between my soft spots and the hard lines of his body. A faint, faraway part of my mind noted that it should have been uncomfortable. After all, hard bunks were uncomfortable, right? Hard floors, too. And the body of Rikkard Ambrose was harder than both put together. So it should have been uncomfortable.

Emphasis on 'should'.

His body was the hammer to my anvil. With every skilful strike of his tongue, every blow delivered by his lips, the passion between us was forged more tightly, connecting us in ways I could never have imagined. My hands, exploring his arms, his chest, his everything were desperately trying to shove him far enough away to remove the barrier of his clothes, and at the same time desperate to pull him closer, pull him against me, into me, until the distinction between our bodies vanished and we became one.

It was more than lust or desire, more even than need. Knowing that this hard, implacable man would never leave me behind, would stand between me and any danger that threatened sent an (entirely unfeminist, but *blast*, nonetheless searing hot) thrill through me. He cared! He cared enough to pick me up and carry me when I needed help, and to set me down on my feet again when I was ready. Not that I approved, of course! I could take care of myself, thank you very much, and I would whack him over the head if he ever tried to do anything like that again. But somehow, right now, I didn't want to whack him over the head at all. Quite the contrary, in fact.

My hand slammed against his top hat, sending it sailing into the bushes.

'What are you doing, Mr Linton?' he demanded against my mouth, his muscles mashing into me.

'Removing the non-essentials!' I panted. 'Clothes! Off! Now!'

He froze.

'Mr Linton...I don't think...'

'Admirable!' Grasping the topmost of his buttons, I slipped it through its hole. 'Not thinking is exactly the thing to do right now!'

'Mr Linton! If we go on now...I don't know whether I will be able to stop myself before...before...'

'Don't worry, I will! Is a knee to the groin all right as a stop signal, or is that too subtle for you?'

All the answer I got was another growl as he claimed my mouth again.

Oh, well, a girl always has to do the hard work herself, it seems. Throwing myself into the kiss, I let my hand slip down his chest, searching for the next button.

My fingers were halted in mid-movement by a metallic *click*. It took me a moment to realise why that sound was so familiar. Then I remembered. I had heard a sound very much like it before – whenever Mr Ambrose cocked his gun. But...both of Mr Ambrose's hands were very much occupied right now.

I froze.

'Well, well,' came a slightly accented voice from beside me. 'What do we have here?'

Brazilian Standoff

My eyes had slid half-shut during the last few minutes of passion. Now, I opened them very slowly and carefully. The first thing I saw was Mr Ambrose, standing even stiller than me, like a statue hewn from bedrock. The second thing I saw was the gun pressed to his head.

'Did you really think,' came the voice of Lieutenant Louis de Alvarez, 'that we would let a treasure like the one you are after slip through our fingers? Oh no. War is a costly business, my friend. Now, hands up, both of you! And don't try any tricks!'

We both followed the order with reluctance. Cautiously peeking past my raised hands, I let my eyes wander from the pistol, along the arm that held it to the figure of Lieutenant de Alvarez. The little man didn't look particularly impressive next to Mr Ambrose, but his gun was loaded and his arm perfectly steady. That more than made up for his diminutive size.

He smirked. 'We had the chance to study that manuscript of yours a little before you managed to escape. What a marvellous thing you've discovered there, my friend! And do you know what?'

Mr Ambrose's mouth was the thinnest of thin lines. 'No. What?'

'We came to the conclusion that we can make much better use of the gold than you greedy Englishmen. So, hand over the manuscript now, and you'll have the thanks of the Piratini Republic.'

To judge by the look on Mr Ambrose's face, he cared as much for the thanks of the Piratini Republic as for mashed snails in garlic sauce.

'And if I don't?'

'Then you'll have a bullet in your brain. Or maybe, I should put one into the head of this lovely young lady here instead?'

'Please do. Her head is worth much less than mine.'

I bridled at his words. I knew of course that downplaying my importance was the wisest course of action to take, that the less important Mr Ambrose made me out to be, the safer I would be. But he didn't have to sound so bloody convincing, damn him!

'Hm...' The lieutenant was stroking his chin thoughtfully, his eyes wandering between me and Mr Ambrose. 'We shall see. No matter what, we shall find a use for her.' His arm still rock-steady, he gave a mocking little bow to me. 'My apologies, by the way, for our inefficient torture methods, *Senhora*. If we had understood the reality behind the mask, I'm sure we would have found something more appropriate to a member of the fairer sex.'

His eyes drifted over me, leaving little doubt about the meaning of his words. From behind him, raucous laughter drifted towards me, and for the first time I realised that he was not alone. Shadows were shifting under the trees, moving steadily towards us. It looked like he had brought a whole squadron along with him.

'Don't worry, Lieutenant,' I assured him. 'I won't hold your negligence against you. In fact, I wouldn't mind you being negligent again.'

'That is extremely unlikely, *Senhora*. But enough of these pleasantries.' He pressed the gun more tightly against Mr Ambrose's temple. 'The manuscript! Now, if you please!'

'*Como interessante*, Lieutenant,' came a voice from further back out of the darkness of the jungle. 'That was just what I was going to say.'

There were more clicks of weapons, and out of the shadows of the trees stepped Colonel Alberto Silveira, rifle raised and aimed straight at the lieutenant's head.

'Hands up!'

'Um...I already have my hands up,' I pointed out.

'Not you! Him!' The army colonel jerked his rifle towards de Alvarez. The man hesitated for just a moment – then dropped his gun with a low curse and raised his hands over his head.

'What's your name?' Silveira demanded.

'De Alvarez, you imperialist scum!'

'Ha! I've heard of you! Wait till the general hears of this. I was only reckoning with the treasure. If I can bag you rebel vermin into the bargain, there'll be a promotion in this for me.'

The only reply to this was an intelligible string of Portuguese profanities. I listened with interest. If I survived this, my vocabulary would be considerably extended.

The colonel did not seem impressed by de Alvarez's tirade, however. His rifle remained steady on the rebel commander. 'Shut up, you filthy dog! And as for you...'

The colonel's eyes drifted to Mr Ambrose. 'Under different circumstances I might drag you back to headquarters and teach you the error of your ways. Someone has to show you that you cannot simply march into a war zone without suffering the consequences. But I'll have my hands full with this lot, so you and your lady will be getting off lightly. Leave Brazil, and you won't hear from me again. But the Brazilian Empire is confiscating that manuscript. We can't have it falling into the wrong hands, now, can we?'

Mr Ambrose met the colonel's eyes. It was hard to say whose gaze was further below the freezing point. 'No,' Mr Ambrose agreed. 'We can't have that.'

In a flash, his hands darted to his belt, and before either of the officers could move, the muzzles of two shining steel revolvers pointed in their faces. Shouts rose from all around us, and rustling broke out in the shadows as dozens of soldiers started to raise their weapons.

'Nobody move!' Mr Ambrose's command cut through the air with the mastery of a dozen field generals. 'One twitch means two bullets in the head! Understood?'

The shapes in the shadows froze, unsure what to do. But if they were taken aback by the new development, it was nothing to how Colonel Silveira seemed to feel. He gaped at Mr Ambrose. 'I just saved your life!'

'And you have my sincerest thanks,' my dear employer told him without shifting his gun an inch from the man's forehead. 'We'll chalk it up against the torture and imprisonment, and call us even. Now, drop the rifle and put your hands in the air. This is your last warning.'

Silveira wavered. He was clearly contemplating trying to sweep the rifle around and shoot down this arrogant Englishman who dared to threaten him like a dog. After all, who was he? Just some big city boy who had gotten mixed up in a matter far, far too big for him. Those were the thoughts clear on Silveira's face – until he met Mr Ambrose's eyes.

'Don't.'

It was just one word, but whispered with such ice-cold menace, it made me shiver. If Mr Ambrose ever pointed a gun at me with that look in his eyes, I didn't know what I'd do. But I probably wouldn't survive.

The rifle hit the ground with a wet *thud*.

Mr Ambrose inclined his head. 'Acceptable.'

'This doesn't mean anything!' Silveira hissed. 'My men outnumber you a hundred to one! Do you honestly believe the two of you are going to get out of here alive?'

'No, not the two of us. But the *three* of us – yes. Karim?'

The last word was a shout over the heads of the soldiers. From somewhere up in the trees came a metallic click, and an answering shout.

'Yes, *Sahib*?'

'Tell our good friend the colonel here what you have up there in the tree with you.'

'As you wish, *Sahib*. I have with me one of your engineers' experimental weapon models, a mechanised gun that can fire several shots per second – without requiring reloading, I might add. Some use the term "machine gun" for this new invention. It seems to be the pet project of the British and American armies, but I doubt the Brazilian Empire has got its hands on one of them yet.'

With every word, the face of the colonel grew paler.

'A bluff!' he hissed. 'This is just a bl–'

Before he could finish the word, an ear-splitting roar cut the night in two. Lightning lit up the trees around, and the muddy ground at our feet spewed upwards, spattering us with dirt and shredded foliage.

Mr Ambrose cocked his head.

'A bluff?'

Colonel Silveira swallowed. 'All right. Maybe...not.'

'I am so very pleased that you agree with me, Colonel. Now – tell your men to throw away their weapons, grab some rope and tie up the rebels!'

'What?' Lieutenant de Alvarez demanded. 'You can't–'

'Except,' Mr Ambrose cut him off, 'for one, who will then take the rest of the rope and tie up all the imperial soldiers.'

'What?' Colonel Silveira exclaimed.

'I thought I spoke perfectly clearly. But if you wish–' Shifting, Mr Ambrose pressed the barrels of his guns against the two men's heads more tightly. '–I can let my two metal associates speak for me.'

'N-no! No need for that. Men, do as he says!'

It all went surprisingly smoothly. I watched, open-mouthed, as enemy soldiers disarmed each other and pulled out coils of rope to tie rebel to imperial and imperial to rebel. Mr Ambrose watched like a hawk, making sure everything went exactly as he had commanded. I had to admire his ingenuity. With only enemies binding each other, it was ensured that nobody would tie a knot too loosely. In the end, all except the officers and one more man were tied up in an impenetrable tangle of ropes.

'Kneel!' Mr Ambrose commanded.

The man did as ordered.

'Now cross your arms behind your back! Mr Linton?'

The call of my name pulled me from the amazed paralysis.

'Y-yes, Sir?'

'Tie his hands behind his back. And don't be afraid to tie the knots too tightly.'

He didn't have to tell me that twice – or once, for that matter. By the time I was finished with the poor man, he was tied up more tightly than a parcel on its way to Australia.

'Karim!' Mr Ambrose called.

'Coming, *Sahib*!'

With an earth-shaking *thud*, the Mohammedan dropped out of a nearby tree, a metal monstrosity clutched under one arm that I assumed was the so-called machine gun. For a moment, I wondered where in hell he had kept this thing hidden before – then I remembered some rather large packages on the back of his packhorse. Of course. Only...there had been more than one such package. What might the others contain?

Mr Ambrose didn't leave me any time to ponder the question further.

'Karim, tie up these two gentlemen here,' he commanded, nodding to the officers.

'I'm an officer of the Brazilian Empire!' Silveira sputtered. 'You can't–'

'And knock them unconscious, for good measure,' Mr Ambrose added.

Silveira shut up.

'And me?' I asked.

'You, Mr Linton, pack everything up and ready the horses. We're leaving.'

I was too busy with my own hasty work after that to pay attention to what Mr Ambrose or Karim were doing. But once I had the horses packed and ready to depart, I glanced back at our former campsite, and saw de Alvarez and Silveira bound up along with their men, glowering fiercely up at Mr Ambrose. Karim stepped behind them, raising the butt of his rifle.

'Not yet,' Mr Ambrose ordered, freezing him in place. 'I have something to say to our two friends yet.'

Kneeling on the ground so he was on eye-level with the two of them. His eyes, already cold before, took on that same merciless look he had had when holding the guns to their heads. I shivered – partly with instinctive trepidation, but far more with anticipation. I couldn't wait to have those dangerous eyes on me again.

'My business,' he told them, his voice coming straight from Antarctica, 'is not your business. And yet you chose to interfere. Be thankful that I am leaving you alive. Others have not been so lucky.'

'You *bastardo*!' de Alvarez growled. 'You will pay for this!'

'I doubt it,' Mr Ambrose retorted, letting his gaze wander over the officers. 'I never pay for goods of substandard quality.'

'You...!'

The officer didn't get out anything more. He seemed to choke on his own indignation, and his nemesis tied up right next to him didn't appear to fare any better.

'I would advise you,' Mr Ambrose continued as if they hadn't spoken, 'not to follow us. Where we are going, there is no place for people like you. The treasure is mine! All mine! And if my man Karim catches so much of a glimpse of any of you, he will not hesitate to use that metal instrument he is caressing so fondly. Do we understand each other?'

The two officers remained silent.

'Adequate.' Mr Ambrose rose to his feet. 'I will have to hope that you use your heads and heed my warning. Oh, and I almost forgot–'

He reached into his pocket with one hand. When he drew it out again, he a held long, shining steel blade. De Alvarez and Silveira shrank back, for the first time since they had been disarmed real fear showing in their eyes.

'Oh, don't be afraid. This isn't for you.' Stepping up to a falling tree trunk nearby, Mr Ambrose placed the shiny dagger on top of it, and let it lie there. 'Or I suppose it is, in a way. After all, we wouldn't want you all to starve to death in the jungle, would we? No, I hope you die much more unpleasant deaths. So I am going to leave this here with you. Once we are gone, you may try to reach it. Whoever gets to it first, rebel or imperial, can cut his bond. And whoever is free first, with a knife in his hand...'

He let his gaze wander over his wide-eyed audience. Something much too cold to be a smile tugged at the corner of his mouth for a millisecond.

'Well, I'm sure I won't have to explain that part to you.'

Without another word, he turned, grabbed the reins of his horse and marched off into the jungle.

'Come on, Karim, Mr Linton!' he called. 'Time to go and leave these gentlemen to their business!'

SOMETHING GOES 'BANG' IN THE NIGHT

We didn't try the river trick again. Since it had not worked twice in a row now, it was clear that the Brazilians, imperialists and rebels both, had excellent trackers among them. Instead, we marched as hard and as fast as we could, and hoped that Mr Ambrose's threats were enough to deter them. They certainly would have been if I'd been the one following.

Still...I did wonder why Mr Ambrose hadn't employed a simpler method of preventing trouble. A method that, usually, he didn't seem averse to using.

'Why didn't you do it?' I demanded, once we were well out of hearing range of our enemies.

'Do what, Mr Linton?'

'Kill them, of course! You could have, after all, easily. They were bound and at your mercy, which we both know is not very considerable. So why did you spare them? You didn't have any qualms about disposing of the pirates.'

'I have business interests in Brazil. I didn't think the Brazilian government would look kindly on my shooting one of its officers, even if that officer is a worthless, greedy worm.'

'And the rebels? You could have shot the rebels.'

'I could have.' He gave me a look. The kind of look that Julius Caesar probably gave his slow-witted little centurions before he explained why he wanted to invade Gaul. 'But if I leave them both alive, maybe we'll be lucky and they'll kill each other.'

I remembered the gleaming blade Mr Ambrose had left behind at our former campsite, and the greedy gazes of the tied-up soldiers. If they did indeed kill each other, it would have little or nothing to do with luck.

We continued through the jungle, keeping up not quite as gruelling a pace as before, but still, it was pure torture for my poor legs. For hours upon hours filled with ceaseless marching, I craved nothing so much as a soft bed to lie on, and three pounds of solid chocolate to forget my aches – at least at first. After a few days, very slowly, a change set in. My legs ached less and less. My behind, which had felt like the dead weight of a mammoth dragging behind me, somehow got...lighter. My steps grew steadier. Only my craving for solid chocolate stayed. But it wasn't nearly as bad as another craving.

'Come here!'

'You are my subordinate, Mr Linton! You cannot give orders to– mmmmph!'

'In case you hadn't noticed before,' I whispered against his smooth lips, 'I like breaking rules.'

'You don't say.'

'Oh yes, indeed, Sir! Now shut up and kiss me!'

We were camping next to a big tree that bore some kind of big, reddish fruit. It smelled invitingly tasty, but Karim had strongly advised against trying it. That wouldn't have stopped me – I wasn't big on following men's advice – but I had my very own forbidden fruit lying right here on the ground beside me, and it was a lot tastier.

'Mr Ambrose, Sir?' Running my nose along the line of his jaw, I breathed in his scent of man, money and power, and felt his hard body quiver beneath me.

'Yes, Mr Linton?'

'Why don't you relax a bit? It's hot here in the jungle. Why don't you take off a few of those stuffy clothes?'

He met my gaze with a cool one of his own. 'Because I'm English.'

'I'm English, too,' I pointed out.

Slowly and lingeringly, Mr Ambrose let his gaze rake over me, from my messy hair down over my torn, threadbare chemise and bare legs to my feet, encased in massive boots. 'Yes, and I'm sure that Nelson and Wellington are turning over in their graves at the fact.'

'What is *that* supposed to mean?'

Grabbing my face with masterful hands, Mr Ambrose pulled me towards him and claimed my mouth with his.

'Try to guess, you wicked little wench!'

I captured his lower lip between my teeth and bit, gently. 'So, I'm your wicked little wench now?'

'You are my little *Ifrit*!'

Warmth flooded my chest, stoking a fire in my heart. Blimey! This seemed to happen more and more often lately. How was it possible that no matter how coldly that man stared at me, it made me heat up inside like a bloody furnace? And every time he used that word, that damn word starting with 'I' that should have been an insult, I felt as if I could fly on fiery wings!

'So?' I whispered, teasing the corner of his mouth with little kisses. 'Are you going to take off that tailcoat, or will I have to burn through it with my fire?'

He groaned beneath me. 'Damn you! A part of me actually believes you could!'

'Out of that tailcoat, Mr Ambrose, Sir! Now!'

'No.'

Growling with frustration, I reared up above him. 'What the hell is the matter? Why won't you...'

My voice trailed off. It wasn't very easy to see anything in the deep shadows of the trees, and it was a task for a clairvoyant with a bloody great telescope to find any expression on the face of Mr Rikkard Ambrose at the best of times, but...

I narrowed my eyes as I knelt there, staring down at him. Then, slowly, very slowly, a smile spread across my face.

'Do you want to know what I think?'

'No. Definitely not.'

'Well, I'm going to tell you anyway.' My smile widened. 'I think you're shy.'

The look he sent back up at me could have introduced a new ice age.

'*Shy?*'

The word was a whisper as sweet as snake's venom.

'Don't get me wrong,' I hurriedly assured him, patting his cheek. 'I think it's very sweet, in a way. I mean, you told me I am your first. But I guess I didn't realize what that meant before. It mustn't be easy for a young, innocent virgin like yourself to trust yourself so completely to someone else for the first time, to put aside all the secret fears about your inadequacies that you've harboured for years and to–'

I didn't get any further than that because I was tossed through the air, rolled around like a rollicking roulade and suddenly found myself pressed against the forest floor with one hundred and seventy pounds of man-muscle pressing into me.

'*Shy?*' an arctic voice hissed at my ear. 'How shy is *this*?'

His hands found their way into my chemise.

'I...oh...I...'

'Tell me,' he rasped, his hands playing me like a fiery instrument, 'what inadequacies of mine were you speaking of exactly?'

'Um...well...I...'

I was sure there were at least three dozen, but right now I couldn't seem to remember. The fireworks going off in my head were too distracting.

'Am I too rich for you? Too powerful? Too strong?'

'N-no...I...'

Underneath the chemise, his fingers found their way to my back, stroking down my spine from the top to the literal bottom. I almost bit my tongue off trying not to moan.

'Am I too beautiful? Too hard? Too perfect?'

With all my might, I tried to gather my scattered wits.

'You're a ch-chauvi...' I muttered, 'chauvinist...'

He just laughed a deep, masculine arrogant laugh that only made me crave him more. Damn him!

'True,' his lips whispered against my skin. 'I do believe that men are stronger than women.' In a lightning-fast move, his hands shot out, capturing my arms at either side of me by the wrists. In just an instant he had them pinned to the ground so I was spread out underneath him, helpless and trembling with need. 'Can you honestly disagree?'

Oh yes, I could! Of course I could! And I would, as soon as I could remember the appropriate arguments and convince my tongue to speak. At the moment, the stubborn thing seemed to be interested in doing one thing, and one thing only.

~~**~*~*

It took me till next morning to remember my feminist principles. But when I saw Mr Ambrose checking and cleaning his gun, a familiar spark of rebellion lit up inside me.

'Why don't I have one of those?' I demanded.

He looked up, his hands freezing.

'Because you are a girl, Mr Linton,' he said and continued with his inspection.

'You know, for saying a sentence like that you should really have your head examined!'

'Indeed?'

'Oh yes, indeed! And not just because you used the words "girl" and "mister" to refer to the same person. We are only three out here in the jungle, and the rebels and imperials might very well still be on our trail! Don't you think it might be better if we had three people with guns instead of just two?'

This time he didn't even bother to look up. 'No. Not if the third doesn't know how to shoot.'

'Then *teach* me how to shoot!'

The sentence hung in the air, heavy with promise.

Teach me how to shoot.

Guns equalled power. A *man's* power. Men could carry guns with them wherever they pleased, could demand satisfaction from anybody and shoot them down in a duel. A lady would fall into disgrace if she even so much as held a pistol. Images I had often dreamt of, but never really dared hope for, suddenly flared in front of my inner eye: me, riding on horseback in a hunting party, a rifle slung across my shoulder. Me, standing across from a man who had dared to threaten my family, raising my pistol. Me, in glorious triumph, standing over–

'No.'

That one word cruelly shattered my nicely bloody dreams. I glared at the stone statue still checking his gun with precision.

'Why not?' I demanded – although I knew the answer before the question was out of my mouth.

'Because you are a girl.'

'And you are a stubborn, chauvinistic son of a bachelor!'

'Thank you for the compliment, Mr Linton.'

He snapped the gun shut with a sharp click and put it away.

'Come on!' I pleaded, knowing that I sounded like I was whining, and not caring. 'It's not as if we're hard pressed for ammunition, is it? We took the Brazilians' weapons, packhorses and bullets. We could shoot down every monkey in this jungle and still have enough bullets left to stage a coup in Rio de Janeiro!'

'Which we are *not* going to do, Mr Linton.'

Placing one hand over my heart, I raised the other in the air. 'If you teach me to shoot, I swear I will abandon all revolutionary ambitions. I'll also promise to never use my newly acquired skills to try and shoot you.'

He cocked his head, giving me a long, long look. 'The fact that you would have to promise that does not exactly raise my confidence in you, Mr Linton.'

'Is that a yes?'

'No. It's a no.'

'But—'

He raised a warning finger, cutting me off in mid-protest. 'No argument, Mr Linton!'

And I didn't argue.

Instead, I practised patience until we camped that night and the sun had set, snuck up to the packhorses and pinched a gun. It was a bloody big thing, and heavy. It didn't have that nice revolving cylinder with the seven bullets that was the prime feature of Mr Ambrose's guns. But it was a gun. I took it off into the jungle until I found a nasty-looking yellow-orange plant that seemed shootworthy and took aim.

Now...breathe deeply. Raise your arm and keep it steady. You've seen men do this, right? So it can't be that difficult.

My eyes zeroed in over the barrel on a poisonous-looking bloom. Holding my breath, I took aim, crooked my finger around the trigger and...

Click.

Hey...Wait just a moment! *Click?* That wasn't right! It was supposed to go *kaboom!*

I shook the gun. Maybe it was a bit stubborn? Well, there was nothing for it but trying again.

Click. Click. Cli–

'I took out the bullets, Mr Linton.'

The voice from behind me came so suddenly, I whirled around instinctively, raised the gun, and–

Click!

'And well I did,' Mr Ambrose said with dangerous calm, 'or my head would be a collection of bloody splatters on the tree behind me right now.'

'Oh. Um...oops. Sorry about that.' My ears started to burn. But then his first words registered. 'Wait a minute – you did *what?*'

'I took the bullets out of all the guns we acquired. Or, to be more precise, I had Karim do it. I knew that sooner or later you would try to sneak off to blow up some innocent tree. I know you.'

'If you know me,' I said sweetly, stepping towards him, clutching the gun like a cudgel, 'do you know what I would like to do to you right now?'

'If I would hazard a guess, I would say it involves inappropriate violence.'

'Violence? Oh yes, it does! But inappropriate? I beg to differ!'

My fist lunged forward, still clutching the gun. Before it even got near that too-damn-perfect face of his and had a chance of leaving a nice scar, his hand shot up and closed around my wrist. I might as well have been clapped in irons.

'Why do you insist on this?' His voice was fierce, his eyes glinting in the dark. 'Don't you think I'll keep you safe?'

'That's not the point!' I growled, punching his chest with my free hand. It was like punching a rock. He didn't even flinch. 'I have to be able to defend myself!'

'Why?'

'*Why?* What sort of question is that?'

'The kind I would appreciate an answer to.'

'Because...because I want to be independent! I have to be able to stand on my own two feet!'

'And what,' he growled, leaning down towards me, his hard chest pressing deliciously into me, 'if I don't want you to stand on your feet?' His foot shot forward, and in one swift move he had tugged my legs out from under me. I fell back with a yelp and landed in his arms. They held me. Hard. Hot. Close. 'What if I want you like this?'

'Too bad! Then you're out of luck, Sir!'

'Really?' He lowered his face until I could feel his breath on my face, caressing my skin. And my heart, the traitorous bloody organ, nearly jumped out of my chest with joy at the proximity! 'I'm feeling lucky tonight.'

And his lips came crashing down on mine.

I didn't think about guns again that night – but there definitely were a lot of explosions going off, trust me.

SNEAKY STUDIES

For the next few days, Mr Ambrose kept me much too busy to think of a new plan. He used me as his personal monkey, sending me up jungle trees at regular intervals to check our course and see if we were being followed. But, after a few days, he seemed content that I had given up, and let up on me a little.

Big mistake.

I had thought long and hard about how to achieve my goal, and finally had come up with a plan that I knew could not fail. I broached the topic one morning while we sat in a circle, consuming our meagre breakfast.

'Mr Ambrose?'

'Yes, Mr Linton?'

'I was thinking...'

'How unfortunate.'

'I was thinking that maybe now would be a good time to start teaching me how to shoot. Have you changed your mind?'

That was about as sensible a question as asking a warthog if it planned on becoming a fairy in its future career, and the answer came quickly, as expected.

'No. Be silent.'

But that was only the first part of my plan. The real fun was just about to start. Ignoring Mr Ambrose, I conjured up a smile on my face and turned to the only other person in the camp.

'Karim?'

Startled, the bodyguard glanced up at me, the look on his face supremely disdainful with a hint of surprise mixed in, like a vestal virgin propositioned by a common plebeian. (Except for the gigantic beard and sabre, of course.)

'Yes?'

'Will *you* teach me how to shoot?'

Karim raised his chin. 'I walk on the path of righteousness! Nothing you can say could induce me to teach anything to a creature like you.'

'Is that so? Well, in that case...' Hopping to my feet, I skipped over to him, and before he could draw away, whispered something in his ear. Under his tan and beard, the Mohammedan went pale.

'You wouldn't! Not even a creature such as you...'

I gave him a charming smile. 'Worse than an *ifrit*, remember? So, what do you say?'

For a moment, just a moment, a titanic struggle took place on the poor man's face – then his shoulders sagged.

'I shall teach you.'

'*What?*' Mr Ambrose's voice was as sharp as a razor. 'You most certainly shall not!'

The bodyguard half-turned towards Mr Ambrose and bowed, his expression mournful. 'Pardon me, *Sahib*. But in this case, I will have to follow this creature's orders over yours.'

For one instant, one brief moment of bliss, I actually saw the expression of surprise cross Mr Ambrose's face. '*What did you just say?*'

'It is so, *Sahib*. The intrigues of this evil creature are too powerful for me to resist. I pray you excuse me now, *Sahib*. I have to go contemplate my future sins.'

And he marched off into the jungle with a mournful expression on his face.

Slowly, Mr Ambrose turned to me, his eyes flashing. 'What did you say to him?'

'I threatened to take the rest of my clothes off if he didn't comply,' I told him, grinning from ear to ear. 'Spiffing idea, don't you think?'

From the non-expression on his face, I gathered he didn't share my opinion in that regard.

'Well...' Sighing, I got to my feet. 'I suppose I'd better go after him and start my lesson. Will you let me have a loaded gun, or will I have to threaten poor Karim further to get one out of him?'

He didn't answer.

'All right, if that's how you want it...'

Shrugging, I started to move away – and jerked to a sudden stop when his hand shot out, closing around my wrist like an iron vice.

'*I will teach you.*'

I tried to tug free – then the words he had just spoken arrived in my brain.

'What did you just say?'

Slowly, he raised his gaze to mine, spearing me with two sharp, dark icicles. 'I said *I will teach you.*'

I blinked at him, confused.

'But a moment ago...'

'That was then. Now is now.'

'But Karim–'

'Forget about Karim!' Coming to his feet, he tightened his grip and towed me away into the jungle. 'Your lesson is about to start. Come along, before you strip naked and start swinging from tree to tree with the monkeys!'

~~**~*~*

Bam!

'No, no, no! You have to hold your arms like *this*, and stand like *this*.'

'I'll look bloody ridiculous!'

'You will also be able to shoot straighter. And in any case, with your current attire, it will be extremely hard to look any more ridiculous than you already do.'

My eyes narrowed, but I didn't turn around to give him a good kick. Instead, I kept my target in my sights – a slim tree, a dozen or so yards away.

'Oh, so you think I look ridiculous, Sir, do you?'

'Your attire is certainly not suitable for polite company.'

Stepping back without looking, I brushed up against him. 'And what about not-so-polite company?'

There was a strangled noise from behind me. Smiling, I took aim at the tree.

Bang!

Splinters and wet bits of leaves erupted from a bush to its left.

'Damn!'

'You still don't have the right stance, Mr Linton. Here, let me show you.'

I felt him step closer, and his arms came up around me from behind.

Oh dear God...! That feeling! Hard muscles pressing into me, pulling me where they wanted me to go...

'Now concentrate. Hold your breath.'

His pectorals pressing against my back, flexing tantalisingly with every minute shift...

My breathing sped up.

'I said hold your breath, not hyperventilate!'

'Yes, Sir! Sorry, Sir!'

Gathering all my willpower, I clamped my mouth shut tightly.

'Now, concentrate! Hold steady, and think only of your target. Think only of what you want!'

Oh, I know exactly what I want right now...

Bam!

'Missed again!' He sounded exceedingly displeased. 'What is the matter with you, Mr Linton?'

~~**~*~*

Lessons with Mr Ambrose didn't go well. Whenever he got near me to show me things, my hands seemed to get shaky and I started to miss targets a lot. It was probably my instinctive urge to turn around and shoot him in the backside, I assumed. Hopefully, it would lessen with time.

Oh really? You think that's what it is? So, it has nothing to do with the fact that your heart starts racing every time he gets close to you? Nothing to do with the fact that every time he touches you, you crave not his death, but the little death?[16]

Well, yes, there might be a tiny little bit of truth to that. Blast!

And the worst thing was that Mr Ambrose was infuriatingly, masculinely smug about it all. Every time I missed he gave me a cool, superior look that, while perfectly unemotional, somehow managed to purvey his belief of the utter and unchallengeable superiority of the male gender over the female one in general, and of him over me in particular.

Finally, I decided I'd had enough! If my silly little heart was going to start acting up every time I was in his vicinity, I would just have to train alone! That very night (making sure that this time, nobody followed me) I pinched a gun from our considerable supply and snuck off into the jungle. Ha! I couldn't wait to see Mr Ambrose's face when I suddenly turned out to be a master marksman!

On my regular nocturnal trips, I had to walk quite a way into the jungle to prevent the shots from being heard back in the camp. Luckily, the racket of the jungle drowned out any other sounds, and the thick trees kept anyone from seeing the light of my little lamp. Mr Ambrose tersely remarked on my tired eyes and slow pace during the day, but that was all anybody noticed.

Thus we moved on, farther and farther westwards. We were almost certain by now that the Brazilians had decided to turn around and leave us alone. I was getting a bit annoyed that Mr Ambrose was still making me shimmy up tropical trees on a regular basis, since it clearly wasn't necessary anymore.

Or at least that's what I thought until *that day.*

It was a routine climb like any other day. (Which goes to show how far Mr Ambrose had knocked me off course. For goodness' sake, I thought of climbing up a tree in the middle of the jungle dressed only in my underwear as 'normal'!) Almost bored, I let my eyes drift over the steaming landscape beneath me, wisps of hot fog drifting past me. I was just about to give it up and slide down the tree again when I saw something glint in the distance.

I froze.

'And?' Mr Ambrose's voice called from below.

'Wait just a second!'

---

[16] 'The little death' – Victorian expression for a certain nocturnal interaction between male and female.

181

Narrowing my eyes, I searched the area where I thought I had seen something reflect the dim half-light. There! Movement, on the bank of that little stream! There were shapes shifting around under the branches of the trees there. Something with two legs that wasn't your friendly neighbourhood gorilla. I caught that glint again, and this time I was certain. Metal.

'Mr Ambrose! Mr Ambrose, Sir!'

I had never climbed down a tree so fast in my life. By the time I reached the bottom, Mr Ambrose was awaiting me, revolver drawn, eyes sharp, scanning the jungle for any danger. As for Karim – well, he was probably out there in the jungle, being the danger (for everybody else).

'Men!' I panted, as soon as my feet touched the ground. 'Armed! Coming this way!'

'Who? Rebels or imperials?'

'Didn't see! No flags. Could be either.'

Mr Ambrose's left little finger twitched. For him, that was as bad as a barrage of curses. 'And you're sure they were armed?'

'Yes.'

'They must have had an arsenal hidden somewhere in the jungle. One? Ha! The rebels probably have several.' His jaw tightened. 'I should have thought of that.'

'There's no sense in torturing yourself,' I told him. 'I'd be more than happy to do it for you.'

'Mr Linton! Now is not the time for jokes!'

'I know.' Before he could pull away or shoot a freezing glare at me, I stood up on my tiptoes and pressed a soft kiss on his cheek. 'Who says I was joking?'

He stiffened under the touch of my lips, so surprised that I had time to slip my arms around him and hold him close.

'I don't know who they are,' I whispered, pressing my face into his chest. 'I don't know where they got their weapons from. All I know is that they're after us again, and they don't look happy. So...what do you think we should do now, Sir?'

Straightening, he snatched up his backpack and slung it over one shoulder. 'Karim? Grab your things! We're leaving!'

After that day, we resumed the same gruelling pace as before. Only – it didn't feel quite as torturous as before. My legs didn't tremble with every step, and didn't have half as much to carry as they had a week or two ago. My strides became longer and steadier, and if I was not very much mistaken, Mr Ambrose now and again sent me looks of what bordered very nearly on reluctant approval.

Only...approval of what? The pace with which I moved, or the way in which? He was still marching behind me, guarding my rear, and he took his duty very seriously. I could feel his gaze on my derrière day in and day out. Only in the night did he take his eyes off me – which was just as well, because you can't sneak off into the jungle for secret shooting practice with the eyes of your employer fastened on your behind.

It had occurred to me that, maybe, it wouldn't be particularly safe to sneak out of the camp with soldiers roaming the jungle looking for us. But then, if I'd wanted a safe life, I probably shouldn't have marched into a warzone to begin with. I needed to be able to defend myself. And I needed to be able to shoot Mr Ambrose's top hat off his head in a fabulously impressive manner. So, as a precaution, I took along a blanket to wrap around the barrel and muffle the noise. It made aiming a little more difficult, but I could use an extra challenge. By now, I had gotten pretty handy with a gun. All right, I probably wouldn't be able to compete with trained soldiers any time soon, but at least I could hit a standing target over a dozen paces away without the recoil knocking the gun out of my hand.

'Die! Die, you ugly orange flower-cabbage-thingy!'

Bam!

'Die, you odd-looking tropical plant of unknown origin!'

Bam! Bam!

The plant exploded as the bullet hit home. Grinning, I whirled the weapon on one finger (which I managed to do about fifty per cent of the time without dropping it) and blew the smoke away. It would have been great to have a scuffed leather gun belt at my hips into which I could casually slip the still-smoking gun, but a girl couldn't have everything, right?

Well, maybe I could get one once I returned to London.

'Well, well...Who do we have here?'

Or...maybe not.

I whirled around and raised my gun – just in time to have it slammed out of my hand by a burly soldier. I threw myself to the side, wanting to lunge for the gun on the ground, but the man grabbed me and held me in place. More soldiers stepped out of the shadows, followed by a tall figure in uniform. Colonel Silveira smiled at me, his white teeth shining in the dark. 'We meet again *Senhora*.'

HEROIC RESCUE À LA AMBROSE

A general piece of advice to tourists and other travellers to the beautiful country of Brazil: avoid getting tied to poles. It's very uncomfortable.

Unfortunately, Colonel Silveira and his merry men had not been so courteous as to give me a choice in the matter when they had dragged me into this tent and twisted my arms behind my back. There had been a definite aura of hostility in the air, unbecoming of an officer welcoming visitors from a foreign country. Really, the way I was accommodated right now, with the ropes cutting into my wrists, the gag in my mouth and the bruise developing on my cheek where a fat sergeant had punched me after I tried to bite off his finger, you might almost think I was a prisoner and not an honoured guest.

'Bloody Brazilians and their bloody civil war!' I growled. Or at least I tried to growl. With the gag in my mouth it sounded more like 'Blwd Brzllns nd dr bdy ceel or!' How very dignified.

And do you know what the best news was?

Not that I had been captured, no. Not even that Colonel Silveira had promised to 'personally attend' to my questioning. No. The best thing was unquestionably, without the smallest doubt, that I'd had the manuscript with me when I went into their nets. Fool that I was, I'd actually thought it would be safest to keep the thing with me at all times! Now it didn't look as if that would turn out to be so safe after all.

And all this had happened because I wanted to learn how to defend myself. How to take care of myself. Now, here I was, tied to a pole in nothing but a glorified nightshirt, a gag in my mouth. Good job, Lilly!

Tentatively, I tugged at the bindings keeping me chained to the pole. It was no use. The ropes cut into my skin and didn't give a fraction of an inch. Bloody Brazilians! Why a pole, anyway? Did they intend to roast me over an open fire? I thought only natives did that kind of thing. And even they should have better sense than to try and roast me. After all, as experienced cannibals they'd have to see at a glance I would make for very chewy, fatty steaks. Now, Mr Ambrose...that was another matter. Once unfrozen, he might actually be rather tasty...

Suddenly, the soft squishing of boots in wet mud came from the entrance of the tent. My head snapped up, just in time to see a dark figure crouching in the entrance, a knife in its hand.

My heart jumped a mile high. Did the sergeant and his cronies come back to have a little fun with the captive?

The dark figure moved forward, blocking out the moonlight completely. 'Mr Linton? Mr Linton, you're alive!'

I breathed in a glorious sigh of relief. That was *not* the sergeant. There was only one man in the world who could pack that much annoyance into a statement of relief.

'Mmph! Mmmp!'

'My God, did they gag you?'

'Ymm!'

'Smart people.'

'Mmmmp! Nmnnn! Mmm!'

I was seriously considering strangling him for that little remark – but a moment later, I decided to forgive him. He was reaching out, his hands wandering searchingly over me, looking for the rope. He was going to untie me.

'Behind my back,' I tried to say. 'Behind my back, at the pole!'

But all that came out was, 'Bnnd ma bbck, t pl!'

His hands slowly wandered over my hips, then my waist. They slid over the belt I usually carried there, with a pouch or two hanging from it, along with a water bottle.

No! No, not there! The ropes are further back!

His hands slid into the first pouch.

Wait just a minute...!

'Hm...' he murmured. 'Not there. Let's see...'

He wasn't untying me. He was *checking my pockets*!

'Mmmmmh!'

Leisurely, his hands slipped into the second pouch. 'Not there either. Pity.'

'Mmmph! Mp! Pfmmm Mmp!'

'Did you keep the manuscript in there, Mr Linton? Or maybe you kept it somewhere a little more private.'

My eyes went wide.

'Wtt? Dnn't drr!'

'Let's see...'

'Dn't y drr! Dn't y drrr! M gna kllya–mmmhhhh...!'

'Hm. No, nothing of interest there, either.'

I really, really, really was going to kill him.

He sighed. 'Well, it wouldn't have made sense for them to leave it here with you, anyway. The colonel is sure to have taken it with him to his own tent.'

'Ntt nm!'

'I'm going to go get it.'

'Wwtt?'

'It will only take a second. Don't move.'

Don't move? Was he serious?

Of course he was. He was Rikkard Ambrose.

'Dn't gg! Nt mm! Nnnmpf!'

'Be quiet! They might hear you.'

And with that encouraging remark, my would-be saviour vanished into the darkness. I mentally started listing ways in which I could maim, torture and kill him just as soon as I got my hands free.

~~**~*~*

The wait was not a pleasant one. It hadn't been before, of course – but back then, the worst thing I could expect was being sadistically tortured for information. Now, I had actually to deal with the possibility of *being rescued*. By a *man*. And not by any man, either – by Mr Rikkard Ambrose!

Please, God, why don't you kill me now?

But God was apparently busy tonight. I remained alive, and very much tied to the pole. A hundred horrific scenes played out in my head: Mr Ambrose cutting my bonds; Mr Ambrose clutching me, the helpless little woman, fervently to his strong, masculine chest; Mr Ambrose whispering 'There, there! You're safe now' into my hair. Ugh! I shuddered. No, I would definitely draw the line there! I might condescend to letting my bonds be cut, but having to be comforted like some dimwitted damsel? No, no, and no again! I would not let myself be rescued in an unfeministic manner!

I had just come to that conclusion when the tent flap was pulled aside, and Mr Ambrose slid inside. I had to admit, now it was proving advantageous that he had kept his tailcoat and trousers during our jungle journey. All in black, he was hardly more than a shadow in the night.

A shadow who had come to *rescue* me. Yuck!

Oh, well, I was going to be firm. As soon as he removed the gag, I was going to explain to him that he wasn't actually rescuing me, but only assisting me in rescuing myself. Furthermore, I would demand that he expunge this unfortunate incident from his memory and that he never ever mention the word 'pole' in my presence.

'Still here, are you?' He knelt in front of me.

'Wll cnt g frr! Gtnn wtht!'

'Keep still.'

A blade flashed in the darkness. A moment later, the ropes that had bound me to the pole fell to the ground and I shuffled away with a sigh of relief. Half-turning, I held out my wrists to him, still tightly bound behind my back, waiting for the knife.

He put the blade away.

What the–?

A moment later that unfinished question was succinctly answered when he grabbed me around the waist, hauled me up and slung me over his shoulder.

Without removing my bonds.

Without removing my gag.

'Nnng! Mmp! Mmmmmph!'

'Yes, you are quite heavy, aren't you?'

'Mmmph? Mmmph mp!'

'But, in spite of that fact, the situation does have a few advantages,' he remarked, his hands sliding over areas of my body that, in this position, were suddenly very accessible to him. 'Don't you agree, Mr Linton?'

'Nnng! Mgmk! Mmph! Rg!'

Swiftly and powerfully, he rose to his feet. If my weight really bothered him, his movements didn't betray the fact. He slid out of the tent, where a shadow was waiting, so big it could only be one man.

'*Sahib?*'

'I have her, Karim.'

'Intact?'

'To judge by the way she's squirming, in mint condition. And you?'

'The manuscript is back in our possession.'

'Adequate. Let's move.'

We slid silently through the night. Even in my current state of blind, disbelieving rage, I was smart enough to realise I had better keep quiet while we were in the enemy camp. If we were captured again, we'd never get out of here. And if we didn't get out of here, I would never get my chance to murder Mr Ambrose. And I *needed* to murder him! I wouldn't even need a weapon! I would simply close my fingers around that velvet throat of his and squeeze hard! And, if my fingers weren't strong enough, I would bite his throat and gnaw and nibble until I reached his lips and then I would–

No, no! Bad Lilly! That's kissing! You wanted to kill, remember? Kill, not kiss! With double-l, not double-s!

Well, it was an easy mistake to make.

Kill. That's what you're going to do. Kill!

186

It wouldn't be long now until I got my chance. I didn't see much of what was going on from my position, but I glimpsed the slumped body of a guard on the ground, and felt the lights of the camp receding. As soon as we were safely away, he would cut my bonds and set me down, and the bloody business of the night could finally begin!

Or that's what I thought.

Only...when the camp had completely disappeared in the dark behind us, and we were safe in the depths of the jungle, Mr Ambrose didn't put me down.

'Mmph! Mmp mph!'

'You know, I could get used to this, Mr Linton.'

'Mmph? Pttt mm dnn!'

'The calm, the incredibly relaxing quiet – yes, this situation really has its advantages.'

'Mmm gna kll y!'

'Pardon, what was that?'

'Rrrrrg!'

'Nothing? Oh, good. I thought you had said something.'

How do you clobber someone over the head with your hands tied behind your back? Difficult question. I would probably have to settle for an alternative. Pulling back my leg with all the force I could muster, I kicked, aiming for his crotch.

He caught my foot long before it hit home. Effortlessly restraining me, he ran his fingers along my bare calf and I – Damn me! – felt butterflies flutter in my stomach.

'Hm...' he murmured. 'Yes, definite advantages.'

His hand slid further up my calf.

Kiss him!

No, no! *Kill*, not *kiss*!

Kiss!

Kill!

Kiss!

Kill!

Kiss!

Kill!

Well...maybe you can do both?

Yes, but which one first?

Who cares? As cold and stiff as he is, it'll hardly matter!

~~**~*~*

I don't know how long I hung over his back like this. An hour? Two? Only a few minutes? It felt like the longest time ever to me. But every time his hands skimmed over my bare skin, every time he murmured to me with that cold, commanding voice of his that could reach right into my chest down to my heart, a tiny part of me wished it would never stop.

Of course, there was also that big part of me that was still dreaming of strangulation!

Kiss!

Kill!

Kiss!

Kill!

Finally, we reached a sort of semi-clearing under the branches of a gigantic tree that had frightened away all trees for several yards in every direction. Mr Ambrose stopped under its majestic branches, glancing up at the hidden night sky.

'We'll make camp here for the night.' Sliding me off his shoulders, he set me on my feet. Blood rushed down in my body, and I swayed. Mr Ambrose's hands shot out, catching me, holding me up. 'Karim?'

'I, um...should scout the area, *Sahib*. See if everything is safe.'

Mister Ambrose's eyes remained focused on me, glittering in the darkness. 'You do that.'

Without another word, the Mohammedan disappeared into the underbrush.

'Well, well, now, Mr Linton...' Raising one hand, Mr Ambrose stroked it down the side of my face, sliding strands of my hair through his fingers. 'You've had quite the adventure. I hope you've learned something from it?'

I tried to spit out the gag and bite him. But the bloody thing stayed firmly lodged in my mouth. 'Grr! Ng! Mph!'

'Apparently not.' Stepping around me, Mr Ambrose slid one arm around my waist. Suddenly, he tugged, pulling me hard against him.

'Don't ever do that again, Mr Linton!' His voice was a satin-covered ice shard in my ear. 'Do you hear? Don't ever leave the camp at night again! Do you have any idea what could have happened to you?'

'Nnng! Mph!'

His lips moved over my ear, whispering against my skin. 'Well? Do you?'

'Ng! Wss pffrct ffnn!'

Something glinted in the traces of moonlight falling through the roof of branches. I tensed.

'Hold still.'

A moment later, I felt cold steel against my skin. There was tearing noise, and – Yes! – the bonds holding my hands fell away. I didn't hesitate a second. My legs were weak, my arms were numb and my head felt woozy. But that didn't stop me from throwing myself at Mr Rikkard Ambrose and punching him in the face.

However, his hand *did* stop me.

It was just suddenly there, closing around my wrist, tight as a torture device and far more dangerous. A torture device would have made me want to scream. His hand made me want to moan and beg for more.

Kiss!

Kill!

Kiss!

Kill!

'Y blldy bstrd!'

Blast! I still had that bloody gag in my mouth! Kicking Mr Ambrose in the shins, I lunged forward. The kick didn't really hurt him, but it distracted him enough for his grip on the knife to loosen. In a flash, I had twisted it out of his hand and raised it to my face, slipping it under the knot that held the gag in place. There was a ripping sound, and the filthy cloth fluttered to the ground.

'You bloody bastard!' *Ah, the bliss of free speech!* 'Chauvinist pig! Dastardly, ditch-digging deviant!'

There was so much fire in my belly I didn't even realise I'd cut myself until I tasted blood. I didn't care! I aimed another kick at Mr Ambrose, but he caught my leg between his.

'Let me go!'

'Why?' he breathed, his hot breath tickling my skin. 'I prefer things like this.' Raising his hand, he slid a finger along the corner of my mouth.

Kiss!

Kill!

Kiss!

Kill!

His finger came away bloody.

'You should be more careful, Mr Linton.'

'To hell with being careful! To hell with you!'

'I told you once already,' he growled. 'The road to hell is paved with good intentions. And right now, I don't have any of those.'

He tightened his grip and pounced. A moment later, our mouths met and we came together in a hot, irresistible mix of blood, sweat and need. The stuff that sin is made of. My lips fought with his, struggling for dominance, neither of us willing to give up. His tongue entered the battle, sliding to the corner of my mouth, tasting my blood. I felt my knees grow weak.

Kiss!

Kill!

Kiss!

Ki–

Oh, to hell with it! You can always do that later!

Giving up the struggle, I mashed myself up against him, throwing my arms around his neck. Only when the blade thudded against the wood of the tree behind him did I realise I was still holding the knife.

I grinned against his lips. Pulling back the blade, I slowly slid it down the side of his head until it rested below his chin. Then I broke the kiss.

'Don't *ever* do something like this again?' I whispered. 'Or next time I'll take the gag and make you choke on it! Understood?'

He growled. 'You're a dangerous woman.'

'Yes, I am. Don't you forget it!'

His eyes, dark as a thunderstorm on the open sea, bored into me. 'I wasn't talking about the knife.'

His hand, still on my face, gently slid to my mouth, caressing my lips. 'I was talking about this.' Moving on, his fingers pointed at my eyes. 'And those.' Moving again, he slid down his hand away from my face, until it rested on my chest, just above my heart. 'And, most of all, this.'

Oh God...

Suddenly, the rage, the violence – it was all gone. But the need for him? That was suddenly so intense I couldn't bear it. I felt a painful tugging in my heart.

'You're dangerous, too,' I whispered, before my courage left me. 'More dangerous than I could ever have imagined.'

'Indeed?' He cocked his head, and his arrogant eyes glittered in the darkness. 'Are you afraid, Mr Linton?'

'Ha! Of you? Never!'

'Is that so...?' Leaning closer, his lips skimmed over mine once more. A ragged sound of need escaped my throat, and the knife slipped from my limp fingers. He gave an arrogant male chuckle that made me instantly wish I was still holding it. 'You aren't afraid at all of what will happen if you let yourself fall? If you forget everything else, and let go completely?'

Mary, mother of God...! What was he talking about?

Whatever it was – a tiny spark of fear did ignite in me. Just enough to make everything that much more thrilling. Damn him!

'Well? Are you?'

'N-no!'

He laughed again. It suddenly occurred to me – had I ever heard him laugh before? I didn't think so. He was Mr Rikkard Ambrose, for crying out loud! The probability of him finding anything funny was about as high as the probability of daisies and rosebushes in the arctic tundra.

'You know,' his voice tickled my ear, 'you aren't the only one who has their moments of...well, I wouldn't say fear. Let's say...agitation.'

'Oh?' I perked up. This was news to me.

'For a moment there,' he murmured against my skin, 'when Silveira captured you, you almost had me worried.'

'Did I?'

'You did indeed. When I discovered you were gone, I nearly lost my mind with worry! I thought I would never ever get the manuscript back.'

I stiffened in his arms.

The manuscript?

The *bloody manuscript?*

If only I hadn't let go of the knife.

'If you don't shut up about that manuscript,' I growled, grabbing him by the collar, 'I'm going to throw you down on the ground and torture you all through the night!'

'Indeed?' His eyes sparked in the darkness. The expression in their swirling depths looked far more like anticipation than fear. He leaned forward and, grasping my chin in one hand, whispered into my ear so low only I could hear: 'Manuscript!'

What was a girl to do?

LOVE IN THE MORNING

Even before I woke all the way up next morning, I knew where I was. There was only one way to connect last night to today, to explain the warm body pressed up against me. I smiled, snuggling closer to Mr Ambrose. The hammock was hardly big enough for both of us, but right then and there, I didn't care. It was enough to feel his warmth beside me, and his strong arms pressing into me. Someone lovingly caressed my cheek, and I felt my body melt. Did he know I could feel it? Did he know I was awake? The same someone bent forward to gently nibble on my ear, and I gave a contented sigh.

Then someone spit in my ear, stuck his finger into it and turned it this way and that.

Suffice it to say that *this* did *not* draw a contented sigh from my lips.

'What the hell do you think you're–'

I shot upright, my eyes spitting fire – and came to an abrupt halt as the fellow beside me greeted me with a smile entirely too friendly, long-toothed and yellow for Mr Rikkard Ambrose.

'Oook!' The monkey said, triumphantly, and proudly held up the finger with which he had kindly cleaned my ear. 'Oook ooog? Oook!'

'Ya! Argh! Argl!'

Scrambling backwards, I toppled clean out of the hammock, slamming into the ground with a resounding *thud*.

The monkey, looking very puzzled that I was not more interested in his ear-cleaning services, climbed down out of the hammock after me and wobbled over to me.

'Oook?' he asked, offering me the smeary finger. 'Oook ok ooog oook!'

Just then, footsteps approached from behind me, and a cool voice enquired: 'I hope I'm not interrupting something?'

Oh God! No, please! Please, let me die now!

'Not at all,' I said without turning around, keeping my voice steady. 'This gentleman was just leaving.'

However, the monkey seemed disinclined to follow my suggestion. It held up its slobbery finger again with a hopeful face. 'Oook?'

'No, I'm not interested!' I hissed. 'Shoo! Piss off, you little furry beast!'

I swear to you, the little furball actually looked *hurt*! It held up its finger one last time, a pleading expression on its hairy little face.

'Seems he doesn't want to take no for an answer,' came Mr Ambrose's cool voice from behind me. There was no hint of amusement in it, but with Mr Ambrose, that didn't mean much.

'He's probably a male,' I growled. 'They all seem to have trouble understanding a certain small two-letter word.

'Or maybe it's just you.' He was closer now, slowly approaching. A hand reached out to gently stroke my cheek, and I quickly glanced at it to make sure it was human this time before relaxing into the touch. 'Maybe you're irresistible.'

'To monkeys?'

'No.' His fingers found their way from my cheek to my lips, stroking their soft curves with sensual precision. 'To males.'

Oh God...! The way he said that...I felt ready to melt into the ground.

Luckily, the monkey didn't seem to appreciate being neglected, and saved me from such an embarrassing display.

'Oook? Ook oook!'

He was holding up his finger again. I looked at the little fellow's big, hopeful eyes and sighed. Normally, I had no problems at all with rejecting interested males of any kind. But with this one chap, I was having increasing difficulties saying 'no'.

Involuntarily, my eyes were drawn over to Mr Ambrose. Well...actually not just with this one.

Blast!

'Sorry,' I told the little fellow. 'But it's really for the best, you know? Trust me, we wouldn't exactly be suited for each other. Find some nice monkey lady with a big, comfy tree of her own. I'm sure she'll let you clean her ears as much as you want.'

The little fellow drew himself up. 'Oook! Oook ook ooog oook.'

I couldn't speak monkey, but I had heard this one so often in English, I knew instinctively what it meant: *I know you love me deep inside! You're just too shy to admit it.*

With that, the little fellow turned and scampered off, probably to gather a few flowers and bananas.

I closed my eyes. 'God! Why do men have to be the same everywhere?'

~~**~*~*

'So, let's examine our situation.'

We were all gathered in our little camp, around a scrap of paper that was supposedly a map of the Amazonian jungle. It bore an astonishing resemblance to a white sheet.

'Not many people have been this way yet, have they?' I enquired, staring at the map.

'No.'

'Is that good or bad?'

'Both, Mr Linton. It means our options are very limited. We cannot deviate too much from the manuscript's instructions, or we will certainly lose our way. But it also means that the further we go, the more difficulties the Brazilians will have with following us. Half the country they claim as their own is really unexplored jungle, owned only by the jaguars and natives that roam this labyrinth of trees.'

'And what does that mean for us?'

'It means that we have lots of space, either to lose our enemies in, or to get lost ourselves. We must use it wisely. And we must, by any means possible, manage to throw the Brazilians off the scent. I think it is clear by now that they won't give up on their own. We can't allow them to capture one of us again. Next time we might not be so lucky, and I will not allow them to lay their hands on my treasure!'

Grim nods from all around. When nobody spoke again, I asked: 'So, what do we do?'

Mr Ambrose took a deep breath. 'There may be a way. A way to throw the Brazilians off our scent for a time, maybe even for good. But it's dangerous. Very dangerous.'

His cool gaze swept our little gathering.

'We'll be going deep into potential enemy territory, giving ourselves into the power of people we don't know and cannot trust. But, if we can persuade them to help us, the soldiers will have no hope of finding us. If – and that is a big if!'

'What if they decide not to help us? What do we do then?' I asked.

Mr Ambrose met my gaze, levelly. 'Dead people don't do anything.'

'Oh.'

'I told you it would be dangerous. That's why I can't make this decision on my own. Your lives are your own. So...what will we do now? Will we forget about the treasure and turn tail? Or will we gather our courage and move forward?'

Karim and I exchanged a look. For the first time in days, he didn't grimace at having to glance at me.

'Forward,' we said in unison.

'Adequate.' Clapping his hands, Mr Ambrose rose to his feet. 'Then let's go. We have no time to waste. I doubt that the Brazilians are more than a few hours behind us.'

'Aren't you going to tell us who these oh-so-dangerous people are to whom you intend to take us?' I demanded.

'No. Come!'

Muttering a curse, I snatched up my knapsack and marched after him. He was already heading off into the jungle.

It didn't take me long to figure out that we had switched directions. Where before we had been heading west, we were now going northeast. And we weren't following my directions from the manuscript, either. Instead, Mr Ambrose was leading now, leaving Karim to protect the back and to perfect the art of walking with his eyes closed. My dear employer seemed to know where he was going. The map he used was almost completely blank, but there seemed to be at least one dot on it that was clear and fixed, and whatever it was, we were heading towards it. Towards one deadly danger, to escape from another.

Oh, the bliss of working for Rikkard Ambrose!

'Sir?'

Mr Ambrose didn't turn around.

'Sir? I have a question.'

'Then ask, Mr Linton.'

Still he didn't turn.

'Tell me, Sir...if we would have voted against the plan, what would you have done?'

He didn't even hesitate. 'I would have ignored your opinions and ordered you to do what I want.'

I had suspected something of the sort. 'Um...Sir? Then why let us vote?'

'To build a sense of community and cooperation among my staff members. It generally is an efficient way of manipulating people into doing what I want while letting them think they do it of their own volition.'

'Ah. Of course. Well done, Sir. I feel very cooperative.'

We continued to march through the jungle at a pace a Roman regiment could have been proud of. Again and again, Mr Ambrose had Karim make forays to the right and left, or made me climb up trees to look as far as the thick roof of plants would allow. He never told me what exactly I was supposed to be looking for, saying only, 'You'll know it when you see it.'

How wonderfully helpful.

Only, he turned out to be right.

The sun was just setting, and I had climbed up one last tree to throw a last look around before turning in when, suddenly, I saw something rising from among the trees that I hadn't seen in a very, very long time.

'Mr Ambrose!'

'Yes, Mr Linton? What is it?'

'Smoke! There's smoke ahead, rising from between the trees!'

'I knew it! I knew he would be here.'

'He? Who, Sir?'

'Never mind that now, Mr Linton! What direction is the smoke coming from?'

Quickly, I pulled the compass from my pouch. 'Northeast! We're marching straight towards it!'

'Get down here now! We're leaving.'

If I thought we'd been moving fast before, I was mistaken. Now that we knew the exact direction, Mr Ambrose took up his usual position at the rear again – and believe me, there's nothing that can make you move as fast as Mr Rikkard Ambrose's ice-cold eyes biting into your behind. Soon I was ready to beg for a break, but I clenched my teeth and carried on, no matter how much my tortured muscles were screaming.

'Stop!'

It took my exhausted brain a few seconds to register Mr Ambrose's abrupt command. Wobbling to a stop, I reached out to support myself against a tree. What was the matter? Had Mr Ambrose suddenly developed a shred of mercy?

Very unlikely.

'Do you smell that? Karim? Mr Linton?'

Smell? I was panting, dragging in big, hot breaths through my mouth. I hadn't bothered to try and smell anything in a long while. Now I tried to calm my breathing and sniff the air. At first, I smelled nothing, but then I suddenly detected a faint odour. Smoke?

'We're getting close,' Mr Ambrose pronounced. 'Let's go! It won't be long now.'

Really? I bloody well hoped so, or my dear employer would have to scrape me off the jungle floor!

Dragging in another breath, I stumbled forward, following Karim's distant figure. It wasn't long before we reached the edge of a small clearing. Here, it wasn't just one big tree keeping the others away. No, a human hand had purposefully cut down a few of the smaller trees, creating a free space in the middle. In the shadow of a bigger tree, someone had built a ramshackle hut. The scrape of metal issued from the sinister interior. Warily, I took a step towards it. Mr Ambrose hadn't said much about the mysterious 'he' we were going to meet here. But, by the sound of it, 'he' was already sharpening his knives in preparation of our welcome. How very nice of him.

PRETTY PRIESTLY

My eyes flicked around the clearing. A saw, hammer, a pair of trousers and a shirt were hanging from a line – whoever was living here, he was clearly not a native. But what would a European, or even a Brazilian, be doing living out here?

Karim seemed to have similar thoughts. 'What is this place?' he rumble-whispered. 'What kind of man would come to live out here, all alone?'

'A madman,' Mr Ambrose told us succinctly.

'*Mad?*' I stared at him. 'And you didn't think to mention this before we came here?'

'No. Let's see if he is at home.'

Mr Ambrose marched forward, seeming not the least bit disturbed by the continued metallic noises from inside the cabin.

'Father?' he called.

My eyes almost bugged out of my sockets.

'His *father* lives here?' I hissed to Karim, who seemed to be having equal difficulties with coming to grips with the situation. 'And he's off his rocker?'

But my theory was crushed a moment later when the curtain in the cabin's doorway was swept aside and out stepped a man in a black robe, holding a rusty goblet in his hand. The man's wide, blinking eyes fell on Mr Ambrose.

'*Oh meu deus!* Visitors? And English ones to boot! Now, this is a surprise. You must excuse me, *Senhores*, I was scraping the rust off the chalice.' He raised the goblet. 'I am afraid I did not hear you approach.'

I stared at the man. It took a few moments to sink in, but then I finally realised: that black robe he was wearing wasn't a robe. It was a cassock. The man was a *priest*. A young, wide-eyed, beardless little scrap of a priest with half a nervous smile on his face and a receding hairline, although he couldn't have been older than twenty-five. If anyone had wanted to capture the perfect platonic idea of the word 'harmless', the incarnation of harmlessness so to speak, this was what it would look like.

'That is the mysterious "he"?' I whispered, gesturing at the little bald man. 'He is supposed to be dangerous? He doesn't look as if he could squash a mosquito!'

Karim shrugged. 'I do not know the *Sahib*'s business. I do not question the *Sahib*.'

'No, of course you don't.'

But I was going to do a hell of a lot of questioning!

The priest was smiling at Mr Ambrose now. Somehow, despite being faced by my employer's cold eyes, he seemed to be labouring under the misapprehension that having visitors was a good thing. But that misapprehension wouldn't last long. It was time to step in, both to save the poor priest from getting squashed, and to find out what the hell was going on here.

'Excuse me,' I began, stepping out of the shadow of the trees and curtsying to the priest. 'I know it is very impolite of us to come unannounced to your, um...home like this, but–'

I didn't get any further.

'*Santa Maria!*' The priest stumbled back, staring at me, eyes wide. He raised a shaking finger to point. '*La puta de Babilonia!*'

I leaned over to Mr Ambrose. 'What did he say?'

'You don't want to know.'

Slowly, his eyes fixing on me one moment, then flickering away the next, the priest sank to his knees.

'*Pai nosso, que estais no céu*
Santificado seja o Vosso nome...'

I leaned closer to Mr Ambrose. 'Is that how priests normally greet visitors in Brazil?'

'I don't think so.'

The priest let his eyes flicker to me again – then abruptly pressed them shut, and folded his hands in front of his chest.

'*...Venha a nós o Vosso reino,*
Seja feita a Vossa vontade,
Assim na terra como no céu...'

'Is he...*praying*?'

'I believe so, Mr Linton.'

One of the priest's eyes opened a fraction of an inch, caught sight of me, still standing there in my shift – and abruptly snapped shut again!

'*...O pão nosso de cada dia nos dai hoje.*
Perdoai as nossas ofensas,
Assim como nós perdoamos a quem nos tem ofendido...'

'What is he praying about?'

Was I mistaken, or was there a slight glint in Mr Ambrose's eyes as he turned to me and let his gaze rake over me?

'Right now, Mr Linton, I believe he is praying not to be led into temptation.'

His gaze swept over me again, meaningfully.

'What? Oh. *Oh!* You don't mean he–'

'In my experience, Mr Linton, devout priests seldom get visits from scantily dressed young ladies.'

'*...E não nos deixeis cair...*'

I glared at Mr Ambrose, then at the priest, who was still kneeling, his hands clutched tightly together, his eyes shut even more tightly.

'Hey, you!'

He ignored me.

'*...em tentação,*
Mas livrai-nos do mal,
Amém.
Pai nosso, que estais no céu
Santificado seja o Vosso nome...'

'Is he starting all over again?'

'Priests have been known to recite the Lord's Prayer up to thirty times in a row, especially in situations of carnal temptation.'

'*Carnal temp*- I'll give him carnal temptation!'

Fuming, I marched over to the young man kneeling on the ground.

'*...Venha a nós o Vosso reino,*
Seja feita a Vossa vontade...'

'Hey, you!'

'*...Assim na terra como no céu.*
O pão nosso de cada dia nos dai hoje...'

'I'm talking to you! Open your peepers!'

'*...Perdoai as nossas ofensas,*
'*Assim como nós perdoamos a quem nos tem ofendido.*
E não nos deixeis cair em tentação...'

'I'm not going to bloody tempt you! I don't even *want* to tempt you! And trust me, you most certainly don't want to be tempted by me!'

'*Mas livrai-nos do mal,*
Amém.
Pai nosso, que estais no céu...'

'Are your ears corked or something?'

'*...Santificado seja o Vosso nome,*
Venha a nós o Vosso reino...'

I decided that extreme measures were necessary. Taking a few determined steps, I positioned myself behind the priest.

'Mr Linton?' Mr Ambrose stepped forward. 'What are you doing?'

'Getting this gentleman's attention,' I told him, and booted the priest firmly in the backside. He ended his prayer in a yelp and flew forward, landing face first in the mud. Spitting out dirt and a few surprised bugs, he rolled around to stare up at me with a mixture of horror and incredulity.

'You...you are real?'

'As real as it bloody gets!'

The priest's eyes wandered up and down my figure, cautiously.

'You are not a figment of my sinful, lust-filled imagination?'

'Would a figment of your sinful imagination have kicked you in the behind?'

'Um...probably not.'

'There you are.'

'But...but...' The priest's eyes didn't seem to be able to make up their minds whether they wanted to fasten on me or jump out of his head and run away as fast as possible. They flickered back and forth with amazing speed. It wasn't really as if he wanted to stare. It was more as if he really, really didn't, but had to, just in order to make sure that what he was seeing was really there. 'But you're a *senhora*, a lady in a...a nightshirt!'

He looked as if he felt sinful even saying the word. I hurried to reassure him.

'Oh, that's not a nightshirt. It's a chemise. You know, it's what women usually have under all their other clothing during the day. You just don't usually see it, unless they take everything else off.'

This didn't seem to reassure him a lot.

'Pai nosso, que estais no céu
Santificado seja o Vosso nome,
Venha a nós o Vosso reino...'

'Are you starting with that again? I thought we had established that I am not a satanic vision sent to tempt you.'

'I would not be so sure about that, if I were you,' Karim advised the priest.

'Oh, shut up, you!'

For the first time, the priest noticed the third member of our little band. His jaw dropped in horror. 'A heathen!'

Karim gave him a hard stare. 'That's a matter of opinion, *Kafir*.'[17]

'Deus, me ajude!' The priest's eyes flickered fearfully from me to Mr Ambrose to Karim, and back to me again. 'What kind of embassy from the pit has come to tempt me off the path of righteousness?'

'A very busy one.' Mr Ambrose stepped forward. 'So, if you'll just give us what I told you we want, father, we'll be out of your hair.' He eyed the priest's receding hairline. 'Inasmuch as you still have any.'

Grabbing the doorframe of his little hut, the priest pulled himself up on his feet again. His gaze went from me to Mr Ambrose once more, and he seemed to realise that we were not about to try and tempt him into satanic rituals.

'Ehem.' He did his best to rally. 'You should not seek what you want, my son. For, as the Evangelist Timothy says, *the desire of money is the root of all evils; which some coveting have erred from the faith, and have entangled themselves in...'*

'Why don't you just get on with your praying and we'll get on with our coveting?' Mr Ambrose cut him off. 'We won't take up much of your time. We only need directions.'

'Directions? Um...I see. Well.' The priest seemed to be floundering, abruptly cut off in his delivery. But he caught himself tolerably well. 'Err...certainly. As

---

[17] An Arabic term, literally 'Concealer of the Truth', but usually translated as 'unbeliever', which is used by Muslims to refer to non-Muslims. It is a matter of debate in the Islamic community whether Christians and Jews should be considered unbelievers, since they do actually believe in God / Allah, but simply worship him in a different way.

you wish. Who am I to deny you help in finding your way? For, as the good book says *Show, O Lord, thy ways to me, and teach me thy paths. Direct me in thy truth, and teach me; for thou art God my Saviour; and on thee have I...*'

'Yes, quite, quite. Can we get on with it, father?'

'Err...yes. Certainly, yes. Please, come into my humble abode, and we will discuss everything like civilised men.'

'And women!' I added sharply.

The priest's eyes slid over me in my ragged, stained chemise, rather doubtfully. 'Um...yes. Civilised women. Of course. Please, follow me.'

~~**~*~*

We followed Father Marcos, for that was his name, into the little two-room cabin, where he served us a meal of corn bread, water and biblical quotations. Except for the fact that he repeatedly tried to foist clothes on me which, really, in this hot weather, were completely unnecessary, he was a model host. I had figured out by now that Father Marcos was not our final destination. It hadn't really been hard. I remembered Mr Ambrose's words exactly.

We'll be going deep into potential enemy territory, giving ourselves into the power of people we don't know and cannot trust.

Father Marcos looked as hostile as Baby Jesus and as untrustworthy as St Peter waiting for you with a smile at the gates of Heaven. Whoever we must be headed towards, it was not Father Marcos. Oh no, he was just supposed to point us in the right direction – a fact that puzzled me exceedingly. How could anyone as harmless and as peaceful as this little priest know anyone dangerous and wily enough to make Mr Rikkard Ambrose hesitate?

I wasn't going to find out any time soon. After the meal, when I was ready to start pelting Mr Ambrose and the priest with questions, Mr Ambrose rose abruptly and tugged him off into the next room. Father Marcos looked only too happy to be dragged out of sight of female temptation. The moment the door shut behind them, I sprang up and ran over to it, pressing my ear against the rough wooden planks.

'Have you no shame?' demanded Karim's outraged voice from behind me.

'Psht!' I waved him away. 'I'm trying to listen!'

Karim grumbled a bit more, but finally shut up when I sent him a glare. However, even when he was silent, I couldn't hear what was said on the other side. The wood was surprisingly thick, and both men kept their voices down. When the priest's cassock rustled, announcing their return, I moved with heavenly swiftness, and by the time they re-entered the room, I was sitting at the table, smiling like an angel. Or maybe like an *Ifrit* with experience as a con artist, depending on your view of things. Who cared?

'We're leaving,' Mr Ambrose announced. 'Now. Father Marcos will show us the way.'

I noticed that, even under his tan, Father Marcos paled at the words. But he didn't object either. It seemed that whatever he was afraid of at the end of our journey, Mr Ambrose was more than a match in the fear department.

'Y-yes,' he agreed. 'I'll be showing you the way.' He brightened a little. 'And maybe I can convince you to search your souls, and help you find not only the path to what you are seeking, but also the path to righteousn-'

Mr Ambrose's hard stare made him cut off in mid-sentence.

'You will show us the way,' my dear employer repeated. 'In a *literal, non-biblical* sense.'

'Of course, Sir. Certainly, Sir.'

THEY

We left about five minutes later. The priest seemed very eager to show us the path to wherever the heck it was we were going, whether righteous or not.

Not that there were any paths that I could see. No, where we were going now the jungle became denser and more difficult with every yard. It wasn't just that the trees were closer together and underbrush thicker. The heat shot up like bullets in a funeral salute, and I felt about ready to be stuffed in a coffin. At least it would have kept the mosquitos away. Oh yes...the mosquitos. Apparently, I had only become acquainted with the more civilised members of that particular species up to this point. Now, however, their cousins were introducing themselves to me, and they weren't being shy about it.

'Ouch!'

'Silence, Mr Linton.'

'You try being silent when some bloody great beast bites you in the kettledrums[18]!'

There was a moment of silence.

'That, I believe, would be anatomically impossible, Mr Linton.'

No need to tell me that. However brief my looks at Mr Ambrose's bare chest had been so far, they had been thorough enough to make clear to me he was all man, with an extra dose of alpha male. If only I could take a closer look! But my seductive skills were slightly squashed by the fact that we had a priest with us. Plus, there were the-

'Ouch!'

Slap!

'Ha! Take that, you bloody beast!'

-mosquitos.

After a few days of this, I was ready to scream! How were you supposed to tempt a man into sin with a priest looking over your shoulder and mosquitos biting your behind? And the worst thing was: Mr Ambrose didn't seem to be bothered by either. He marched along as if the mosquitos around him didn't exist, and the only time he acknowledged Father Marcos' existence was when he glared at the priest to keep him on track.

---

[18] A Victorian word for a lady's breasts.

Father Marcos, for his part, followed Karim's example and did his very best not to look at me. In fact, he did his very best not to look at any of us, or exist at all. If he could have vanished into empty air, I was sure he would have jumped at the chance. He didn't actually try to preach morals to me, or to lead me to the path of righteousness, but I only had to take one look at his poor little face to know I couldn't throw myself at Mr Ambrose in front of him. It would scar the poor man for life. Damn!

But, apart from the fact that he thought I was a succubus from hell and that he was inhibiting my insidious attempts at seduction, Father Marcos was actually a pretty decent fellow. He was polite, obliging, and not once did he mention anything about women having to keep their mouth shut, which the vicar back home was prone to do every other Sunday.[19]

'Why did you tell me he was crazy?' I whispered to Mr Ambrose, after we'd been marching a few days and a particularly nasty mosquito had just bitten me on the nose, leaving me with an urgent need to distract myself. 'I mean...he's a bit shy, and apt to see satanic temptations where there aren't any, but crazy?'

Mr Ambrose gave me a level look. 'He lives alone out here in the jungle to teach a useless doctrine to a couple of half-naked primitives. Of course he is crazy. But that does not mean he cannot still be useful to us.'

I couldn't help but agree. Living out here wouldn't be my idea of a sane, healthy life. If I tried to imagine living without my friends, my sister, my whole world back home in London – I couldn't even finish the thought! There was no one else out here in the jungle to distract you from the heat and the rain and the ravenous mosquitos. Not a single soul you could ask for shelter or help. Except, maybe...

Oh no.

That couldn't be, could it? Surely, not even my granite-head of an employer would risk going to *them* for help, would he? No, surely not!

Really?

It wasn't long before I got an answer to my question. Only a few hours later, Father Marcos stopped next to a small tree. With a small shiver I noticed that it had a tiny, red feather attached to it.

'Here we are.' He glanced around nervously. 'This is how far I dare to go. I've tried to talk to them in the past, but they, um...don't seem very interested in hearing the Lord's word.'

'I can't imagine why,' Karim growled.

'Just continue in that direction,' the priest continued, pointing, 'and you'll find them sooner or later. Or rather, they'll find you.'

Mr Ambrose gave the priest a cool look and a nod – his version of a 'Thank you'.

---

[19] Corinthians 14:34-35, King James Version of the Bible: 'Let your women keep silence in the churches: for it is not permitted unto them to speak; but they are commanded to be under obedience as also saith the law. And if they will learn anything, let them ask their husbands at home: for it is a shame for women to speak in the church.'

'Adequate, priest. You can leave now.'

'I can't persuade you to turn around?' the priest enquired, tentatively. 'They're not fond of visitors in general, and a group like yours might–'

'No.'

'Please, Sir, reconsider! For the young lady's sake if not for your own. These are dangerous people you are getting mixed up with and–'

'No.'

The priest blinked. 'No? You don't think that they are dangerous?'

Mr Ambrose slid his hand along his belt until it came to rest at the holster of his gun. 'Not in comparison.'

The priest swallowed. 'Ah. Um...I see. Well, in that case...' Hurriedly, he took a few steps away from Mr Ambrose and then turned to me. His eyes flicked timidly along the edges of my figure, finally landing on my face as the only part of me that was moderately decent. 'And you, *Senhora*, can I not persuade you to turn back?'

'I'm afraid not.'

'Well, then, for pity's sake, will you at least put on some more, um...covering garment before I leave you? A gentle lady such as you should not...I mean I wouldn't be able to live with myself if you...'

He broke off, hopelessly, and just held out his cloak to me.

I shook my head, trying to suppress a smile. 'Thank you very much, father, but I like myself just the way I am.'

As if he hadn't expected any other answer, Father Marcos's shoulders slumped. 'Oh, well.' He sighed. 'Maybe it's just as well. You won't need many clothes where you are going.'

And with that encouraging comment, he turned away and hurried off into the forest, back towards his little cabin.

I stared after him.

'*You won't need many clothes where you are going?* What's that supposed to mean?'

Mr Ambrose gave me a calculating look. 'You'll understand soon enough.'

And with that, he turned away and marched off into the direction the priest had pointed out. I followed, walking more cautiously than before. I didn't know why, exactly, but I felt...nervous. When I reached the tree with the feather, I hesitated for some reason.

'Come on, Mr Linton!' Mr Ambrose's voice came from farther ahead. 'We haven't got all day!'

With a shrug, I shook off the strange feeling and stepped past the tree. Bah! What was a measly little feather? I wasn't going to let myself be intimidated by that! It probably had no significance anyway.

Or that, at least, was what I thought for the first five minutes of marching. Then, I began to feel them: the eyes on me. And I don't mean the eyes of Mr Ambrose or some love-struck little monkey. Oh no. These eyes were far more secretive. I never actually saw them. I heard a rustling here, saw a branch twitch there – but no glimpse of any curious eyes. They stayed out of sight, hidden in the shadows of the trees. But they were there. They were.

Are they? Or are you just hallucinating, Lilly? It wouldn't be the first time, after all.
No. That couldn't be. I could *feel* them. I knew I could.
Snap!
I whirled around. 'What was that? Did you hear that? What was it?'

'A snapping branch,' Mr Ambrose answered without bothering to stop or turn around. 'Calm down, Mr Linton.'

'Calm down? You want me to *calm down*? We're stuck in the middle of the Amazonian jungle, with no help for miles around, surrounded by God only knows who and you want me to *calm down*?'

'Yes.'

'We could be killed!'

'They won't kill us.'

'How do you know?'

'Because they're too curious to know what we want. They won't kill us until they've found out.'

'Oh, thank you, Sir! That makes me feel so much better!'

'You're welcome.'

Gah! I would really have loved to strangle him right then and there. Only, I knew if I got that close to him, even with mosquito bites all over me and anger boiling up inside, I would go for his mouth instead of his throat.

'I am gratified to hear that you have such a high opinion of our survival chances,' I said in the sweetest voice I could manage. 'Who are these mysterious "they" you are taking us to?'

No answer.

'Tell me! Now!'

No answer.

I was just about to reach for my gun, when my question was suddenly answered for me – but not by Mr Ambrose. It was answered by a man dropping out of a tree only a few yards ahead, blocking our path. More men followed, dropping from trees and appearing from behind bushes all around, their eyes narrowed and as sharp as the spears in their hands. All the men were dark-skinned, with strange, flat faces and slitted eyes. And, oh yes, one tiny little detail...They were all stark-naked.

'Mr Linton,' Mr Ambrose said, raising his hand, 'let me introduce you to "they". "They", meet Mr Victor Linton.'

GOING WILD

We reached the village by sundown. It sat atop a cliff high, high above the rain-forest, and the sinking sun cast everything into a golden light. That didn't make the two dozen or so sharp spears pointed at us any more visually appealing in my mind, however.

Mr Ambrose had been right in one respect – the natives were curious. They also, however, as suggested by the raised spears, the half-drawn bows and the searching gazes they directed at us, were immensely suspicious. They muttered to each other in hushed voices, using a strange, completely alien tongue that I had no hope of understanding.

'What are they saying?' I hissed at Mr Ambrose as we were slowly escorted up a path to the top of the cliff.

'How should I know?'

'*What*? You don't understand their language?'

'Strange though it might seem to you, Mr Linton, I do not, in fact, know everything there is to know.'

'How the hell do you expect to talk them into helping us if you don't speak their language?'

'Father Marcos told me that their leader speaks Portuguese.'

'And if they decide to kill us before we reach this multilinguistic gentleman?'

'That would be most unfortunate.'

We were at the edge of the village by now. The ring of men around us split at the front, giving me, for the first time, a view of an Indian village.[20] Honestly, at first glance, it wasn't much to write home about. About as much as this:

Dear XYZ,

My holiday in South America is going splendidly so far! I'm standing here with mosquito bites all over me and a spear jabbing into my back, struck dumb in awe at the sight of a few round, mud-brown huts with thatched roofs. Oh, and have I told you yet that there are mud-streaked paths leading from door to door? Isn't that wonderful? Oh, and of course, there are weapons leaning against the outside of the huts – really lovely weapons, with which we'll probably soon be violently killed.

I hope everything is going well with you at home, too? Hoping to hear from you soon, I remain,

Yours truly,

Lilly Linton

There, you see? Not much at all. Oh, except, of course:

P.S: There are a lot of naked people staring at me!

P.P.S: I don't just mean scantily dressed. I mean stark-buck-blasted naked!!!

P.P.P.S: I hope you had fun at the ball last week?

It wasn't just naked men anymore, either. Oh no. Women and children, scattered all around the village, were gathering quickly to stare at the newcomers, whispering excitedly to each other. The children weren't the problem. Eve's cousin was married with about half a dozen babies, so I had seen (and smelled!) my fair share of bare babies' bottoms in my life, although it wasn't exactly an experience I was keen to repeat. The women, however...

---

[20] I am aware of the fact that nowadays, 'Indian' or even 'native' are not exactly considered to be polite terms for the original inhabitants of the American continent, and that 'indigenous people' is the politically correct word. However, back in the 1850s, political correctness towards indigenous populations was not exactly high on anyone's agenda, and the two former terms were much more common. Therefore, I use them here in an effort to maintain historical accuracy.

Let me put it this way: in London, if a woman shows too much of her unmentionables – also known as legs to the uneducated – she would be decried as a loose woman. If any of these women here were to show up in London, people wouldn't get to the decrying. They would faint at the first sight of these ladies.

They were completely, utterly stark-naked.

Well – maybe it wasn't *strictly* true. They did wear something. A leather strap, about one inch wide, resting loosely on their hips. I was not one hundred per cent sure whether to count this as clothing, since it didn't actually cover more area than two or three postage stamps. The rest of them was visible. Very visible. In fascination, I watched a woman detaching a baby from her breast with no more ceremony or secrecy than I would use to open a letter or wave a fan. She met the eye of one of the armed men surrounding us, and sent him a meaningful look.

I pursed my lips, thoughtfully.

'Don't go getting any ideas, Mr Linton,' Mr Ambrose voice came in a growl from behind me.

'Whatever do you mean, Sir?'

My fingers strayed to my chemise. It really was still quite hot, even up here on the cliff. And, if I was going to be killed soon, I might at least be comfortable in my last few minutes...

Mr Ambrose's hand closed around my wrist like a vice.

'Don't even think about it!'

'About what?' Half turning towards him, I fluttered my eyelashes up at him. 'I'm afraid I really do not know what you could mean, Sir.'

He snorted. 'Yes, of course you don't! And my tailcoat has pink pig tails!'

'That could be arranged, if you want. I know a tailor back in London who is open to unusual requests.'

A spear jabbed me in the small of the back. I winced.

'However, that will probably have to wait until we're back in London. If we get out of here alive.'

'Oh, we'll get out of here alive all right.' Flexing his fingers, Mr Ambrose stepped towards the biggest of the huts, from which a large man with sharp, dark eyes had just stepped into the murky sunlight. 'Just don't take any more clothes off while I negotiate!'

'I'll do my best to restrain myself.'

Another jab in the back made it clear that we had better get moving. Armed men still hovering around us, curious women and children gazing on from everywhere, we were led to the big hut. The big man waited for us with arms crossed in front of his solid bulk.

'Their leader,' Mr Ambrose murmured. 'Let's see what he is made of.'

He came to a halt a few steps away from the big Indian, and met his gaze. The Indian, eyes hard, stared at Mr Ambrose. Mr Ambrose stared back. The man also stared back. Upon which Mr Ambrose reacted by staring back and narrowing his eyes infinitesimally. The Indian also narrowed his eyes infinitesimally, which made Mr Ambrose cock his head, threateningly. And then he continued to stare. Whereupon the Indian also continued to stare, to which Mr Ambrose responded by staring some more.

'Um...' I cleared my throat. 'Is this going to go on for long? Not that I mind – you have fun with your staring contest, if you want. I'd just like to have an opportunity to step behind a bush for certain necessary business in the not-too-distant future, if you get my meaning.'

Mr Ambrose gave a snort. 'I'm surprised you'd bother with a bush! Why don't you just do it here?'

Beside me, I saw all colour drain from Karim's face.

'Now, that wouldn't be at all ladylike, would it?' I asked, sweet as sugar. 'Can you please speed things up? You can growl at each other to find out who is the more manly man later.'

'Very well, Mr Linton. Let's see what this leader of theirs has to say.' Showing the big Indian both of his hands, presumably to demonstrate he was unarmed, Mr Ambrose took a step forward and asked: '*Você fala português?*'

The Indian studied him for a moment – then shook his head. Motioning for us to follow, he ducked into the hut. The three of us followed, Karim and I throwing each other puzzled glances. But our confusion didn't last long. Inside the gloomy hut, a hunched figure sat on the ground, legs crossed. As we approached, the figure lifted his head–

And I saw it wasn't *his* head at all.

It was *hers.*

The old woman smiled a crooked, gap-toothed smile. The big Indian marched to her side, gestured down and said, in a voice that brooked no argument: '*Português!*'

Behind Mr Ambrose, I grinned. 'Oh yes, let's see what that leader of theirs has to say, Sir. Go ahead, Sir. This should be interesting.'

'Mr Linton?'

'Yes, Sir?'

'Be silent!'

'Yes, Sir! As you wish, Sir!'

A muscle in his cheek twitching, Mr Ambrose folded his long legs and settled down in front of the old woman, who met his icy glare with another gap-tooth smile, totally unperturbed.

I liked these Indians already.

~~**~*~*

It took a while to get the preliminaries out of the way. Apparently, the natives in these parts had certain customs which included having the face of any passing visitor you welcomed into your home painted with red and yellow stripes. I must say, I hadn't thought these diplomatic negotiations would be that much fun. Mr Ambrose, suffering in silence, glaring at a wall of the hut as if it were solely to blame for all the problems of the world, was one of the most amazing sights I had ever seen. Karim was nearly as much fun. When the old lady was done with him, he looked like a demon from (a very colourful part of) hell.

'You look very handsome, Sir,' I congratulated Mr Ambrose when my own makeup was finished, trying my best not to laugh.

His icy gaze cut into me like a knife into butter. 'I would not have put up with this tomfoolery,' he growled, 'if it did not have some practical value!'

'Practical value?'

'Why do you think they paint the faces of their guests?'

'Um...because they like to watch people squirm?'

'No. Because it's a signal to the whole tribe that they shouldn't kill you at first sight.'

'Oh.'

Yes, I could see how that could have some practical value. Indeed.

'So, they have decided not to kill us?'

'For now, Mr Linton. The paint can easily be washed off.'

'True. So...what now?'

'Now?' Mr Ambrose flexed his fingers and fixed his cold gaze on the little old Indian lady. 'Now that they are finished, I will have my fun. It is time to negotiate. Karim, bring out the bag, please.'

The Mohammedan reached into his knapsack and pulled out a small leather bag, which he handed to Mr Ambrose. Mr Ambrose undid the knot that held the bag closed, but didn't pull it open yet. Instead, he focused on the old lady.

'Estamos à procura de um lugar. Um lugar secreto escondido na selva. Precisamos de alguém para nos guiar no cofre caminhos. Você pode fazer isso?'[21]

'What did you say to her?' I whispered.

I had learned some Portuguese on my way up here, but nowhere near enough to understand this.

'I told her what we want from them. That we need guides to see us on safe paths through the jungle.'

'You didn't mention the Brazilians, did you?'

'No. Why should I?'

That manipulative, scheming bastard...!

The old woman regarded him through narrowed eyes. They were old eyes. Eyes, which, I did not doubt, had seen much.

'É que todos?'

My Portuguese was good enough for that one. Is that all?

Oh, this old lady was good. Very good.

'Não,' Mr Ambrose was forced to admit, grudgingly. 'Há homens nos seguindo. Homens perigosos. Eles querem nos matar e tomar o que buscamos.'[22]

The old woman nodded, sagely.

---

[21] We are looking for a place. A secret place, hidden in the jungle. We need someone to guide us on safe paths. Can you do that?

[22] No. There are men following us. Dangerous men. They want to kill us and take what we seek.

'Estou entendendo.'[23]

'They know about the Brazilians now, don't they?' I enquired sweetly.

'What did I tell you about keeping quiet, Mr Linton?'

'Oops. Sorry, Sir, I forgot.'

'I'm sure you did.'

The old lady had watched our exchange with interest. If I wasn't very mistaken, I saw amusement twinkling in her eyes. They focused back on Mr Ambrose alone, not quite as hard and sharp as before.

'O que você está oferecendo?'[24]

What are you offering?

This was the prompt that Mr Ambrose had apparently been waiting for. With an air of reverence that made me think he was handling the Crown Jewels, he opened the leather bag on his lap and pulled out a small, shiny necklace of glass beads.

That was it.

That was all.

Still holding the thing as if it were made of diamonds, he handed it to the old lady with a little bow. The old lady for her part, without betraying any emotions, took the small necklace and lifted it into the air, gazing at it thoughtfully.

'What are you doing?' I hissed at Mr Ambrose.

'I am negotiating, Mr Linton.'

'You want them to lead us dozens, maybe hundreds of miles through the jungle, to risk getting in the way of professional soldiers for *that*?'

'Certainly.'

'Sir?'

'Yes, Mr Linton?'

'You are the most mean, miserly, stingy, tight-fisted and avariciously greedy bastard I have ever met in my life.'

'Flattery won't get you anywhere with me, Mr Linton.'

The old woman was still holding up the glass beads, watching how a ray of sunlight that fell in through a tiny gap in the roof sparkled on their surface. I could see it in her eyes – the almost childlike fascination for western marvels that had cost so many Indians their lands and freedom. Inside, I was fuming! I didn't want this old lady to be cheated! But what could I do?

Finally, she nodded, seeming to come to a decision. Returning her gaze to Mr Ambrose, she smiled.

'Eu aprecio seu senso de humor. No entanto, se você não quer acabar pendurado de cabeça para baixo de uma árvore com uma cobra morta enchido na sua bunda, eu sugiro que você se abstenha de piadas como esta no futuro.'[25]

Mr Ambrose stiffened, his eyes freezing over completely.

---

[23] I see.

[24] What are you offering?

[25] I appreciate your sense of humour. However, if you do not want to end up hanging upside down from a tree with a dead snake stuffed up your ass, I suggest you refrain from jokes like this in the future.

'Mr Ambrose?'

No reply.

'What did she say, Mr Ambrose, Sir?'

Still no reply.

'Karim? What did she say?'

The bodyguard cleared his throat. It sounded like a mountain belching. 'Um...I don't know if I should...'

'Tell me now, or you-know-what happens!'

Reluctantly, Karim yielded to superior force.

'She told the *Sahib* that she appreciates his sense of humour, but that if he does not wish to end up hanging upside down from a tree with a dead snake stuffed up his, um...posterior, he should refrain from jokes like this in the future.'

'Did she indeed?' As inconspicuously as possible, I peeked at Mr Ambrose out of the corner of my eye. His face was as unreadable as a book written upside down in coded Chinese with invisible ink. 'My oh my.'

This old lady was *really* good. If she kept this up, she would end up on my list of role models, right next to Jeanne D'Arc and Mary Astell.

I sent a smile to Mr Ambrose. 'That didn't go quite as expected, Sir, did it?'

A muscle in Mr Ambrose's jaw twitched. 'Indians aren't what they used to be,' he growled.

'Yes, just imagine, they don't want to be used and exploited anymore. Shocking, isn't it?'

'Indeed, Mr Linton.'

I didn't think he was joking.

'So? What now, Mr Ambrose, Sir?'

The old lady seemed to be interested in the answer to the very same question. Smiling her toothless smile at Mr Ambrose, she raised one eyebrow. The meaning was clear to everyone: *Anything else to offer?*

Mr Ambrose sat there, studying her for a moment in cool silence. He raised his hand and thoughtfully stroked two elegant, long fingers along that chiselled chin of his. Then, suddenly, he leapt to his feet and strode to the door. The big Indian stepped in his way, raising his spear, but the old woman barked a command at him, and he pulled back, letting Mr Ambrose pass. Without hesitation, he ducked through the doorway and stepped outside.

'What is he doing?' I demanded.

'I do not know,' Karim rumbled, looking just as puzzled as I felt. Jumping up, we started after our dear employer. To judge by the rustling and thumping from behind us, the old lady and her bulky guard were hot on our heels.

Outside, we found Mr Ambrose standing next to the extra packhorses we had acquired after our encounter with the Brazilians. Pulling back the leather coverings of one of the packs, he pulled out something long, sleek, and dangerously metallic. He had his back turned towards me, so I couldn't see exactly what it was – but I didn't need to. I knew what was on that horse.

Ka-cluck!

The metallic sound made my heart leap into my throat.

Good God! What is he doing? Is he going to...no! He can't threaten them! He can't be insane enough to try and force them to do what he wants at gunpoint!

But maybe he thought he could. He was Rikkard Ambrose, after all.

KABOOM

Mr Ambrose whirled around, a shining rifle in his hand. Shouts rose from the natives all around. Apparently, they had seen rifles before. From the looks on their faces, I would guess they had felt them, too. Bows, arrows and spears went up in a perfect symphony of threatening violence.

Mr Ambrose didn't seem perturbed. Swinging the rifle upwards, he fired, once, into the sky. I jumped, and so did nearly everyone else. Only the old woman remained standing still near the entrance of the hut, watching Mr Ambrose with a speculative glint in her eyes.

Mr Ambrose lowered the rifle until it was pointing straight ahead. Bowstrings all around were suddenly drawn back, arrows ready to be fired. But Mr Ambrose wasn't aiming at any of the natives. As best I could tell, he was aiming at a spot about a dozen yards to my left, where nothing stood but an old, empty bowl on the ground.

Bam!

The muzzle flashed, the rifle bucked, held in place only by Mr Ambrose's strong hands. With a *crack*, the bowl splintered into a dozen pieces and mud splattered up into the air. Mr Ambrose, as if completely unaware of the danger he was in, with hundreds of probably poison-tipped arrows aimed straight at him, marched over to the old Indian lady and held out the rifle to her, offering it with both hands. The old lady took it, and, a gleam in her eyes, ran her withered old hands along the shiny metal. Mr Ambrose marched back towards the packhorses and flung back the covering over their load all the way.

An excited murmur went up from all around as the sun sparkled on the barrels of at least forty rifles. Mr Ambrose focused his cool gaze on the old lady. She gazed back at him, clutching the rifle. He cocked his head in a gesture as clear as hers had been, earlier: *good enough for you?*

The old lady gazed down at the rifle in her hands once more – then nodded. From all around, cheers erupted.

~~**~*~*

I had to hand it to him. I really had to. He was hands down the hardest, coldest, most devious negotiator I had ever met in my entire life. He had basically managed to get everything he wanted in exchange for something that didn't actually belong to him. Nice trade, that, right?

I didn't know whether to be angry, impressed, or simply relieved. I probably would have been all three if I hadn't been busy being so thoroughly exhausted.

The effort of hiking hundreds of miles through the jungle was finally catching up with me. As soon as a good-hearted Indian lady showed me two suitable trees, I hung up my hammock, fell into it and was dead to the world. I think not even a lovesick monkey cleaning my ear could have woken me up right then and there. When I woke up, I was confused for a moment. The sun was just about where it had been when I had fallen asleep in the middle of the day – but the clouds were totally different, and so was the colour of the sky.

'What...?' My voice was nothing but a drowsy drawl. 'What time is it?'

'The real question,' came a cool voice from nearby, 'would be "what day?".'

Blinking, I hauled myself up until the statuesque form of Mr Rikkard Ambrose came into view not far away, sitting on a rock so still you might think he was part of the stone.

'I've slept more than one day?' I demanded.

A snap announced the opening of Mr Ambrose's silver pocket watch.

'Two days, three hours and twenty-seven minutes, to be precise, Mr Linton. But don't feel the need to end your nap prematurely. It's not as if we are in any hurry, with a horde of bloodthirsty soldiers on our track and an enormous treasure to find.'

I sat up all the way, shaking off the sleep. 'Why didn't you wake me?'

Mr Rikkard Ambrose never had an expression on his face. Never. But, if such a thing were possible, purely hypothetically, I would say that he looked a tiny bit sullen.

'That woman wouldn't let me.'

'Woman?'

His left little finger twitched. 'The old hag that gives the orders around here. She was quite firm in her admonishments in regard to your state. Seemed to think that I have overworked you in some way, which apparently isn't proper in our situation.'

I stared at him. 'In our situation?'

His cold, sea-coloured gaze met mine. 'For some reason, she seems to be labouring under the misapprehension that you are my...intended.'

'Intended?' My eyes almost bugged out of my sockets. 'Intended as in *engaged*?'

'I do not think they take things quite so formal here – but yes, in essence that is what she meant.'

I felt heat rush up to my face, and not for the first time was profoundly glad that my tanned skin didn't blush easily. Instinctively, my eyes flitted away from his, hiding under my lashes. 'What did you say?'

'Well, I put her straight, of course. And do you know what she did then?'

'No. What?'

A muscle in his jaw twitched. 'She *patted me on the head*, turned, and walked away!'

'Dear me.' I did my very, very best not to laugh as I visualised Mr Rikkard Ambrose being patted on the head. I didn't think I was entirely successful, though. 'That must have been...upsetting for you.'

Arctic eyes met mine, making it clear that I had better be quiet if I wanted to live to see the next day. Clearing my throat, I quickly changed the subject.

'So...this is why we are still here?'

'Yes.' His voice was less than pleased. 'She flatly refuses to help us before you are properly rested. She has threatened to instruct me in the proper way for a man to treat his...woman.'

An image flashed in front of my mind, of Mr Rikkard Ambrose sitting at a table, me beside him, being taught how to properly eat *mousse au banana* and roasted monkey bottoms by a little old Indian lady in a governess's outfit. I disguised my laughter as a cough as best I could.

Then I realised that the image didn't just make me want to laugh. It also made my stomach growl.

'Come on,' sliding out of my hammock, I stretched, yawning. 'I'm hungry. Time to find something to eat.'

However, apparently roasted monkey bottoms weren't exactly the main staple of the local tribe. Instead, the menu consisted mainly of roots, some big kind of fruit that grew on dark, gnarled trees and something that looked a bit like a potato, but tasted a lot sweeter. These were supplemented with various small birds and other animals, brought in every day by the hunters and roasted over an open fire.

The old Indian lady sat next to me during the whole meal, chattering away in Portuguese and force-feeding me choice morsels. Every now and again she would pat me comfortingly and glare at Mr Ambrose. I had to say, I hadn't enjoyed a meal like this in a very, very long time.

It turned out that the old lady had meant what she said. We were staying in the village for now, no matter how many frosty glares Mr Ambrose shot at the old lady. I was a bit worried about that, myself – after all, we did have half a battalion on our trail – but here we were probably as safe as we possibly could be. The Indian village was high up in the hills, up on a rocky cliff, where we would see any pursuers coming from miles away. Plus, our native friends had done their best to conceal our tracks on their way in. And, to judge by the way they slithered silently through the jungle, their best was probably the best there was.

So I decided, as long as we were here, I might as well put the time to good use. Every day I went to shooting practice with Mr Ambrose, and with my ultimate threat – emulating the native dress code – I got Karim to start teaching me Portuguese. And I wasn't just talking about curse words! It wasn't that I felt a deep-seated need to expand my language skills – it just pissed me off that I was the only one who could only communicate with hand gestures! The old Indian lady spent most of her time talking to me, and yet I didn't understand a single word she said! And...I would have liked to. Unlike many of my fellow females at home, who frittered away their lives on balls and buffoonery, I had a suspicion she was someone I could really talk to.

And what do you know? After a while it paid off. It only took me a few days, and I started to catch a word here and there in her conversations with Mr Ambrose. A few more days, and I spoke my first word in Portuguese. It was

'Bastard!' Oh, what a proud moment! If my mother still been alive, I'm sure she would have cried.

Mr Ambrose didn't appreciate the special moment fully, however.

I started helping out around the village, making a few really awful pots and bowls, and helping to weave a few cloths that were only fit for scarecrows. The other women found my attempts amusing enough not to mind. It turned out that a few of them also spoke broken bits of Portuguese, and with their help, I slowly started to be able to communicate. As long as the sentences were short and to the point, I could manage.

Communication had its dangers, however, as I learned a few days later. The men were just returning from the hunt. Mr Ambrose had gone with them, since, as he put it 'if I have to spend another minute in unproductive idleness, I will murder someone, just to have something to do!' The other men had been quite amenable, interested, I supposed, in seeing how one of the palefaces hunted with their exploding sticks. And, apparently, the hunt had been quite success-ful.

'Ay! Ay!'

The excited cries of a child were the first signal announcing the return of the hunters. Putting aside the pot I had been able to form, and which looked more or less like a pelican trying to commit suicide by tying itself into a knot, I stood up and, shielding my eyes against the sunlight, looked over to the distant entrance of the village, where an excited gaggle of naked children was already gathering.

His head – tall, dark and proud – was the first to appear out of the jungle. Then followed the long staff that was resting on his shoulder, and only then came the other men, helping to carry the staff. And then...

My mouth fell open, and I gaped at the shape of the enormous wildcat hang-ing limp from the stake that had to be carried by at least half a dozen men. The beast's face was twisted into a snarl in death, its fangs visible even from where I stood. The children were gaping in awe – but just for a moment. Then they started screeching in excitement and rushed forward, wanting to touch the enormous beast. Unlike them, I didn't stare at the leopard. I only had eyes for Mr Ambrose.

Light, slow footsteps approached from behind me. I didn't have to look around to know who it was. The old Indian lady hobbled to a halt next to me, supporting herself on a gnarled old stick. She regarded me with shrewd eyes.

'He.' The old woman nodded at the tall, dark figure striding at the head of the hunters. 'Strong. Quick. A good hunter.'

'He...good at...getting what he wants,' I grudgingly admitted in halting Portu-guese. 'No matter what.'

'Then why the two of you not make small things yet?'

I looked at her, nonplussed. 'Small things?'

'You know.' Letting go of her stick with one hand, she mimed the shape of a round, extended belly in front of her own, and winked.

Good God! She wasn't asking why we hadn't made 'small things'! She was ask-ing why we hadn't made 'little ones', as in...

I felt heat rush to my face.

'I...we...well...um...'

'Yes?'

The old lady regarded me like an owl, her head cocked to the side, her wide, wise old eyes looking disturbingly deep inside me. I tried to think of a way to explain the intricacies of feminism, women's rights and the men who denied them to this little old Indian lady – and couldn't. All those things seemed suddenly very far away.

'He arrogant!'

She waited – then, when I didn't say anything else, she prompted: 'Yes?'

'And stubborn! And greedy, and merciless and convinced he is always in the right!'

'Yes?' She was still watching me as if waiting for the important part of my explanation.

'Umm...that's it.'

'Girl, you just describe every great hunter.'

I blinked, desperately searching for more arguments, desperately trying to express what was my problem with Mr Ambrose.

'Um...he not...' I struggled, trying to find the right words. 'He not believe women as good as men.'

The old lady didn't seem very impressed. Instead, she just winked at me again. 'Well, then someone had better teach him differently, eh?'

~~**~*~*

The words of the old lady stayed with me, and over the next few days, I found myself watching Mr Ambrose again and again.

That was nothing new in a way – I'd had my eyes on him often enough in the past, to glare at him or glower or make sure he wasn't doing anything chauvinistic. But now I wasn't doing any of those things. I was simply...looking. Not at my employer. Not at the chauvinist, or even the businessman, but at the man beneath.

Rikkard Ambrose.

What kind of a man was he?

It startled me to realise how little I still knew about him. I had no idea where he came from, if he had family, what he had done before he had started dominating the world trade, and what had driven him to become the most powerful man in the British Empire. I had no idea who he really was.

And yet...

And yet, in another way, I knew exactly who he was. I knew he was hard and strong and unforgiving. I knew that he would take whatever he wanted and protect what was his to his last breath, and possibly beyond. I knew that he expected the best of himself and others, and did not forgive failure. I knew he breathed power like other people breathed air. And I knew that he had spectacularly firm pectorals. Oh yes, in a way, I knew Rikkard Ambrose. I knew him very well.

Well enough to help him change?

Good question, Lilly. But here's an even better one: do you want him to change at all?
Of course I did! He was a bloody chauvinistic son of a bachelor!
And you like him just the way he is, don't you?
No! No, of course I didn't!
Really? Think about how it felt, unbuttoning his shirt, sliding your hand over those smooth, hard pectorals of his...
Well, all right, maybe I did like *parts* of him. But purely in a sinful, lusting manner! It didn't have anything to do with really liking him or, God forbid, any of that yucky romantic stuff! That would be just...Ugh!
The thought of romance alone made me shudder. I felt like I needed a bath to wash the filthy thought off my skin. Actually, there were a lots of other things stuck to my skin – including sweat, little twigs and dead mosquitoes – that could do with washing off. But it wasn't very likely that I was going to find a bathtub in this wilderness, was it?
Sighing, I settled back against the wall of the hut outside of which I had been conducting my little foray into personal philosophy. Someone stepped out of the hut and I felt a familiar presence settle beside me.
'Something bothering you?' asked the old lady, a kind, if gap-toothed, smile on her face.
'I need a bathtub!' I sighed. *'Badly!'*
'Bath...tup?' The old lady repeated, puzzled. For once, it seemed, I had hit on a Portuguese word she didn't know.
'I need to wash,' I explained. *'But I not think there are things like bathtubs or showers here in village.'*
'Wash?' Her face brightened. *'Of course you can wash.'*
'I can?'
'Of course. You see there?' She pointed towards the centre of the village, where a little stream meandered through the huts. *'Stream run into lake. Lake spill over cliff. Waterfall come down from cliff. Small waterfall, not dangerous unless it rain. Go there and wash. Take your time. My grandson show you way to bottom of cliff.'*
I was so elated to be able to wash all the grime of my skin that I didn't even notice the devious twinkle in her eye. In retrospect, of course, I know I should have. Oh yes, I definitely should have.

~~**~*~*

The path down to the foot of the waterfall was winding but not long. The old lady's grandson guided me down as promised, grinning all the way. Normally, I would have been more than a bit concerned about being shown to a bathroom without doors or walls by a grinning adolescent boy, particularly if there were convenient bushes nearby to hide behind. But, in this particular case, the adolescent boy ran around butt naked among a community of equally butt naked people. Even if he were to spy on me, I doubted very much he'd see anything he hadn't seen before.
The boy called out and pointed ahead. I couldn't see anything yet, but then we rounded a corner and my mouth fell open.

The water fell down over the sharp, ragged cliff in a rainbow of glittering colour and silver, collecting in a charming little pool below that was so clear I could see the scales on every fish waggling their fins in the water. Flowers in golden-yellow, red and purple bloomed around the pool, interspersed here and there with a fresh spot of green. The scene looked like something out of an ancient Greek myth – a spring so clear only the gods would dare drink from it. But it was far more than a scene from a storybook. It was alive. In a flash, one of the fish jumped, water spraying in all directions, and before I could blink he had swallowed a mosquito and disappeared into the silver waters again.

Awed, I approached the beautiful spot. With care, I knelt down and slipped a finger into the water.

My eyes slid shut in bliss.

Oh...

Cool. Blessedly cool.

I slipped in my whole hand, then my arm, splashing the water all over my dirty face, and then, suddenly, there was no holding me back: I tugged off my boots, and without even bothering to pull off my chemise, plunged into the water. What the heck! It could do with a wash, too, anyway.

The water was like balm on my skin. No, actually better than balm, because balm is medicine, and medicine itches, and usually stinks into the bargain. This was...pure. Soothing. Cool. Clear. Wonderful.

The pool was not deep – just above waist height. I let myself sink back into the water and drift under the cool spray, just letting the water soothe my aching muscles, luxuriating in every second. I heard scuffling and, cracking one eye open, saw the boy running back up to the village. I was alone with the fish and the water and the wonderful, wonderful coolness all around me.

For a while I just drifted. Then I slowly forced my eyes open.

Get a move on, Lilly! You came here to clean up, not just to float around like the Lady of Shalott on holiday!

Taking a deep breath of the cool air – yes, even the air was cooler here in this heavenly spot – I got to my feet and started washing my hair, strand by unruly strand. My chemise was soaked by now, and while it was blissfully cool against my skin, it was also just about as see-through as you could get. So, just in case any of the boys from the village were spying on me after all, I moved behind a picturesque rock that rose out of the centre of the pool.

It took a while to get the worst tangles out of my hair. Finally, when I no longer felt as if I had a mop plastered to my head, I leant back against the rock with a sigh and for a few minutes just enjoyed the feeling of being (partially) clean. After a while, I decided it was time to stop lazing about, and started to pull off my chemise, to give it a thorough wash as well. The moment I began to pull the thing up, the water rushed in from all around me, tickling me deliciously. I was so lost in the bliss of cool air around me and clean water on my skin that, for a moment, I didn't even register the sound of approaching footsteps.

Wait a minute...*footsteps?*

And not any footsteps, either. No. These were quick, hard, determined foot-steps. Footsteps that I knew very well.

My hands dropped the chemise, and it fell back down, clinging to my wet skin.

No. No. No, no, nonononono *no*!

Clutching my skimpy garment to my chest, I peeked around the rock, pray-ing that I was wrong. Praying that I was right, too. The first prayer was denied. The second was answered.

There, right in front of me under the glittering shower of the waterfall, stood Mr Rikkard Ambrose, his back towards me, his shirt half unbuttoned. As I watched, he swiftly grasped the hem of the shirt and pulled it over his head, revealing all that lay beneath.

Oh dear God...

How did Father Marcos put it again?

Our Father, which art in heaven,

Lead us not into temptation.

Well – it was a bit too late for that now. Mouth dry and skin wet, I watched as droplets of water ran over hard, impenetrable muscles.

SIGHTSEEING

It wasn't like I had never seen a half-naked man before. All right, so most of the ones I'd seen had been made of marble and placed on pedestals in art museums, but so what? I knew pretty much what the male chest looked like. From some of the racier pieces I even had a pretty good idea of what was going on below the waistline.

Still...

None of that could have prepared me for *this*.

All those other sculptures had been made out of simple, soft marble. This one was made out of granite from the very centre of the earth. All those other sculptures only depicted heroes, kings, or paltry gods. This one depicted Rikkard Ambrose, in the flesh. And do you know what the best thing was?

Yep. It was alive.

The granite statue shifted, the perfect muscles in its back flexing with every movement. It – he – cupped his hands together and gathered up some of the clear, cool water of the pool. In a move so fast my eyes could hardly track it, his hands came up and splashed the water into his face. Droplets ran down his neck, over his broad, strong shoulders and down over his back. They twinkled on his skin like diamonds, calling me forward, begging to be touched.

I should go. I should definitely go. I should *not* be watching this.

Are you nuts? Of course you should! This is better than a week's worth of solid choc-olate! Who knew? Men are useful for something after all.

For watching them naked? No! No, no, no! That was *not* feministic!

Why not? They've been using and objectifying us poor women for a few thousand years. It's time we got a bit of our own back, don't you think?

No! I did most certainly not think that!

Are you sure?

Yes! Yes, absolutely sure! I should leave now. I should leave right away.

Then why aren't your feet moving?

Damn inner voice and her logical arguments! Why couldn't she just shut up and go away for once?

Because I'm too busy watching those delicious muscles flex. Yummy!

Oh, bloody hell! I should leave! I really should! It was just...the sight of Mr Ambrose standing there, water droplets running down his broad, bared back, the soaked cloth of his trousers clinging tightly to body parts I didn't even dare name, for fear of fainting – it was something you could not turn away from. Not if you were female and under the age of ninety-nine.

But I couldn't just stay here watching, could I? If I wasn't going to go, I should at least make my presence known, right? Standing here behind the rock was just so...

...the best bloody experience of your life?

No, no, nononono!

All right, being pressed up against a tree with his hands all over you and his lips devouring yours was the best. But this is a close second.

No! Shut up shut up shut up!

And I did shut up. Both my conscience and my seductive inner voice, and any other part of me that might have had something to say on the matter. They all shut up, because at that very moment, Mr Rikkard Ambrose took a step back, right into the waterfall.

My breath caught.

Where before there had only been a few single, solitary droplets running over his granite skin, there now was a shower of diamonds raining down upon him. Never in my life had I seen anything so magnificent. That was, until a second later, when he raised one of his arms and stretched, his biceps flexing, gleaming with sweat and sparkling water in the sunlight.

For a moment, standing there motionless, his fist raised into the air, he looked like some hero of old, triumphing over an ancient enemy. Then he lowered his arm again and once more looked like what he was: an arrogant, miserly son of a bachelor with a heart of stone and a body of even harder stone, perfectly sculpted to the last detail. He raised his other arm to stretch, and water droplets flew everywhere, surrounding the king of miserdom with a glowing halo of diamond.

Go on! Reach out! Touch him!

I just stood there, staring, behind the rock. Even if I'd had the willpower, I wouldn't have dared to move a muscle.

God! Get a grip, Lilly! Preferably on him, below the waistline!

A shiver ran down my spine – a shiver of need and want and must-have-right-now-or-else! This truly was better than the first time I had tasted solid chocolate. The chocolate had melted like heaven on my tongue. But if I were to taste *him*, take *him*, I knew it would be like heaven, and still he wouldn't melt. He would be there for another trip to cloud nine, and another, and another. My eyes bored into his back, devouring him with my hungry gaze.

I had to stop this. This was wrong. Profoundly wrong, and unfeminist. But I was like an addict sucking on an opium pipe, desperate for more. What to do? Damnit, what to do?

Stay!

No. I had to go, I had to...

Stay!

I had to...I...had...to...

Taking up handfuls of water, Mr Ambrose began stroking his body. Well, I guess he was rubbing the dirt off, but it *looked* like stroking to my over-heated, overactive mind. The voice of my conscience gave a desperate squeak and then went silent forever. I stayed in hiding, my eyes pinned to the delicious sight in front of me, my hands clutching the rock for support.

I was staying to watch.

I was staying in hiding, and I was going to watch until Mr Rikkard Ambrose had cleaned every last morsel of dirt from his smooth granite skin. What was the harm? I was safely hidden behind the rock, right? He would never know.

I should have known better. This was Rikkard Ambrose – the man who could smell money a mile away, the man who walked through the jungle as if he owned it, and had more eyes and ears than I had ambitions.

'Why don't you come out from behind that rock?'

I sucked in a breath. His voice was as cold as midnight moonlight in the arctic. My fingers dug into the rock painfully hard.

Calm down! He can't know it's you! He's just guessing!

'Well, Mr Linton? What are you waiting for?'

Damn and blast!

I didn't move.

But he did.

Slowly, so slowly I thought I could almost hear the stone of his bones grating against each other, he turned around, his shirt still clutched in one powerful fist.

I felt my knees go weak.

Mr Rikkard Ambrose from behind was a sight you could never forget. But Mr Rikkard Ambrose from the front? He was more than unforgettable. He was unforgivable. The moment you clapped eyes on him, you would feel honour-bound to your fellow females to hunt down and kill any deity who had dared create anything that male, perfect and irresistible. It was simply not fair! It was inexcusable, a mortal sin no woman could forgive, unless...

...unless, of course, this man could be hers, and hers alone.

Now you're talking!

For the first time in a very long time, my inner voice and I were in complete agreement. Both she and I were speechless from awe as my eyes raked the perfect, chiselled statue that was Rikkard Ambrose. His broad, hard chest, the valleys and ridges of his abdomen – all was as smooth and hard as diamond, and just as impenetrable and unmoving. The only sign that there was life underneath the shell of smooth stone was a light trail of hair, rising up to his navel from underneath his trousers, from the place where...

All right, Lilly, best stop thinking there, if you want to stay upright and conscious! One step after another!

With difficulty, I raised my eyes from his body to his face, and saw that I had been mistaken. The trail of hair was not his only sign of life. There also were his eyes, roiling with a dark storm of epic proportions, promising to swallow me whole.

'I cannot help but notice,' he said in a voice as deadly as a boa constrictor, 'that you are still behind that rock, Mr Linton.'

I nodded, unable to form a single syllable. I didn't know whether he even saw it from where he stood. The only thing he could see of me was probably one wide eye and a few wild strands of hair. Whereas what *I* could see of *him*...

My thoughts ran away and started frolicking.

Mr Ambrose fixed those dark, sea-coloured eyes of his on mine. They bored into me with the force of a thousand crashing icebergs.

'Come!' he commanded.

As if pulled by invisible puppet strings, my feet started to move. Slowly, hesitantly, I stepped out from behind the rock, clutching my sodden chemise to me. It didn't do much in the way of concealment.

'Closer!'

I took another hesitant step forward. My eyes devoured every inch of him.

'How long have you been standing there, watching me, Mr Linton?'

Suddenly, I found a small smile playing around the corners of my mouth. 'Not nearly long enough.'

He smiled no answering smile – but the storm clouds in his eyes started swirling, forming a hurricane.

'Is that so, Mr Linton?'

'Indeed it is, Sir.'

I took another step forward, without waiting to be invited. He shifted, his muscles tightening, his eyes narrowing infinitesimally.

'And why in Mammon's name are you here at all? Is it a habit of yours to watch half-naked gentlemen bathing?'

'Not yet. But I might take it up in the future. It's quite...interesting.'

A growl ripped through the air. I looked around, panicking, trying to make out the panther or tiger – until I realised the growl was coming from Mr Ambrose's throat.

'Answer my question, Mr Linton! *What are you doing here?*'

I took another step forward, my chin rising. I didn't like his tone! Not one bit!

'I came here to bathe! The old lady sent me down here and told me–'

'She did *what?*'

I blinked at him, taken aback by the vehemence in his voice. 'I told you. She sent me down here and told me I could shower under the waterfall. She told me I wouldn't be disturbed.'

'That old witch!'

'Witch?' I stared at him, nonplussed. 'Why? What's wrong with telling me I could shower here in peace?'

'Nothing.' His eyes, for the very first time, left mine and slid over me. I could feel his gaze, like a sweet, cold finger gliding over me, touching every inch of my skin. 'Except she told me the exact same thing when she sent me down here not five minutes ago.'

'Oh.'

Mr Ambrose's left little finger twitched – not once, or twice, but three times. 'That conniving little old...! When I next see her, she is going to regret this.'

Funnily enough, though, it didn't seem as though he particularly regretted it. His eyes were still fastened to me, and deep down in their unfathomable deaths, I could see something wild. Something hungry. Something that didn't regret coming here at all.

'Well...' I licked my lips. 'I guess one of us should probably go.'

I didn't move.

'Yes,' he agreed after a while. 'Someone should.'

He didn't move either.

'Well, go on then!' I told him.

His dark eyes flashed. 'What? *I* have no intention of leaving!'

'I was here first!'

'And I outrank you, Mr Linton.'

'Ladies first, Sir, remember?'

'And do you remember, Mr Linton, that while you work for me, you are not in fact a lady?'

'Really?' Without warning, I lowered my arms from around my body, for the first time giving him a full few of me in my wet chemise. 'Are you sure about that?'

'Gnk.'

'Sorry Sir? What was that?'

He cleared his throat.

'Go! Go, Mr Linton! That is an order!'

'Oh, an order? Well, all right, then.'

I took a step towards him.

'I said *go*, Mr Linton!'

Another step.

'I am going, Mr Ambrose, Sir.'

'I meant *away*, not *towards me*!'

'Oh, did you?' I took another step forward, moving sinuously through the water, like a siren on the prowl. He was almost within reach now. 'What a shame that you didn't express your original instructions more precisely.'

'Mr Linton, I'm warning you! Be careful or–'

My finger brushed his lips.

One brush of my fingers against his lips.

That was all.

That was all it took to silence his protests. His eyes blazed with cold fire and silent thunder. Even though I was only touching one infinitesimally small patch of skin, I could feel his whole body tense under my touch – a granite predator, ready to spring. The water droplets clinging to his skin quivered as his chest heaved, sucking in a harsh breath. Slowly, very slowly, my finger travelled down from his lips, over his throat and down to the great, smooth expanse of his chest. There was power in this hard stone marvel. Leashed power, tight and controlled, just waiting to be released. I could feel it, pulsing just under his stony skin. What if I were to step forward? What if I were to unlock that power and–

A hand shot up, catching my finger in mid-movement. My eyes flicked up from a stone statue's bare chest to meet the very alive eyes of Mr Rikkard Ambrose. There was no compromise in them. No room for doubt or hesitation. Only desire, and the power to get what he desired – no matter what!

'I told you to be careful!' he growled. 'You wouldn't listen!'

In a flash his arms were around me. I felt myself being hauled up out of the water and then I was suddenly pressed against a bare granite chest, and we were under the waterfall, in a world of flying diamonds and shining dreams. Good God! Was this really happening?

My common sense said no. My inner feminist said no. But his dark, deep, unfathomable eyes screamed yes with a thousand silent shouts. His hands slid up underneath my chemise, and his skin against mine was hot and cold and scolding and icy all at once, making me burn with a need for this solitary iceberg of a man that was so intense I could almost taste it.

Almost?

Scratch that!

His lips came crashing down on mine and they were sweet, sweeter than any solid chocolate ever produced by man. Now I *could* taste my need, and what's more, I could taste *his*. It was there, on his lips devouring mine, on his tongue claiming my mouth for his own. My mouth was fighting back, wanting not to be conquered but to conquer, to take possession of this man and never let go. My hands swept greedily over him, bared to me by the luckiest of chances. Who knew when I'd have an opportunity like this again? I needed to take advantage of it now! Or better yet, I needed to take advantage of him!

I mashed myself more tightly against him, and through the sheer material of my chemise I could feel every hard line of his body. My hands started roaming over his smooth, powerful torso, claiming every inch for my own. But it still wasn't enough! Breaking our kiss, my lips slid from his and raced down over his throat, towards his shoulder.

'Aar!' The groan he let out as my teeth sank into his muscled shoulder was sweet music to me. 'Mr Linton! What the hell are you doing?'

Licking my lips, I grinned up at him. Bending to his shoulder again, I placed a soft, gentle kiss on the place where the bite mark, *my* mark, was beginning to form.

'Mine,' I whispered.

I didn't think it required any more explanation.

A ravenous growl erupted from his throat, and he hauled me up against him, claiming my mouth once more.

'My little *Ifrit*!' he whispered against my lips.

'Really? I thought *ifrits* were supposed to have fiery wings. We're under a waterfall.'

'Doesn't matter!' His voice was harsh and chopped, his breathing unusually heavy. 'You burn hot enough to light an ocean on fire!'

'So, my wings are still there?' Smirking, I captured his lower lip between my teeth, just for a moment. 'I can still fly?'

'Yes!'

'Then come fly with me!'

His answer was lost in an animalistic sound out of the back of his throat. His hands on my back travelled up and further up, until they were clutching my neck, securing my lips to his, making escape impossible. As if I wanted to! My chemise was pushed up dangerously, deliriously high now. I could feel bare skin on mine where I had never felt it before, where no young unmarried lady should ever feel it.

'Come!' he demanded.

I tightened my grip on him. 'Need you!'

We were only able to speak in monosyllables now. Anything else got lost in our short, hot, panting breaths. The thrill shooting through me nearly set my head on fire. Despite all my carefully laid plans, my decision not to lose my head, I was going to do something forbidden. And I was going to do it with Mr Rikkard Ambrose!

'Closer!' he ordered again.

'C-closer?'

'Now!'

It wasn't a question – but I answered anyway.

'Yes!'

We were so tightly pressed against each other now, you couldn't have fit a knife blade in between. We didn't fit together perfectly – not at all! I was soft, and he was hard. I was curvy, and he was flat as a washboard. It would have been hard to find two people who fit together less well. But who the hell cared? Even as a child, I'd had the most fun hammering rectangular toy blocks through round holes! And right now, I wanted nothing so much as to hammer him good and proper!

'Not here!' he growled.

'What?' I was so delirious now, I could barely understand single words.

'Out of sight! Behind rock!'

'No! Now! I need–'

My words ended in a squeal when, in a move too fast for me to blink, his hands slid down behind my thighs. He lifted me out of the water as if I were just another little fish caught with his spear, and we were off. In a moment we were behind the rock, effectively hidden from the eyes of the world. He continued until we were standing in the centre of the waterfall, the spray of water less than gentle here. I frowned. Was it stronger than before? Or was that just my imagination, feeling everything stronger in this whirling, glittering whirlpool of lust?

'Why here?' I whispered. 'Still feel the need to wash, do you?'

'No!' His answer was raw. His hands still had hold of my thighs and didn't seem to want to let go. 'If I don't cool off a little, I'm going to do something I'll regret.'

Cool off? As in...he felt hot? Mr Rikkard Ambrose?

My fingers skimmed over his wet skin. It was true. His voice was cold, his eyes were cold – but his body with burning. Burning for me.

'Do it!' I demanded. 'No regrets!'

'But–'

I stretched until my lips were at his ear, caressing his earlobe. 'Do it!'

His eyes found mine. Even through the downpour all around us, I could see their swirling depths, calling me, demanding all of me.

'Hold on!' he commanded.

I clenched my legs around his hips, clinging to him like a little lovesick monkey. Removing one hand from under my thighs, he reached for the buckle of his belt. A cheap-looking, tarnished old thing that no London tailor in his right mind would put on for sale. But right then and there, I didn't care how cheap his belt buckle was. I only cared that it would be opened pronto!

Torturously slowly, he slid one finger underneath the strap and started to pull. Inch by inch, it pulled back, taking the buckle with it.

'Get a move on!' I growled. His hand under my thigh was like a living, breathing brand burning into my skin. His fingers flexed, sliding up my thigh, and I couldn't keep a small moan from escaping my throat. To hell with it! There was no way he could have heard over the roar of the waterfall.

'Getting impatient, are we?' his cool, composed voice whispered into my ear.

He'd heard! How the hell had he heard?

'No!' I denied.

He flexed his fingers again, and I sucked in a breath.

'Indeed? I do believe you're misreading the situation, Mr Linton.'

'Get that blasted buckle open!' I groaned. 'And stop calling me Mister!'

His hand slid further up my thigh. 'Hm...we might just come to an agreement on the latter point. A modification of terminology seems appropriate.'

Good God! His words set my body on fire, burning me up from tip to toe. I heard, from very far away, like a distant echo, the *click* of metal on metal. The belt buckle!

I glanced down, trying to see if it was open yet – but I could hardly see anything. For a moment I thought a haze of passion was clouding my eyes – but a haze of passion would be red, right? Or maybe a nice shade of purple. But certainly not brown! No self-respecting haze of passion would be brown, right?

I opened my mouth to ask what was going on – and got a mouthful of water in reply. Muddy water. Good God, the waterfall really had started spouting like crazy for some reason. And it wasn't quite as clear and wonderful anymore as a few minutes ago.

Still, I'd be damned if I let a few drops of water keep me from my goal! My hand reached out and grabbed Mr Ambrose's hair, directing his attention down towards the belt buckle.

'Get on with it!'

His dark eyes met mine. Or at least I thought they did. It was a bit hard to tell through the increasing shower of mud. 'I intend to Mr Linton. I–'

He was abruptly interrupted when a great bucketload full of dirty water hit him straight in the face.

'Pfft! Brrz! Rg!'

His hand abruptly let go of my thigh and suddenly I was falling. Something hit the back of my head, and then everything was blue and brown and green and I couldn't breathe anymore. A fish darted past me, casually waving its fins at me. I didn't really feel like being courteous and waving back.

'Bfft!' Resurfacing, I spat water and mud, and probably a few smaller fishes. 'What the hell...?'

But nobody heard my words. They were drowned out by the roar of the waterfall and the background music of a torrential downpour. With a speed only a rainforest can offer its guests, it had started pouring. Water hammered down on the little pool, turning its surface into a turbulent, liquid drumhead. The waterfall was quickly turning from a sprinkly little fountain into a sledgehammer made of water.

No! No, we're not giving up! Not for a bit of bloody water!

Not waiting for his opinion on the matter, I grabbed Mr Ambrose's belt buckle and pulled. Damn, those things were difficult to operate! How did men ever get them open?

I had just one second for wistful thoughts of my corset laces before a pair of strong hands grabbed me and pulled me up, away from the buckle. Mr Ambrose claimed my mouth with need, desire, and dirty water on his lips. Somehow, he still managed to taste delicious.

'Get that damn buckle open!' I demanded against his lips. 'I want to–ppft!'

I gagged on a mouthful of mud.

'Yes!' he growled! 'One second and I'll–Rrrg!'

Bloody hell! It was getting increasingly difficult to whisper sweet, hot nothings at each other without getting a mouthful of fertiliser.

Mr Ambrose's fingers released me, fumbling at the buckle.

'Do it!' I commanded. 'I want you so badl–mmpf! Grk!'

Damn! How come heroines in romance novels never had to deal with this kind of stuff?

'Doing...best...I...can! I am–ppft!'

'What's the – mfff! – matter?'

'Damn...slippery thing...won't...opmpff! Grks!'

'Do you need a – pfft! – manual?'

'Mind your – Grk! Mpf! – language!'

Exasperated, I rolled my eyes upward – which was why I was the first to see the piece of driftwood tipping over the edge of the waterfall and hurtling down towards us.

'Look out!'

I shoved Mr Ambrose in the chest – which had about as much effect as a chick shoving a Rottweiler. I catapulted myself back, landing hard against the rock.

'What is the meaning of this, Mr Linton?' Mr Ambrose demanded, regarding me through the downpour with narrowed eyes. 'Have you lost your mi–'

That was when the piece of driftwood hit his head with a dull *thunk*.

'Oh my God, Sir! Are you all right, Sir?'

'Ng...!' he said – and collapsed into the pool.

FAREWELL

Pulling that blasted granite block of a man to the shore took me nearly half an hour – partly because he weighed about a ton, partly because I was so busy cursing every atom of water in the pond and the waterfall. But the most difficult problem was the man himself. No matter that he was only half-conscious and bleeding from the head, he was apparently quite well enough to know he did not wish to be saved from drowning by a girl. I pointed out that while I worked for him, I technically was no girl, correct? He had said so himself, after all.

For some strange reason, this didn't seem to soothe him.

'L-let g...of m...me.'

'Shut up!'

I tugged on his collar, hard. Reluctantly, he slid a few more inches out of the water.

'Th-that is an ordl...ordo...order!'

'And this is a better one: shut up right now!'

Amazingly, he did. Though, to judge by the way he sagged and his head lolled to the side, I guessed it wasn't one hundred per cent voluntarily.

'Help!' I yelled, though there was little chance of anybody up the cliff hearing me over the roar of the waterfall. 'Help! *Socorro! Socorro!*'

It turned out I needn't have worried about nobody hearing me up on the cliff. I had hardly dragged Mr Ambrose onto the bank when, from behind a bush a little up the path, a familiar head of grey hair appeared.

'Ah!' The old Indian lady looked from me to the prone figure of Mr Ambrose, impressed. '*You wear him out? Good girl!*'

'*No. The piece of wood did that for me.*'

'*Wood?*' The old lady grinned. '*You use piece of wood? What you up to, you naughty girl, eh?*'

'*Will you help me to get him up to the village? Or call for help, please?*'

'*No worry! He no have stamina? He fine in morning.*'

For the first time I was profoundly grateful that Mr Ambrose was unconscious. I shuddered to think what he might have said – or done! – if he had been awake for that particular part of the conversation.

'*His, um, stamina is fine. He got a knock on the head.*'

'*Oh?*' Stepping forward, the old lady bent over to examine Mr Ambrose's head wound – and then shrugged. '*No worry! I did same with my first husband sometimes. Three good knocks on head, and he be good husband.*'

Deciding that it probably wouldn't be very fruitful to continue this conversation, I took a tighter hold on Mr Ambrose's arm and tugged. Slowly, he began to slide farther up the bank. The old Indian lady, after a few minutes, sighed and grabbed the other arm, helping me to pull him through the downpour, away from the muddy waterfall. We didn't make it very far, though. We had only got to the start of the cliff path when Mr Ambrose slipped out of our exhausted arms and slumped to the ground. We promptly followed, panting like race horses after the Derby.[26]

'*He...heavy!*' the old lady grunted. '*Lot of muscle! Make good children, will he!*'

I did not venture an opinion on the matter.

'*Just you wait and see.*' Reaching over, the old lady affectionately patted my stomach. '*A few months, and you see what I mean.*'

Groaning, I covered my eyes with my hand.

~~**~*~*

It took a while for me to digest what had almost happened.

Congress.

And not the kind they had in America, either, with the delegates and the boring speeches. No, this was far worse. *Amorous* congress. With *Mr Rikkard Ambrose!*

What kind of demon had taken temporary possession of my mind?

I didn't know. But I knew it had to have been a damn devious one! There was simply no other way to explain what had happened. I mean, me? Me playing the blanket hornpipe? Basket making? Getting my bread and butter?[27] With *Mr Rikkard Ambrose?*

And it wasn't even as if he had wrestled me to the ground and overwhelmed me with the overwhelming force of his dark, ice-cold eyes and delicious body. *That* I could have understood. Instead, it had been me who had attacked him,

---

[26] The Derby Stakes, popularly known as The Derby, is a British horse race open to three-year-old horses. It was established in 1779 and named after Edward Smith-Stanley, 12th Earl of Derby.

[27] Every one of those three expressions is a Victorian euphemism for 'having sex'.

and practically ordered him to dance the fandango de pokum[28] with me. In the middle of the jungle! *Under a waterfall!*

Not for a moment had any of the repercussions crossed my mind. And to be honest, if I thought of Mr Ambrose's hot mouth on mine, devouring me in the sweetest way possible – they still didn't seem all that important to me. Which was, of course, completely ridiculous. If we really and truly did it, I could end up pregnant – or worse – married! I mean, if there was a way to live in sin for the rest of my life without blowing up like a balloon...now, that would be interesting. But *marriage*? Ugh!

Really? Are you sure that's how you feel, Lilly?

Yes! Marriage was an instrument of the patriarchy designed to oppress womanhood!

Is it? Is it really?

Yes! I had only to think back on that *Times* article on 'quarrelsome wives', and the idea of marriage made me want to get a bucket to puke in. I would die before I ever became a slave to a man!

But spending the rest of my life side-by-side with one...

Strange how the idea didn't seem quite as abhorrent as it had a while ago. Especially if we were talking about one particular man.

Getting Mr Ambrose up the cliff hadn't been half as difficult as I had thought. He had woken up shortly after we had dragged him ashore, and after the old lady had called two of her people down, had managed to stagger up to the village with two strong natives supporting him. I had to admit, I enjoyed the sight. It was probably the first and last time I would see Mr Rikkard Ambrose staggered.

I wasn't particularly worried about his head wound. That man had a skull as thick as a rock, and I was betting he would be up and about again in no time, ready to order me about and stare at people just as coldly as ever. Still...when the old lady asked if anyone would sit up with him during the night, for some reason I volunteered.

So now I was sitting next to Mr Ambrose in the dark silence of the hut, gazing into space, lost in thought. Mr Ambrose was a dark form against the wall, lying on a thin mat, as stiff in sleep as he was awake. He didn't snore, didn't move, gave no sign of life at all – but I still wasn't worried. He would pull through. Of course he would. I definitely absolutely totally wasn't worried.

Is that so?

Bloody inner voice of mine! Couldn't it shut up for two minutes?

Swallowing hard, I shifted closer to Mr Ambrose. A strip of moonlight was falling into the hut through the door, illuminating his face. There was no trace of blood now. The tribe's doctor, or medicine man, or whatever he was called, had washed it off, and applied a nasty-smelling poultice to the head wound. But in my mind's eye, I could still see the line of blood trickling down the side of his face. His hard, cold, incredibly beautiful face...

---

[28] Another nice little Victorian euphemism for getting hot and sweaty with someone.

Suddenly, my hand started to move. I had no idea why. *I* certainly didn't tell it to sneakily creep out of my lap and across the floor. I most definitely didn't tell it to skulk across the floor and sidle up to Mr Ambrose's cheek like a thief in the night. This was outrageous! Who had taken control of my bodily parts?

My hand didn't seem to share my outrage. In a manner that was altogether too self-satisfied for my taste, it settled down on Mr Ambrose's cheek and – of all things! – began to *stroke* it! In a way that was suspiciously reminiscent of tenderness.

But things didn't stop there. Oh no! My hand had the bloody cheek to slip away from his cheek (no pun intended) and slide down, over his chest and abdomen, until it reached his hands, lying folded on his taut belly. And what did it do then? It took his hand, and squeezed it, *sweetly*, almost *lovingly*.

'Wake up, will you?' I whispered. 'There are plenty of people left in the world for you to fleece and terrorise.'

~~**~*~*

Mr Ambrose woke up the next morning, grouchy as an old bear who had just woken out of hibernation to find out he'd had a full-body shave. Luckily, by then my hand had started to behave itself again, and I was sitting in my corner of the hut, where I belonged. I greeted him with the brisk efficiency of a secretary who *hadn't* spent the day before half-naked in a pool with her employer, and informed him straight up that, no, we couldn't leave right away, not until he could stand up on his own two feet and walk in a straight line for more than three steps.

'Don't be ridiculous, Mr Linton,' he snapped, and pushed away the blanket my traitorous hand had pulled over him during the night. 'I feel perfectly fine.'

Bracing himself against the wall, he pushed himself up and started forward. 'There, you see? Perfectly finnng...!'

There was a thud as his face collided with the floor. I had to admit, I felt a bit sorry for the poor floor. It didn't deserve such a harsh beating.

'Back to bed with you, or I'll be calling Karim!' I threatened. 'He'll tie you down if he has to.'

'Unlike you,' Mr Ambrose informed me, his voice muffled against the floor, 'Karim is a loyal employee. He will follow my orders, not yours.'

'Not if I threaten him with you-know-what. Back to bed, now!'

'This is mutiny. If we were on a ship, you could be hanged for this.'

'How fortunate for me that we are not on a ship, then, Sir.'

He continued to grumble a bit, and then contented himself with being icily silent at me. Nobody could be icily silent like Mr Rikkard Ambrose. I swear, he brought the temperature in the hut down to minus twenty degrees. Fortunately, after nearly a year in his employ, I was almost immune to frostbite, and was able to change his bandage without my fingers turning black and falling off. The old Indian lady came in after a while and told Mr Ambrose in no uncertain terms that he was not going to leave until he had fully recovered.

Of course, I should have expected him to make a record-time recovery out of sheer contrariness. After only a day, he was back on his feet, and after two days, he was ordering Karim about, gathering supplies and making other preparations for our departure. Our time in the Indian village was coming to an end. I had to admit, I was a bit sad about that. I had grown really fond of the old lady who was in charge here. On the other hand, maybe it wasn't such a bad idea we were leaving. I wasn't completely sure Mr Ambrose would survive her next attempt at matchmaking.

The last few days I spent taking long walks, building up my muscles, gathering supplies and using every free minute to expand my Portuguese vocabulary. I had a feeling I was going to need it before this journey was over.

Finally, the day of departure arrived. The old lady would not be coming with us. She had – with considerable regret – explained that her bones were too old and creaky for adventure. But she had hand-picked those of her people who would be accompanying us, among them the big fellow with whom Mr Ambrose had had a staring contest on the first day, and a girl called Amana, for whose company I was profoundly glad, since she was one of the few women who hadn't smiled condescendingly at my failed pottery attempts. Her name meant 'rain' in their language – but to judge from her temperament, 'gentle, nice little shower' would have been more appropriate. Except for being stark-naked and brown as chocolate from head to toe, she reminded me of my little sister Ella.

We were all gathered in front of the old lady's hut, our weapons ready, our packhorses laden with provisions. I felt a little tug in my heart as I looked around at all these people, many of whom had somehow become my friends, although we only spoke a word or two of the same language. It was strange. I didn't make friends easily, back in London. But here...

The curtain covering the hut's door was swept aside and the old lady stepped out, using a rifle as a walking stick. The sight of her brought my meandering thoughts to an abrupt halt. She flashed me a brief, warm smile, then shot one at Mr Ambrose which wasn't quite so warm.

'We gather,' she began in her throaty voice, 'to say goodbye to friends. They have been good friends. Some good hunters-'

She nodded at Mr Ambrose and Karim.

'-and some good company.'

She nodded at me. I couldn't suppress a smile.

'We will welcome them back at any time - if they bring me such nice presents again.'

Her fingers flexed around the rifle. Mr Ambrose's left little finger twitched.

'They have asked to be guided to the city in the mountains, far away to the west. What do you say, my people? Do we grant their request?'

Unanimous shouts of agreement went off from all around. Shots rang out as bullets pierced the sky.

'Then it is decided! They will set off immediately, guided by the very best of our people. Chandresh, step forward!'

The big Indian we had met on our first day in the village stepped towards the old lady, his chest proudly puffed out.

'Chandresh, my grandson, you will guide our friends on their journey. Do not lead them astray. Their lives are in your hands.'

I had expected him to bow, or clap his fist to his heart, or do something equally dramatic. But all he did was nod and gesture to his men. Immediately, five Indians ran off into the jungle, scouting ahead.

'As for you,' the old lady continued, turning back to Mr Ambrose, 'I leave you in good hands. You will reach your goal safely. Whether or not you find everything there that you are looking for - that is your business. However, before we part, I have one more thing to say to you.'

Standing up on her tiptoes, she leaned towards Mr Ambrose and whispered something to him in Portuguese, too fast and low for me to understand. Whatever it was – it made his eyes flicker to me, just for a split second. He said something back to her, sharply, and the old lady shook her bony finger under his nose.

Bloody hell! What on earth was that about?

I didn't get a chance to wonder about it for long. Mr Ambrose nodded to Chandresh, the big Indian barked a command and we were off, marching between the village huts towards the jungle. The remaining tribe cleared a path for us, waving their bows and guns in the air and shouting encouragement. We passed the last hut. The line of trees loomed ahead, beckoning to us. Slowly, the shouts of encouragement from behind us grew dimmer and dimmer, until finally, they faded into the distance. The first trees began to rise up on either side of us, their tops towering above our heads. Following Chandresh's lead, we marched deeper into the shadow, until mist and hot, green shadows surrounded us.

The jungle had swallowed us again.

~~**~*~*

In a lot of ways, our journey through the jungle was a good bit nicer than it had been before. For instance, I was by no means so worried about the Brazilians finding us, with dozens of Indian guards around us, leading us by safe paths and obscuring our tracks. Then, there was the fact that my days as a tree-climbing monkey were over. The Indians were perfectly able to find their way through the jungle without clambering up trees. And when it did prove necessary once in a while, Amana pushed me aside with a gentle smile. She was the fastest tree-climber and best jungle-sneaker in the whole tribe. A spider monkey couldn't hold a candle to her (even if spider monkey were in the habit of using candles).

But there were still some aspects of the journey that were as bad as ever. In fact, they grew worse. Foremost among those were the heat and the mosquitos. We had to be getting closer and closer to the equator. With every step, it seemed, the jungle seemed to be more determined to cook me alive and suck my blood. I even briefly wondered whether these mosquitos here in the Amazonian jungle were distantly related to the vampires that had become so popular in penny dreadfuls[29] back home recently. They definitely seemed pretty determined to suck an innocent, helpless virgin dry!

Maybe you should just do something about that virgin thing, then...

That method of insect protection was very tempting, admittedly. But there were a few too many people around to implement it speedily. Besides, there were still those pesky little issues attached to losing your virginity – like pregnancy or becoming a social pariah. So I marched on and bore the mosquitos as patiently as a martyr. Except for the complaining. Lots and lots of complaining.

'Damn blasted blood-sucking beasts! Blast, blast, blast you all the way to hell!'

'Um...Lillian.' Amana glanced at me nervously, not sure what my one-hundred-per-cent English cursing was all about. She was marching beside me, appearing miraculously serene, although mosquitos were crawling all over her. *'Is something the matter?'*

'You bet something is the matter!' I repeated my curses in Portuguese forthwith, and did a pretty good job of translating, if I do say so myself. Boy, I was turning into a bloody good linguist! *'I'm being eaten alive!'*

'The mosquitos? They are bothering you?'

'They are sucking me dry!'

'Why don't you keep them away?'

'Keep them away? Ha! That's easier said than done. How am I supposed to keep a whole swarm of those blood-thirsty little suckers at a distance?'

'There is a way.'

Amana's voice was so quiet and matter-of-fact that it took a moment or two for the meaning of her words to sink in. When it did, I froze in my tracks. The man behind me bumped into me, cursing in the Indian's native language, and I hurried forward to catch up with Amana.

'Are you serious? Please tell me you're not joking!'

She smiled at me shyly. *'No, no. I'm not joking. Haven't you wondered why the mosquitos don't bother me?'*

I hadn't, actually. I was far too busy cursing and aching all over. But now that she mentioned it, I did wonder. I wondered a hell of a lot!

'What?' I demanded 'What is your secret? Please! Please, tell me! I'll do anything! I'll pay you a million pounds! I'll kill somebody for you! I'll give you my firstborn! Just please, please tell me! How do you do it?'

'It's not difficult. You just have to...'

Sidling closer, she whispered into my ear.

My jaw dropped open.

'You're serious?'

'Yes.'

---

[29] 'Penny dreadful' was a name during the Victorian era for cheap stories (i.e. available for a penny) that were not very refined (i.e. dreadful). They were often printed as cheap leaflets and were the literature of the working masses. One of the most (in)famous and successful penny dreadfuls was a supernatural story called *Varney the Vampire*.

'Oh my holy...! And that works?'
'Yes.'

My eyes flickered to Mr Ambrose. Slowly, a smile started to spread over my face. This method had...possibilities.

~~**~*~*

The next morning, I rose before anybody else and made my way into the jungle until I found a nice bit of ground, moist enough for my purposes, but not swampy enough to sink in. Following Amana's advice, it only took a couple of minutes to complete my business.

And you know what?

She had been right!

It was an instant relief. Sighing at the pleasurable feeling of peace all around me, I gathered up my things and started back towards the campsite. Karim and a few of the Indians were sitting around a map, their backs to me, talking in low murmurs. My dear employer was nowhere in sight.

'Where is Mr Ambrose?' I asked.

Karim jabbed his thumb westwards. 'Gone to the stream to take a drink.' He half turned to look at me. 'Why, what do you want from hi-'

His voice died in his throat. His eyes, almost hidden under his huge eyebrows a moment before, turned as wide as saucers.

'Is something the matter, Karim?' I asked, sweetly.

'Grk. Ng. Err...um...'

The Indians turned to look at me too, to see what all the fuss was about. None of them seemed to be particularly shocked by what they saw. A few nodded at me. One smiled. Amana winked. I winked back, then turned another beaming smile on Karim.

'Well, if there's nothing else, I'll be going now, all right? I have a sudden inexplicable desire to see Mr Ambrose.'

'Ng!'

'Toodle-pip!'[30]

I slipped away, off into the jungle, before Karim could blow the alarm, or do something else to derail my devious plans. Sneakily, like a slithery snake, I made my way down to the little stream that wound through the jungle not far away from our camp. Mr Ambrose was kneeling at the bank, refilling his water bottle.

Stepping out of the underbrush, I cleared my throat.

'I'm busy!' he snapped, not bothering to turn around to see who it was.

I cleared my throat again.

'Yes?' This time he did turn. 'What is the ma-'

His voice died on a strangled choke in mid-sentence. His eyes didn't turn as big as saucers – that would have required too much facial movement – but they did widen at least 0.00451 inches. For Mr Ambrose, that was quite something.

I smiled at him.

---

[30] Old British slang for 'goodbye'.

'Good God!' Springing to his feet, he stumbled back, almost falling into the stream. 'Who...what...?'

My smile grew wider. This was going better than I had expected.

'Good morning, Sir.'

THE LUSTY GOLEM

'Mr Linton?'

'You didn't recognise me?' I took a step forward. 'Well, I suppose I do look a bit different from before.'

He tried to take a step back. But taking a step back is difficult with a stream behind you. 'You could say that!'

'It's the hair, isn't it? It's the hair that makes me look so different.'

'Not particularly. I'd have said it was the fact that you are covered from head to toe in mud!'

'Ah. Yes, that, too.'

'What in God's name happened to you? You look like an Indian coming back from a ten-day hunt in the jungle!'

'Funny you should mention that, because, you know, that's actually where I got the idea from.'

'What idea?'

I shrugged. 'It's those bloody mosquitos. I was pretty desperate for a way to make them a little less bloody – at least as long as my veins were their favourite diet. I could have put on more clothes, of course, as a protection – but it's already more than hot enough in this green pot of hellstew. Then Amana mentioned this trick the Indians have: they don't wear any clothes either, of course, so they roll around in the mud until they're covered by a nice, thick, protective crust. That not only keeps the mosquitos away, but also has a nice cooling effect as it hardens. Then it just falls off.'

I smiled, proudly, hoping for a compliment on my acclimatisation skills or something like that. But Mr Ambrose, like always, had right away picked up the essential part of the conversation.

'They don't wear any clothes either?' His voice was as cold as midnight in the middle of an arctic winter. 'Mr Linton, do you mean to tell me that underneath that layer of mud, you are...you are...?'

He didn't finish the sentence. He didn't need to. His eyes did all the talking for him. They swept over me, taking me in this time not just as the friendly neighbourhood mud-monster, but as the woman beneath. The moment he realised what he was seeing, his gaze whipped away, and a muscle tightened in his jaw. Desperately, he rolled his eyes from left to right, trying to find anything for them to land on that wasn't me.

'You are naked!'

'Yep,' I confirmed cheerily. 'It's really comfy. You should try it.'

'Comfy? Comfy?'

234

'Why do you think the Indians do it?'

'I wouldn't know! I, Mr Linton, am not an Indian! I am an English gentleman of good breeding.'

'What a shame.'

'Put something on immediately! That is an order!'

I put a finger to my arm. It came away sticky, covered with a nice, brownish extra layer. 'I have plenty on.'

'I meant clothing, not half-dried mud!'

'Doesn't that count?'

'No!'

I smiled at him innocently. 'Oh dear. I'm so sorry, I'm a bit behind on Brazilian fashion.'

'I'm serious, Mr Linton!'

'So am I.' I took a step forward, still smiling. 'You had better get used to seeing me like this. After all, we still have a long way ahead of us.'

'*What?*' He tried to glare at me without looking at me, which even for a glarer as experienced as Rikkard Ambrose is something of an impossible feat. 'You are not travelling the rest of the way like a...like...like *this!*'

'I most certainly am.' I took another step forward, my smile slowly morphing from amused to flirtatious. 'Don't you like me like this, Sir?'

'No!'

'Liar.'

He said nothing in answer. Silence reigned in the jungle, loud and clear. I saw his throat move as he swallowed hard.

'Why won't you look at me, Sir?'

'You know perfectly well why!' Was it just my imagination, or was his voice the slightest bit hoarse? 'Put some clothes on, right now!'

'Actually, I don't think I will.' I took another step forward.

'Don't come any closer! I'm warning you!'

'Why?'

He took a quick step back, right into the stream. Water splashed around his black shoes that, somehow, even here in the jungle were still shiny. 'Because...because...'

'No need to be afraid.' I placed a hand on my chest, right over my heart. When I pulled it away, it left a very strategically placed bare patch. 'It's just me.'

'Yes. *Just* you. Nothing else. That's the problem!' He took another step back into the stream, his eyes focused firmly on the treetops above my head. 'And I am not afraid of a *girl!*'

'Indeed?' Another step forward. 'Then why don't you stop?'

'Because...because...'

His teeth ground together in the fruitless search for an answer. He shifted, torn between the instinct to run, the instinct to fight, and the instinct to peek. I took another step forward, quite curious to see which instinct would win.

He took another step back, but only a small one. He was knee-deep in water now, and I was only a few yards away from him. It was becoming quite difficult for him to not look at me. Tension sparked through the air.

'Mr Ambrose?'

My voice was soft. Breathy. I had come here with the intention of having a bit of fun at his expense – but now that didn't seem so important anymore. I suddenly realised that we were alone, far away from the others, and the protective covering of mud on my skin wasn't at all as thick as I had thought. When I had been with the others, it had almost felt like clothing. But in the presence of Mr Rikkard Ambrose, it felt like nothing more than the shell of an egg – easily shattered.

'Mr Linton?' His voice was cold and raw and sharp-edged, like the cliffs of a freshly calved iceberg.

'Look at me!'

The strength of my voice took even me by surprise. Had I ever dared give Mr Rikkard Ambrose an order before? But if I was surprised at my own words, it was nothing compared to the surprise of seeing them obeyed.

Slowly, torturously slowly, his eyes came down from the roof of leaves above and settled on me. And all of a sudden it didn't matter that, technically, there was a layer of protection between him and me. It didn't matter that it was only his eyes caressing me, not his hands. I could feel him. Could feel his gaze slide over my tangled, mud-capped hair, down my throat, over my chest and farther down, until...

Under the mud, I felt my skin heat.

My legs moved, as if of their own account, carrying me forward.

'Do you like what you see, Sir?'

'No!'

But his eyes kept devouring me, as if I were the key to the vaults of the Bank of England.

I smiled, continuing to advance. My gait had somehow become lithe and predatory, like that of a jungle cat. 'Liar!'

He took another step backwards. Soon, he'd almost be waist-deep in the water. 'I'm not lying, Miss– I mean, Mr Linton! I find you repugnant!'

I took another step forward, still smiling.

'Do you?'

'Yes, indeed I do! I also find you grisly, grotesque, hideous, horrid, unsightly, appalling, and, and...'

Never before in my life had I seen Mr Rikkard Ambrose struggle for words. Usually, he didn't need them – especially to insult. Just his icy glare was enough. But the look in his eyes right now was anything but insulting. Any woman who felt this gaze on her could only feel heat and need inside.

'Beastly?' I suggested. 'Foul?'

'Yes! Exactly!'

I took another step forward. He was almost in reach now. But instead of reaching out for him, I reached out for myself. I ran a hand down my throat and towards an area of my upper body that seemed to hold particular interest for him. His left little finger twitched.

'And tell me, Sir...why is it that you find me so repugnant? Which part of me–,' using my other hand, I traced the curve of my hips, '–repels you so?'

236

He cleared his throat.

'You...you are dirty!'

From underneath, I smirked up at him. 'I bet you like it dirty.'

'Mr Linton!'

My hand slid away from my chest, pointing further down. '*Miss*,' I corrected him. 'The proof's right there.'

'Mr Linton!'

'*Miss*. You really *are* a stubborn man.'

Another step forward brought me within reaching distance. I lifted my hand from where it had been resting and raised it towards Mr Ambrose. He twitched back as if it were an adder. 'Stop! You, um...you can't touch this suit! It's still in mint condition. I won't have it ruined.'

'So take it off,' I purred.

'I, um...I...'

Bloody hell! Being the seductive siren was fun. Why didn't more women do this? Seeing Mr Ambrose squirm was just about the most delicious sight of my life. Now, if he would only take off his shirt...

My hand reached for his top button, and he ducked out of the way, stumbling back farther into the stream.

'No!' he ground out between clenched teeth. 'Impossible! What if somebody came...if somebody saw us...saw you, like *this*!'

'Oh, yes, that would be a real tragedy.' I followed him, my eyes sparkling. 'Those poor natives have probably never seen anybody naked before. I bet it would scar them for life.'

'What about Karim? If he came–'

'He already saw me.'

'*What?*'

For one moment, Mr Ambrose wasn't flustered. For one moment, his eyes flashed with cold, ruthless fire.

'Don't worry. I packed the mud on thick.' Stretching on my toes, I whispered in his ear: 'But I'll let you wash it off, if you want. *Everywhere.*'

The promise of vengeance vanished from his eyes, and instead, another cold fire started to burn there. One that lit me up inside, drawing me closer.

'What do you want to start with?' Reaching out, I took his unresisting hand. It was unnaturally still. I could feel the power in it, barely contained under a shell of cold stone. Slowly, I raised it until it hovered just over my belly.

'Here?'

Softly brushing over his palm with my thumb, I raised his hand high until it hovered over a far more interesting area.

'Here?'

He made a low noise in the back of his throat. I smiled. The first cracks were appearing in the stone.

'Oh, no! I have a better idea. Here...'

Raising his rather unwilling hand up even farther, I brought it to my lips and with his wet fingertips, brushed off the specks of mud on my lips. The first touch was incredible. His fingers brushing across my mouth were like the tips of angels' wings. They sent a blast of heavenly fire through me, making me crave more. Languidly, I parted my lips and slid one of his fingers inside, my tongue flicking against its pad.

His breath hitched – and I pounced! He was so dazed, he didn't have a hope of evading me. My arms locked around his neck before he'd had time to blink, and then my lips were on his, taking him, devouring him, in the most wanton kiss we had ever shared. He fought. Not to get to me this time, but to get away. Trying to protect his precious mint-condition shirt, I guessed. Or he just couldn't deal with a woman going for what she wanted.

Ha! He would just have to! I was not going to let his rock-hard stubbornness get in the way of this. This was too good to end.

'Mr Linton...Lilly...no, I...'

'You what?' Freeing his lips, my mouth raced down his throat, scattering kisses all the way. My arms came down from around his neck, and the first button of his shirt popped open in a moment. 'You want more? Coming right up!'

'No!' he growled. 'We can't do this!'

'Can't we?' I softly bit him on the neck and felt him quiver against me. Oh boy, this was fun! 'Why? It's not as if we haven't done a bit of this before.'

'That was different,' he groaned.

'Why?'

'You weren't covered in mud!'

I smirked against his granite skin. 'What? You can't engage in amorous congress while you're dirty?'

'Not if you're English, no!'

'I must say,' I whispered, my lips moving slowly further down to the hollow at the base of his throat, 'I disagree.'

I started forward, and was just about to mash my dirt-covered body against him, when he – damn him! – slipped from my grasp like an eel, ducking down into the water and coming up with a splash a few yards away.

'Hey! Don't you move!'

Ignoring my order, he flung himself head-first into the water. I lunged after him, but he was already darting away, swimming the crawl faster than I had ever seen anybody do in my life.

'Come back! I promise to wash before we do it! Hey! Come back!'

He didn't respond. Instead, he continued on until a few fast strokes had brought him to the opposite bank. Ducking down, he slid into a thicket of reeds and lianas, and was gone. All that remained was a whiff of his smell in the air and the sound of wet footsteps, fast receding into the distance.

I punched the water.

'Damn!'

~~**~*~*

Needless to say, I wasn't in a particularly good mood when I got back to the camp. After my little trip into the river, the lower half of my body had lost most of its mosquito protection and was now itching for an entirely different reason than I had originally hoped for. Quickly I returned to my little patch of mud and restored my protective package, taking care to punch the mud a few times, imagining that it was Mr Ambrose's face.

And the worst thing was: I couldn't even be officially miffed at him. Because, no matter how much he protested that it was all about his mint-condition suit, I knew what it was really about: he had been protecting my virtue.

The nerve of him! If my virtue needs protecting, I'll do it myself, thank you very much!

Yes, but...right then and there, did I have the strength to do it myself? Did I even want it? All I knew was that I wanted him. Desperately. I wanted to get dirty with him and paint myself all over his body, mark him forever as mine.

Biting my lip, I punched the mud again. Damn him! Damn him for being so reasonable and controlled. Damn him for thinking of what I needed, instead of what I wanted!

I finished my insect protection measures, and, getting to my feet, started back towards the camp. I hadn't got half the way when a dark figure stepped out from the trees, blocking my path. My hands instinctively rose in defence – when dark, deep, sea-coloured eyes met mine and I immediately recognised the figure on the shadowy pathway.

He stood there, silent as an empty grave. His eyes, though, weren't empty. They were swirling with dark storm clouds, speaking their own secret language.

The silence was lengthening. I supposed I had better say something before it reached the length of Loch Ness.

'Mr Ambrose, Sir.'

That was it. I didn't really know what else to say. The look in his eyes was slightly disturbing.

'Mr Linton.'

That was it. That was all he said. His voice was perfectly cool and controlled again. He stepped out of the shadow, and I saw that he had somehow managed to clean and dry his oh-so-precious mint-condition shirt and tailcoat.

Slowly, he took a step forward. My whole body tensed, prickling with the feeling of his proximity. What was he doing here? Not half an hour ago, he had run away from me. And now he was coming towards me, with a look in his eyes that made me shiver inside? What was his game?

Whatever it was – he intended to win.

He was only a few feet away from me now. His hand came up, and, mesmerised, I stood there as his fingers approached. They touched my cheek – my dirty, mud-stained, unladylike cheek – and stayed there for an immeasurably long second. When his fingers came away again, they were stained with dirt. He raised them to his own face and I watched, spell-bound as he drew a long, devilishly dirty, line of mud across his cheek. He began just under his eye, and drew downwards, until his path ended right next to his mouth.

Or so I thought.

His fingers moved on, until they rested against his lips, and he bestowed a gentle kiss on the finger that had grazed my cheek, leaving his lips mud stained and dirty. His eyes met mine, searing into me. Then, without saying a word, he turned and marched away back up the path.

With trembling fingers, I reached up to touch my cheek, where I could still feel his fingers burning into my skin with cold fire.

What the hell was that?

CAUGHT IN COBWEBS

If I had thought the little episode on the path meant that Mr Ambrose was now fine with my new apparel (or lack thereof), I had been vastly mistaken. I had hardly time to wake up the next morning before he pounced on me. He more or less arm-wrestled me into wearing my chemise over my mud-package. It was a bit wet and sticky, but on the whole I had to admit it felt nice having something to cover my girly bits. I guess I wasn't completely cut out for life as an Amazon Indian.

That didn't mean, however, that I wasn't more than ready to forego cover in the presence of Mr Rikkard Ambrose. Not at all. The longer we travelled together, the stronger became my desire to push him to the ground and rip his clothes off. Unfortunately, Mr Ambrose didn't seem to share my desire, or at least had much better control of it than sweet little me. How could I possibly get this craving under control? *How?*

I tried logic. It had served me well in the past:

Men and women deserve equality. Men won't give women equality. Ergo, men are bastards.

See how well it works?

So I tried it on this situation.

I want to dance the fandango de pokum with Mr Rikkard Ambrose. I want it really, really bad. But if I do, I will probably get pregnant and have to do the unspeakable m-thing. You know the one that involves churches and priests and vows of obedience. Ergo: I can't get my hands on him.

But...I still wanted to! Blast!

Logic didn't seem to work here. Instead, I secretly started plotting ways of getting him to take his clothes off. For days and days, I brooded over dozens of plans, one less likely to succeed than the last. But it turned out that I needn't have bothered. All I had to do was wait, for fate was on my side.

~~**~*~*

'Take care where to step.'

Those were the first words I had heard Chandresh say for several days. He was almost as tight-lipped as Mr Ambrose. So, I had to admit, I was curious why he was speaking up now.

'Why?'

He didn't look at me. Instead, his eyes kept doing what they had been doing before: scanning the ground.

'*There are dangerous animals here.*'

'*What kind of animals? Jaguars? Leopards?*'

He pointed upwards. I followed his finger with my gaze, but all I could see were a couple of cobwebs stretched between tree branches.

'*I don't see anything. What-*'

Then it clicked.

'*Oh.*'

'*Yes. As I said - take care where you step.*'

I was tempted to ask whether the little fellows we should be on the lookout for were poisonous or not - but then I decided that, on the whole, I'd rather not know. Once or twice I saw something dark scuttle past underfoot, but the day passed without a major incident. It was towards evening that events took a more interesting direction.

We had made camp near a clump of tall, dark trees, just right for hanging our hammocks from. Our supplies were beginning to run low, so Chandresh posted a few guards some distance away around the camp, and then took the rest of the men hunting into the jungle. Karim went with them, but Mr Ambrose, for some reason, decided to stay behind. Maybe he wanted to lean back, relax and calculate how many millions of pounds he was going to make from this trip. Maybe he had found a stain on his tailcoat that he needed to eradicate. Most likely, though, it was fate.

I was lying in my hammock, contemplating the unfairness of life and the perfection of Mr Rikkard Ambrose's profile when I heard a noise from the direction of his hammock. I turned and saw that he wasn't lying down like me, but standing upright. In fact, you could hardly have stood more uprightly uprighter. His posture was as stiff as a board, his eyes fixed on some point in the distance. His hands, his arms, his face - they were all perfectly still. Even his left little finger didn't twitch.

'Mr Ambrose?'

He didn't reply. What was the matter with him? Had he finally truly turned into stone?

'Mr Ambrose, Sir? What is the matter?'

He parted his lips, infinitesimally, and whispered so low it was hardly more than a tickle against my eardrum, 'Drr ss smsm crlnp mm lg.'

'Pardon?'

His cool eyes bored into me. Every other part of his body still stayed perfectly still. 'I said *there is something crawling up my leg.*'

Swinging out of the hammock, I examined his lower half with a frown. 'I don't see anything on your trousers.'

'It's *inside* the trousers.'

'Oh.'

'Indeed.'

For some reason, a smile twitched at the corners of my mouth. 'You do real-ise that if you hadn't been so stubborn about keeping your clothing on, this wouldn't be a problem? You could just reach down there and sweep away the–'

'This is not the time to discuss my sartorial choices, Mr Linton. Take my trousers off!'

It was very hard to keep my lips from breaking into a full-fledged grin. Very hard indeed. 'Sir! Are you trying to persuade me to get you naked? I'll have you know that I am a decent girl, and not in the habit of pulling down the trousers of any gentleman who asks.'

'Mr Linton!'

'Though I might consider it, if he looks nice enough.'

'Mr Linton! It's at the knee already. Get a move on.'

I sighed. 'All right, all right. Don't get your knickers in a twist. I'll be taking them off now anyway, so it's not worth the bother.'

A seraphic smile on my face, I started forward. I didn't hurry, particularly. I had been waiting a long time for this and was going to enjoy every moment.

'Mr Linton!'

'Coming, coming...'

Stopping a few feet away, I eyed the belt buckle of Mr Rikkard Ambrose. Oh dear. This looked as if it was going to take some work. Checking for spiders on the ground, I knelt down in front of him. From under my lashes, I looked up at him.

'Oh dear.' I smiled an innocent little smile. 'What a compromising position.'

'If you don't get on with it,' Mr Ambrose ground out from between clenched teeth, 'I'm going to find a *really* compromising position to put you in!'

My smile widened. 'Don't tempt me.'

'It's on my thigh now!'

'Lucky spider.'

'Mr Linton...!'

'All right, all right.' Batting my lashes up at him one last time, I reached for his buckle. The thing was just as stubborn as its owner, and felt as if it was rusted shut, although it gleamed like freshly polished silver. Still, I was nothing if not determined. With a *clink*, the buckle opened, and a moment later, Mr Rikkard Ambrose's legwear slid to the ground with a soft rustle.

Aah...

Closing my eyes, I took a second to appreciate this unique moment. He was there, right in front of me. And he couldn't move.

Then I opened them again to see what he had to offer.

My mouth went dry.

'Mr Linton?'

'Wrgsfgl?'

'Mr Linton! The spider!'

'S-spider? What spider?'

'*The* spider!'

'Oh, *that* spider.' I blinked, trying to shake of the daze. It was hard. Very hard. After all, I was only human. 'Well...let's see, where is it...?'

My eyes swept over his thighs, taking in the sleek, smooth skin, the hard muscles, and, oh, of course also looking for spiders. But...there weren't any.

'There is no spider,' I informed my dear employer.

'That's,' he ground out between clenched teeth, 'because while you were staring, it decided to move up into my tailcoat. Get my shirt open! Now!'

Dear me! This spider was a clever little fellow.

'Why don't you open it yourself? Buttons aren't complicated like a belt. You should be able open them without shifting too much.'

'I'm not going to move an inch. Didn't you hear Chandresh? Some of those beasts are poisonous. I do not intend to end my days in the Amazonian Jungle, brought down by a mere spider bite.'

Rising to my feet, I lifted an eyebrow.

'And you're not worried that I'll be bitten?'

'I doubt one poisonous spider would suffer much from the bite of another.'

'Has anyone ever told you that you are a real gentleman, Mr Ambrose?'

'No.'

'Well, don't expect them to.'

My eager fingers started on his tailcoat and vest.

'You know,' I muttered, 'you're the only man I've ever known who wore a black vest under a black tailcoat – apart from undertakers.'

'We can discuss fashion later, Mr Linton. Get the shirt off!'

'Why, Sir! I never thought you'd be so forward with an innocent maiden like me.'

'You're going to pay for this later, Mr Linton.'

'No, you are. You are the employer, remember? You pay me, not the other way around.'

He gave me an arctic glare as good as a dozen curses. After that, I decided it would be politic to indeed get a move on. Besides, if you got a chance to fondle Mr Rikkard Ambrose's naked chest, would you pass it up?

That was a rhetorical question.

I unbuttoned his shirt and cautiously slid it off, taking time to appreciate his marvellous musculature in the process. He was so impressive, it took me a moment to notice the large, hairy black spider sitting on his chest.

'Eew.' I pulled a face. 'Nasty little beast!'

'Precisely my opinion, Mr Linton,' he managed to get out without moving his lips. 'Now *will you get it off me?*'

'Yes, Sir! Right away, Sir!'

Picking up a stick from the ground, I slowly slid it under the spider's hairy belly.

'Three...two...one...*now!*'

One flick of my wrist, and the spider flew away, landing a few feet away on the soggy ground. I could have left it at that. But if I had, I wouldn't have been me. So instead, I whipped out my gun, levelled it at the little beast and fired.

Bam!

When the echoes of the shot had died away, all that was left of the spider were a few hairy remnants. Lifting the gun to my mouth, I blew the smoke away and batted my eyelashes at Mr Ambrose.

'Will you look at that? The heroine has saved the day. Now, all that remains for the hero to do is to fall into her arms, weep on her chest and offer up his virtue in gratitude.'

Mr Ambrose stepped forward, his eyes glinting coldly. 'Don't count on it.'

'The weeping, or the offered virtue?'

'Both.'

'Dear me. You really are a skinflint. Don't I even get a "thank you"?'

He said something in reply – but I didn't catch it. Because in that moment, I turned away from the dead spider to face him and got my first real eye full of Mr Rikkard Ambrose in his new, much less restrictive state of apparel.

Now, as mentioned some time ago, I had seen naked men before – well, statues of them, anyway. But never, not once in my life, had I seen a real man in underwear. Especially not this one. The sight hit me like a sledgehammer, squeezing my heart into a painful pancake.

Good God...!

Why didn't he just sell half-naked pictures of himself to young single ladies? No matter how much money he had made in other ways, it had to be a pittance in comparison to what he could make with such a business model. His figure was cast in half-shadow under the roof of the jungle, but that only accentuated the subtle, hard curving of his muscles. Slowly I dragged my eyes up from his powerful thighs, over his drawers, faded white and much too tight, to his bare abdomen and pectorals.

I nodded at his drawers.

'Let me guess...ten years old and still in mint condition?'

'Twelve, actually.'

'Of course.' My eyes were drawn back down there, enamoured by the way the cotton was stretched tightly over hard muscles and...other things. 'And I bet you haven't grown a bit since then.'

'Not significantly enough to warrant a new purchase. Why are we discussing my underwear, Mr Linton?'

'The real question,' I murmured, taking a step closer, 'is why we're still discussing, and not exploring.'

Our eyes met, and for the first time he seemed to realise what I had noticed quite some time ago – that we both were alone, hot, sweaty and very nearly naked. I watched the realisation enter his eyes, spread through his body and settle in his bones. I watched as a dark storm started to whirl in the depths of his eyes, and a muscle just over his jaw began to twitch.

'Well?' I raised an eyebrow. 'What are you waiting for?'

'I can't!' he ground out from between clenched teeth. 'I shouldn't...'

'Don't waste time with should or shouldn't.' Taking another step forward, I stood up on my tiptoes and, caressing his chest with one dirty hand, whispered into his ear, 'As a very intelligent man once said to me...*I hate time-wasters.*'

His arms were up and around me faster than I could blink. His *bare* arms, hard, smooth and unspeakably strong. Even if I'd wanted to, there wouldn't have been a hope of resisting as he crushed me up against his bare chest, devouring my mouth.

'Let up a bit!' I growled against his mouth, then kissed him back voraciously.

'Why?'

'Because I want to feel you!'

A deep sound came from back in his throat, almost like...a chuckle? No!

'Find something else to feel! I'm not letting go of you!'

'Bastard!'

I tried to squeeze my hand in between him and me, tried to find my way to his chest, but you couldn't have squeezed a knife blade in there. He was clutching me so tight it was almost hard to breathe, and – damn him! – I loved every minute of it.

Well, I'd simply have to find something else to touch.

With a slap, my hands came down on his derriere. I felt a jerk go through his whole body, smiled to myself, and squeezed.

'Mr Linton!'

'What?' I enquired innocently. Well, as innocently as I could, under the circumstances.

'Your hands–'

Was it my imagination or did his voice sound a little bit rougher than usual?

'What about my hands?' I squeezed again. Hm...nice. One thing was for sure: Mr Rikkard Ambrose didn't eat solid chocolate. Not one ounce. I should have despised him for being such a philistine, but at that moment, my hands were loving it.

Still...there was the problem of that annoying bit of cloth between me and my fun. Time to travel on, to the wide open spaces. Squeezing one last time, my hands started to move up the broad expanse of his back, claiming, exploring, pressing him even tighter against me (and leaving a few claw marks in the process). All the barriers were gone for once. I could feel his muscles flexing, could feel his blood pulsing under my fingertips. All the barriers were gone.

Or were they?

True, his skin was heated, his breath was hot, his lips burning on mine – but his eyes? They still were cold and calculating, filled with the same barrier of ice and stone that he build up between himself and everything else.

And part of you loves that, don't you? You want to climb that wall, and stand on top of it, shouting your victory to the world!

On top of it?

Scratch that! On top of *him*!

Grabbing his shoulders, I pushed him back, trying to get him down to the ground. I might as well have pushed at the foundations of a mountain. Only – a mountain wouldn't have pushed back. With the ease of infinite power, he captured my arms and pulled me down, bestowing another earth-shattering kiss on me. My knees buckled, as much from his kiss as his powerful hands. Slowly,

I slid down to the soft ground, and he loomed above me, a granite monument to masculinity.

His hands still gripping my arms, he lowered himself until he hovered over me, his arms and legs caging me in as effectively as iron fetters. I watched, mesmerised, as he slowly, inexorably, sank down towards me. The moment his body touched mine, a jolt of heat surged through me, so intense I thought I'd be incinerated.

How the hell could this be? How could Rikkard Ambrose, coldest block of ice in all of Britain, make me feel like this? Like I was burning? Like I was ready to explode?

I didn't know. I didn't care. I simply grabbed him, and pulled him down on top of me. Leaves rustled. Skin slid against bare skin. And a little time later, the world did indeed explode. And when the shards came back together again, it didn't look the same as before. Not in the slightest.

~~**~*~*

Question: a man makes you feel two different ways. When he is fully dressed, he makes you climb up walls and evokes a strong desire for manslaughter. When he is undressed, he makes you want to climb up on top of him and evokes desires that are much more desirous than homicide. What do you do?

The simple answer would be: see to it that he never has clothes on. But this, I thought gloomily while watching the erect figure of Mr Rikkard Ambrose marching along before me in his tight black tailcoat, was something he wasn't likely to go along with. Right now, maybe he would. But right now wasn't the problem. Here in the wilderness, far away from the watchful eyes and wagging tongues of London society, everything was easy. March. Eat. Drink. Enjoy wicked delicious moments in the depths of the jungle. The big question was: what would I do once we returned to England? What would we do?

I had never been a procrastinator. If something needed doing, I did it. No questions asked. But this? I didn't know what to do. I didn't even know if something could be done.

So I procrastinated. Every time thoughts of England crept into my head, I told myself: *It's far too soon! We'll be stuck in the jungle for ages. After all, we've still got an incredibly long way to go!*

But the days drifted by, and the incredibly long way became a long way. The long way became a longish sort of way. The longish short of way became a rather short way. And the rather short way...

Well, you get the idea.

Snow-covered peaks appeared out of the jungle in front of us. I was terrified of what that would mean, and after I saw Chandresh and Mr Ambrose exchange a significant look, I knew for certain. In no time at all, we were ascending into the mountains that, according to the ancient manuscript, held the great treasure we were seeking.

Not fair! So totally not fair! Treasure hunts should be more difficult than this. We should have at least a few more hundred miles of jungle to cross before we find the gold. Before we have to go back to Eng-

But I couldn't even think it. England meant a world in which Mr Rikkard Ambrose couldn't pull me into his arms and plunder my mouth whenever he wanted to. England meant a world with rules and regulations, and hundreds of other people watching our every move.

We would have to end it! Whatever 'it' was, exactly, we would have to stop. That was the only way. If we didn't, if someone caught us at 'it', we would have to...

At this point, my already exhausted imagination wheezed its last breath and collapsed in a crumpled heap. It was simply too much! Too much to contemplate, and most certainly too much to do. If only something, anything were to happen, to distract me from this torture!

Did you ever hear the saying 'Be careful what you wish for, you might just get it?'

I perfectly understood the wisdom of this saying one second later. We had just turned into a path leading high up into the mountains, when, from behind us, a commanding voice called out in Portuguese:

'Halt! In the name of His Majesty the Emperor.'

I whirled – but already before I looked, I knew what I would see. And my fears were not disappointed. There, only a few dozen yards below us, stood Colonel Alberto Silveira, his soldiers behind him, weapons raised and aimed straight at us.

THE AMBROSIAN KNOT

For a moment, I was frozen. Incredible, right? I mean, it was hot enough in the jungle to melt an iceberg. But where ice crystals failed, the muzzle of a gun seemed to be wonderfully effective. I felt a chill go down my spine – and I was not as grateful for the relief from the heat as I probably should have been.

How did this happen? How did they catch up to us?

The question answered itself almost as soon as it was posed. Of course, they didn't catch up! They must have been able to decipher enough of the manuscript to figure out it led into these mountains. And then, they had simply moved on the swiftest path, and lain in wait for us. No wonder we had taken longer, with all the roundabout paths we had taken to avoid detection.

'Well?' Colonel Silveira raised an eyebrow. 'Surrender!'

Mr Ambrose? Surrender?

Yes, of course! And elephants could walk on water.

Mr Ambrose, Karim and Chandresh shared a brief look. One of those 'We're men! We can do this!' looks that only the most infuriating, chauvinistic males on this earth have mastered to perfection.

'Go, *Sahib!*' Karim called out, whipping a rifle off his back and aiming in a blink. 'Get out of the line of fire! We'll take care of this!'

I wanted to growl: 'Not bloody likely!' No way in hell was I leaving someone else to fight my battles for me. But Mr Ambrose apparently had a more practical, less heroic approach to matters. Grabbing me by the arm, he pulled me behind a rock and off up the mountain as the bullets started flying.

'Let go!' I demanded, struggling against his hold. 'They need our help!'

'They're doing their job,' he told me coolly. His grip did not relax, and neither did his stride slow down for an instant. 'We're doing ours. Where is the treasure, Mr Linton?'

'Who cares about the stupid treasure?'

'I do. And since I pay your wages, mine is the only opinion that matters.' He spoke perfectly calmly, as if the barrage of gunfire behind us wasn't hammering on our ears, deafeningly loud. 'Now, and I am not going to ask this again, *where is the treasure?*'

Grinding my teeth, I pointed up one of the paths ahead.

'Adequate.'

He made a slight course correction, and started pulling me up that way.

'You really are a ruthless son of a bachelor, aren't you?' Without the slightest intention on my part, the words came out sounding almost admiring.

'Eloquently put, Mr Linton. And correctly.'

'What if Karim dies?'

His grip on my arm twitched. 'Then I will have difficulties finding an adequate replacement.'

'Is that all?'

His fingers twitched again. 'Yes.'

Liar!

But I didn't say it out loud. If there was one thing I had learned from Mr Ambrose it was that, sometimes, silence was golden. Especially when there were bullets flying and you had to run.

Running wasn't easy. The path was rocky, every step a dangerous experiment. But no matter how tough it was, Mr Ambrose never let go of my arm. Eventually, the ground became smoother. The path opened up in front of us and, a moment later, we were standing on the edge of a cliff, staring at a gorge spanned only by a single, rickety rope bridge.

We dashed forward, but had hardly reached the bridge when footsteps came thudding up the path behind us. Mr Ambrose whirled around, shoving me behind him with an air of masculine superiority which I deeply resented. I probably would have resented it even more if the people behind us hadn't had guns.

'Stay behind me!' In a flash, Mr Ambrose had his revolver drawn and cocked. His hand was as steady as a rock as he took aim at the opening of the path.

Shrugging, I slid my hand into my pocket and pulled out my own gun. He had said to stay behind him. He had mentioned nothing about not shooting the sons of bitches that were after us!

But when the first figure burst out from between the rocks, it wasn't Colonel Silveira or one of his men. It was a mountainous man with a big beard and a turban on his head.

Karim looked even grimmer than usual. He was bleeding out of a gash on his forehead, and there was more blood scattered over his clothes which I guessed probably wasn't his. Mr Ambrose lowered his firearm a few inches as the Mohammedan came hurtling towards us.

'There are too many, *Sahib*! They're coming up other paths to the side! We can't hold them! Run! Run!'

Mr Ambrose wasn't one to ever take commands. But I guess he chose to view this as a friendly recommendation, because he turned and, grabbing my hand again, started to dash across the bridge, Karim hot on our heels. We were half-way across when the sneering voice of Colonel Silveira stopped us in our tracks.

'Halt! Halt or you'll all die!'

We whirled around, the bridge swaying precariously underneath us. My eyes zeroed in on Colonel Silveira. He was standing at the edge of the bridge, holding something shiny to one of the ropes. I squinted. It was difficult to make out at this distance, but that almost looked like a...

'Oh crap!'

Beside me, I saw a muscle in Mr Ambrose's jaw twitch. 'My sentiments exactly, Mr Linton.'

The colonel was holding a knife.

'One step farther,' he shouted, 'and I'll cut this rope! All of you will plummet to your death!'

'Then you'll never find the treasure!' Mr Ambrose called back, his voice as cool as a cucumber on ice. 'Without the manuscript, nobody can!'

Even at this distance, I saw the colonel's eyes glitter. 'I'll find it eventually. There are only so many peaks in these mountains. The only reason you are still alive is that I don't want to waste time with an unnecessary search.'

His eyes met those of Mr Ambrose. For a few moments the two men just stared at each other, locked in a silent battle that needed no swords or fists or guns.

'Throw away your weapons,' the colonel commanded. 'Come back and surrender, or I will cut through this rope, and you will plunge to your death!'

It all felt a bit like one of the scenes from my favourite adventure novels: the manic villain, the beautiful heroine with her hero sidekick in deadly danger – only in real life, it wasn't quite as enjoyable.

'Last warning!' the colonel shouted. 'Throw away your weapons, or I will cut through the rope.'

'I don't think so.' With an ice-cold stare at Colonel Silveira, Mr Ambrose raised his gun, pointing it straight at the rope next to him. 'Leave now, or *I* will sever the rope!'

'What?' the colonel demanded.

'*What?*' I demanded. This hadn't happened in any of my adventure novels!

Mr Ambrose cocked his head, like a schoolmaster glancing down at an ignorant pupil. 'Didn't you know? This bridge is the only way to the treasure. If I destroy it, you will never get to your goal. Leave. Now.' He rested the muzzle of the revolver against the old, fraying rope. 'Or I shoot.'

'If you shoot, you will all die,' the colonel pointed out with what I thought was admirable logic. I had been about to make that point myself.

'Maybe.' Mr Ambrose gave a barely perceptible shrug, glancing down at the chasm beneath us. 'Maybe not. I have been told my head is quite hard. It might withstand the impact.'

That might actually be true. But that didn't exactly make me feel more comfortable about what would happen to the rest of us.

'What are you doing?' I hissed at him. 'Haven't you read any adventure novels? He's the villain! He's supposed to be the one threatening to plunge us into a deadly chasm, not you!'

'Sorry to disappoint you, Mr Linton,' he said, his tone, or rather the lack of it, making it clear he wasn't sorry at all. He directed his gaze at the colonel, hard. 'Well, colonel? I am waiting.'

An immeasurably long second passed. A second in which anything was possible. The colonel's aristocratic face was completely unreadable. There was no telling what he might have done if not, at that very moment, from the other end of the gorge, a familiar voice had shouted: 'Everyone drop their weapons, or I will cut the ropes!'

I whirled around, just in time to see Lieutenant de Alvarez step up to the rope on the other side of the bridge, raising his knife. Behind him, his men fanned out, covering the edge of the gorge, a mirror of the Imperialist troops on the other side.

'Is that who I think it is?' Mr Ambrose hissed out from between clenched teeth, his gaze still fixed on Colonel Silveira. The two of us were standing back-to-back now, with Karim standing beside us, looking exceedingly unhappy at being unsure whom to shoot first.

'I'm afraid so,' I whispered back. 'What should we do?'

But before either of us could do anything, the decision was taken out of our hands.

'He lied!' I heard the triumph in Colonel Silveira's voice, and, whirling back to face him, saw the gleam in his eyes. 'There must be another way across, and those rebel rats found it! His threat is empty! Charge, men! Charge!'

The Brazilian troops raised their weapons, bellowed a battle cry and charged onto the bridge. Lieutenant de Alvarez, who was not about to be outdone by an imperialist pig, shouted: 'Kill the royalist scum! Charge!'

Both groups rushed onto the bridge, bayonets, raised, ready for the kill. They had apparently forgotten that sweet little me and company still stood in the middle of the bridge, right in their way. Or maybe, they just didn't care.

I looked at Mr Ambrose. Mr Ambrose looked at me. We both looked at the bloodthirsty hordes of charging soldiers. I saw the resolution form in his eyes a moment before his fingers squeezed the trigger. A shot rang out, rope tore, and then we were falling, falling, falling, and I was thinking: *Bloody stinking hell! I'll never read adventure novels again!*

Did you know that Brazil is one of the largest countries on the planet, and most of its provinces are landlocked, far away from large bodies of water? I had never paid much attention to this fact before, but when I came up sputtering on the shore of whatever river I had plunged into, I had reason to be thankful for it. I was sopping wet, and aching and dirty, but – Yay! – I had managed to hit a river and not be smashed to death on the rocks.

No welcome party of Brazilian soldiers awaited me, rifles raised. No rebel placed his knife at my neck, ready to slit my throat at the first sign of trouble. The only Brazilians who greeted me were a few blueish corpses, strewn across the bank.

'Hello, fellows,' I rasped. 'Had a nice swim, did you?'

Unsurprisingly, none of them replied.

'Well, it was really nice seeing you. But I'm afraid I'll have to go now. Just in case any of you are still alive, you know.'

I tried to push myself up – and promptly landed on my face. If I had expected someone to rush to my aid, I was sorely disappointed. No Mr Ambrose came dashing towards me, eager to help me up. Ha! Who needed him anyway? I was not a helpless damsel in some cheap novel! I was a strong woman and could stand on my own two feet. At least after a couple of tries.

When I finally managed to stagger to my feet, every bone in my body was aching from the effort. I hobbled along the bank in a meandering path, avoiding dead Brazilians left and right. A bit farther downstream, I came upon Mr Ambrose, who was glaring at a few mud stains on his ten-year-old mint-condition tailcoat, and Karim, who was wringing water out of his beard.

'Hello there,' I croaked.

Mr Ambrose looked up. 'Ah. You are alive.'

'Don't overdo it with the joyous shouts of welcome and happy dancing. I know you're delighted to see me.'

'Indeed I am. You have the manuscript.'

'Ah, yes. A woman's greatest worth lies not in her looks, but in the contents of her pockets.' Reaching into my backpack, which I had somehow managed to cling onto, I pulled out the sodden bundle of pages. Incredibly, most were still legible. 'I am happy to be of service.'

Mr Ambrose gave me a curt nod. Karim gave me a look which said clearly that he could have done without the manuscript, if he could have got rid of me.

Ah, friends! Aren't they wonderful?

'We will move into the jungle and rest,' Mr Ambrose ordered. 'It's almost sunset, and we can't climb up into the mountains at night.'

'Not to mention the fact that I'm wet as a drowned weasel and aching all over,' I pointed out, politely. 'Thanks to the brilliant plan of a certain someone, which got us all dunked into the river.' He ignored me.

'Let's go. We haven't got all day.'

Turning, he started to walk away – but I made a grab for his arm.

'You don't think you're going to get off as easily as that, do you?' I hissed into his ear. 'Shooting through the rope of the bridge while we were standing on it? What kind of insane idea is that! Did you lose your mind?'

He cocked his head, coolly. 'Do my ears deceive me, or do I detect a certain amount of criticism in your voice, Mr Linton?'

'You bet you do! We could have been killed!'

'But we were not.'

'Pure luck!'

'I prefer to call it a calculated risk.'

'A calculated risk, eh?' My grip tightening, I stepped closer. My eyes burned into him, screaming the words that my lips were too afraid to say: You could have died! I could have lost you! 'Well, tonight, when the two of us are alone, I'm going to show you exactly what I think of your calculated risks!'

And I did show him. All night long. The problem was: he didn't seem properly chastened. Not at all. On the contrary, he only wanted more.

~~**~*~*

When I opened my eyes next morning, a light mist lay over the jungle and the mountains. I yawned, dragging in big mouthfuls of the cool air streaming down from the peaks.

'What time is it?'

'Time to go mountain climbing,' Mr Ambrose's voice came from above me. My clothes landed in front of me with a thud. 'Get dressed. Up in the mountains, you'll need all the warmth you can get.'

'Mountains?' I blinked up at him groggily. 'You honestly mean for us to go climbing up into the mountains this early in the morning? My bones feel like lead and I'm sore all over!'

'Really?' His face remained perfectly expressionless. '*I* feel perfectly fine. Whatever can you have been up to last night?'

I gave him a glare, which he ignored.

Bloody hell! Oh, well. If he could pretend he was perfectly fit after last night's shenanigans, then so could I! Groaning, I pushed myself onto my feet and slipped into my clothes. They felt alien on my skin after so much time spent walking around half-naked. I could only hope that once we were back home again, I would get used to them quickly, and not accidentally come down to breakfast one morning dressed only in my drawers.

Wait a minute...half-naked. That reminded me of something. And no, I wasn't thinking about Mr Ambrose.

'What about the Indians?' I demanded. 'What happened to them?'

'They slipped away once it became clear that the Brazilians were too many to handle,' Karim grunted. 'I cannot blame them, really. They only signed on to be guides, not bodyguards.'

Very true. I wasn't one for praying, usually, especially not to a patriarchal God who kicked humans out of paradise because a woman wanted to satisfy her perfectly natural curiosity, but I sent up a quick prayer to whatever heathen gods the natives prayed to, asking them to guide Amana and all the others safely back to their village. These people had truly been my guides, and not just through the jungle of South America.

'Let's go!'

Mr Ambrose's command pulled me from my reverie. I looked up, just in time to catch the end of the rope he threw at me.

'What am I supposed to do with that?'

'It's a safety measure. Tie it around your waist – if it's long enough.'

My eyes narrowed. 'Thanks so much for the compliment.'

'You're welcome. Some of those mountain paths look pretty steep to me. If one of us falls, hopefully the other two will be able to catch him–' he glanced at me and reluctantly added, 'or her.'

Well, well, well. Will you look at that? Mr Rikkard Ambrose has learned a new pronoun. So miracles do happen, after all.

Smiling, I tied the rope around myself.

'Enough chit-chat. It's time we got moving.' And he marched off towards the nearest mountain.

'What about breakfast?' I demanded.

'There's a piece of bread in your knapsack. We have no time to waste.'

'But– ah!'

Feeling a sudden tug on the rope around my waist, I stumbled forward.

'No buts, Mr Linton!'

Another tug, and I staggered forward again.

Safety measure my foot! This was why he had done it! So he could tug me around on a leash, like a little obedient puppy! And the worst thing was: I couldn't even find reasonable grounds for complaining! Gah!

TO THE TOP

I might have been a little hasty in my judgement. The mountain paths we started to climb were steep, and the rope did come in handy. More than once I stumbled, and it was the only thing that prevented me from sliding back down the gravelly path, towards a fate that included a cracked skull and several broken bones. The one time that was really dangerous, however, was not when I slipped and fell, but Karim. The sudden, violent tug on the rope nearly ripped me off my feet, and only by combining all our strength did Mr Ambrose and I prevent our favourite turbaned giant from plummeting down the mountain.

Mr Ambrose never slipped. Mr Ambrose never fell. It was as if the mountain's rocks, knowing that it was just another rock walking around on them, extended him special privileges. He never even teetered or showed the slightest hesitation in his movement. Briskly he strode up the path, his eyes cold, his face set in stone.

We took a brief break around noon, and then started up again, up, up and farther up. The path grew even steeper. Often now, we were more climbing than we were walking, pulling ourselves from rock to rock. Sweat was streaming down my back in rivers, every drop caused by exertion, and not one by heat. The stifling hot jungle was long behind us. Up here, the air was starting to become bitterly cold. Of course, the only one who didn't seem to notice the temperature was Mr Rikkard Ambrose.

It was probably about 1 pm, just as the sun was starting to sink towards the horizon after reaching its zenith, that we came to the wall.

Not a man-made wall. Oh no, that would have been manageable. We did have rope after all, and two tall men who, if one stood on the other's shoulders, could probably have topped most walls that weren't built to deter hordes of barbarian invaders. But this wall was another matter entirely. From top to bottom, it was made out of solid, rough, unbreakable rock, with scarcely a handhold in sight anywhere. Somewhere deep down I knew it was simply a natural rock formation, but it looked as if it had been placed here by some ancient race of giants to block anyone from going farther. Our path ended at the bottom of the wall. There was no other way in sight.

'What do we do now?' I demanded. This couldn't be it! We couldn't be forced to give up now, after all we had been through!

'Climb,' was Mr Ambrose's cool reply.

I stared at him, then let my eyes wander to the wall and finally back to him.

'Have you lost your marbles, Sir?' I enquired, politely.

'I have never been in the habit of collecting marbles to begin with, Mr Linton. Look.' And, raising his arm, he pointed up the wall to a spot I could hardly make out from down here. I squinted.

'Something is up there.'

'What impressive cognitive capabilities, Mr Linton. Yes, there is something up there. A ledge.'

'A *ledge*?'

'To which we are going to climb up.'

'You're joking!'

'It is a mystery to me why you insist on accusing me of such a useless habit. Well, Mr Linton?'

'We are seriously going up there?'

'Indeed we are. Unless your manuscript can point us a different way?'

I scowled. 'No. This is where it said to go.'

'Then what are you waiting for?'

My eyes went wide. 'What? You're not expecting me to go first!'

'Certainly, Mr Linton. When climbing a mountain, the least experienced climber always goes first. That way, the experienced climbers can catch them if they fall.' His eyes slid over me, assessing, lingering particularly long on my generous derriere. 'Don't worry. It won't be easy, but I'm strong. I'm ninety-nine per cent sure I'll be able to manage.'

I stabbed him with a dagger-like gaze. Unfortunately, it didn't leave any flesh wounds. 'Thanks *so* much!'

'You are welcome. Now move!'

I moved.

Don't ask me how I managed it – because I couldn't tell you. Afterwards, I spent considerable time and effort expunging every single little horrifying detail of that climb from my memory. I'm good at expunging, it turns out.

All I know is that after endless millennia of terrifying torture (which, in reality, probably lasted about thirty minutes) I lay on top of the ledge above the precipice, panting like a panther, clutching a large boulder next to me as if it were my dear sweet mother.

Karim stuck his bearded head above the edge of the ledge. 'Why are you lying on the ground, woman-who-is-worse-than-ifrit?'

'Bite me!'

'I would rather bite a donkey's arse.'

'Be my guest.'

'If you two do not stop wasting time and move,' came a noise from below, out of the precipice, 'I will employ you both as donkeys. You can carry the treasure to England on your backs!'

That got Karim moving. Even I, tortured wreck that I was, somehow managed to pull myself to my feet. A few moments later, the top of a top hat appeared above the edge of the abyss, followed by the hard head of Mr Rikkard Ambrose.

'How in God's name did you manage to keep that thing on while climbing up there?' I demanded.

All I got in answer was a cool look and silence. Mr Ambrose pulled himself up the rest of the way and, unlike me, didn't seem to feel the need to collapse on the spot. Instead, he surveyed the ledge, which led up the steep mountainside, forming a path about two feet wide.

'This is...inconvenient,' he stated.

'Inconvenient?' That was not the word I would have chosen for this harrowing ordeal of a hellish climb.

'Indeed. It will be difficult to transport all the gold back down there.'

'Oh yes, indeed, Sir. It will also be difficult to transport ourselves back down there. Especially without cracking our heads open.'

'Well, no sense in wasting time. Let's move!'

He started forward, and I, forgetting I still had the rope around my waist, was nearly tugged off my feet, stumbling after him.

'Keep up, Mr Linton!'

'You're really enjoying this, aren't you?'

'I have no idea what you mean, Mr Linton.'

~~**~*~*

We climbed for hours upon hours. When the sun was setting and the whole mountain was being flooded in red-golden light, we finally approached the top. My heart was hammering a frantic rhythm against my ribs, and not just from the exertion. This was it. The venture I had, to some extent, staked my fortunes on was reaching its climax. I had talked Mr Ambrose into this expedition. If we were not going to find gold at the top of this mountain, he would be, to put it mildly, displeased.

I did not want to see Mr Rikkard Ambrose displeased. Not at all.

But when we climbed the last stack of rocks and finally had our first view of the mountaintop, all thoughts of treasure and gold, yes even all thoughts of Mr Rikkard Ambrose, flew out of my head, because there, right in front of me, stretched a sight the like of which I had never seen before. For a moment I thought we had been magically transported to Egypt, to the great pyramids of Giza. But no, the stone here was grey, not the colour of sand. And besides, even though I had been to Egypt, I had never got to see the pyramids of Giza. But I could see this one. Oh yes, I definitely could.

Like a crown atop the head of an ancient king, a majestic stone pyramid rose on the highest point of the mountaintop. Around it stood various smaller buildings, impressive monuments in their own right. They stood atop a broad grassy stretch of land that once had been tamed by rows upon rows of stone terraces, but was now slowly being reclaimed by the wild. Mist drifted between the ancient monuments. The sun sparkled on dew.

I was awestruck.

'Why are you standing there with your mouth open, Mr Linton?' enquired a cool voice from beside me.

Ah. Apparently Mr Rikkard Ambrose was not quite as awestruck.

'I was inhaling the fresh mountain air, Sir.'

'Stop inhaling and start moving. We have work to do.'

He strode past me, off towards the largest of the pyramids. Under a wide stone lintel, there gaped an opening. I hesitated to call it a door, because for that, in my humble British opinion, you usually need a slab of wood with a knob attached to it. But it definitely was an entrance. Mr Ambrose stopped a few feet in front of it and pulled something out of his backpack that looked like a stick of wood. Only when I saw sparks fly from the flint in his hand did I realise it was a torch.

A flame flared up and, in its light, the entryway suddenly glowed, bright and red like the gates to hell. All that was missing were the words 'All hope abandon, ye who enter here' over the doorway. But if there had been treasure in hell, I doubt even that would have deterred Mr Rikkard Ambrose. He strode forward with confident steps. Karim and I threw each other a look – and then hurried after him, each determined to be the first to follow.

Inside, it was dark. No matter that a torch was burning – the room we were standing in was so vast that its light was simply swallowed up by the darkness. Somewhere, high in the shadows above me, I could guess at a stone ceiling, but other than that, there was only blackness.

Or was there?

Out of the corner of my eyes, I caught a glint in the shadows. The eye of an animal? No. It was too cold for that. Too...metallic.

'Karim? Mr Linton?' Mr Ambrose's voice echoed in the great darkness. 'You have torches in your knapsacks, too. Light them.'

'But...'

'Light them *now*, Mr Linton.'

Without further argument, I pulled the torch out of my knapsack and, after several failed attempts, managed to light it. Slowly, I raised it over my head – and my eyes went wide.

Gold.

In the light of three torches, there was no doubt anymore. Gold and gold and more gold. It glinted on the walls, was heaped on the floor, yes, even hung from the ceiling. There were heaps of coins, mountains of jewellery, great statues of ancient heathen gods in jewels and precious metals – more than the eye could see. And trust me, my eyes were capable of seeing pretty damn much!

'Bloody hell...!' I murmured.

No answer. I glanced sideways at Mr Ambrose. This time, even he seemed to be somewhat awestruck. I could practically see the pound symbols blinking in his eyes. His gaze was fastened to the gold and precious jewels with a look I recognised. It was the same one he sometimes got when I started to take my clothes off. I wasn't entirely sure whether I should be offended or flattered by this.

'How are we ever going to get all that down the mountain, *Sahib*?' Karim murmured.

Mr Ambrose's face hardened in an instant. 'We are. Somehow, we are going to. We have to.'

He left unsaid what would happen to any employees who didn't come up with ingenious ideas towards that end.

'Let us go outside,' Karim suggested. 'Maybe, among the ruins, we will find something that we can use to transport all this.'

He didn't sound too hopeful. I had to admit, I shared his pessimism. What could we possibly find to help us carry several hundred pounds – no, probably several tons! – of gold and jewels? We had no packs, no saddlebags, no horses, and even if we had, how would horses ever be able to get down that steep cliff that was the only way up to the mountain. No, unless a miracle occurred, we were stuck up here. Because one thing I was certain of: Mr Ambrose would rather tear out his heart with hot irons than leave one single little coin of this treasure behind.

Well, look on the bright side: you won't be returning to England for a good, long time. You can keep frolicking in the jungle as much as you wish.

Strange. For some reason, that didn't make me as happy as I thought it would. But what could I do? In this ancient, long-lost ruin, there was no one to help us. Not a single soul. Sighing, I turned back towards the entrance and trudged out into the sunset. I was so lost in my own thoughts that I almost ran head-first into the shepherd.

I screamed. The shepherd screamed. His sheep screamed (or rather bleated), and ran away up the hill. The man stumbled back and fell on his butt.

'What is happening here?' Mr Ambrose appeared behind me, gun raised, ready to shoot. At the sight of the gun, the shepherd stopped screaming, and his eyes widened to the size of saucers.

'No, don't! Don't shoot!' I grabbed Mr Ambrose's arm, pointing it away from the man. Or...no. Not a man. He was really only just a boy, I realised as I studied his face more closely.

Karim appeared beside Mr Ambrose, his gun drawn as well.

'Put that away, will you?' I hissed. 'You're frightening the poor boy.'

Karim ignored me.

'What is he doing here, *Sahib*?' he demanded, jerking his firearm towards the frozen figure of the shepherd boy. 'How did he get up here with those beasts?'

'I have no idea,' Mr Ambrose said coldly. 'But I intend to find out!'

He snapped a few brief phrases in Portuguese. The boy stared at him uncomprehendingly. So Mr Ambrose tried again, this time in Spanish. This time, the boy's eyes lit up and he started to chatter. I was pretty fluent in Portuguese, by now, but my Spanish was still restricted to words like 'bastard' and 'donkey's arse'. I didn't understand a word of what was going on. But by the look in Mr Ambrose's eyes I could tell it wasn't going the way he expected. Not at all.

Karim didn't look too pleased, either. 'What in the name of...' He uttered a few unpronounceable words in his mother tongue. 'What is the brat rambling on about, *Sahib*? I thought...'

'Yes.' Mr Ambrose's voice was hard as steel. 'So did I.'

'*She* said...'

'Yes. She did.'

Slowly, very slowly, Mr Rikkard Ambrose turned towards me, the icy cold of the entire arctic wasteland gathered in his deep, dark eyes.

Uh-oh...

'Can you explain something to me, Mr Linton?'

His voice was deceptively calm.

'Um...I'll try to. If I can.'

'How very kind of you. Well, then, explain this to me: this boy says there is a perfectly good, easy path down the mountain on the other side. So easy to use, in fact, that the people in the neighbourhood often drive their sheep up here to let them graze. He saw us climbing up the rock cliff and was quite surprised we would risk falling to our deaths when it is so perfectly easy to get up here.'

'Oh.'

'Oh indeed, Mr Linton. And that's not all. Do you know what he also told me?'

'Not really, no.'

'He told me that to the west, in the direction of his village, it is only a few miles to the ocean. Imagine that, Mr Linton. We are only a few miles away from the sea. It makes one wonder why a certain someone would send us hacking through hundreds of miles of jungle, including a deadly warzone.'

I cleared my throat. 'The directions in the manuscript didn't say anything about coming from the west coast.'

'And were these instructions by any chance old enough to have been written before the passage to the west coast of this continent around its southern tip was discovered?'

I cleared my throat again. 'Err...they might be.'

'Ah. And you didn't see fit to mention this fact because...?'

'I, um...might not have noticed.'

His calm façade vanished. Fiery ice blazed in his eyes. He took a step towards me, a muscle in his jaw twitching.

'You...you...' He was trying to come up with a bad enough word to describe me. I was about to help out (after all, I had learned quite a lot of interesting swear words on this journey), but he found one without my help. 'You...*female*! You sent us all this way through the jungle for nothing?'

And suddenly, inexplicably, a grin tugged at the corners of my mouth. I probably should have been scared. I mean, he was a big man and pretty near to the edge, apparently. But all I could do was smirk.

'Really, Sir? Nothing?'

My hand reached out, gently caressing his face, then moving over his chest and down, down, down. He jerked, and stiffened.

'Well...' Suddenly, his voice, although still cold, sounded a bit strained. 'Maybe "nothing" was the wrong word.'

'That's what I thought, too. So...how about we start getting the gold off this bloody mountain, now?'

'Adequate idea.'

'And then, maybe, we can do a bit more of the "nothing" we did in the jungle.'

'Indeed. Yes.'

~~*~**~*~*

Getting the gold down the mountain wasn't difficult at all, it turned out – not once we had got the help of the villagers. They weren't the least bit interested in the heaps of cursed yellow metal lying around up in the old ghost city. But they were interested in sheep. Very interested indeed. Once Mr Ambrose had promised to double their herds, they were more than willing to help us cart the stuff down the mountain, pack it up, and bring it into the next city, where Mr Ambrose had both an agent and several of his fleet of merchant ships.

At first, when Mr Ambrose stormed into the captain's cabin and demanded that he throw overboard his cargo of salted fish, the man was less than willing. However, once he had understood that this tall, dark, cold individual in front of him was the man who owned the company that owned the company that owned the company that owned his arse, and if he didn't do as he was told he was the one who was going to be thrown overboard, he hastened to comply.

From then on, it all went so fast I felt slightly dizzy. The treasure was labelled 'salt fish', and snuck onto the ship in the middle of the night. When I suggested to Mr Ambrose that we should perhaps report to the authorities that we were removing historic artifacts from their soil, he gave me a look that shut me up in a flash.

We set sail that very same night. My heart was pounding as we drifted out of the harbour. I thought that any moment a hue and cry would go up, and the Navy would be after us, trying to recapture stolen national treasures. But nothing of the sort happened. We sailed out into the darkness with nothing but the whisper of the wind as company, and soon were out on the open sea, bound for England. Bound for home.

The days passed. I'm not going to waste time describing another sea voyage, because one is pretty much like another. And besides, I've been reliably informed that knowledge is power is time is money. I wouldn't want to waste any of the above, now, would I?

'Land ahoy!'

The call from the top of the mast brought me out of my cabin. And indeed, there it was: just a faint white line, as yet, but I could already recognize the cliffs of Dover. My heart sped up, and I glanced at Mr Ambrose, who stood next to me at the railing, like a stone monument to masculinity.

'So...we're back home.'

'Indeed.'

'Back in England.' *Where it is not usual to run around half naked covered in mud all the time.*

'Indeed.'

'Are you happy to be back?'

Silence.

Well, I suppose it was a stupid question. In order to be happy to be back, you would first have to know what it means to be happy.

'When you're back in London, are you going to publish your discovery? Are you going to write about our adventure? I'm sure the Royal Geographical Society would be interested.'

He turned his head an inch or so in my direction, inquiringly. 'What profit would that bring?'

'Fame! Publicity! Scholarly recognition!'

'How much is that in pounds sterling?'

'Hrumph.'

'Besides, I doubt the government back in South America would agree with my personal "finders keepers" philosophy.'

Well, he was probably right about that.

My eyes were drawn back to the Cliffs of Dover, and all thought of discoveries and adventures vanished from my mind. This was England. I would have bigger things to worry about than whether or not my name appeared in the journals of the Royal Geographical Society. Glancing sideways at Mr Ambrose, I tried to detect one crack in his armour, one little hint that he wasn't as perfectly cool and composed as he appeared to be. There was nothing.

He hadn't touched me once on the journey back from South America. He hadn't even tried. True, a stifling little cabin that smelled of salted fish wasn't exactly an environment conducive to violent romantic passion, but still...I had expected at least something to happen. At the very least, I had expected him to say something. Instead, all I had got was...

Can you guess?

Yep. Silence.

Really very extraordinarily silent silence. How surprising.

I wondered what would happen if I were suddenly to grab him by the ears and plant a big, fat, fiery kiss on him. And then I wondered why I was wondering these things. I was a feminist, bloody hell! I should have got this annoying habit of plastering my lips to those of my chauvinistic employer out of my system by now! Even if I wanted anything to do with men – which I most definitely absolutely and totally did not, no, never, thank you very much for not bothering me with it and going to hell *right now*! – he and I were about as well-suited to each other as a Siberian tiger and a firebird!

And yet, and yet...

I glanced at Mr Ambrose again, and as I did, something contracted around my heart, squeezing painfully.

Oh no.

My tastes leaned more towards adventure novels. But I had read enough romances to know what that feeling meant.

There it went again! One look at Mr Ambrose, one painful squeeze around my heart.

Oh, no, no, no, never in a thousand million billion years! It was simply impossible! And even if it were possible, it was completely and utterly intolerable! I would rather drown myself in the Thames or go into exile in the Sahara than admit that I might actually be...that I might feel...for him? No! No, no, and triple *no*!

My hand clenched around the railing. I stared ferociously forward, towards the white Cliffs of Dover, trying to make them explode with the force of my glare alone. It didn't work.

No! This can't be happening! This can't be happening! This can't be hap-

Something touched my hand, and my thoughts fizzled out like a wet fuse. My eyes darted down, and with horror I watched Mr Rikkard Ambrose's hand closing over mine.

He was holding my hand.

He was holding *my* hand.

He was *holding my hand*.

And what was worse, I didn't even try to slap him for it! I didn't even want to, because it felt...good.

My mind flashed back to that day in the Chapel Royal. He had held my hand while the minister pronounced the wedding vows.

Not yours! I thought, fiercely. *They weren't your wedding vows!*

No. Not yet.

261

It took me a few moments, but then I realised: hang on, what had that traitorous mind of mine just thought? *Not yet?* As if...as if this might lie in my future?

My ears started to burn. I felt sure that if Mr Ambrose looked my way, he would be able to read every single little stupid thought on my stupid face. But he didn't look my way. He just stared straight ahead, and I, too, stared straight ahead. But our hands didn't part.

~~**~*~*

I suppose you'd think there was a big fuss when I suddenly returned home after a few months of mysterious absence, and I suppose, in a way, there was. If she could have, my aunt would have had me up in front of a hanging judge for disappearing just when she had found a nobleman to marry me off to. Since not marrying rich people was fortunately not a hanging offence, she instead dragged me into my uncle's study, so he could visit his worst punishments on me.

And what did my uncle do?

Well, our conversation went something like this:

Uncle Bufford (raising his eyebrows threateningly): 'Where have you been, girl?'

Me (smiling innocently): 'Busy.'

Uncle Bufford: 'Busy? What is that supposed to mean?'

Me: 'It means I earned some money.'

Uncle Bufford: 'Earned money? How?'

Me: 'If I give you ten per cent of it, will you not ask that again and forget about this whole business?'

Uncle Bufford: 'You think you can bribe me, girl?'

Me: 'All right, fifteen per cent.'

Uncle Bufford: 'Twenty-five, at least!'

Me: 'Twenty, and that's my last offer.'

Uncle Bufford: 'Done.'

Me: 'Let's shake on it.' (shaking hands)

Uncle Bufford: 'Where did you learn to negotiate like that?'

Me: 'I'm learning from the best, trust me.'

Uncle Bufford: 'Good girl! And now get out of here, I have work to do.'

You know what? I really love my uncle.

My sister Ella wasn't quite so easy to deal with. Since she actually (for some strange reason) genuinely cared for me, a cut of my monthly payment probably wouldn't be the right approach to soothe her tears. Instead I tried a mixture of pats on the back and 'there, there's'. It seemed to work quite well. I decided that next time I went on a dangerous journey into the South American jungle, I should probably warn her beforehand.

Soon, my little sister was so overtaken by joy that I was not dead in a ditch somewhere that she had forgiven me for my disappearance. Normal home life resumed.

At work, too, the usual office routine was back in place. Mr Ambrose pelted me with little notes demanding for me to get this and note down that, and I ran around doing my best to soothe his tyrannical disposition. Only one thing was a little different: in my absence, a whole mountain of correspondence had accumulated. I was a bit puzzled as to why, at first – after all, we hadn't been gone that long – until I started to dig through the pile and came across the pink letters.

Dozens upon dozens were heaped onto my desk – maybe even hundreds! With a sigh, I started to deposit them in my full-to-bursting bottom drawer. Three days later, I was still busy trying to find a place to stash the last of them so Mr Ambrose would think I had destroyed them all. I was just contemplating whether I could nail some of them to the underside of my desk when a brisk knock came from the door.

'Y–' I began. That was about all I got out of my intended 'Yes, who is this?' before the door burst open and a young woman strode into the room as if she owned the place (and the rest of the world besides).

My mouth dropped open.

She was a girl, of course, so she had curves and long hair, but apart from that...the determined, chiselled jaw, the perfect face, the dark, sea-coloured eyes with the look inside them that could freeze your butt off at fifty paces...

I swallowed, hard.

She was young, probably a bit younger than me, and her face was still too round and childlike for the resemblance to be perfect, but no matter. I knew. I just knew.

'Where is he?' the girl demanded, eyes blazing.

Not for one moment did I doubt to whom she was referring. Unable to manage speech, I lifted one slightly trembling hand and pointed to the connecting door to Mr Ambrose's office, which he had (very unwisely, as I currently believed) left unlocked.

'All right.' The girl cracked her knuckles. I am not joking. She actually *cracked her knuckles*. Her gaze fell on the stack of unanswered pink letters on my desk. Her eyes flashed with anger, and then darted to the connecting door. 'You stay here and don't interrupt! I have a few things to say to this brother of mine!'

And, marching to the door, she tore it open and marched inside. It slammed shut behind her like a thunderbolt.

This time, unlike with his mother, I didn't try to listen in. But that was only because this time, unlike with his mother, the whole conversation was perfectly audible through the thick stone walls. If you could call something a 'conversation' that rattled the windows and probably shook the building to its foundations. I winced, for the first time in my life feeling genuinely sorry for Mr Rikkard Ambrose. When the girl stormed out of the office half an hour later, I had stuffed my fingers in my ears so as not to go deaf from the noise.

She stopped at the door to the hallway and turned around one last time. 'If you're not there by the end of the month, I'll come and drag you there by the ears!' she shouted. 'Mother is hurting! Enough is enough!'

With that, she stormed out into the hallway and slammed the door behind her.

Silence descended over the office.

It's funny, really. In my time with Mr Ambrose I'd had plenty of experience with it, but still, I had never realised until now what a wonderful thing silence could be. Cautiously, I removed my fingers from my ears.

Even more cautiously, I glanced at the half-open door to Mr Ambrose's office. It was quiet as the grave in there. Maybe quite literally. I wouldn't put much past that little raven-haired vixen, including blackmail and manslaughter.

But then, to my infinite relief, I heard footsteps approaching from inside the other office. Slowly, the door creaked open, and there he stood: Mr Rikkard Ambrose, looking as cool and controlled as ever, not betraying a hint of the fact that he was just ravaged by a mad fury from hell. Except...well, his left little finger was twitching. Fast.

'Mr Linton?'

'Yes, Sir?'

'Pack your bags. It appears we are going on another trip.'

'Indeed, Sir?'

'Yes, indeed.' His eyes as he looked at me were as deep, dark and unfathomable as the farthest depths of the ocean. 'It is time I pay a visit to my family.'

THE END

SPECIAL ADDITIONAL MATERIAL

THREE CHAPTERS FROM

MR AMBROSE'S PERSPECTIVE

'Happily Ever After with Whiskers',
'Really Hot Jungle Heat',
and
'Interesting Ideas'

A Royal Waste of Time

'Name, Sir?'

Now here was a rare specimen – someone who dared to step in my way. I regarded the royal guard before me and wondered if he knew he wasn't going to keep his post for long.

Karim, ever the efficient employee, spoke a few curt words to the man and, for the first time, he took a good look at my face. His visage under the ridiculous pelt hat paled. Ah. Recognition. Too late.

Quickly, the unfortunate guard took a step back. Wise decision.

'Mr Ambrose, Sir. So you could come after all.' He gave a salute, more snappy than a thousand snapped fingers. 'We are honoured, Sir.'

'Yes, you are.' I strode past the guard without giving him a glance. Right now, I had more important things on my mind. Like the opportunity this ridiculous ceremony afforded me to advance the New Zealand project. There was no time to lose. Sliding out of my coat, I thrust it at the nearest walking hallstand in butler uniform. 'Let's get this over with. Where is the Queen?'

'Um...Her Majesty is preparing herself, I believe, Sir.'

'What does she need to prepare herself for? She's had three months of engagement time for that.'

The butler cleared his throat delicately. 'I couldn't say, Sir.'

My patience, already strictly rationed for the last few years, was rapidly running out. 'Well, where is this whole thing going to happen?'

'In the Chapel Royal, Sir, but – Wait! Wait, Sir! You can't go in there yet!'

I can't, can I?

Behind me, I heard *her* snicker at the poor butler. She knew me well.

Too damn well.

Quickly, I banished that thought from my mind. Without paying any attention to the lackey's protests, I marched into the palace.

The place was predictably pretentious. Colour and glitter everywhere. Portraits of self-important people on the walls. I didn't give them a glance. I had a purpose here.

Hurried footsteps sounded behind me, catching up. 'Where are we going?'

Ah. She apparently had a purpose, too. Distracting me.

'The Chapel Royal, Mr Linton.'

'Um...are we allowed to simply go in there?'

'I don't believe so, no.'

'But you're going to do it anyway, aren't you?'

She knew me well indeed. For some reason, it didn't irk me as much as it probably should have. Why would I not object to someone seeing through me this easily? Why didn't it make me feel suspicious and distrustful? I had always reserved a healthy portion of distrust for everybody.

'Yes,' I told her briskly.

I didn't glance at her, keeping my eyes straight ahead. The corridor in front of me, the paintings, the sparkling chandelier, those were all just slight distractions, easy to ignore. But her in that dress...

I squashed that thought before it could fully form and hastened my steps. We were heading down a long corridor now. At the end of it, a set of double doors awaited us. Pushing them open, I strode inside and surveyed the Chapel Royal – the place where, since time immemorial, the kings and queens of England had married, if they didn't want to bother with Westminster Abbey.

For a moment, I stood still, gazing up at the high, arched windows and dark, wood-panelled walls – then I shook myself. Why would I care where some self-important royal tied the knot?

Get a grip, or this deal might slip through your fingers!

'Ah. Welcome, welcome!' My head snapped around, and I saw some cleric in robes coming towards us. I didn't keep track of the clergy, focusing more on keeping them at arm's length. They had the annoying habit of asking for alms for the poor. 'Come in, Sir, Miss. What a joyous occasion! Such a happy day deserves to be celebrated, does it not?'

'No, it does not.' Snatching my top hat off my head, I clamped it under my arm and gave the priest a cool look. 'But I presume it is going to happen anyway.'

'Err...well...'

And that was about the extent of my conversation for the next half hour. People came over to get an introduction, get a loan, or get me to marry their daughter, but I was highly skilled in rebuffing the first two kinds of overtures, and in regard to the last, Miss Linton proved to be a convenient buffer. I would have to remember that for the future.

Still, I had to admit as I glanced over at her and caught her vigorously rubbing her wet hair, after which she turned to offer the wet towel to the Comtesse de Gramont, she couldn't just be an asset. She could be a disaster, if she wanted to.

'What's wrong with the towel?' She demanded when the comtesse raised her nose and stomped off. 'It still has some dry patches! And my hair doesn't smell that bad.'

'I presume it is not the towel of which she disapproves,' I informed her coolly. 'But the idea of rubbing her hair into haystack style in the middle of the Chapel Royal.'

'Haystack st...! You really know how to compliment a lady, you know.'

'Yes, I know. Do you have a comb with you?'

The question had slipped out before I really knew why or how. Why the heck would I care what she looked like in front of these people?

Well...it only made sense, didn't it? She was my escort tonight. I couldn't let her run around looking like that. Her appearance would reflect directly on me. That's why I had asked. Yes.

'Why on earth would I bring a comb to a royal wedding?'

'I thought so. Well, no matter. Hold still.'

Almost instinctively, I reached up. The familiar movements came easy. Memories flashed in my mind, memories of being dirty, drenched and cold, long, matted clumps of hair clinging to my scalp, sometimes even freezing in the icy air. The mountains had been rough. I'd had no one to help me then. But she had someone now. Gently, I took hold of her hair.

'Hold still? Why...' Her words cut off as I started combing through her hair, squeezing out the last remnants of water with a practised hand, straightening rebellious curls with ease. It was all so familiar – and yet all totally new. My gut tightened as I felt a strange feeling grow inside me. It felt...warm?

What was wrong with me? It was just hair! And damn clammy hair, to boot!

My insides didn't seem to agree. Something tugged at my very core. I didn't want to stop. I wanted to go on sliding my fingers through her soft hair even when it was completely dry. That made no sense! It was just normal, average hair. I had never had the urge to extensively tickle Karim's beard, had I? So why now? Why her? Was I losing my mind?

Knowledge is Power is Time is Money, I reminded myself. *And hair is just hair. Get a grip, and not on her! Remember who and where you are.*

'There you go.' With a swipe of my forefinger I slid a final stray lock of hair behind her ear, completing the image. 'Much less faeneumerial.'

'Faene*what*?'

'Haystackish,' I told her, my tone colder and more brusk than usual.

'Ha!'

The little sound of laughter that escaped her took me off guard. Instinctively, I took a step closer and–

'Attention please!'

I froze. What was I doing? Shaking myself, I turned towards the voice that had called. The Royal Herald. Of course. We were in the Chapel Royal. Wedding. Prince. Queen. Business deal. Concentrate! 'Attention, everybody. The Royal Couple is approaching. Please take your places.'

For a moment I hesitated, not knowing whether it would be a huge mistake – then I offered my arm to Miss Lillian Linton. 'Come.'

And she did. She slipped her arm into mine without the slightest hesitation and walked beside me, taking me aback. I was used to women wanting me, to them being eager to catch my attention – but if and when they had it, they were always overcome by shyness, or even fear. They knew who I was and what I was capable of. Miss Linton moved so easily beside me...almost as if she...as if she *trusted* me?

Then she's a fool. And you're a fool for wasting time on thoughts like this one right here.

Abruptly, I realised we had reached our row of chairs – and she was trying to sit down. By Mammon and Midas! I grabbed hold of her arm.

'No!'

'But...that man said for us to take our places.'

'Yes. *Standing*. You don't sit in the presence of royalty.'

'But...that's stupid!'

'Yes, it is. But until and unless someone successfully explains this to the reigning monarch, we stay upright.' With my free hand, I reached up and, gently, with the back of my knuckles, caressed her hair. Hair that was, for some reason, so much more interesting than my own hair, or Karim's beard, or the fur of a stray cat. 'Understood, Miss Linton?'

She gazed up into my eyes, and once again, I felt that warm tug deep inside. Warm like her eyes.

'Yes, Sir.'

'Adequate.'

The Royal Herald pounded the floor with his staff, tearing me from my paralysis. Royals. Wedding. Business. Remember! 'His Highness, Prince Francis Albert Augustus Charles Emmanuel of Saxe-Coburg and Gotha, Duke of Saxony!'

Miss Linton leaned towards me, so close I could almost feel the warmth of her through my tailcoat. 'Is that two people he just announced, or three?'

Don't look at her! Don't look into her eyes! 'One! Be quiet, Mr Linton!'

'*Miss* Linton to you, Sir.'

As if I could ever forget. 'Be quiet!'

The prince entered the room. Beside me, Miss Linton gave him a thorough once-over, then leaned over towards me again.

'Why would anyone want to marry *that*?'

Be. Quiet. Two words. Not a command that should be difficult to follow, correct? In this case, apparently, it was. And why, by all that was valuable in this world, didn't that annoy me?

'Miss Linton?'

'Yes, Sir?'

'Shut up!'

'Yes, Sir. Right away, Sir.'

She fell silent. Just in time, too. The prince was moving towards us, and however affable he was, I doubted he would be open to business offers after being referred to as 'that'.

'Follow my lead,' I hissed into Miss Linton's ear. 'Do exactly what I am going to do!'

'What? Stare at him icily?'

That woman...!

'Just do what I do!'

'Yes, Sir.'

Taking a deep breath in preparation for the approaching ordeal, I pulled her towards the Prince – and smiled at him.

Or at least I showed him my teeth. I hadn't smiled – really smiled – for longer than I could remember.

But sometimes you want to. When you look at her.

Business. Prince. Concentrate!

'Your Highness!' I inclined my head in a bow. 'I am so delighted that you were so kind as to invite me to your special day.'

The silly smile on the Prince's face broadened. 'You are welcome, Herr...'

I waved my hand, humbly. For some reason, monarchs seemed to like it when you pretended that you weren't more important than they were. 'We've only met once before. I doubt Your Highness would see fit to remember me.'

'But of course I do! Herr Rikkard Ambrose, isn't it?'

'Yes. You honour me, Your Highness.' *Now, if you'll only honour me a little more by helping me to seal this deal, we can all go home and spend the rest of the day on sensible matters.*

'Not at all!' Reaching out, Prince Albert grasped my hand and shook it energetically. Unlike with most of my other business partners, I didn't try and see how hard I would have to squeeze to break his fingers. He'd need at least one of them, after all, for his bride to stick a ring on. 'After your generous contribution to the orphanages in my home city, how could I not remember? Thank you, Herr Ambrose. *Ich danke Ihnen von ganzem Herzen.* You are a truly good and generous man.'

At that insult, I truly had to control myself not to break his fingers.

Queen, I reminded myself. *Wedding. Finger required.*

'It was my pleasure, Your Highness,' I lied. 'How could I stand idly by and let little children suffer when it was in my power to help?' *After all, I can just as well work while they suffer.*

A strangled noise came from the lady beside me. Part of me was tempted to glance at her, just to see the expression on her face in her reaction to my heartwarming kindness to poor little street brats – but I resisted. Instead, I kept spouting meaningless platitudes, making the prince beam like a beam of wood. When I came to mention the sum I had donated, Miss Linton made another strangled noise.

I just couldn't resist. Glancing sideways, I smiled – at her. Somehow, it took a lot less effort than smiling at His Royal Highness. 'Something wrong, my darling?'

She blinked up at me as if she'd never seen me before. 'N-no. Nothing at all.'

'Wonderful.' Taking her by the arm, I steered her a step closer towards the Prince – and she actually *let* me. She really had to be in shock. 'Your Highness, please allow me to introduce my lovely companion for today,' – *and general bane of my existence* – 'Miss Lillian Linton.'

The Prince's gaze took in Miss Linton for a long moment, and for an instant I wondered whether I would have to break his fingers after all. But his eyes didn't wander. Lucky prince. 'How do you do, *Fräulein* Linton?'

Sher curtsied – and smiled. I felt something twist in my stomach.

Fingers must remain intact. Fingers must remain intact!

'When I invited you, I had no idea that you would appear in such charming company,' the Prince added, turning to me.

'Neither had I.' My grip on Miss Linton tightened. *If I had, I would have tied up my charming company and stored her in my cellar.* 'But the Fates play with the string of one's life as they please, sometimes.'

She grinned. The little vixen *grinned.*

Concentrate! Focus on the matter at hand. Prince. Business. Marriage.

My face twitched. All right...maybe not the last one. Refreshing my mask of a smile, I once again grasped the prince's hand and shook it in congratulation.

'But not even Miss Linton can hope to outshine your bride on her big day. May I congratulate you, Your Highness, on your good fortune, and wish you perfect happiness in marriage? There is nothing as important in life as finding a good woman to love, and you have found the best of noble blood in the whole wide world.'

'Thank you!' The Prince looked deeply touched. Fine by me, as long as he didn't try to touch me for some money in return. 'You don't know what this means to me, *Herr* Ambrose, coming from a man like you. I truly hope that once the bustle of the wedding is over, you will come visit me and my bride at Buckingham Palace?'

There we go.

The first return on my investment. The first of many to come.

'I should like nothing better.'

'Attention, please!' I glanced around. It was the herald again. All eyes focused on him, and there was a prickle in the air. 'I have just received word that Her Majesty is approaching. Would everyone return to their places, please?'

I squeezed the Prince's hand once more – but not too hard. How fortunate I had resisted the temptation. Giving him a last bright smile, I started to steer my 'charming company' away, back towards our seats.

'What is this?' she whispered, staring suspiciously up at me. 'What's wrong with your face?'

'Miss Linton?'

'Yes?'

'Shut up!'

'I won't shut up! I want to know what – Hey!'

Ignoring her protest, I manoeuvred her into a corner and only stopped when we were firmly situated at the left end of the front row of guests, well out of hearing distance of the prince.

'What is the matter with you?' she demanded. 'Three thousand pounds sterling? You gave three thousand pounds sterling to an orphanage? Did someone knock you over the head with an iron bar?'

For a moment, I considered knocking *her* over the head an iron bar. But then, knowing her head, that would probably only destroy an expensive piece of ironwork. So instead, I did something far more dangerous. I smiled at her.

Was that...?

Was she blushing?

It was just a hint under her sunny tan, but yes. It was definitely there. A slight, almost imperceptible blush. I felt a tug in my chest.

Heartburn. Ignore.

'Is it so unbelievable that I would do a generous deed out of the goodness of my heart?'

'Frankly – yes!'

'I see you've come to know me well, Mr Linton.'

'I have, unfortunately. And that's *Miss* Linton to you, Mr Ambrose, Sir.'

Don't remind me. I was already having a hard enough time concentrating. The way she looked in that dress... *Ignore, dammit! Ignore!* 'Miss. As you wish.'

'Why did you give away three thousand pounds?'

'You cannot catch fish without bait on the hook, Miss Linton.'

She gave me a sceptical look. 'Three thousand pounds is a pretty big bait.'

I flashed her another smile, this one as hard and dangerous as a shark's.

'Oh, the three thousand pounds aren't the bait, Miss Linton.' Half-turning, I nodded towards Prince Albert. 'He is.'

Her eyebrows shot up. 'Then you have to be catching a fish with pretty strange tastes!'

'Indeed. There she is.'

I pointed discreetly to the door, just as a figure in white appeared in the archway. Miss Linton's eyes went to the figure – then shot to mine, incredulous.

I nodded.

Her eyes flicked back to the door, just as the herald pounded his staff onto the floor. 'Her Majesty Alexandrina Victoria, Queen of the United Kingdom of Great Britain and Ireland!'

The Queen gave a supercilious smile and honoured her subjects with a royal nod, in answer to which the crowd bowed deeply. Hm. She didn't really look worth three thousand pounds. Hopefully, I hadn't paid too much. Maybe I should demand a refund.

'Tell me why you think of the Queen of England as a fish?' a persistent voice beside me enquired.

'Later, Miss Linton.'

'But–'

'Later!'

Finally, she was silent. Like the loyal subject I was, I fixed my eyes on the centre of the chapel, where the Queen was slowly advancing towards the altar. Still...out of the corner of my eye, I could still see Miss Linton. The silence around us began to expand, and as it did, for the first time in my life, it wasn't my refuge. It wasn't the place I could flee to. The longer she was silent, the more I wished she would speak.

The Queen reached the altar. Music had started to play in the background. The reverend pulled out his bible.

Don't look at her. Don't look at her. Don't look at her.

Out of the corner of my eye, I saw her glance at me. Stonily, I stared ahead, not acknowledging her in the least.

And what did she do?

She *smiled.* Smiled at me, glowering into empty air.

Why the heck would she–?

The priest cleared his throat.

'Dearly beloved, we are gathered together here in the sight of God, and in the face of this congregation, to join together this man and this woman in holy matrimony.'

A muscle in my jaw twitched. This man? This woman? Why in Mammon's name couldn't they use labels, serial numbers or at least names in that little speech? I shifted uncomfortably. Only when my feet were done shifting did I realise they had deposited me several inches closer to Miss Lillian Linton.

This man. This woman.

Stop. Stop now. Irrational. Cease this!

I shifted again.

Damnation! What was the matter with me? Did I have the fidgets?[31]

No. I didn't. Because the fidgets only affected the legs. But now, my hand was moving, too, shifting slowly towards hers.

Stop!

I waited. It shifted again, towards that small, soft hand that was so close to mine.

Stop! That is an order.

But my hand seemed to have spent too much time in contact with Miss Lillian Linton already. It stubbornly refused to do what it was told.

But...she seemed to have the same problem. My breath caught as I noticed her small hand inch towards mine, seeming unable to resist. What was this?

'*...which is an honourable estate, instituted of God in the time of man's innocency, signifying unto us the mystical union...*'

My hand moved another inch closer. By King Midas' throne! Why couldn't that infernal priest shut up?

'*...that is betwixt Christ and his Church...*'

My hand moved another fraction of an inch closer.

Out of the corner of my eye, I caught her glancing at my face. I was sure it was cold and hard as ice. All my heat was in my fingertips, burning to move, to close the distance.

Control! Control! Ignore her!

'*...which holy estate Christ adorned and beautified with his presence, and first miracle that he wrought, in Cana of Galilee; and is commended of Saint Paul to be honourable among all men: and therefore is not by any to be enterprised, nor taken in hand, unadvisedly, lightly, or wantonly, to satisfy men's carnal lusts...*'

Wild images flashed past my inner eye. Images that had no place in a chapel – and most certainly not in my mind!

Don't move! That is an order!

But my hand jumped two whole inches forward, and I could be thankful it was only my hand. I trembled, fighting to control the rest of me.

'*...and appetites, like brute beasts that have no understanding; but reverently, discreetly, advisedly, soberly, and in the fear of God; duly considering the causes for which Matrimony was ordained. First, it was ordained for the procreation of children...*'

So much for control. My eyes flew to her. Her face. Her eyes. Images swept past my inner eye that were far more dangerous than the ones I had to endure a moment ago. She and I, and we together with our...

Stop! There will never be an 'our'! There will never be a 'we'!

---

[31] Victorian-era name for RLS (Restless legs syndrome).

Except maybe as in *We are extremely sorry to inform you that, due to budget cuts, your position has been terminated forthwith. We wish you the best of luck with your future career. Good riddance to bad rubbish.*

Because she was bad. Bad for my peace of mind. Bad for my composure. Bad for my control over my infernal extremities!

'...to be brought up in the fear and nurture of the Lord, and to the praise of His holy Name. Secondly, it was ordained for a remedy against sin, and to avoid fornication...'

Very bad for my control. Very bad indeed.

'...that such persons as have not the gift of continency might marry, and keep themselves undefiled members of Christ's body. Thirdly, it was ordained for the mutual society, help, and comfort...'

Comfort? Comfort? Ha! She had been nothing but a pain in my rear!

'...that the one ought to have of the other, both in prosperity...'

Plus, I had to pay her for it!

'...and adversity...'

And why, pray, was I thinking about marriage in combination with Miss Lillian Linton? The concepts were about as related as tin plates and elephant turds! What was I still doing here, anyway? My business was concluded. I should sneak out through the back door, get back to work, and–

'...Into which holy estate these two persons present come now to be joined.'

–and my hand moved another inch or two closer to hers. Now our fingers were only fractions of an inch away from touching. My heart beat against my chest like that burglar I had trapped in my bank vault and left to suffocate. What a shame the peelers had gotten him out. My heart, for some reason, seemed just as determined to escape my chest as he had been to escape the vault, in spite of my indisputable rights of ownership. This was intolerable!

'Therefore if any man can show any just cause why they may not lawfully be joined together, let him now speak, or else hereafter forevermore be silent.'

Now here, finally, was something easy. Something I could do. Just stand here, be silent and don't move. That I could do, right?

Incorrect.

My hand moved to close the last bit of distance. As tumultuous cheers exploded all around us, and a choir started singing, my fingers interlaced with hers. I didn't need to speak. With silence, my hand said more than my lips ever could with words. For one moment, one blissful moment, it all made sense.

'Wilt thou have this Woman to thy wedded Wife, to live together after God's ordinance in the holy estate of Matrimony?' The priest enquired. *'Wilt thou love her, comfort her, honour, and keep her in sickness and in health; and, forsaking all others, keep thee only unto her, so long as ye both shall live?'*

'I will!' rang out a voice over all the cheers in the chapel – and instinctively, my hand squeezed hers.

SARTORIAL RATIONING

An insect settled on my hand and started sucking blood. Without even glancing at it, I squashed the thing and flicked it away. Only one person here was allowed to suck blood in my book – and that was me, from people who owed me money. The other insects got the message and kept their distance.

Crack!

At the noise of breaking branches from behind me, I froze. A predator approaching?

'Bloody hell!' a lady's voice behind me uttered a distinctly unladylike curse.

Ah. Not a predator. Just another pest.

You should never have brought her on this journey.

As if I'd had a choice. For a female, she could be quite persistent.

'Bloody, stinking hell! And I mean that literally! How can it be this hot in here? I thought the desert was supposed to be hot!'

'High humidity,' I answered without turning or slowing down. She had wished to come on this trip. She would have to deal with it. 'The higher the humidity, the hotter human senses perceive it to be,'

'Perceive it to be? You mean it's not really this hot?'

'Exactly. Your body is a fallible animal. Simply ignore its false information.'

'Oh, thanks so much! That's a great help!'

'You are welcome, Mr Linton.'

That should have settled the matter – or at least so I thought, until, after a few more moments, I heard another sound from behind me.

Thud!

Unless a monkey had just toppled out of a tree, that was the sound of a falling secretary. I felt a muscle in my jaw twitch. She had come on this trip. It was her burden to bear, her task to accomplish alone. That's what I paid her for, after all.

And yet...

And yet...

Muttering a low invective, I turned around and marched back to the spot where Miss Linton lay on the ground, panting and gazing blearily at my feet.

'In case there was a miscommunication, Mr Linton,' I told her, my voice cold enough to freeze the constant rain dripping from the leaves overhead, 'we are not stopping for the night yet. Because, as you might have noticed, it isn't night yet. Get up!'

'Pfft...!' she said. Normally, I would have appreciated such brevity. Right now, however, I would have preferred a 'Yes, Sir! Immediately, Sir!'

'Mr Linton!'

'Ffff...fff...Pfft...!'

I cocked my head, regarding her coolly. 'Am I to infer from your excessive panting that you do not have the wherewithal to continue?'

'Pff...pff...'

Glaring balefully, she raised her head to look at me. 'I'm not weak, darn you! This is inhuman! Nobody can manage this!'

I looked down at her, trembling on the ground – and suddenly, I was seized by the insane urge to kneel down and hold her in my arms. Had I gone mad? Bodily contact would provide additional heat, and would be completely counter-productive in these surroundings! What was the matter with me?

Shaking off the mad idea, I gave her another cold look.

'Indeed? I seem to be managing. And so, believe me, do the numerous native tribes living in this jungle.'

'There are people *living* in this hell? Of their own free will?'

She looked so horrified and lost...

No bodily contact. No. Bodily. Contact!

'Indeed there are.'

'How do they stand it?'

You'd be surprised what people can stand, when they've never known anything else.

I shrugged and turned away. Better not to see her. Better not to stand too close. 'Unlike you, they are resilient. And I believe they wear somewhat less clothing than you or I. Now, are you going to get up, or will I have to drag you up?'

There was a moment of silence. Long, thoughtful silence. When finally she said, 'All right. I'll get up,' I felt as if I'd missed a part of the conversation. What was going on in her mind?

Better not ask. It's probably safer.

Still...

I found out soon enough, anyway.

It was twenty-eight minutes, seven seconds and three hundred seventy-five milliseconds later when I suddenly heard a gasp from behind me. Not her gasp, either. No, that was what truly put me on alert: it was Karim's. There weren't many things which could make that gnarled, hardened fighter afraid. Whatever he had seen had to be truly horrifying.

I turned around and–

Holy golden throne of Midas!

I felt my whole body stiffen. Before I could get my face under control, my eyes widened infinitesimally, and, even in this humidity, my mouth went dry.

Miss Linton stood there, sliding off her tailcoat as cool as a cucumber, a devious little smile on her lips that made my insides churn. The waistcoat she wore beneath suddenly seemed a lot more revealing than it had in London, and the linen shirt clung to her skin, wet from top to bottom.

'What do you think you are doing, Mr Linton?'

'Why, removing some unnecessary clothing, of course, Sir.' Still smiling that insidious little smile, she slid the rest of the way out of her tailcoat and let it hang loosely from one hand, swinging back and forth, as if baiting a bull. 'Thanks so much for giving me the idea, by the way.'

My left little finger twitched. 'I? I did nothing of the sort!'

'Of course you did. Don't you remember?' Stowing the tailcoat away in her backpack as if she were merely packing away a pesky piece of luggage, she took a deep breath of air and stretched herself. 'You said the natives do it, didn't you?'

'True.' With considerable effort, I raised my eyes away from where her shirt clung to her body in a way that... *No! Think pounds. Think gold bars and high-return investments.* Yet, whereas these thoughts had always helped to clear my mind of anything else before, they suddenly seemed to have lost their allure. Clenching my teeth, I forced myself to continue. 'But there are two important differences between you and a native of South America, Mr Linton.'

'Indeed, Sir?'

Oh, that tone of voice...

I took a step towards her. 'Yes, indeed, Mr Linton! Firstly: you are English!'

'You don't say.'

Another step. Why was I moving towards her? I had to stop! *Gold bars. Big, glinting gold bars decorated with diamonds.* 'And secondly: *they don't work for me.*'

'How disappointing for you. Haven't you opened a branch down here yet?'

That infuriating little...!

A noise erupted from my throat, somewhere between a growl and the grinding of stone on stone. I stared at her for a moment, not knowing what in Croesus's name to do with her – then I whirled around and gave a curt shrug. 'Fine! If you wish to run around the jungle without your tailcoat, Mr Linton, be my guest. But be warned that such improper attire will not be tolerated in my office.'

'Of course not, Sir,' she purred from behind me, sounding like a wildcat on the prowl. I would have to keep an eye on her once were back in the London office. But right now, what I had to do was keep my eyes and my mind off her. I needed to think of other things. *Gold. Diamonds. People who pay their debts on time. Big, chocolate brown eyes gazing at me from under teasing lashes-*

No! No! Rubies and diamonds! Rubies and diamonds!

We continued on. For several hours, we marched in silence through the jungle, the only noises around us the chirping of the birds in the trees and the rustling in the underbrush as unknown animals slipped by us in the darkness. Maybe she had given up. Maybe she had seen the foolishness, the danger in acting as she did, and had decided it was better to stop while she still–

The rustling of cloth from behind me interrupted my thoughts. A moment later, Karim cleared his throat, sounding urgent.

'Um...*Sahib? Sahib!*'

I froze. 'What is it, Karim? Is there a problem? Did you see something suspicious?'

'Err...in a manner of speaking, *Sahib*, yes. *Sahib*, she–'

She.

Of course. She.

Slowly, I turned around to face her – just in time to see a pair of trousers fall to the ground. Not too extraordinary an occurrence, you might think. During my time in the west of America, I had seen plenty of trackers and cowboys discard their trousers when they wanted to swim, fish, or were just too damn hot in the burning sun. But the sight that met my eyes now wasn't a pair of typical cowboy legs, to put it mildly.

'Aahh!' The little minx stretched her legs. I felt my fingers twitch, itching to wrap around...what? Her throat? Other, more intriguing places? *Concentrate! Gold. Diamond. Rubies.* 'Much more refreshing like this, don't you think?'

'I–cannot–agree,' Karim managed to get out between clenched teeth. He was holding one hand clamped over his eyes, and the other outstretched towards Miss Lillian Linton, as if to ward off evil. Ridiculous! She was far too evil for that to work. 'Put those back on *now!*'

'Oh, I don't know.' Making a little pirouette, she glanced down at her new attire, a spark twinkling in her eyes. *Warm eyes. Mesmerising eyes.* Damnation! 'I like it like this. Nice and breezy.'

'You...you...*ifrit*! Temptress! Demon in human form!'

I couldn't agree more.

She raised an enquiring eyebrow. 'How would you know? You haven't taken a good look at my form yet.'

I have. Trust me, he's right.

Karim only muttered a string of Punjabi curses. Clearly not considering being insulted in a foreign language a matter for concern, Miss Linton turned her back on him and turned her sweet smile and lack of trousers on me.

'And you, Sir? What do you think?'

What I think right now is not fit for a lady to hear, Miss Linton.

For she was a lady. There was no doubt about that now. No amount of my calling her 'Mr Linton' would burn from my mind the image which met my eyes when I looked at her. I didn't even want it burned from my mind. I wanted it burned into me, seared deeply like a brand that would never disappear. My eyes slid down her form, taking in everything as if I were a bank vault and she a substantial cash deposit. Finally, I managed to tear my eyes away and meet her gaze, teeth gritted. Midas, Croesus and Mammon! It shouldn't be legal for her to walk around like this.

Well, it probably isn't. But why would she care?

'What in the name of all that is properly attired do you think you are doing, Mr Linton?'

She gave me a smile as bright as diamonds. 'Why, simply adjusting to the climate, Sir, as you suggested.'

'I didn't suggest for you to run around displaying your unmentionables to the world!'

'The world?' She raised an eyebrow, playing the innocent. 'But it's the middle of the jungle. There's no one here except Karim–' A groan came from the direction of my long-suffering bodyguard, which she completely ignored. '–me, and of course.... you, Sir.' She gifted me with another sweet smile. I had never trusted gifts.

'You can't have anything against seeing my legs, now, can you? After all...' She stepped closer. Damn her to hell, she stepped closer! So close that our bodies were almost touching. Leaning forward, she whispered: 'It wouldn't be the first time, would it?'

I swallowed hard.

'Are you going to continue with this lunacy?' It cost me all my power to speak. All my power to look at her, and not reach out towards her. 'Or are you going to remember what behoves a decent young English lady and give up now?'

'I don't really think wearing these–' she told me, holding up her trousers '– is what most people think behoves a decent young English lady, Sir – but I'm doing it anyway. Besides...' She grinned at me impishly. 'Have you ever known me to give up?'

I felt my left little finger twitch. Probably my hand was considering mutiny, itching to wrap around her throat and...

I cut off that thought before it turned from homicide to more dangerous ideas.

'Karim!' I barked.

'Yes, *Sahib*?'

The bodyguard snapped to attention, his hand still firmly clamped over his eyes.

'Take your paw away from your face, man, and get to the front! I'll be guarding the back from now on.'

And she had better guard her tongue, or I'll...I'll...

'Oh, *Sahib*! A thousand blessings upon you! Thank you! May your soul be saved and find its way to the Garden of Eternal–'

My soul isn't what's on my mind right now.

'Yes, yes! Move!'

Thumping against a few trees in the process, Karim made his way around the *ifrit* tormenting the two of us. Only when he was well ahead and out of the danger did he lower his hand.

'Well, now I know what to do if I ever want to get the better of you.' Miss Linton told his back. 'I'll just have to drop my trousers, and that'll be it.'

I stiffened. My fist clenched, overcome with the sudden urge to slam into Karim. What nonsense! The man was my bodyguard! I paid for him. Why would I wish to damage him?

It was her! Her, who was making me feel all these irrational...things. What were they called again?

Ah yes. *Emotions.*

Bah! To hell with them! To hell with her!

Only...we were already in hell. The green hell. And I, I realised as Miss Linton bent over to pick up her knapsack, taking care to waggle her posterior in my face while she was at it, had signed up for my very own personal torture.

Over her shoulder, she threw me a smile. 'Shall we go? Or were you to planning on lazing around here all day?'

Whistling, she started northeastward, Karim fleeing before her.

As for me...

I did what I hadn't done in my entire life.

I went after a woman. I went after her, and somewhere, deep down, had the suspicion that I would be running after her for quite some time.

Nonsense!

Shaking my head, I rid myself of those silly thoughts. Whyever would I run after her? I was the one in charge here. I was the one with all the power. What could she possibly do to rein me in?

THE METHODS OF MISS LILLIAN LINTON

The sun was just starting to set when she made her next move. There was no warning. No chance to prepare. She just took off her hat and shook out her hair, the mahogany strands gleaming like gold in the warm light of the sinking sun. Really, really gold, begging to be touched. For an instant, I felt the insane urge to pluck off a single hair and place it in my most secure bank vault.

Nonsense! She isn't El Dorado.[32]

But she wasn't done yet, apparently. I watched, unable to look away, as her hands slid around to her back, searching for buttons to open.

'Stop!'

It took me a moment to realise that the voice had come from my own mouth. It must have been one of those instant, unconscious decisions. A survival instinct.

She glanced at me, raising an eyebrow. And I felt...

I didn't how. I just felt. Which was infuriating enough. Why the hell did I suddenly have to go around *feeling* things?

Hurriedly, I cleared my throat.

'I...ehem. I mean we'll stop here for the night.'

'Already, *Sahib*?' Karim asked, and started to turn – then remembered the temptress in our midst and whirled to face away again. 'It'll be quite a while till the sun is down yet.'

'Don't question my orders! Do as I say!' *Because even I don't have a logical reason for those orders right now. Damn that female!*

'Yes, *Sahib*. As you wish, *Sahib*.'

I breathed a sigh as her fingers dropped away from the buttons at her back. But...was it a sigh of relief, or of disappointment? I should know that, shouldn't I?

Concentrate. Rest. Camp.

Reaching into the right bag, I pulled out a hammock and threw it at Miss Linton. It was pure coincidence, I'm sure, that it happened to hit her in the back of the head.

'Sling this! Go on, don't laze about!'

---

[32] Most people know El Dorado as the name of the mythical, fantastically rich city in the South American rain forest. However, it is also the name of the ruler of this mythical city, a man who supposedly covered his skin regularly in gold dust, and thus slowly collected a coating that made him the most valuable individual in the world.

She gazed at the hammock for a moment – then her eyes lit up in a dangerous way.

'There's one for each of us,' I informed her, before she could get any ideas.

Too late. She glanced up at me and fluttered her lashes. Deep inside, I felt something tug at my insides.

'Oh, really? Could you maybe help me and show me how to hang one of these up? I'm afraid I've never done it before, and I might do it wrong.'

Another tug, harder – and without a doubt in her direction. I wanted to go to her. I wanted it like I wanted gold and diamonds and world domination.

Well, maybe not quite as much as world domination.

'If you do it wrong,' I told her, keeping my expression hard as stone, 'you'll land on the forest floor. A course of action I would advise against, considering the poisonous snakes.'

With that, I turned and marched away. I had my own hammock to hang. Far away from her. As far as possible.

~~**~*~*

They say revenge is a dish best served cold. They're wrong. There was no place on earth hotter than this jungle, and revenge could not have tasted more delicious. As we sat and ate our breakfast the next morning, I watched with relish as Miss Lillian Linton wiggled and squirmed under the onslaught of insects buzzing around her scantily-clad figure as if she were an all-you-can-eat buffet. She had wanted to attract attention with a lack of clothing? Well, she had definitely succeeded.

Negligently, I brushed off the single little insect that had dared to land on my mint-condition, barely ten-year-old tailcoat. Apparently, I was not nearly as appetising to the buzzing vermin as Miss Linton. Glancing up, I let my eyes rest on her for a moment.

I had to admit – mosquitoes had good taste.

Things were going smoothly again. The insects kept Miss Linton occupied. If all went well, we would make good time today.

I should have known it was too good to last. As if a few insects would be enough to deter her.

'Dear oh dear.' Sighing, Miss Linton rose from the tree root she had been sitting on, put her breakfast bowl away and stretched. Stretched long and lavishly.

I will not look. I will not look.

'Hm...' her voice came from my left. 'It's really hot this morning, don't you think?'

'No!' Karim protested. 'No, I don't think so at all! In fact, I detect a definite chill in the air this morning! Isn't that right? *Sahib*, you know best! It's chilly, is it not?'

'I concur,' *I will not look. I will not look.* 'Positively freezing.'

'Strange. I somehow feel that I'm too hot. You know what? I think I'm wearing too many clothes. I should...'

Out of the corner of my eye, I saw a giant form dash off into the trees. Karim, that cowardly traitor! I was going to get him for this.

'That's south!' She called after him. 'We're going northeast!'

Abruptly, I rose to my feet. 'I had better be going, too.'

'What?' She turned to look at me and, from under lowered lashes, gave me a distinctly insubordinate look. It made me want to grab her and... *No! No, stop thinking about that! That's not what you do with insubordinate employees. You do not want to do that with Mr Rogers from accounting.* 'Don't you want to guard my rear today?'

On the other hand, maybe I should change my methods for dealing with insubordination according to the circumstances.

A muscle in my jaw twitched. 'I think your rear will be much safer without me as a guard.'

'Well, that's too bad.' Grabbing her backpack, she whirled around and flitted after Karim. 'I guess I'll just have to live in danger.'

Always.

We once again set out on a northeastern route, Karim at the front, and I, Rikkard Ambrose, the richest and most powerful man in the entire Kingdom of Great Britain and Ireland, trudging after my secretary, who flitted through the forest like a chocolate-addicted sprite with the dress-sense of an inebriated monkey. How the mighty have fallen.

'Are you enjoying the view, Sir?' came a cheerful voice from farther up ahead.

Oh yes, I do. Far too much.

'I've seen jungles before.'

'I wasn't talking about the jungle,' she was kind enough to point out.

'Mr Linton?'

'Yes, Sir?'

'Be silent!'

'Yes, Sir!'

'And, Mr Linton...'

'Yes?'

'When we return to London, you are buying more underclothes!'

'I don't know, Sir... Underclothes are quite expensive. Will I get a raise?'

The r-word. It sent a badly needed shock through me and, for a few moments, brought me back to my senses. I shuddered.

'Don't stretch my patience, Mr Linton!'

'Oh well, I'll stretch something else, then.' And, leaning against a tree, she stretched herself. Stretched herself like a cat, purring, wanting to be stroked.

My hand was halfway up already when I noticed what I was doing. Clenching my teeth, I jammed it into my pocket.

March. Treasure. Gold. Concentrate!

She apparently didn't intend to make it easy. Not long after our midday meal, I caught a movement out of the corner of my eye. My gaze flicked up to her just in time to see her undo the top button of her waistcoat.

'Mr Linton!'

Of course, she did the only thing such a loyal and obedient secretary could do – ignore me and open the next button.

'Mr Linton, what are you doing?'

'I'm adjusting my attire. Don't you remember?' Slowing to a languorous stroll, she half-turned to glance at me. 'I said this morning that I thought it had got even warmer.'

'It hasn't!'

'Really?' She undid another button, revealing the soft, sodden fabric beneath, which clung...*No! Don't look. Don't think.* I needed a distraction – anything! Counting gold nuggets, calculating the inflation rate of Paraguay, *anything*! 'I feel positively *hot*.'

'Mr Linton,' I commanded, my teeth clenched, 'cease that immediately!'

'What?' Reaching for another button, she teased it with her finger. 'This?'

A muscle in my jaw twitched. 'Yes.'

'But why?' The button popped open. *One gold nugget, two gold nuggets, three gold nuggets...* 'They're just buttons.'

What number came after three again?

'It's not the buttons I'm concerned about,' I bit out. 'It's–'

'Yes?'

'Nothing!'

'Oh, well, if that's the case...'

She let the last button pop open, and slid the waistcoat completely off. Dangling like bait from the hook of her finger, she let it swing while striding through the jungle with the confidence of a tigress. I tried to start counting gold nuggets again – but found that I had forgotten math altogether.

By all that was valuable and pricey! This had to stop! I had to rid myself of this illogical fixation. I was losing the one thing I could not afford to lose. My most precious possession and most dangerous weapon – my mind.

~~**~*~*

Something was tickling my nose.

It was not a sensation I was accustomed to. Blisters on my hands – yes. Knives at my throat – certainly. But something tickling my nose? That wasn't something the people I had associated with over the years normally did. Except perhaps for...

No. She had better not be doing this.

I opened my eyes.

It wasn't her. She was nowhere in sight. Something was hanging from a branch above my hammock. Something white and, and thin and...

I stiffened.

She didn't. She wouldn't dare.

Half a second after the thought crossed my mind, I realised how ridiculous it was. This was *her* we were talking about. Was there anything she wouldn't dare?

'Mr Linton?'

'Yes, Sir?' came her voice from somewhere behind me.

'Remove this item at once!'

'Item? What item, Sir?'

Fixedly I gazed up at the shirt dangling above my head.

'You know exactly what item I am referring to, Mr Linton. Remove it, and get dressed. We're leaving.'

'Certainly, Sir. There's just one tiny little problem with that...'

'Yes?'

'I am already dressed.'

'*What?*'

Ripping the shirt from the branch above me, I sat up abruptly and slid out of the hammock.

Don't turn around, I told myself. *Don't turn around. You know what you'll see if you turn around.*

I knew my own limits. Giving credit at less than twenty percent interest was one of them. This was another.

'Do you mean to tell me,' I enquired, keeping my voice as cold and controlled as possible, 'that you intend to skip through the jungle with nothing more to cover you than a piece of skimpy lingerie?'

'Oh no, Sir. I still have my corset on.'

My little finger twitched, no doubt betraying my hand's desire to wrap around her neck and start squeezing. 'What a tremendous comfort to us all!'

Balling up her shirt, I hurled it over my shoulder and, with some satisfaction, heard it hit her in the head with a muffled noise.

Think! Think about normal things. Sane things. Things that do as they are told.

'Where's Karim?' I demanded. 'Has he gone to dance tango with the monkeys, or is there at least one person in this group besides me who has not lost their mind yet?'

'He's gone scouting ahead.'

'This early? Why?'

'I, um...' Did she actually sound embarrassed? No, my ears had to be malfunctioning. The rest of my body seemed to be doing whatever the heck it wanted lately, so why not my ears as well? 'He woke up just as I was pulling my shirt off. Gave the poor man quite a shock.'

I had been about to open my knapsack. At her words, I froze.

'Yes.' I whispered, my voice oddly calm. 'I would imagine so.'

The 'poor man' and I were going to have a chat when when next our paths crossed.

'I, err...don't think he saw very much.'

'Is that so?'

Lucky him.

'He ran off into the jungle as soon as he had untangled his legs from the hammock he dropped out of.'

'I see.'

'So...what about you?' Footsteps crunched behind me on the forest floor, approaching slowly. 'If you see me, are you going to run off into the jungle, too?'

I didn't answer. My fingers clenched around my knapsack. I should run. I should. I should never have let things get this far.

But then...I had never been one to run. Especially not from something I wanted. And I did want her, for whatever infernal, illogical reason. I wanted her more than gold, more than diamonds, more than a three per cent reduction of income tax.[33]

'What's the matter, Sir? Are you afraid?'

Afraid?

In front of my inner eye flashed an image from long ago. A boy with sea-coloured eyes cowering in a dirty alley. A starving boy, facing two grinning opponents with wicked grins and wickedly sharp knives.

'What's the matter, runt?' asked the bigger of the two. *'Are you afraid?'*

The boy that was me glared up at them – then, without warning, jumped to his feet and charged.

I whirled around. The knapsack dropped from my hands. Before it thudded to the ground, I was already in front of her, eyes burning with icy fire. Afraid? Me? I almost wanted to laugh. Fear had been beaten out of me a long time ago. And she thought I was afraid of her? She looked so small, so breakable standing in front of me. Afraid? Ha! I'd show her who was in charge here!

'Don't play games with me, Mr Linton!' I warned, my voice low and dangerous.

'Oh yes? Why not?'

'Because if you do, you might soon find yourself the plaything rather than the player!'

She smiled at me. Rising on her tiptoes until she was almost level with me, she lifted her eyes until she met mine straight on.

'Who says I want to play games?' she asked, and...something touched my lips.

Something soft.

Something warm.

Something incredible.

She was kissing me. *She* was kissing *me*! Intolerable! Absolutely outrageous! If she wasn't going to stop immediately, I was going to–

–kiss her back?

No! No, that was not what I was going to do. I was going to take charge, remind her that I was a gentleman, and she was a well-bred young lady! I was going to do the right thing and–

–kiss her back.

Her lips were dancing over mine. Playing. Playing with me. Blood started to pound in my ears. My hand shot up to grasp her chin. To grasp her.

She wanted to play?

All right, Miss Linton. Let's play!

...THE MIDDLE...

---

[33] Just so you know – back then, the income tax was at about three per cent.

ABOUT THE AUTHOR

 Robert Thier is a German historian and writer of historical fiction. His particular mix of history, romance, and adventure, always with a good deal of humour thrown in, has gained him a diverse readership ranging from teenagers to retired grandmothers. For the way he manages to make history come alive, as if he himself lived as a medieval knight, his fans all over the world have given him the nickname 'Sir Rob'.

For Robert, becoming a writer followed naturally from his interest in history. 'In Germany,' he says, 'we use the same word for story and history. And I've always loved the one as much as the other. Becoming a storyteller, a writer, is what I've always wanted.'

Besides writing and researching in dusty old archives, on the lookout for a mystery to put into his next story, Robert enjoys classical music and long walks in the country. The helmet you see in the picture he does not wear because he is a cycling enthusiast, but to protect his literary skull in which a bone has been missing from birth. Robert lives in the south of Germany in a small village between the three Emperor Mountains.

OTHER BOOKS BY ROBERT THIER

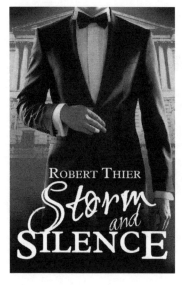

Storm and Silence

Freedom – that is what Lilly Linton wants most in life. Not marriage, not a brood of squalling brats, and certainly not *love*, thank you very much!

But freedom is a rare commodity in 19th-century London, where girls are expected to spend their lives sitting at home, fully occupied with looking pretty. Lilly is at her wits' end – until a chance encounter with a dark, dangerous and powerful stranger changes her life forever...

The award-winning first volume of the *Storm and Silence* series! Winner of the *People's Choice Award* and *Story of the Year Award* 2015.

ISBN-10: 3000513515   ISBN-13: 978-3000513510

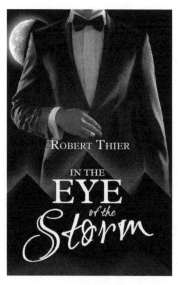

In the Eye of the Storm

Egypt... land of romance, mystery, and exploding camels. Lilly Linton thought she'd be ready for anything after one month of working for her boss – cold, calculating businessman Rikkard Ambrose. But when they embark on a perilous hunt through the desert, she has to face dangers beyond anything she has encountered before: deadly storms, marauding bandits, and worst of all, a wedding ring!

Can the desert's heat truly be enough to melt the cold heart of Britain's richest financier?

The long-awaited second volume of the acclaimed *Storm and Silence* series.

ISBN-10: 3000513515   ISBN-13: 978-3000513510

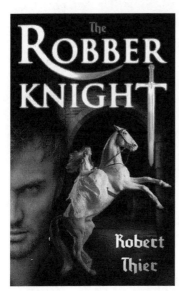

The Robber Knight

When you are fighting for the freedom of your people, falling in love with your enemy is not a great idea.

Sir Reuben, the dreaded robber knight, has long been Ayla's deadliest enemy. She swore he would hang for his crimes. Now they are both trapped in her castle as the army of a far greater enemy approaches, and they have only one chance: stand together, or fall. Welcome to *The Robber Knight*—a tale full of action, adventure, and romance.

Special Edition with secret chapters revealed and insights into Sir Reuben's mysterious past.

ISBN-10: 1499251645   ISBN-13: 978-1499251647

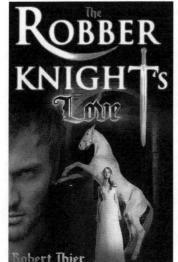

The Robber Knight's Love

Ayla has uncovered a terrible secret: the man she loves is in fact her worst enemy. As a mighty army gathers to destroy her and her people, she must ask herself: will he join them to destroy her? Must she cut him out of her heart to survive?
Or is there another way—a way to forgiveness and...love?

Special Edition with secret chapters revealed and insights into Sir Reuben's mysterious past.

ISBN-10: 3000536590   ISBN-13: 978-3000536595

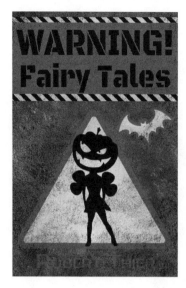

WARNING! Fairy Tales

WARNING! Please be advised that this is not a bedtime story about sparkly fairies and pink unicorns. This book may contain graphic descriptions of poisoned apples and witches' ovens. It is not appropriate for supernatural beings under the age of 377 (excluding vampires and werewolves).

DISCLAIMER: Wicked Witches Inc. and Evil Stepmother Enterprises are not responsible for any maiming, mass murder or permanent insanity resulting from the reading of this book.

The first volume of Robert Thier's *WARNING! Fairy Tales* series.

ISBN-10: 3000547118

ISBN-13: 978-3000547119

WARNING! Fairy Tales 2

WARNING! Please be advised that big bad wolves, wicked witches, and harmless-looking little girls are roaming the pages of this book. It may contain graphic descriptions of wolf teeth and grandmothers with big ears. This book is not appropriate for supernatural beings under the age of 388 (excluding anyone wearing a red hood).

DISCLAIMER: *Wicked Witches Inc.* and *Evil Stepmother Enterprises* are not responsible for wolf bites, vampirism or witch curses incurred during the reading of this book.

The second volume of Robert Thier's *WARNING! Fairy Tales* series.

ISBN-13: 978-3962600013

UPCOMING TITLES

At present (2017), the titles listed above are Robert Thiers's only books published in English. However, book three of the Robber Knight Saga, *The Robber Knight's Secret*, as well as his latest project, *Black Diaries*, are being edited for publication. Keep updated about the books' progress on the internet.

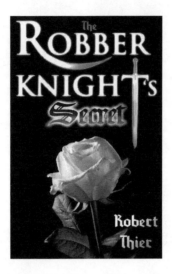

Website: www.robthier.com

Facebook profile: www.facebook.com/robert.thier.161

Facebook page: http://www.facebook.com/TheSirRob/

Twitter: http://twitter.com/thesirrob

Goodreads: www.goodreads.com/author/show/6123144.Robert_Thier

Made in the USA
Columbia, SC
02 May 2021